THE
JANSON
COMMAND

By Robert Ludlum

The Jason Bourne Novels

The Covert-One Series

Paul Garrison Novels

ROBERT LUDLUM'S™

THE JANSON COMMAND

PAUL GARRISON

GRAND CENTRAL
PUBLISHING

NEW YORK   BOSTON

Grand Central Publishing
Hachette Book Group
237 Park Avenue
New York, NY 10017

www.HachetteBookGroup.com

Printed in the United States of America

Originally published in hardcover by Grand Central Publishing.

RRD-C

First International Trade Edition: February 2012

10 9 8 7 6 5 4 3 2 1

Grand Central Publishing is a division of Hachette Book Group, Inc.
The Grand Central Publishing name and logo is a trademark of Hachette Book Group, Inc.

The Hachette Speakers Bureau provides a wide range of authors for speaking events. To find out more, go to www.hachettespeakersbureau.com or call (866) 376-6591.

The publisher is not responsible for websites (or their content) that are not owned by the publisher.

ISBN 978-0-446-57358-0

For AMBER EDWARDS
Bob celebrated beauty, hard work, love, and talent.
He'd have thought you were the cat's meow.

THE
JANSON
COMMAND

PROLOGUE
The Rescue

Three Years Ago
41°13′N, 111°57′W
Ogden, Utah

"Ogden's a great town if you like hiking and mountain biking and skiing." Doug Case gripped the broken armrests of his secondhand wheelchair and pretended they were ski poles. "That's what I'm doing here, since you ask. How'd you happen to track me down? I wiped my names from the VA computers."

Paul Janson said, "When it all goes to hell, people go home."

"The place where they have to take you in? Not me. I'm not asking any favors."

"I don't see you getting any, either."

Case's home was the mouth of an abandoned railroad tunnel with a view of a garbage-littered empty lot, a burned-out Kentucky Fried Chicken, and the snowy Wasatch Mountains. He hunched in his chair with a frayed backpack on his lap, stringy hair down to his shoulders, and a week of beard on his face. His dull gaze flickered occasionally toward four muscular teenage gangbangers who were eyeing them from a Honda parked beside the KFC.

Paul Janson sat on an upended grocery cart. He wore lightweight assault boots and wool trousers, a sweater, and a loose black ski shell.

"Kill me and get it over with," Case told him. "I don't feel like playing games."

"I'm not here to kill you."

"Just do it! Don't worry; I won't defend myself." He shifted the pack on his lap.

Janson said, "You are assuming that I still work for Consular Operations."

"Nobody quits Cons Ops."

"We have an arrangement. I went private. Corporate security consulting. Cons Ops calls me now and then. Now and then I call back."

"You never were one to burn bridges," Case conceded. "You work alone?"

"I have someone to bring along if I need a sniper."

"Good?"

"As good as I've ever seen."

"Where from?" Case asked, wondering who of that caliber Janson had recruited.

"Top of the talent pool," was all Janson would reveal.

"Why'd you quit Cons Ops?"

"I woke up one morning remembering all the people I killed for the wrong reasons."

Case laughed. "For Christ's sake, Paul! The State Department can't have covert operators *deciding* who to kill. When you have to kill somebody to do the job you kill him. That's why they're called sanctioned in-field killings."

"Sanctioned *serial* killings was more like the truth. I lay in bed counting them up. Those I should have. Those I shouldn't have."

"How many in total? Shoulds and shouldn'ts."

"Forty-six."

"I'll be damned. I edged you out."

"Forty-six *confirmed*," Janson shot back.

Case smiled. "I see your testosterone hasn't passed its sell-by date." He looked Janson up and down. The son of a bitch hadn't aged. Paul Janson still looked thirtysomething, fortysomething, fifty. Who knew with his close-cropped hair a neutral iron-gray color? And he still looked like somebody you wouldn't look at twice. Unless you were another professional, and then, if you were really, really good, you'd look twice and see the shoulders under the jacket and the watchful eyes and by then it might be too late.

Janson said, "We have company."

The gangbangers were strutting toward them.

"I've got 'em," said Case. "You got lunch." The empty Sonic burger bags were neatly folded under one of his wheels. Doug Case let them get within ten meters before he said, "Gentlemen, I'm offering one free lesson in survival. A survivor never gets in the wrong fight. Turn around and go away."

Three of them puffed up. But their leader, the smallest, shot an appraising glance at Case and another at Janson and said, "We're outta here."

"The guy's in a fuckin' wheelchair."

The leader punched the dissenter hard in the ear and herded them away. "Hey, kid!" Case shouted after him. "You got what it takes. Join the Army. They'll teach you what to do with it." He grinned at Janson. "Don't you love raw talent?"

"I do," said Janson, and called in a voice accustomed to obedience, "Come here!" The kid came, light on his feet, wary as a stray. Janson gave him a business card. "Join the Army. Call me when you make buck sergeant."

"What's that?"

"A rung up the ladder that says you're going places."

Janson waited until the Honda squealed away on smoking tires. "I remembered something else. I remembered every idea I used to believe that I turned my back on."

"You could use a dose of amnesia."

"There's none available."

Case laughed, again. "Remember when that happened to an operator? Forgot everything. Woke up beating the crap out of people. Couldn't remember how he learned close combat. What the hell was his name? . . . I can't remember. Neither could he. Unlike you; you remember everything. Okay, Paul, if you're not here to kill me, what are you doing in fucking Ogden?"

"Telling the truth about what I did is pointless if I don't atone."

"Atone? What? Like an AA drunk apologizing to people he was mean to?"

"I can't change what I did, but I can pay back the next guy."

"Why not just buy a pardon from the pope?"

The sarcasm button didn't work. Janson was deaf to it. He said, "You take the skills of observation we learned and turn them into yourself, it's not a pretty sight."

"Saul on the road to Damascus discovers his moral compass and changes his name to Paul? But you already are Paul. What are you going to change? The world?"

"I am going to do my best to save every covert government operator whose life was wrecked by his covert service. Guys like you and me."

"Leave me out of this."

"Can't."

"What do you mean?"

"You're my first project."

"A million people hold top-secret clearances. If one in a hundred work undercover that's ten thousand covert agents you could save. Why me?"

"Some people say you were the worst."

Case returned a bitter smile. "Some said I was the *best*."

"Fact is, *we* were the worst."

"I don't need saving."

"You're living outdoors. Winter is coming. You're hooked on Percocet and the docs have cut you off. When this month's prescription runs out you'll be scrambling to find it on the street."

"Paul Janson's famously accurate research?"

"You'll be dead by Valentine's Day."

"Janson's renowned discerning analytic tradecraft?"

"You need saving."

"I don't want saving. Get out of here. Leave me alone."

"I've got a van with a ramp."

Doug Case's pale, grizzled cheeks flamed angry red. "You got a van with a ramp? *You got a van with a ramp?* You got shooters in the van gonna help you wrestle me up your fucking ramp?"

An awkward smile tightened Janson's face. For the first time since appearing at the mouth of Doug Case's railroad tunnel, he looked unsure. The man they called The Machine was suddenly vulnerable, and Doug Case pressed his attack.

"You're falling down on the planning end, fella. No assaulters in the van. No rehearsal. No quick-reaction force backup. No contingency. You're kind of, sort of, fumbling on impulse. Should have gone about this the way you'd plan a Cons Ops job. Tortured soul muddles toward atonement? And you're going to get *me* straightened out?"

"More than straightened out. We're going to put you back together with a life."

"With a *life*? So first you'll get me off the Perc? Then you'll have shrinks fix my head? And when the docs get through you'll find me a career that will employ my considerable talents? Go to hell."

"You will be made whole."

"Maybe even find me a girl?"

"If you want one, you'll be whole enough to find one on your own."

"Jesus, Paul, you're as wired and freaked out as I am. Who in your mental wilderness do you imagine would pay for this fantasy?"

Janson said, "On my last job someone deposited a ton of money in my overseas accounts to make it seem I turned traitor. That someone no longer exists. Money will not be an issue."

"If you ever do rope some poor fool into your pipe dream, you'll need more than money. You'll need help. Lots of it. You'll need a staff. Hell, you'll need an entire company."

Again Janson looked unsure. "I don't know about that. I've had it with companies. I've had it with institutions. I've stopped trusting any more than two people in one room."

"Poor, tormented Paul. Trying to make everything right by saving the worst guy you know, single-handed? What are you going to call this outfit? The Paul Janson Institute for Raising Fucked-up Former Field Agents Out of Deep Shit? No, keep it simple: the Phoenix Foundation."

Janson stood up. "Let's go, my friend."

"This guy ain't going anywhere. And I'm not your friend."

"Maybe not," Janson agreed. "But we've worked together and I could be sitting where you are, so we are brothers."

"Brothers? Is your halo pinching?" Doug Case shook his head, scratched an armpit, and covered his face with his dirty hands. After a while, he lowered his left hand and spoke through the fingers of his right. "They called you 'The Machine.' Remember? Some operators they call an animal. Some a machine. A machine usually beats an animal. But not always."

In a blur of coordinated movement drilled ten thousand times, Case's left hand flashed from his knapsack, pinching the barrel of a Glock 34 9mm automatic between thumb and forefinger. His right hand closed around the butt, forefinger curling into the trigger guard, and his left pulled back the slide, loading a round into the chamber and cocking the pistol with the speed of liquid flame.

Janson kicked it from his hand.

"*Fuck!*"

Doug Case rubbed his wrist where Janson's boot had connected. Should have remembered that Cons Ops combat instructors, the best in the world, had a saying. Lightning fast, nano fast, Janson fast.

Janson scooped up the gun. He was suddenly grinning ear to ear, optimistic, full of hope, and absolutely convinced he could fix what was broken. "I see you're not completely screwed up."

"What gives you that idea?"

Janson tapped the Glock. "You replaced the crappy factory sights with ghost rings."

He removed the magazine and pocketed it, removed the round from the chamber, snapped the knapsack off Case's lap, removed two spare magazines from a side pocket, pulled a third from the waistband of his sweatpants, and handed the empty gun back to Doug Case.

"When do I get the rest of it?"

"Graduation Day."

PART ONE

The Mother of All Reserves

Now
1°19′ N, 7°43′ E
Gulf of Guinea, 260 miles south of Nigeria, 180 miles west of Gabon

ONE

"Vegas Rules," said Janet Hatfield, captain of the *Amber Dawn*. Her three-thousand-ton offshore service vessel was running up the Gulf of Guinea on a black night, pitching and rolling in following seas. Her voice rang with quiet authority in the near silence of the darkened pilothouse. "What you saw on *Amber Dawn* stays on *Amber Dawn*."

"You already swore me to Vegas Rules when we sailed from Nigeria."

"I'm not kidding, Terry. If the company finds out I snuck you aboard, they'll fire my ass."

"And a lovely ass it is," said Terrence Flannigan, MD, nomadic corporate physician, globetrotting womanizer, world-class snake. He raised his right hand and gave Janet Hatfield a sleepy-eyed grin. "Okay. I swear, again, to keep my mouth shut about *Amber Dawn*, about oil in general and deepwater petroleum exploration in particular, cross my heart and hope to die."

The captain, a solidly built blonde of thirty-five, turned her back on the snake and ran an uneasy eye over her radar. For the past several minutes the screen had been throwing out a ghost target. The mystery pinprick of light fading and reappearing was too dull to be another ship yet bright enough to make her wonder what the heck was out there. The radar was a reliable unit, a late-model Furuno. But she had the lives of twelve people in her care: five Filipino crew, six American petroleum scientists, and one stowaway. Thirteen, if she counted herself, which she tended not to.

Was the hot spot only sea clutter? Or an empty oil drum bobbing in the heavy seas, topping crests, hiding in troughs? Or was it something bigger, like an unreported, half-sunken hulk that she did not want to run into at fifteen knots?

It glowed again, closer, as if it was not merely drifting but moving toward her. She fiddled the radar, playing with range and resolution. Otherwise, the sea looked empty, except for some large oil tankers a safe twenty miles to the west. A single land target at the top of the screen marked the summit of Pico Clarence, the six-thousand-foot volcanic mountain at the center of Isle de Foree, tonight's destination. " 'Foree' rhymes with 'moray,' " she told visiting company brass new to the Gulf of Guinea oil patch. "Like the eel with the teeth."

She glanced at her other instruments. Compass, autopilot, and a wide panel of gauges monitoring the diesel generators that powered the twin three-thousand-horsepower electric Z-drive thrusters all gave her normal readings. She stared intently at the night-blackened bridge windows. She grabbed her night-vision monocular, shouldered open a heavy, watertight door, and stepped out onto the stubby bridge wing into equatorial heat, humidity she could slice with a knife, and the brain-numbing roar of the generators.

The southwest monsoon was blowing from behind, swirling

diesel smoke around the house. The following seas had gathered ponderous momentum rolling three thousand miles up the African coast from Cape Town. They lifted the ship's stern and plunged her bow nearly to the foredeck. The heat and humidity had the captain sweating in seconds.

Her night-vision device was an eighteen-hundred-dollar birthday splurge to herself to help spot navigation buoys and small craft. It did not magnify, but it pierced the dark dramatically. She glassed the sea ahead. The 2-gen image intensifier displayed everything green. Nothing but whitecaps swirling like lime chiffon. Probably just a barrel. She retreated back into the cool quiet of the airconditioning. The red glow of the instruments reflected in Flannigan's come-here smile.

"Don't even think about it," she warned him.

"I am merely offering to express my gratitude."

"In four hours you can express your gratitude to the ladies of Porto Clarence's massage parlors."

Low-rent Eastern European and Chinese cruise ships had discovered the capital city. A mix of poverty, an embattled dictator desperate for cash, and the legendary beauty of Isle de Foreens' West African and Portuguese bloodlines had sex tourism booming in the old colonial deepwater port.

Terry paced the pilothouse. "I've been company physician on enough oil jobs to know to keep my trap shut. But this voyage is the most secret I've ever seen."

"Stop saying that."

"You spent the week towing hydrophone streamers and air guns. When was the last time your OSV was Rube Goldberged into a seismic vessel?"

"Last month." Janet Hatfield kicked herself the instant she admitted it.

Terry laughed. "The 'captain's curse.' You love your boat too much to keep a secret. This isn't the first time? Are you kidding? She's an offshore service vessel, not an oil hunter. What is going on?"

"Forget I said that. I shouldn't have—so it's weird. So what? When the company makes me vice president of marine services, I'll ask why. Till then, I'll drive the boat. Now shut up about it. Jeezus, I should have left you in Nigeria."

"I'd be dead."

"Roger that," Janet Hatfield agreed. It was easier than ever to die in the oil-soaked Niger Delta. Militants kidnapped petroleum workers right off their rigs, drunken soldiers strafed their own checkpoints, and fanatics rampaged in the name of Jesus and Mohammed. But catnip-to-women Dr. Terry had come close to getting killed the old-fashioned way: a jealous husband with a machete, a rich chief, no less, with the political connections to get away with hacking up the wife poacher.

"Janet, where did we go wrong?" Terry asked with another soulful smile.

"Our relationship collapsed under its own lack of weight."

He made a better friend than lover. As a boyfriend he was treacherous, head over heels in love with himself. But as a friend Terry Flannigan had something steady deep inside that said he would take a bullet for you. Which was why Janet Hatfield had not hesitated to bundle him aboard before the angry husband killed him. For ten days she had hidden him from the crew in her cabin, "airing" him when it was her watch.

The bridge and her attached cabin stood in splendid isolation atop a four-story deckhouse near the front of the ship. Under it were crew cabins, mess and galley, and the lounge that the petrologists had taken over as their computer and radio room. The scientists had declared it off-limits to the crew. They even told her that the captain had to ask permission to enter. Janet Hatfield had informed them that she had no plan to enter unless it caught fire, in which case she would not knock first.

"You know what the petrologists are doing now?"

Terry was staring out the back windows, which looked down on the hundred-foot-long, low and flat cargo deck, empty tonight but for the OSV's towing windlass, deck crane, and capstans.

"Get away from the window before they see you."

"They're throwing stuff overboard."

"What they're doing is their business."

"One of them is crawling around with a flashlight— Oh, he dropped something."

"What are they throwing?" she asked in spite of herself.

"Computers."

* * *

BELOWDECKS, JUBILANT PETROLOGISTS peeled off their sweat-soaked shirts and did a victory dance in the now-empty computer room. They had worked 24-7 for ten days, trapped on a boat where possession of booze or drugs or even a bottle of beer would get you banned from the oil business for life. Now they were headed for a well-earned party in the brothels of Porto Clarence, having successfully uploaded multiple terabytes of the hottest 3-D seismic data on the planet.

The data acquisition was done, the client's seismic model refined, the success of what oilmen called an elephant hunt confirmed beyond any doubt. The client had acknowledged receipt of the densely encrypted satellite transmissions and ordered them to throw the computers into the sea. Every laptop, desktop, even the

fifty-thousand-dollar subsurface-modeling workstation that took
two men to lift over the side of the ship. The monitors went, too,
so no one would see them and ask what they were for, as did the
hydrophones and air guns and their mil-spec satellite transmitter.

In a few more hours the petrologists would celebrate the discovery of the "mother of all reserves"—billions and billions of barrels
of oil and trillions upon trillions of cubic feet of natural gas that
would transform Isle de Foree from a remote plantation island
trickling oil through a neglected infrastructure into a West African
Saudi Arabia.

* * *

"HEY, JANET. How many dinosaurs died to make the oil patch?"

"Algae. Not dinosaurs."

Terry Flannigan stared at the dark ahead of the boat. The big secret could only be about oil. The water was miles deep here, but if
you took the long view in eons, eras, and epochs, the seabed was
actually an extension of the shallow African coast. For more years
than there were stars in the sky, the Niger River had been dumping
sediment into the Atlantic Ocean. This slurry of mud, sand, and
dead plants and animals had filled the troughs, rifts, and clefts of
the Atlantic and had kept spilling across the continental slope into
the deep and continued seaward, drifting, filling. A lady petrologist
once told him that the compacted fill was eight miles deep.

"What did dinosaurs make? Coal?"

"Trees made coal," Janet Hatfield answered distractedly, her
eyes locking on the radar. She switched on the powerful docking
lamps. They lit a brilliant hundred-yard circle around the OSV.
"Oh, shit!"

"What?"

An eighteen-foot rigid inflatable boat driven by enormous Mercury outboards swooped out of the dark bristling with assault rifles and rocket launchers. Janet Hatfield reacted quickly, grabbing the helm to override the autopilot. The RIB was struggling in the heavy seas. Maybe she could outrun them. She turned *Amber Dawn*'s heels to it, locked the new course, rammed her throttles full ahead, and yanked her radio microphone down from the ceiling.

"Mayday, Mayday. Mayday. This is *Amber Dawn, Amber Dawn, Amber Dawn*. One-degree, nineteen minutes north. Seven-degrees, forty-three minutes east.

"One-degree, nineteen minutes north. Seven, forty-three east. One-degree, nineteen minutes north," she repeated her position, "Seven-degrees, forty-three minutes east." They couldn't help if they couldn't find her.

"Pirates boarding *Amber Dawn*. Pirates boarding *Amber Dawn*. One-degree, nineteen minutes north. Seven-degrees, forty-three minutes east."

There was never a guarantee that anyone was listening. But the 406 MHz satellite EPIRB, which was out on the bridge wing in its float-free bracket, would broadcast her position continuously in case of sinking. She pushed through the door again to switch it on manually.

The inflatable was so close she could see eight soldiers dressed in camouflage. *Jungle camouflage on a boat?*

They had to be from Isle de Foree, she thought, the only land within the inflatable's range. But they couldn't be government troops in that little commando boat. Free Foree Movement rebels? Pirates or rebels, what did they want? The only thing valuable on an offshore service vessel was the crew. To hold hostage or for ransom. So they wouldn't kill her people. At least, not yet.

Muzzle flashes lit the inflatable like a Christmas tree and all the windows in *Amber Dawn*'s bridge shattered at once. Janet Hatfield felt something tug hard in her belly. Her legs skidded out from under her. She pitched backward into Terry's arms and she almost laughed, "You never stop trying, do you?" except she couldn't speak and was suddenly afraid.

* * *

A CARGO NET edged with grappling hooks cleared the low side of *Amber Dawn*'s main deck, clanged onto steel fittings, and held fast. Seven FFM insurgents scrambled aboard with their assault rifles, leaving their rocket launchers with one man in their boat. They were lean, fit, hard-faced fighters with the distinctive café-au-lait coloring of Isle de Foreens. But they took their orders from a broad-shouldered South African mercenary named Hadrian Van Pelt.

Van Pelt carried a copy of *Amber Dawn*'s crew list.

He sent two men to the engine room. Bursts of automatic fire echoed up from below and the generators fell silent, but for one powering the lights. The men stayed below opening sea cocks. Seawater poured in.

Two others kicked open the door to the improvised computer room. Van Pelt followed with the crew list. "Over there! Against the wall."

The petrologists, shirtless and terrified, backed against the wall, exchanging looks of disbelief.

Van Pelt counted heads. "Five!" he shouted. "Who's missing?"

Eyes flickered toward a closet. Van Pelt nodded at one of his men, who triggered a short burst, shredding the door. The ship rolled and the body of the scientist hiding there tumbled out. Van Pelt nodded again and his men executed the rest.

A burst of gunfire from the quarters on the levels above spoke the end of *Amber Dawn*'s Filipino crew. Eleven down. Only the captain to go. Van Pelt drew his pistol and climbed the stairs to the bridge. The door was locked and made of steel. He signaled a soldier, who duct-taped a chunk of C-4 onto it. They sheltered halfway down the steps and covered their ears. The plastic explosive blew the door open with a loud bang and Van Pelt vaulted through it.

To the mercenary's surprise, the captain was not alone. She was sprawled on the deck, a pretty blonde in blood-soaked slacks and blouse. A man was kneeling over her, working with the sure-handed economy of a battlefield medic.

Van Pelt raised his pistol. "Are you a doctor?"

Terry Flannigan was holding death in his hands, and when he looked up from Janet's riddled chest to the gunman standing in the door he was staring death in the face.

"What kind of doctor?" the gunman demanded.

"Trauma surgeon, you asshole. What does it look like?"

"Come with me."

"I can't leave her. She's dying."

Van Pelt stepped closer and shot Janet Hatfield in the head. "Not anymore. Get in the boat."

TWO

221 West 46th Street
New York City

Paul Janson descended a steep flight of stairs to Sofia's Club Cache in the basement of the Hotel Edison. The curly-haired brunette knockout who took his fifteen-dollar cover charge with the dazzling smile she reserved for new customers saw him as he intended to be seen: an out-of-town businessman hoping that Vince Giordano and his famous hot-jazz Nighthawks would liven up a lonely Monday evening. His navy suit, artfully cut to conceal his powerful frame, looked like a classic soft-shoulder Brooks Brothers sack suit, neither dapper nor expensive. His tailor had seen to that by eliminating bespoke sleeve buttons and bound buttonholes. The creases in Janson's brow marked a man somewhere past his thirties, and he could have acquired the faint lines of scar tissue playing college sports.

Janson took his change, returned an unmemorable smile, and remarked, like half the people who came down the stairs, "The joint is jumpin'."

Across the wide, deep low-ceilinged room the tuxedo-clad eleven-piece band of saxophones, clarinets, trumpets, trombone, banjo, piano, drums, and an aluminum double bass was storming through "Shake That Thing." A hundred people ate and drank at the tables. A dozen couples danced to the music, many with great skill. The dancers older than thirty wore dresses and suits befitting the hot-jazz era. The younger favored T-shirts and cargo pants.

One of the younger, an attractive woman with strong, regular features, high cheekbones, full lips, and spiky brown "bed hair," was dancing a high-speed 1920s one-step with the intensity and precision of a laser cutting machine. Janson concealed an appreciative smile. Jessica Kincaid demanded of herself, "Go fast till it hurts, then put on some speed and do it better."

Kincaid shot Janson a glance that mingled fascination and envy. Paul Janson was master of the nondescript, and it drove her crazy. She worked hard at being a chameleon. With adjustments of clothing, hair, jewelry, and makeup she could make herself look twenty-five or thirty-five and pass for a Brooklyn video artist or a good ol' girl juke-joint bartender or a buttoned-down banker. But she could never look nondescript, and when she tried Janson laughed that "nondescript" and "interesting" did not fit the same sentence.

Paul Janson was just there. Except when he was not there. Janson could hide in plain sight. If he chose to, Janson could fill a room, but he was more likely to enter without anyone noticing—as he had just now—and leave the same way. He even had a trick of shifting his shoulders to make his height look average. She glanced at him again. He returned it this time and drifted toward the stairs.

"Gotta go," she told her dance instructor. Duty called.

The Town Car looked identical to a thousand black livery cabs in Midtown. But the kid behind the wheel had driven armored security vehicles for tanker convoys in Iraq and the interior lights did not go on when Kincaid opened the door.

"Where we going?" she asked the sturdy shape of Janson in the shadows.

"First stop: Houston, Texas. American Synergy Corporation's HQ."

Biggest oil company in the country. Snapped up the richest leases after BP's Gulf of Mexico disaster. "Then?"

"West Africa is my guess. If we take the job. Home if we don't. We probably won't."

"Why go at all?"

"ASC's president of global security is an old friend."

Kincaid nodded in the dark. Janson had lots of them, and when old friends called he ran to them. He passed her a thick towel. "Don't catch cold." Soaking wet from dancing a heart-pounding two beats to a second, she was shivering in the AC.

"Y'all telling me I smell?" While a fluent student of several languages and possessing an invaluable gift for mimicking accents, Jessica Kincaid had not entirely erased from her own voice the Kentucky hill twang she had grown up with, particularly when she was alone with Janson.

"That's why we have a shower on the plane."

The car caught the green lights up Madison Avenue, crossed over to the Major Deegan, and swung onto the Hutchinson River Parkway. Late-night suburban traffic was light. Forty minutes after leaving the Edison, they pulled into Westchester Airport, bypassed the passenger terminal, and continued on to a fenced-off section with a chain-link gate. A voice on a security speakerphone asked who they were.

"Tail number eight-two-two-Romeo-Echo," the driver answered, and drove through when the electric gate slid open. An attendant opened a second gate that led to the runways, a vast expanse of darkness dotted with blue, yellow, and green lights marking taxiways and runway edges and thresholds. The car parked beside a silver Embraer Legacy 650 jet with two enormous Rolls-Royce AE 3007 engines in the tail. The pilots were completing their checklists. Janson and Kincaid climbed aboard, retracted the self-contained deployable entry steps that permitted fast exits independent of airfield facilities, and locked the door.

The long-haul executive jet built to carry fourteen passengers had been made extremely comfortable for two. Embraer had reconfigured it to Janson's specs, outfitting it to deliver two or three operators well rested and fed, suited up, and thoroughly informed for any kind of work anywhere in the world. The galley directly behind the cockpit had been upgraded, and the lavatory and the rearmost of the three seating areas had been converted to a dressing room and full bath. The forward seating areas had been turned into a study and dining room. The middle section had fold-down beds for transocean runs.

The plane had climbed to forty-one thousand feet and their pilot was radioing, "New York center, Embraer two-two-Romeo level at four-one zero," when Kincaid came out of the shower wrapped in a terry-cloth robe. Janson looked up from his green leather easy chair, where he was studying a dossier labeled: "ASC—American Synergy Corporation." A laptop was open on the table beside him and he had a glass of water close at hand. An identical dossier and laptop were waiting beside Kincaid's red chair along with water and a stack of lemon-lime Camelbak Elixir electrolyte tablets.

Janson peered over the wire-rimmed reading glasses that Kin-

caid called his innocent old guy specs and said, "If we could bottle
the aroma of a woman in a shower we would be rich."

"Folks I know would think we're rich already." She touched a
fingerprint reader to unlock an overhead luggage bin, opened a hidden interior cabinet, and took down her Knight's M110 semiautomatic sniper rifle. The weapon was spotless, but she fieldstripped
it anyway, laying the parts on the fold-down galley table, cleaned
and oiled each, checked for wear, and reassembled them. Janson
likened her ritual to an already clean cat grooming itself into a
hunting trance.

Kincaid would have preferred, before she locked the weapon
up again, to open the accessories case and put her day and night
scopes, bipod, and laser sight through the same close inspection.
But the dossier was still sitting there beside her chair demanding
to be read.

"Okay if I open one of your shirts?"

"Of course," he answered without looking up.

From a built-in chest of drawers she took a freshly ironed pale
blue Burberry dress shirt, carefully removed the laundry's cardboard stiffener, and put the shirt back. She settled in her leather
chair, covered her ears with noise-canceling headphones to help
her concentrate, and opened the dossier on the American Synergy
Corporation. She held the cardboard at the top of the first page and
began sliding it down the page, covering each line of text as she read
it. If she didn't cover each line after she read it, she would go back
and read over and over fearing she must have made a mistake.

"Not severely dyslexic," she had explained when she first told
Janson. "Just dyslexic. They didn't call it that back in Red Creek.
They all thought I was a little slow. Didn't bother me much," she
added quickly. "I could outshoot the boys and fix any vehicle in my
daddy's gas station."

She had taught herself the cardboard trick while struggling through college equivalency courses to join the FBI—her first step up the ladder to Cons Ops.

She read the ASC report cover to cover. Whenever she double-checked a detail on her laptop, she placed the cursor at the bottom of the screen and scrolled with the down arrow, concealing what she had already read. She knew she was getting too tired to continue when a letter *b* flopped upside down and became a *p*.

At that point she loaded in a promotional Blu-ray video titled *American Synergy Corporation—New Energy for a New Tomorrow*.

Paul had reclined his chair and fallen asleep. She pressed a button that laid her own chair flat and listened to Kingsman Helms, the president of ASC's Petroleum Division, give a speech to shareholders. The handsome smooth talker reminded her of evangelical preachers down home.

"It isn't a matter of telling our story better. We have to create a better story. Long-term growth means long-term survival. Oil is one type of energy we develop, along with wind, solar, biomass, nuclear, and coal. Our mission is to supply secure, safe, environmentally sound, *cheap* energy—not just today, but twenty years down the road.

"A lot has gone wrong, lately." Helms paused to look straight into the camera with an expression that said that everyone knew that he meant Wall Street screwups, government meddling, and oil spills by mismanaged competitors. "Americans are counting on us more than ever. ASC will not let them down, because at ASC we never forget that leadership is not about now, not about today. Leadership is about then, about the future, about tomorrow."

CatsPaw researchers had attached to the DVD a voiced-over addendum: "Of wind, solar, biomass, nuclear, and coal, the global corporation has steered clear of biomass, which a secret company memo rated 'a huge joke perpetrated on the Congress by farm states,' invested just enough to appear green in multiple solar-tech startups and wind turbine manufacturers, and has recently amassed huge holdings in Appalachian coal companies." Kincaid's hackles rose; that meant strip mining and blasting the tops off mountains. The researchers had highlighted ASC's biggest challenge: direct competition for access to new "ground resources" from the China National Offshore Oil Corporation. "In plain language, as big and powerful a global as it is, ASC is being squeezed overseas by China. To remain on top 'twenty years down the road' ASC will have to conduct business ever more ruthlessly."

* * *

THE EMBRAER LANDED at Houston's Hobby Airport at three in the morning. Janson's pilots taxied to the Million Air private aviation terminal and woke their bosses for breakfast at six, cooked by the senior man. "My biggest fear, Mike," said Janson, knotting a club tie with a small repeating pattern, "is one of these days you'll quit flying and open a restaurant."

"Car in two minutes," said Kincaid, exiting the dressing room in a seersucker skirt and jacket. Her bed hair was now a sleek junior-executive bob that exposed her ears and high brow. Her manner was brisk.

The Million Air car delivered them to the Hilton Americas-Houston hotel. They walked through the marble rotunda, crossed the lobby, and joined crowds of businesspeople hurrying from breakfast to the adjoining Brown Convention Center. But when they emerged from the connector corridor Janson and Kincaid skirted the registration desks and went outside for a taxi.

They found American Synergy Corporation headquartered in a

round thirty-story building set back from the Sam Houston Toll-way like an enormous bronze silo. Surveillance cameras enfiladed the driveway, the front entrance, and the lobby. The lobby guards operating the metal detectors wore sidearms. Those manning the reception desk carried theirs concealed.

"Paul Janson and Jessica Kincaid to see Douglas Case."

Printed visitor badges were waiting for them.

They rode a private elevator to the executive offices on the twenty-ninth floor. The foyer overlooked low-lying smog, which a hot sun was turning orange. The near-silent hum of a belt-driven electric power chair was punctuated by a glad shout of, "Paul!"

Janson intercepted the custom-built six-wheel vehicle and thrust out his hand. "Hello, Doug. How are you doing?"

"Great. Great. Terrific."

They clasped hands and searched each other's faces for a long moment. Two well-dressed white guys nearing middle age, thought Jessica Kincaid. Doug Case looked as rugged as Paul, clean shaven, with an expensive version of a military buzz cut, a four-thousand-dollar suit, a crisp white shirt, and a shimmering yellow necktie.

"Thanks for coming so fast."

"Our pleasure. This is my associate Jessica Kincaid."

Doug Case's hand had the flexible power of laminated Kevlar. He inspected her with a piercing gaze, then called over his shoulder to Janson, "What does she know?"

"About us?" Janson asked with a significant glance at the empty but still-public space. "Special Forces. You got shot and I didn't."

"What about you, Jessica? Where've you been?"

"Where she's been is not your business," Janson answered for her, in a tone both friendly and final.

Case said, "Did you know, Jessica, that my former, your present, 'associate' was once know by his fellow covert field officers as 'The Machine'?"

"That is a lame probe," Kincaid retorted. Taking a cue from Janson, she said it with a smile.

"The Machine was the best of the best. You've heard that?"

Janson said, "Drop it, Doug. Off-limits."

"Anyhow," Doug said, "we've all moved on, haven't we. These days my derring-do exploits are more along the lines of compromised SCADA systems."

He looked challengingly at Kincaid, who kept her smile in place. "Supervisory Control And Data Acquisition is increasingly vulnerable to cybersecurity incidents as corporations switch from secure private networks to Internet-based networks to save costs."

"But," Janson said, "SCADA is not why you asked us down here, Doug."

"Right about that. Come to my office."

They followed Doug Case's wheelchair down a wide hall lined with closed doors.

"How was your flight?" he asked over his shoulder.

"On time."

In Doug Case's front office an elegantly dressed middle-aged woman he introduced as Kate presided over a pair of assistants with polished Junior League smiles. His private office faced south. "You can see the Gulf of Mexico on a clear day."

"But at this moment," Janson said, "you would prefer to see the Gulf of Guinea."

"Where did you get that idea?"

"What shape is ASC in?"

"Terrific shape. Our safety standards are the highest. We're don't screw up in the field and we're tops at controlling costs so we pull more profit out of a barrel of oil than anybody. Plus, American Synergy kept its head when everyone else was going nuts for alternatives and sinking dry wells."

"But you didn't sink that many wet ones, either, and if there is anywhere in the world right now where ASC can boost its dwindling oil reserves it's West Africa. Cullen hit it big off the Ivory Coast and you're probably hoping for the same, before the Chinese snap it up. So your problem is in the Gulf of Guinea."

"You've done your homework, Paul. Per usual. But not for this assignment. It has nothing to do with oil reserves."

"What is your problem?"

"You may have heard that we lost an offshore service vessel last week."

"I saw a report that an OSV sank with all hands in the Gulf of Guinea. I was not aware it belonged to American Synergy. It was registered to a Dutch firm."

"We've since learned that the boat was attacked by Free Force Movement insurgents."

"Why?"

"They murdered the crew."

"Why?"

"Who the hell knows? The problem is, the murdering lunatics snatched one of our people. We've got to rescue him. That's where you come in."

"That will be a tall order if the Free Forces took your man to their base on Pico Clarence," said Janson.

"Pico Clarence is exactly where they have him, high on that mountain, deep in the interior."

"Getting back to my questions, why?... FFM insurgents murdering your boat crew doesn't make sense. FFM is winning its war. 'President for Life' Iboga is roundly hated."

"Eating the testicles and brains of your political rivals tends to piss people off," Case agreed. "Even in Africa."

"Iboga is losing," said Janson. "He's about to be toppled."

President for Life Iboga had wrecked the economy of Isle de Foree, which had broken away from Equatorial Guinea, backed by the Nigerian military. Iboga, opposition leader in Isle de Foree's parliament and former fighter in the Angolan wars, seized power in a coup. Renaming himself Iboga after the rain-forest hallucinogen, the dictator had handed the coffee and cocoa plantations to his corrupt friends and let the island nation's small, antiquated oil infrastructure go to hell.

"As I understand it, the rebels are buying munitions from Angolan and South African gunrunners. They've already cleared the sky around Pico Clarence of Iboga's helicopters. And they just broke their leader out of Black Sand Prison, which is another reason why killing your people doesn't make sense. Ferdinand Poe is a beacon of democratic hope. Why would Ferdinand Poe's fighters endanger his righteous rebellion by slaughtering innocents? He can't afford to outrage nations he needs to recognize his new government as legitimate."

"Good question," admitted Case. "But I repeat, who knows? Fog of war? A signals screwup? Revenge? It's been a long, bitter fight with plenty of brutality on both sides."

"Have they demanded ransom?" asked Jessica Kincaid.

"No. Our guy is a doctor. Looks like they wanted a doctor for Ferdinand Poe. You can imagine what the Black Sand jailors did to him."

"But if the boat sank," said Kincaid, "and the crew was murdered and the rebels didn't ask for ransom, how did you learn that FFM took one of your people?"

"Guess," said Douglas Case.

"Guess?" she said, shooting Janson a who-is-this-jerk? look.

Janson, already aware that Jessica and Doug had formed an instant dislike for each other, answered soothingly, "Since ASC holds positions in several Gulf of Guinea Joint Development zones, I would imagine that Doug takes time off from his SCADA exploits to maintain contact with African arms dealers to keep abreast of events in the insurgent camp. Correct, Doug?"

Douglas Case winked. "Score another for The Machine." He turned to Kincaid and said, "The guys supplying FFM's artillery reasoned that I'd be interested in what was happening on Pico Clarence."

"Why don't you hire the gunrunners to rescue the doctor?"

Case laughed and winked again at Janson. "Out of the mouths of babes."

"What?" snapped Kincaid.

"They're *gunrunners*. They sneak stuff in; they don't sneak it out. Besides, they won't do anything to disrupt the next sale. If FFM is winning like Paul thinks, the gunrunners are going to tread very lightly, hoping to move up the food chain from runners to dealers by selling more expensive weapons to their victorious friends in the new government."

A cell phone buzzed. Case snatched it from a molded dock among the buttons and controls that studded his chair's armrest. "I said no calls.... Right, thank you." He hung up and said, "You're about to meet Kingsman Helms, president of ASC's Petroleum Division."

"We saw the video," said Kincaid.

Case grimaced. "Corporate arrogance embodied," he said, and mimicked Helms's speech, " 'It isn't a matter of telling our story better. We have to create a better story.' How about this for a story: Big oil and coal have squelched production of American natural gas for twenty years. For some reason the shareholders think the sun rises and sets on the son of a bitch."

"You seem conflicted about your employer." Janson smiled.

"Helms is top snake in Buddha's nest of vipers."

"Who," Jessica Kincaid asked, "is Buddha?"

"That's what we call the Old Man."

"By 'the Old Man' you mean American Synergy's CEO, Bruce Danforth?"

"Correct. Kingsman Helms is one of four men and two women who would eviscerate their own mothers if that's what it took to replace Buddha as American Synergy's CEO."

"Are you another of those men?" asked Kincaid.

Case returned a cold smile. "Security is not on that career track."

"Security," Kincaid shot back, "just phoned you a heads-up that Helms is coming. You're keeping tabs on the competition."

"Security chiefs—and security consultants—are servants, Jessica. Which is something you'll come to understand if you stay in our business. We protect; we don't command."

The door flew open. The tall, blond thirty-eight-year-old Kingsman Helms barged in without knocking. "Doug, I understand you've called in the Marines."

Helms's piercing blue eyes lingered on Kincaid. "Hello, Marines." Then he bore down on Paul Janson. "Kingsman Helms," he said, thrusting his hand out. "Who are you?"

Kincaid hid a smile as she watched Janson step into the space Helms was heading for, blocking his rush, forcing him to pull up short. "Paul Janson. CatsPaw Associates."

"Which cat's paw would that be? Keats's 'quick cat's paws' that kill the fat straggler? Or the cat's paw the pope's monkey used to pull his nuts out of the fire? Or our modern pry?"

"We're a full-service outfit."

Helms grinned appreciatively. "Nice."

"This is my partner Jessica Kincaid."

"Nice to meet you, Jessica." Helms smiled, then turned on Janson in a tone all business. "So who are you two with, Janson?"

"CatsPaw Associates is independent."

"Independent is small."

"The clients we accept trust us to be nimble."

"I question," Helms replied coolly, "whether a small outfit can field the resources to do the job."

Douglas Case surprised Janson by interrupting, curtly: "Back off, Kingsman. This is my call."

Helms ignored him. "I cannot imagine the reasoning behind paying two individuals—one middle-aged, the other a woman, no offense to either of you—to execute the sort of military operation required to rescue our employee."

Douglas Case spun his wheelchair in a half circle to face Kingsman Helms. Then Case stabbed a button in the armrest that raised his seat hydraulically while the base extended wheeled outriggers to balance the higher center of gravity. Eye to eye with the executive, Case spoke in a voice dripping with sarcasm.

"Imagine this: Our doctor is trapped in a war zone in the middle of a remote island by a bloodthirsty rebel army surrounded by a vicious dictator's army. The kind of 'resources' you're spouting civilian fantasies about would blow it into a three-way war and get the doctor killed in the process."

"I am merely—"

Case cut him off, again. "Isle de Foree is two hundred and fifty fucking miles offshore and none of the jumping-off points on the African coast are all that amenable to corporate bullshit. Corporate won't save our guy. Quick and light will. He's in a hell of a jam, and

I don't know anyone better qualified to get him out of it than Paul Janson. I'll stake my job on it."

"That's quite an endorsement," said Helms. "It sounds like you got the job, Paul. What's this costing us?"

"Nothing until we produce your man. We cover our expenses. Doug gets the family rate. Five million dollars."

"That is a lot of money."

"Indeed it is," said Janson.

"All right! Here are your marching orders: Save the doctor at any cost; spare nothing. ASC stands by its people. We are a family."

"We haven't accepted the job," said Janson.

"What? What's stopping you?"

"We need to know more about the circumstances. What was the doctor doing out there?"

"Doing? He was doing his job."

"What is his name?" asked Kincaid.

Helms glanced at Doug Case, who then said, "Flannigan. Dr. Terrence Flannigan."

Janson asked, "What was Dr. Flannigan doing on an offshore service vessel? Six-man boats don't carry company doctors. Or was the OSV ferrying him somewhere?"

Again Helms looked to Doug Case as if the job description of a company doctor was not his concern. Case said, "We're presuming they were ferrying him out to a rig to care for somebody who got hurt."

"Why didn't they helicopter the victim to shore? That's how it is usually done."

"Look into it, Doug," Helms told Case. "Find out where Dr. Flannigan was going." He showed his teeth in a grin. "Better yet, Paul, if you manage to rescue him quickly you can ask him yourself. Pleasure meeting you. And you, too, Jessica. I must go. I really do hope you take the job," he said, and left.

"What do you say, Paul?" asked Doug Case. He was deferential all of a sudden, even pleading. *He* certainly wanted Janson to take it. Janson did not put much weight on that. People preferred working with people they knew.

"We will look into the feasibility of the operation," he said. "You'll have our answer in twelve hours."

Jessica got to the door first and held it for him. But Doug Case called, "Paul, could you wait a moment? I'd like to speak with you alone."

Janson stepped back into Case's office and closed the door. "What's up?"

"I really appreciate what you're doing."

"I will do what is feasible."

"Once again, I owe you."

"I told you before: If you owe anything, pay the next guy."

"Thank you. I will do that. Now, listen, whether or not Helms is our next CEO has no bearing on this kidnap situation. Buddha is not retiring tomorrow. So don't worry about Kingsman Helms."

"I'm not."

"What I told him is true. I can't think of anyone else who could pull this off without accidentally embroiling the company in a fucking civil war. All we want is our man back. And I don't have to tell you that it would solidify my position here."

"If I feel I can pull it off, I will take the job."

"Is Jessica Kincaid the sniper you told me about? The one who was the best you'd ever seen?"

"None of your business."

"I'm only asking because I'm hoping for both our sakes that if you're working with a woman she's someone you've worked with long enough to really count on."

"I count on her," Janson answered patiently. "She excels at everything she turns her hand to."

"A Machine-ette?" Case grinned.

Janson reflected momentarily. As he had told Case already, Kincaid's operator training, mastery of the "deadly arts," and service record were nobody's business. But Janson saw no reason to hide his admiration. "She is a perfectionist and hungry to learn—dance, saber, telemark skiing, swimming, boxing. She takes elocution lessons from an acting coach to learn how to mimic body language, she throws herself into foreign languages most people never heard of, and she's close to getting certified to fly jets."

"Are we a smidgeon smitten by our protégée?"

"Awed," said Janson. "Is there anything else? I need to get going."

He headed for the door and had his hand on the knob when Case said, "I've worked with women. They're smart. A hell of a lot smarter than we are."

"Based on all the evidence, I agree."

"But I never worked with a woman in the field. At least not under fire, never when the lead was flying. What's it like?"

Janson hesitated. Doug's question—even if he was asking in general what it was like to work with a woman—caught him off-stride. That surprised him. He was a man who reviewed his life in small ways on a constant basis. But the survival habit of compartmentalizing his thoughts and emotions and desires ran deep. Was it possible that until this moment he had never fully considered, or allowed himself to consider, how central Jessica Kincaid had become to his life as protégée, business partner, and friend?

"Do you have a dictionary in that computer?"

Case rolled across the office, lowered his chair to desk height, opened a computer window, and poised his powerful hands over the keyboard.

Janson smiled, suddenly clear in his mind. "What is it like? Look up 'Comrade-in-arms.'"

Doug Case typed in the old-fashioned warrior phrase, scrolled down the entry, then read aloud: "'An associate in friendship, occupation, fortunes'?"

"That nails it."

"But," Case said, "the downside I see to working with a woman is that in the clutch, when the lead is flying, it's only natural that you'd be distracted, worried about her getting hurt. Particularly if she's your protégée. Devoted followers have a habit of getting killed in our line of work. I've lost them; so have you."

"Jessica is predator, not prey."

* * *

DOUG CASE TOUCHED his telephone the instant the door closed behind Paul Janson.

Bill Pounds, one of his ex-Ranger ASC field agents, was watching the lobby. "Yes, sir?"

"They're on their way. Report where they go. Don't let them make you."

"No one makes the invisible man."

THREE

Bill Pounds walked quickly to his metallic-green Taurus parked in the No Parking zone. His partner, Rob, a hard-eyed moonlighting Houston Police Department detective, was at the wheel. They watched a red and white Fiesta Taxi pull up to the building's entrance. The middle-aged businessman and the gal in the seersucker suit climbed into the cab.

The Fiesta Taxi driver had been instructed to leave his cell phone on. Pounds and Rob heard the woman say, "Brown Convention Center."

Rob wheeled the Taurus onto the Sam Houston Tollway after them and followed at a distance. "The Brown's got two conventions showing this week, National Association of Black Accountants and the Texas Towmen, and they don't look like either."

"Pass 'em," Pounds ordered. "I'll wait for them in the lobby."

* * *

Jessica Kincaid leaned close to whisper, "What did he say?"

"Tell you later."

Janson sat back and watched the scenery, such as it was. Outside the taxi window Houston looked hot and dry, a flat, new land empty of people and full of cars. Janson looked through it, past it, to London with crowded sidewalks, ancient stonework, and lush green Regent Park the day that Cons Ops sent Jessica Kincaid to kill him.

She had been good then, already, among the best of the younger operators, but lacking the instincts acquired in the course of the miles that he carried. She was still ready to believe the bosses, completely sure of herself, and fiercely defiant. When he had pulled her out of her sniper perch and taken away her guns and put one to her head she responded, "You're overmatched, Janson. No embassy lardasses this time. This time they cared enough to send the very best."

The very best was Sniper Lambda Team. And Jessica Kincaid was their Janson expert, having made him the subject of the "Spy Bio Paper" required by the Cons Ops instructors. The Lambda snipers were operating as singletons—one reason he was still alive—each tasked with the complicated job of finding their own targets, instead of relying on a spotter. There were five of them, stationed on buildings and in trees. If he got out of the park they had strollers with Glocks waiting on the sideways.

He had pulled Jessica out of her tree not knowing she was a woman until he was on top of her. She had been astonishingly strong and agile, an extraordinary marksman, quick thinking, and a practiced liar. When he had taken his eyes off her for one second, she brained him with the nearest weapon at hand.

"What?" she said.

"I was thinking about our blind date in London," he said with a smile for the benefit of the driver, whose eyes kept shooting to his rearview mirror. Janson could not see over the back of the seat, but he assumed that the cell phone was still lying faceup in the driver's lap.

Jesse grinned back. "Remember laying in the grass?"

Janson touched his temple where she had dealt him half a concussion with a length of steel rebar. "Vividly."

They had met next in Amsterdam. She had caught him flatfooted and he had seen death in her rifle barrel. He remembered looking back calmly. The memory sustained him. He was proud of how he had accepted the inevitable. For he had had no doubt he was about to die. She had been built to kill and nothing could stop her.

The cab slowed for the convention center exit.

Jessica Kincaid watched him peel two twenty-dollar bills off the roll he always carried. Cash for the driver. No receipts, no tracks, and a fast exit. Janson saw her watch the money. Cash had memories for her. Sixteen years old, lighting out of Red Creek, Kentucky, the day she graduated high school, buying a Greyhound ticket with a wad she lifted from the cash register in her father's ramshackle gas station. The father who had raised her alone when her mother died, and taught Jessica to hunt, fish, fix cars, and shoot. The father who wouldn't allow her to do anything girls did because the sight of her cooking, cleaning, keeping house, would twist a knife in the wound of losing his wife.

"You know, you could drive down there one day and pay it back with interest."

"Don't think I haven't thought about it."

"One of these days you'll do it."

"Is that a fact, Janson? And how do I pay back betraying him?"

"I've seen you do harder."

"It only looked harder."

"You'll find a way."

"Yeah. One of these days."

* * *

BILL POUNDS WATCHED Janson and Kincaid pay off their taxi, enter the Brown Convention Center, and head down the connector to the Hilton, where they were either staying or going to another meeting or just maybe switching taxis. He followed, well screened by the crowds hurrying back and forth. All of a sudden they stopped. Rest rooms. The woman ducked into hers. The guy kept going. Pounds stuck with him. Seconds later the guy stopped, too, ten yards past the restrooms, turned around, and headed back like he'd decided to take a leak after all.

The ASC security agent did not break stride or swerve but continued coolly ahead, intending to pass close, avoiding eye contact, innocent as the others hurrying through the corridor. The guy bumped into him. The ex-Ranger was a well-built two hundred pounds, but it felt like crashing into a cinder block wall.

"Tell Doug Case to grow up."

Slate-gray eyes were boring into him.

Pounds tried to bluff it out. "What?"

"I said, 'Tell Doug Case to grow up.' "

"Do I know you?"

Now the woman was behind Pounds, calling in a friendly country drawl, "Hey, hon, how you doing?" and taking his elbow, and sending a jolt of unbelievable pain through a nerve he had not known existed in his arm. For half a second he couldn't see straight. Then he was leaning on the wall and they were walking unhurriedly toward the Hilton.

* * *

THE JOB WOULD not be feasible without routes in and out of FFM's
Pico Clarence camp.

In the cab to Hobby Airport, Paul Janson exchanged circum-
spect text messages with a weapons dealer he trusted more than
most, Neal Kruger, and the deputy national commissioner of the
South African Police Service, Trevor Suzman. Jessica Kincaid
Googled maps and charts on her iPhone, routed them to her computer on the plane, and queried the Frenchman who handled their
helicopter needs in Europe.

They followed up with voice links as the Embraer soared off the
runway. The plane's secure Inmarsat satellite telephones employed
IP Tor protocols in a virtual private network. Kincaid produced a
slide show of maps and charts on their Aquos 1080 monitors.

"Ready."

Janson had a pretty good idea how he would prefer to go in—
quick and light on the backs of the gunrunners—but to stay alive
he and Kincaid would consider every available alternative, from the
least obvious to the unlikely. Sometimes something better came
along. And when the ground shifted and you had to change tactics,
you could keep moving ahead if you didn't waste time dreaming up
options.

"Helicopters?"

"The EC 135 with a long-range fuel tank will give us five hundred miles round-trip," Kincaid answered. "It's a powerful twin-
engine machine, easy to get in Europe and findable in West Africa.
Tough, but not impossible, to land in the jungle. I see three possible sites near the foot of Pico Clarence, but the topo maps suck
and there's no satellite shots that penetrate the canopy."

Janson studied the topographic maps of Pico Clarence she had put on the screen. What was known about the volcanic mountain's terrain was based on Portuguese government surveys in the 1920s. Then he scrolled through her maps of the African coast. "The problem with the helicopter is where do we base from? Five hundred miles round-trip, two-fifty one-way, tops, limits our takeoff point to Nigeria, Cameroon, Equatorial Guinea, and Gabon. Cameroon, Equatorial Guinea, and Gabon are waiting to see who wins, so definitely won't give permission to launch from their territory. Which means if we launch from them we have to return elsewhere. Nigeria seems to have sided with Dictator Iboga. But I would hate to have to trust the Nigerians to keep their word."

"Isn't there a Nigerian lady you know sort of well?"

"She's in London these days. Besides, even with the extra tank, the EC 135 will not offer much leeway range-wise."

"The Super Puma doubles our range. So will a Sikorsky S-76. Plenty of them in the oil patch. Your pal Doug could get us one easy."

"The S-76 would put Ghana, Togo, Benin, and Congo within striking distance, but those governments also want to be hands-off until someone wins the revolution. The Puma is an eighteen-passenger machine. Too big."

"Another possibility is an EC 135 from a ship passing offshore."

"Much better. Except how do we persuade FFM not to shoot it down thinking it belongs to Iboga? They've done a thorough job of clearing the sky."

"Scratch the helicopter. What if we fly commercial or private into Porto Clarence? Drive inland to the end of the road. Walk into the jungle. Grab the doctor and walk back to Porto Clarence."

"What if President for Life Iboga wants to interrogate the doctor about the insurgent camp, or Ferdinand Poe's state of health?"

"We'd have the same problem with an airdrop. If we chute in

we'll still have to walk out. That leaves a boat. Boat ashore. Walk inland. Walk back. Boat out."

Paul Janson said, "I'm wondering if we should draft in on the gunrunners. Somehow they're getting on and off the island and in and out of the camp. They must be bribing Iboga's coast guard patrols and soldiers."

"But your pal Doug says they're hands-off."

"I was talking to Neal Kruger. The Swiss? He claims he knows where to get some Starstreaks still in the crate."

Kincaid's eyes widened. "Cool."

"We could trade them to the gunrunners for passage in. The FFM would be happy to buy man-mounted laser-guided surface-to-air high-velocity missiles. We land on their boat, split off from them once we're close, go in light, and come out fast."

"What if the gunrunners run into trouble?"

"We have our own boat waiting and rendezvous offshore with an OSV."

"Supplied by Doug?"

"No. The client pays for deniability."

Kincaid said, "Another problem: FFM is not going to be happy when we skedaddle with the doctor. Would the gunrunners risk pissing off their client?"

"We'll have to find some way to persuade them to take the chance."

Janson studied the topo map until he became aware that Jessica was staring at him.

"What is it?"

"Why did Case have us followed?"

Janson shrugged. "Old warhorse stuff. Just trying to keep his hand in."

"Why did he keep asking about me?"

"Same thing. Old reflexes. I noticed you took a strong dislike to him. Why?"

"He's a jerk."

"Have you ever met a top operator who was not a pedal-to-the-metal, Type A, supercompetitive personality?"

"I'm not a jerk. Neither are you."

"Some of us hide it better than others. Just like some hide what it feels like sitting in a wheelchair better than others."

"That's a cool chair. Did you see the balance wheels come out when he raised the seat?"

"Typical Doug. He threw unbelievable energy into designing it, while he was still recovering. He said, 'Damned if I've going to sit when everyone's standing.' Went about it like it was an operation."

"Did the foundation back it?"

"Sure. Doug wants everyone who can't walk to have one, but at a hundred-and-forty grand a pop it's going to be a while. Anyway, they're still working out the kinks. What did you think of Kingsman Helms?"

"Good-looking. Going places. I pity who gets in his way.... Paul?"

"What?"

"Is Doug Case one of the 'saved'?"

"The 'saved'?"

"Is Doug Case one of the former agents who you've rescued with your covert MacArthur-genius grants?" Jessica said.

"Covert MacArthurs? I like that." Paul Janson showed his pleasure with a smile. "Good a name as any."

Jessica stared at him, demanding an answer.

Janson was not inclined to answer. Rules kept him alive. Both of them alive. Need to know was the primary rule. "*Why* do you ask?"

"This doctor rescue is not a good job."

"I would not call it a piece of cake," said Janson. "But it's not as grim as Doug made it out to Helms. Strict in-out. Insertion and extraction."

"A rebel camp that successfully defends itself is a hornet's nest."

"You and I have done worse."

"I'm trying to figure out why you want to take the job."

"The doctor deserves rescuing."

"So do a lot of people. Lucky for him ASC can afford our fee. But that's not why you want the job. Is it because Kingsman Helms and Douglas Case are cooking up something they didn't tell us about?"

"I don't know about 'cooking up.' They're probably just holding something back."

"They are lying," she said firmly. "You know it and that intrigues you."

Kincaid knew Janson so well she could see on his face the lupine gleam of the hunter catching movement on the periphery of its vision. No, she corrected herself. Not lupine, he's not an animal in the woods; he's more like a pirate: Something was out there and he was sailing closer, wondering was it something he wanted?

But Janson only shook his head. "I don't *know* that they're lying."

He extinguished the gleam so thoroughly that even she could not tell what he was thinking. "But yes, I am intrigued. For the U.S. and China, and anyone else trying to corner a stable source of oil, the Gulf of Guinea looks more and more like an end run around the mess in the Middle East. The stakes are huge, potentially."

Kincaid knew that. It was obvious. What was not obvious to her, and it drove her crazy, was what he was really thinking. What did Janson want? He was as complicated a person as she had ever known. She had learned that his apparent straightforwardness was more a factor of acute decisiveness. Like her, he thought and acted quickly. It was necessary to survive. But in Paul's case, she thought, decisiveness masked complication.

"But it's more than that," she pressed him. "I think you are also influenced by concern for Doug Case. Isn't that the truth?"

"The truth?" Janson returned a bantering smile. "Our old friend."

"*Your* old friend," she retorted, and watched his thoughts sink inward.

To keep healing Paul Janson knew that he had to brave the truth daily: Crimes he had committed to serve his country were still crimes; assassinating even the most deserving of termination was murder; a successful assassin was a serial killer; and unless an agent possessed the empty heart of a sociopath, murder after murder exacted a fierce toll on the murderer.

But as he had explained years ago to Doug Case, admitting the truth could only save him if he atoned. He could not change the past, but he could work with every fiber in his being to make amends. That was his dream, one that was battered daily by reality, human failings, moral conundrums, and the paradox of atoning for violence with violence.

"Yes," he admitted. "Doug is one of the 'saved.'"

"I *knew* it!" she said triumphantly. "The Phoenix strikes again."

"Doug was my first. Back when I was blundering around on my own."

Doug Case had been right about one thing: Janson had soon discovered that it was impossible to do it alone. The man who loathed institutions had to create one. He had recruited experts to help create the Phoenix Foundation to seek out and rehabilitate former covert officers suffering the mental wounds of dehumanizing service. Astute management of the money planted in his overseas accounts, bold moves at moments of financial meltdown, and some astonishing good luck helped pay for Phoenix grants to former covert operators to set them up in academia or public service or community institutions. Jobs like this one to rescue ASC's doctor earned the money to maintain facilitators, specialized operators, computer wizards, and hackers.

None knew the whole story. Jessica was special and knew more than most.

"Doug is also a major success. Head of global security for the biggest oil company in the world. In his so-called spare time he's big brother, dad, and uncle to an entire halfway house for former gangbangers crippled in shoot-outs. At Christmas everybody gets an electric superchair."

"What did he do? What did you save him from?"

"Nothing you need to know."

"Of course I don't *need* to know. Except if I'm suddenly hanging upside down by my ankles watching you get tortured and waiting for my turn, I would like to think that we went into this job with our eyes open."

"Funny you should mention torture."

"What is funny about torture?"

"Doug Case was against torture. Vehemently. He believed that everyone—citizen, soldier, covert agent—was in the war against terror. Therefore, he claimed, we should not destroy the best part of ourselves—our civilization, our morals—just to save ourselves. He said innocent victims who are killed because a terrorist was *not* tortured into giving up information die serving the greater good."

"Which is?"

"Our decency."

"The boys must have loved him at Cons Ops."

"You may recall," Janson reminded Jessica drily. "Consular Operations was not a debating society. He only spoke about it after."

"After what?"

"After he shot his partner to stop him torturing an asset they had captured in Malaysia."

"He *shot* a fellow agent?"

"Twice in the head."

"He shot an *American*? Jesus, Paul. No wonder he's in a wheel-chair. Who put him there?" Her eyes got big. "You?"

"Vengeance ain't my style, Jesse. You know that. There is no revenge. Not on this earth."

"Yeah?" She stared at him probingly. "Then who did it?"

"He put himself in that wheelchair."

"Come again?"

"Doug stepped off the roof of our embassy in Singapore."

"Suicide?"

"That was his intention. But the body doesn't always obey the mind. He'd done too many parachute jumps to auger passively into the ground. His body remembered how to fall. Saved his life, if not his spine."

"Wow...But you said he got shot."

"That was a different time."

"When did you step in?"

"When I found him begging on Washington Boulevard in Ogden, Utah."

"How'd you track him down? VA hospital?"

"He grew up in Ogden. When it all goes to hell, people go home."

Jessica Kincaid shook her head. "Sometimes I feel guilty."

"For what?"

"All the good stuff you do that I don't."

Janson laughed. "One crusader in the outfit is plenty—Seriously, Jesse, you're young. You're in a different place; you're still honing yourself, learning your craft. Go tell Mike we're going to Africa."

Jessica Kincaid stepped to the front of the plane and opened the cockpit door. Forty thousand feet under the Embraer's long nose fenced farmland stretched for as far as she could see. Fields were green in the sunlight. Creeks and rivers were fringed with trees.

She laid a hand each on the shoulders of Mike and Ed. "Boys, you know where Africa is?"

"Heard of it," said Ed.

"The boss wants to go there."

Mike asked, "Any particular part of Africa?"

"Port Harcourt, Nigeria."

She observed closely as Ed brought the changed destination up on the Honeywell Flight Management System. New-generation software integrated the Embraer's WAAS GPS, waypoint data, and the Future Air Navigation System for flying under transocean Procedure Control. He began charting a course to minimize distance and fuel burn.

"Hang a right," he told Mike, showing him the course. "We'll fuel up in Caracas."

Mike said, "Better get some sleep."

"Soon as I enter our passenger manifest for Customs and Border Protection."

Mike tossed a grin over his shoulder at Kincaid. "Miss Jessica, if I were to move over while Ed sacks out, would you like some left-seat flight time?"

"You bet!" she said, always eager to fly the plane. She listened while Mike radioed Atlantic Air Traffic Control Center, through whose airspace they were flying, to request permission to change their route. When he received clearance to turn to a new course, he eased the big silver jet onto its starboard wing.

"Be right back," said Kincaid. "Soon as I check on the boss."

She hurried to the main cabin, braced against the tilt. Janson was seated on the high side, staring out the window at nothing but sky. It's more than Doug Case, she thought. It's more than the doctor. The Machine sensed that something didn't fit. She thought of challenging him, of saying, "Something else is going on. What is it?" But even if Janson was ready to admit it, she knew by the tilt of his head that he could not put it into words, yet.

FOUR

In the Free Foree camp, hidden in the caves that honeycombed the densely forested mountainous center of the island state, seven frightened men waited with their arms tied around the trunks of broad-leaf evergreen ironwoods.

Shafts of sunlight pierced the ragged canopy seventy-five feet above their heads where rampant vines were killing the treetops. The drone of a swift stream racing down the mountain muffled the sounds of nearby activity, heightening the prisoners' sense of isolation from events that would determine their fate. They could not hear the shouting in the cave that sheltered the field hospital.

"What did they do to my father?" an angry Douglas Poe demanded of Dr. Terry Flannigan. The son of the leader of the Free Foree Movement was a tall, dark-skinned twenty-five-year-old with a wiry build, a hard mouth, and cornrowed hair.

"About everything you can do to a man and not quite kill him," the doctor replied, working hard at maintaining enough detachment to keep his head on straight. When you were trying to put a patient back together again it did not pay to dwell on the nature of his fellow human beings who had taken him apart.

Flannigan glanced warily at the son. Douglas Poe seemed thoroughly unhinged by the sight of his tortured father. One false move, thought the doctor, and he, too, would end up tied to a tree with the others waiting to be shot. Flannigan shivered. The air was markedly cooler on the slopes of Pico Clarence and even cooler inside the cave.

About the only part of the poor devil they hadn't tormented was his face. His eyes were closed—Flannigan had given him enough morphine from *Amber Dawn*'s first-aid kit to see to that—but if you didn't look at the rest of him what you saw in his face was a once-vigorous sixty-eight-year-old with salt-and-pepper mustache and eyebrows, a thick head of kinky hair, dyed black and growing out at the roots, big elephant ears, a narrow Portuguese nose, a strong jaw, and the double chin and round cheeks of a man who enjoyed himself at the dinner table. Flannigan found it hard to believe that Ferdinand Poe had given up his pleasures to lead a revolution. Almost as hard to believe that he was their prisoner.

"If he dies, you're next!" vowed the son.

"Fuck you!" said the doctor, who had nothing to lose. He could say what he wanted. They wouldn't hurt a hair on his head unless the old man kicked the bucket. But even though they needed a doctor for dozens of wounded, angry-son Douglas would pull the trigger if his father died. Just as Douglas was about to pull it on the jerks tied to the trees. Not that the doctor would grieve for those bastards. They were the commandos who had boarded *Amber Dawn* and shot everybody, so whatever they got they had coming.

But where it got strange was that Douglas the son, Ferdinand

Poe's son, was accusing his own soldiers of going rogue. Terry Flannigan did not know what the hell was going on. Except that the
commandos' leader, the South African psycho who had murdered
Janet, had disappeared before the rest got tied to the trees. Poe
had sent a hundred men out combing the jungle for him with orders to shoot to kill. But the doctor had seen the South African
operate on the long boat trip into the island and the dangerous slog
through the swamps and forests and he would be very surprised if
they caught the animal.

Douglas Poe reached for his father's hand and felt him flinch
as he touched him. "I thought you gave him morphine!" Douglas
shouted accusingly.

"I told you not to touch him," said the doctor. "If I give him any
more he'll fall into a coma. Your cave is not equipped to monitor a
patient in a coma."

"But when—?"

Terrence Flannigan resorted to an answer as old as Hippocrates
and probably still current with witch doctors: "He needs time."

Douglas Poe drew his pistol from the holster strapped to his
thigh, spun on his heel, and stormed out of the cave. The soldiers tied to the trees craned their necks to watch him coming.
They tugged at the ropes holding them to the rough bark. A
man cried out. Another groaned. Their sergeant addressed Poe
in measured terms: "Douglas, Comrade, we only did what you
ordered us to do."

"I did not order you to kill them."

"Yes, you did. You said to kill the oil boat crew and sink the boat."

"I did not."

"Douglas. Brother. Comrade. I heard you with my own ears on
the radio."

"Liar. I never spoke to you on the radio."

"I heard you say it to Sergeant Major Van Pelt: 'Shoot them. Sink the boat.' "

"You have ruined everything my father worked for. All of you!" Douglas shouted. He strode from tree to tree, waving his gun in their faces. "My father planned to bargain with the oil company to free and rebuild our ruined nation. And what did you do? You killed the oil workers."

"You gave Sergeant Major Van Pelt the crew list."

"I did not."

"He told me you did."

Douglas Poe cocked his pistol, pressed the barrel to the sergeant's temple, and jerked the trigger. Then Poe hurried from tree to tree and shot the rest. It was over in thirty seconds. Terry Flannigan watched from the mouth of the cave, sickened and terrified. He wondered if he was strong enough to run for it like the South African?

Isle de Force was thirty miles long and twenty wide. Six hundred square miles. The insurgents held the highlands in the middle, and held it tightly if the scores of heavy machine guns Flannigan had seen mounted in treetops and the burned-out wreckage of Iboga's helicopters was any indication. The dictator controlled the lowlands that descended to the Atlantic Ocean, which seemed a very long way away. In between, where it was hotter and wetter, the forest thickened into lush jungle. Above the plantations. On the way up that had appeared to be no-man's-land. The insurgents had been cautious moving through it.

Should he run for it?

He was in lousy shape. He hadn't worked out in years and he drank too much. He was no soldier, no jungle fighter. They would catch him and kill him if he didn't get a long lead. Problem was, if the old man died they'd kill him anyway. He resolved to make a run for it, the sooner the better. A boy tugged at his arm, one of the kids who acted as orderlies. The only thing Flannigan liked about FFM was that they did not employ child soldiers. These were orphans kept safe in the camp running errands and bringing food and water. "He awakes."

"What?"

"Minister Ferdinand awakes." Ferdinard Poe had been foreign minister before Iboga seized power. They called him Minister.

Flannigan hurried to Poe's cot.

Ferdinand Poe was staring at him, peering through the drug like an ancient mariner piercing the fog. He had a strong voice that seemed appropriate to the strong jaw and the double chin and the round cheeks. The voice of a man who believed in himself. "Who are you?"

"I'm your doctor," said Flannigan, with a sinking heart. He wasn't going anywhere. "How are you feeling, sir?"

FIVE

Janson's diggers discovered that among the gunrunners supplying the Free Foree Movement was a tight-knit team of Angolans and South Africans. That explained their success in repeatedly breaking an island blockade. Tenacious Angolans had been fighting civil wars since the days of competing superpowers. Rebel diamonds and government oil had paid for tanks, helicopters, and fighter jets and they knew weapons and escape and evasion tactics like no one on the African continent. With the possible exception of the South Africans whose experience with advanced weaponry made them the mercenaries of choice.

The actual transporters were a young, recklessly brave pair—Agostinho Kiluanji and Augustus Heinz—nicknamed the Double As, of whom little was known, though Kiluanji was probably a nom de guerre taken from a heroic sixteenth-century defender against the invading Portuguese. Janson knew the type, poor but ambitious men putting their lives on the line to earn the money to become full-fledged weapons dealers. Money would talk.

But before the Embraer landed in Nigeria, the word came back on the sat phone that the Double As were not interested in ferrying two covert operators into the rebel camp.

"Increase the offer," Janson ordered.

His negotiator in Luanda did and reported back that they still weren't interested. "They're afraid it's a sting."

"Offer them the Starstreak missiles."

When his negotiator called back he sounded anxious. "What's wrong?" said Janson.

"They turned down the Starstreaks."

"And?"

"They say they'll kill me if I ask again."

"I like these guys," said Janson.

"What?"

"They're not greedy. Catch the next plane out of Angola. I'll deal with it."

Kruger in Zurich revealed the name of a Lebanese arms dealer, Dr. Hagopian, who supplied Augustus Heinz and Agostinho Kiluanji the weapons they delivered to FFM. Janson was surprised. Business must be tough. Selling contraband to warring Africans, while profitable, was one-shot bottom-feeding. Hagopian had been a key player since the days of arming Saddam Hussein against Iran on behalf of the United States. Maybe Dr. Hagopian was betting that FFM would win and become a sovereign client, where the steady money was. Maybe he needed the dough. Janson recalled a lavish estate on the Mediterranean and a mansion in Paris, elaborate security for both, and an equally costly wife.

His past dealings with Hagopian had left both of them satisfied. Now Janson instructed his eyes and ears in Europe to check

Hagopian out, seeking leverage, some new chink in his armor that had not been known before. He, of course, had cultivated excellent contacts among U.S. intelligence, which allowed him to operate relatively openly, and no legitimate regime had him on its arrest list. And yet weapons was a slippery, fast-changing world. Word came back that Hagopian had acquired a chink, a deep one. Of his two sons, one was in the business with him; the other, Illyich, was reported to be a "troublemaker."

"Troublemaker?" Janson asked. "How does an arms merchant's son make trouble: join the clergy?"

"No," answered the humorless Frenchman on the telephone. "The son has fallen in with thieves."

* * *

JANSON PRIED SOME details out of the Frenchman, then polled a few others in Europe. Then he telephoned a beneficiary of the Phoenix Foundation and told him he needed his help.

All Phoenix "graduates" had telephones fitted with an encryption chip that made conversations with Janson impenetrable to surveillance. Not all beneficiaries knew that Paul Janson was behind the foundation, but Micky Ripster, like Doug Case, was an old friend.

"Why me?"

"I need it done immediately in London and you're in London."

"Well, that's not very flattering, is it? Geography trumps talent."

"It's my good fortune you're on site. No one else could pull this off."

"But you forget that you paid me to retire."

"I am paying for your rehabilitation, not your retirement. Don't worry; it's for a good cause."

"And now you expect my help killing for 'a good cause'? Isn't that how we got into trouble in the first place? What's different about killing for your causes?"

"The difference is that now we play by Janson Rules."

"Which are?"

"No torture. No civilian casualties. No killing anyone who doesn't try to kill us."

"No torture?" Micky Ripster repeated. "No civilian casualties? No killing anyone who doesn't try to kill us? Don't be put off by that strangling noise you hear on the telephone. It is not the encoder chip. It is merely me smothering my laughter."

"You owe me," Janson said in a voice suddenly cold. "I'm collecting, now."

There was a long pause. "So, uh, what Janson gives Janson takes back?"

"What *Phoenix* grants Phoenix retrieves to pass on to the next guy."

Ripster sighed. "All right, Paul. Who do you want killed?"

"No one."

"I thought—"

"It's not a killing job. It's a gamesman job and I never met a better gamesman than you. Syrian intelligence still believes that Israeli bombs destroyed their Dayr az-Zwar plutonium collection."

"Ah, well," Ripster demurred modestly, "it's what they want to believe."

Janson laid out what he needed.

Ripster asked, "And what do I get out of this? Other than the pleasure of what I must admit is an interesting challenge."

"The satisfaction of doing the right thing. And five times your day rate."

"*That's* generous."

"Not at all. You've got one day to do it, starting this minute."

* * *

ILLYICH HAGOPIAN, WHO had received his Christian name from his doting Russian mother, pedaled a three-speed vintage Raleigh bicycle with a wicker basket round and round London's Berkeley Square. Hagopian was young, handsome, and had the pouting mouth of a spoiled child. A yellow cashmere sweater was draped over his shoulders, its arms tied carelessly across his chest. The few people seated on park benches who noticed his repeated circles assumed he was posing for a commercial photo shoot or rehearsing until the photographer arrived.

It was a perfect day for setting a magazine advertisement in Mayfair. The afternoon sky was deep blue, immense plane trees filtered the sunlight that shimmered on limestone houses and green grass, and it might have been a long-ago afternoon when Queen Victoria reigned, except for the center-city buzz of taxis, delivery vans, and motorbikes.

On nearby New Bond Street, at the exclusive Graff Jewellers, a security guard and a salesclerk were unlocking the door with pounding hearts. If that wasn't Mick Jagger climbing out of a black BMW and heading for their shop with a bejeweled blonde on his arm, he surely looked like him. They opened the door and ushered the fabulously wealthy rock star and his expensive-looking girlfriend inside. Seen up close Jagger's skin looked oddly crepey, even for a performer who had been at it since the sixties. But the pistol he was suddenly holding in his gloved hand seized their attention, as did the blonde's. She, the clerk reported later, might have been in drag.

The guard, a retired Royal Marine, was having none of it. He grabbed for their pistols but saw reason, the clerk reported, when Mick Jagger fired a single shot into the carpet. Things moved quickly after that. The thieves filled velvet bags with the best neck-laces, bracelets, rings, and watches. Guard and clerk were made to lie down behind the counter, and the pair were out the door and into the BMW in moments.

The black car shot down New Bond Street, turned right onto Bruton, and right again onto Bruton Place to Berkeley Square. They jumped out, leaving latex masks, guns, and wigs on the floor, bumped into a bicyclist who was waiting to cross the street, apol-ogized politely, and climbed into a waiting London black cab. The cabdriver pulled into the traffic heading down Berkeley Street to-ward Piccadilly. The bicyclist untied the sleeves of his cashmere sweater and dropped it in his basket.

As police sirens began echoing shrilly in the narrow streets, he walked his bicycle across Berkeley Street and into the square. Be-hind him, a yellow and blue Smartcar police car hooked around the corner of Burton Place and stopped beside the abandoned BMW.

The bicyclist, a cool-headed young man—despite appearances and the disappointments he had dished out to his father—stared innocently at the commotion over his shoulder and kept walking the bike. A Flying Squad car came down Berkeley Street at high speed, a large Volvo with siren screaming. Armed robbery special-ists jumped out, pistols in hand, and peered into the empty BMW. Pedestrians pointed toward Piccadilly. The Flying Squad roared off.

Having crossed the narrow square, Illyich Hagopian was mount-ing his Raleigh when two men, one dressed in a pinstripe suit, the other in jeans and windbreaker, rose from their benches and took his arms.

"Don't yell," they told him. "Or we'll call the cops."

"And show them what's in your basket."

A van pulled up. It had room for his bicycle. They snapped a set of handcuffs to his right wrist and the bike, ending any thought of jumping out of the van at a traffic signal. Then they took the velvet bags out of the basket and sealed them in a number of small padded postal envelopes. When Illyich Hagopian saw the printed address labels he thought he had lost his mind.

Graff Jewellers
New Bond Street
London W1
(Attention: Lost & Found)

The van stopped. The man in pinstripes hopped out and stuffed the envelopes through the slot of a post office pillar box and walked away. The van continued on. The mystified would-be jewel thief noted that they were following the signs to the M4 and Heathrow Airport and, once there, toward Airfreight.

"Where are you taking me?"

"Home to Mummy."

* * *

PAUL JANSON'S EMBRAER flew eleven hundred miles from Port Harcourt, Nigeria, into Luanda, Angola. It landed at Quatro de Fevereiro Airport, with Mike and Kincaid, who was sitting in for Ed in the first officer's seat, paying strict attention to tall oil derricks poking into the sky. They taxied through crowds of giant 747 air freighters and oil corporation passenger charters.

Dr. Hagopian's Angolan agent, operating under the guise of a translator of Portuguese, met Janson in the terminal and ushered him through a special section of passport control. He was half-Portuguese, half-Angolan, of the Fang tribe, a tall and handsome man in middle age with courtly manners. In the car he professed astonishment at the high regard in which Hagopian held Paul Janson: "The doctor said I am to treat you as if you were he. I will admit freely to you, sir, that he has never said a thing like that before."

"Don't worry; I'll be gone soon."

They drove twenty minutes to O Cantinho dos Comandos, a restaurant in the Old City, situated on the ground floor of a pink stucco building that housed an Angolan Army club.

The gunrunners themselves were not there but were represented by a young guy in a cheap leather jacket. Janson would have pegged him for a nightclub manager or car salesman. He seemed eager to please and started by saying, "I am in your debt, mister. A very important supplier who has both First Class and Economy Class clients informs me that from this day on I will fly First."

"My pleasure," said Janson. "You know what I want. I give you my word we will be no trouble. Just get us onto the island and set us loose. We will not get in your way and no one will ever know that you helped us."

The young man spread his hands in a gesture that feigned emotional devastation. "If only I could help you, I would. But the ship has sailed."

"When?"

"Yesterday. She is approaching Isle de Foree as we speak."

"Why didn't she wait?"

"The captain, he decided..." The man trailed off. Janson exchanged looks with Hagopian's agent, who appeared mortified by the screwup or betrayal, whichever it was.

The gunrunner said, "It is as well, my friend—the situation has changed on the island. Iboga has acquired a shipload of tanks."

"What kind of tanks?"

"Amphibious snorkel-equipped T-72s."

A tank attack on the FFM stronghold would be bad news for the doctor, thought Janson. There was no time to lose if they were going to get him out of there. "Where'd they get T-72s, the Nigerians?"

Hagopian's agent nodded. "Nigerian Directorate of Military Intelligence has not, shall we say, kept its fingers out of that pie."

"You would not want to be there when the tanks come," said the gunrunner.

"I want to be there."

"As I say, if there is anything I could do to help, my friend." He opened hands even wider to Hagopian's agent. "Anything. You need only to ask. But the ship has sailed." He turned back to Janson. "Anything."

"I'm taking you up on that right now," said Janson, which elicited a tentative, wary, "If I can . . ."

"You can and you will. Radio your captain that we will catch up with his ship. Tell him to stay fifty miles off until we get there." That would put the ship well beyond Isle de Force's territorial sea and contiguous zone.

"I don't know how long he can stall. There are schedules, rendezvous."

"He can wait eight hours," said Janson, and Hagopian's agent nodded cold agreement.

Back in the car on the way to the airport, Janson said nothing until Hagopian's agent finally broke the silence. "The tanks?"

"What shape do you suppose they are in?" Janson asked.

"Usable," said the agent. "And, of course, as everyone knows, Isle de Foreens are excellent mechanics."

Janson nodded. Island people were always good mechanics. "Who will drive them?"

"The presidential guard are Angola veterans. They are no strangers to Russian tanks."

Janson pondered that. Not that he was looking for a fight with the dictator's forces, but if he ran into them he had to be prepared.

"May I propose a thought?" the agent said.

"Please."

"It is possible that Dr. Hagopian might know of some respectable, trustworthy individual at the airport who might have access to some RPG-22s."

"I would rather Dr. Hagopian know of someone who has access to AT-4s." The excellent AT-4, a powerful anti-tank recoilless rifle made by Saab, was capable of stopping the Russian-built T-72s. Six warheads and launchers would weigh ninety pounds, the absolute limit they could carry in on top of the rest of their gear.

"I would strongly doubt that AT-4s could be available in time for a rendezvous in eight hours."

"Would there be any already on the ship?"

"Sadly, no. She is not an arsenal, but mainly conveying legitimate cargo."

The Russians made the less powerful RPG-26 and there was no shortage of Russian and older Soviet arms in Angola. "Do the gunrunners have any?"

"Not on this run. All they're carrying are machine pistols, ammunition, and drugs for malaria and infection."

"Would Dr. Hagopian know anyone in Angola with access to six RPG-26s?"

The agent shrugged. "Perhaps he could find one or two."

"With HEAT?" A shaped-charge warhead to penetrate the tanks' armor.

"Yes. But his associate would possibly be forced to complete the order with RPG-22s."

An older version, out of production since Jessica was in elementary school. Janson frowned. Hagopian's agent said, "In perfect condition, recently uncrated and thoroughly inspected."

"I would expect no less of a trustworthy associate of Dr. Hagopian," Janson said sternly.

Back at the airport twenty-five minutes later, Janson ordered, "Port-Gentil soon as we load up." The seaport was on the coast of Gabon, which lay north of Congo, and closer to Isle de Foree. Mike and Ed already had their course punched in.

Within the hour a truck with a noisy refrigeration unit backed up to the Embraer and unloaded six dripping crates onto the tarmac in the shade of the plane. Ed and Mike began humping them aboard.

"This is a hell of a lot of lobsters, Boss."

"Nothing like Angolan seafood," said Janson.

The pilots carried the crates into the plane before locking up and taking off for Gabon. "How'd you do?" Janson asked Jessica.

"Found a helicopter. How about you?"

"Found out the dictator got tanks."

SIX

The Sikorsky S-76 had worked long and hard in the oil
patch.

Fresh from the factory, the twin-turbine machine had
flown ChevronTexaco executives out to the seismic vessels exploring Angola's deepwater blocks. When the company started drilling,
they replaced the fancy leather seats with aluminum ones and used
the S-76 to ferry crew to the floating rigs. Long hours and salt water took their toll, as had dicey landings on sloped and slippery
helipads. Eventually the company downgraded the helicopter to
cargo runs before common sense dictated they sell it to an independent Italian company that traded it after several hard years to
settle a debt to an equipment-leasing outfit. AngolLease ran it until
a near-fatal hard landing bent its landing gear and shoved one of
the struts through the cabin floor, which had led to jury-rigging the
retraction mechanism. AngolLease passed it twelve hundred miles
up the coast to Port-Gentil, Gabon, into the hands of LibreLift, a

service operation owned by the pilots: an anorexic Frenchman with a sun-blasted face and a nicotine-yellowed walrus mustache, and a beefy Angolan wearing a patchwork of army uniforms, who also served as the helicopter's mechanic.

Janson had no desire to take the panels off to confirm how worn its guts were. Judging only by loose rivets, oil streaks along its tail boom, and crazed Plexiglas, he figured he had flown in a lot worse. Jessica Kincaid had not and she mentioned as soon as they had their headsets on that she smelled a fuel leak.

"No problem," said the pilot.

"You're smelling the extra tanks in the cargo bay," Janson explained. But the co-pilot/mechanic was quick to defend his brand-new composite tanks with crashworthy fuel cells that LibreLift would inherit after the job along with their mounting rafts. "Not auxiliary," he assured Kincaid. "Main tank leak. No problem."

She looked at Janson. "Am I supposed to be relieved?"

Janson pointed at the instrument panel. "You can relax unless you see one of these chip sensors light up."

"Chips of what?"

"If they sense chips broken off the main bearings floating around the oil pan, the manual says: 'Land while you still can.' "

"Glad to hear it." Kincaid checked their rigid inflatable boat, the RPGs they'd separated from the lobsters, and her personal weapons, then strapped in and closed her eyes. The S-76 got clearance and lifted off with a racket of loose turbine bearings. Despite the ominous sound effects, Janson and Kincaid exchanged an approving glance. The pilot had a nice smooth touch. By the time his helicopter was whining and thudding west making 130 knots at four thousand feet above the Atlantic Ocean both agents had fallen asleep. They awakened simultaneously in one hour.

"*Bateau délesteur*," said the Frenchman, pointing down at a little gray ship plodding through the murky sea. Janson glassed her. She was rust stained and heaped with cargo, a two-hundred-foot former OSV converted to freighting up and down the African coast. The main deck was crowded with used cars, pallets of bottled water, and lumpy shapes covered in blue poly tarps. With a three-deck wheelhouse sticking up in front and a fixed cargo crane in back, it offered no place to land a helicopter.

"Fast rope," Janson said, and handed the glasses to Kincaid. The wheelhouse roof, the highest point on the ship, was the safe choice for the helicopter to hover while they went down the rope. But it was small, and in the middle spun a horizontal four-foot radar dish.

Janson radioed the ship's captain on the short-range VHF channel the Angolan had specified to avoid transmitting on the general marine channel that anyone could monitor. The captain spoke only French. Janson passed the radio to Kincaid.

"Démonter la radar antenne, sil vous plait?"

The radar dish stopped spinning. While seamen climbed to the roof with tools and removed it, Janson and Kincaid attached the helicopter's cargo hook to the inflatable's harness. Then Janson and Kincaid put on their packs and rifles and rope gloves and snap-linked the bitter end of the fast rope to a cable donut ring anchored to the helicopter floor. Janson instructed the pilot to hover twenty meters above the wheelhouse.

The machine approached obliquely, angling in from the side. By now it was clear that the Frenchman was an exceptional pilot with light feet on his pedals, applying and reducing power smoothly. But unlike a ship captain, whose first responsibility was to his passengers, a helicopter pilot's priorities were machine and crew first, customers second. The Frenchman would do anything he had to to keep from crashing, which would include a sudden departure while Janson or Kincaid was still on the rope.

Kincaid dropped the running end of the fast rope, which was coiled around a length of firewood, out the door. The thick, braided line uncoiled down to the roof of the wheelhouse and snaked around violently, whipped by the rotor wash. Janson took it in his rope gloves, clutched it to his body after running it between his thighs and around his right calf. Assault rifle hanging from a strap over his shoulder, barrel down, face turned aside, he swung away and slid down, controlling his descent on the rough surface by squeezing the line in his gloves. His weight straightened the rope. Sixty feet under the helicopter he landed on the roof.

Kincaid tipped the heavy RIB pack out the door and lowered it with the electric cable winch. Janson guided it to the deck beside him, signaled for her to crank the cable up, then steadied the fast rope for Jessica. She came down in three seconds and touched lightly beside him. He signaled the pilot to go up, and let the rope ease out of his hands.

They climbed down the ladder behind the house, stepped into the wheelhouse, and greeted their reluctant hosts.

* * *

THE CAPTAIN WAS so nervous that his small store of English deserted him. His first mate, a Congolese, spoke no English at all. Janson's French was not up to the task. Kincaid took over and the captain quickly calmed down.

"Nicely done," said Janson. "How'd you get him smiling?"

"He likes my French accent. He thinks I live in Paris. He wants to have dinner next time we're both in the city. But we've got a problem. There's a U.S. Coast Guard cutter patrolling between us and Isle de Foree."

"I've been watching him on the radar," Janson replied. The

screen beside the silent helmsman showed a large ship twelve miles to the west. They had not seen her through the haze from the helicopter.

"What's our Coast Guard doing six thousand miles from home?"

"Must be part of the Africa Partnership Station, maintaining a 'persistent presence,' as they call it. In other words, showing the flag in the oil patch."

"Yeah, well, the captain's concerned they'll board us. Particularly if they spotted our helicopter on their radar. He wants to stash us in a hidey-hole down in the engine room."

"Ask him where are the gunrunners?"

"Already hiding."

Janson nodded to the captain and said to Jessica, "Assure the captain that we, too, have no desire to explain our presence to the United States Coast Guard. Tell him we'll hide if the cutter decides we're a Vessel of Interest. Let's hump the boat under-cover."

The captain ordered seamen to help and they got the RIB pack onto the main deck under a blue tarp. The radar target drew nearer. At eight miles the cutter appeared as a light dot on the horizon. At five miles she raised a tall, knife-like narrow silhouette. At four miles a helicopter took off from her, circled out around them, and went back.

Then the cutter radioed a boarding hail identifying herself as the U.S. Coast Guard Cutter *Dallas*, asserting their authority under the African Partnership Station. The captain answered requests for his ship's name, cargo, port of departure, and destination.

Janson could hear chatter on the cutter's bridge. It sounded like a lot of people were gathered around the radio. The captain muttered to Kincaid, who translated, "He says it's probably just an exercise—they've got local sailors visiting."

The *Dallas* announced their intention to board and requested the captain to heave to.

"*Merde!*" said the captain.

"*Merde* for sure," said Janson "All right, let's check out the hidey-hole."

They put on their packs. The Congolese first mate led the way, down four deck levels of stairs, at the bottom of which he swung a heavy door on the deafening roar of two three-thousand-horse-power 16-cylinder Electro-Motive Diesel engines. He led them through the engine room and out the back into a quieter, dimly lit tween-decks space. Halfway to the stern, he rapped his knuckles on a gray-painted bulkhead, waited thirty seconds, and rapped again. The bulkhead, which appeared to be an immovable slab of steel welded to scantlings, slid aside with a grinding of metal on metal. Janson was relieved to see that the gunrunners knew their business.

Two men stepped into the light, a black Angolan and a mulatto South African.

"What is this?" asked the South African in nasal English. His eyes widened at the sight of Jessica Kincaid, who had stepped back and drawn a pistol to cover Janson.

"Room for two more?" asked Janson.

"Are you the bloody American mercs?"

"We are the bloody American mercs," said Janson. "You are our bloody highly paid guides, Agostinho Kiluanji and Augustus Heinz. And the bloody Coast Guard is boarding. Why don't we continue this conversation undercover?"

The Congolese mate who supposedly spoke no English nodded emphatically.

The South African asked, "Any chance of the crumpet putting away the artillery?"

"Soon as we are all inside." Janson stepped past them into a gleaming stainless-steel chamber six feet in diameter and thirty feet long. He realized it was a tank originally installed to transport drilling mud.

"Clear!" he called to Kincaid. It was just the two men and a heap of gear, no one else holding a weapon. She and they stepped inside. The door slid shut with a clang that echoed. A single electric lantern provided light.

* * *

THE CONVERTED OSV stopped briefly ten miles offshore to hoist first the gunrunners' heavily laden rigid inflatable and then Janson and Kincaid's smaller RIB over the side. Then, as the ship hurried on toward Porto Clarence, Janson and Kincaid and Agostinho Kilu-anji and Augustus Heinz paid out a long line between their boats so they would not get separated in the dark and motored toward the invisible coast. They navigated with handheld GPSs, but with no lights marking the channels, Janson and Kincaid would have to rely on the experienced gunrunners ahead to find their way in the swampy mouth of the shallow river.

The shore was dark, devoid of lights, apparently uninhabited, which was to be expected, as 90 percent of the population lived in Porto Clarence. The outboard motors were relatively quiet at moderate speed and their noise would be blown away from the shore by the land breeze descending from the mountainous interior, but not quiet enough to hear surf pounding the beach. Instead, the warning they were near came in the form of the seas steepening as the water grew shallow. Janson shortened up the line, while Kincaid drove, until the lead boat was only a few meters ahead and he could see the silhouettes of the men steering for the river.

Suddenly they could hear the surf. The water grew violent, tossing the rubber boat, and just as suddenly the sound moved to either side. They were inside the mouth. The gunrunners throttled back, quieting their motor. Kincaid followed suit, swearing quietly under her breath as she shoved the motor left and right, trying to follow the twisting route of the boat ahead. Then they were under trees, out of the wind, and the warm air grew warmer and gathered like soap on the skin. Mosquitos descended, buzzing angrily around the repellant they had slathered on their necks and faces.

Pale lights shone through the trees—oil lamps, Janson guessed by their yellowish glow. If their owners heard the mutter of the slow turning outboards, they did not come closer to investigate. After what his carefully shielded GPS showed was a mile of movement inland, the boat ahead stopped and the engine went silent. Kincaid immediately choked their engine. In the quiet they heard insects sing and then the hollow grating sound of rubber on gravel as the boats drifted into a bank.

Moving quickly, they pulled the boats inside a cave-like space that the gunrunners had cut under mangrove knees that arched into the water. Janson sensed more than saw men waiting there and for an awful split second thought they'd been discovered. Instead, whispered greetings were exchanged and the men started unloading the gunrunners' boat.

Janson tapped Kincaid's shoulder. She stepped into his cupped hands, onto his shoulders, and pulled herself up between the mangrove knees. After a minute of silent watching, she toe-tapped his shoulder and he passed up her pack, then his, and hoisted himself after her. When Kiluanji and Heinz and their helpers finished loading backpacks they started inland on a path that led away from the river. Janson and Kincaid followed them. He checked the time. Three more hours of dark.

The path was at first a sort of narrow causeway across swamp with water on either side. But within a mile the land began to rise gently, and they left the water behind. They came to a dirt road, watched carefully, and crossed it quickly. Shortly they came to another, this one laid with a surface of oil, and crossed it, too, the land still rising. Dawn arrived abruptly, revealing geometric rows of green shrubs interrupted by wooden shacks. A familiar aroma indicated they had reached the cropland that supported Isle de Foree's coffee plantations.

They forged inland, skirting shabby buildings, quickening their pace as the strengthening light shredded cover. At a raised concrete road, the gunrunners signaled a stop while they listened for vehicles. Heinz came back and said to Janson, "You should go ahead at this point. You'll make better time climbing than we will with our lot."

Janson gauged the land ahead. It appeared to rise more steeply and the belt of plantations came to an end. He nodded to Jessica, who quickly removed thirty thousand euros in banded one hundreds from his pack and passed them to the South African. It represented more than Heinz and Kiluanji would make carrying the pistols and drugs.

Janson offered his hand. "Thank you."

"Strange."

"What?"

"No patrols. No presidential guard. Not even the guys we bribe. Haven't seen a soul."

"What does it mean?"

"Busy somewhere else. Cranking up an offensive."

"With the tanks?"

"All I know is I want to get in and out fast and you ought to do the same."

"In other words, speed it up," said Kincaid.

They bounded up the bank, crossed the concrete road, and broke into a run.

* * *

ABOVE THE CROPLAND belt thick jungle thrived in the humid heat. Kincaid's pack weighed seventy pounds, Janson's ninety. Streaming perspiration, they alternated a mile of running with a mile of walking up the ever-steepening trail. They covered three and a half miles in the first hour, two in the second as running became climbing. The reward was a slight drop in temperature and humidity as the jungle began thinning into rain forest with a high canopy. Here among the tall trees they stopped. They were beyond the reach of the dictator's troops that FFM had fought to a standstill at this level. This was a narrow no-man's-land. Beyond it FMM ruled their closely guarded territory that rose to their camp on the mountain of Pico Clarence.

From this point on they should wait until dark, when their night-fighting gear would give them the advantage of seeing while not being seen. But if the dictator was launching an offensive, did they have time to wait? So far things had gone like clockwork. They had gotten every break. Now was thank-you time. They had to pay back their good luck by taking a chance.

In half a mile, Kincaid, who was on the point, suddenly froze. There was no need to signal Janson, no need even to *tsk* a warning from her wireless lip microphone to Janson's earpiece. Her body language said it all—hidden sentries positioned to ambush—and Janson stopped moving instantly.

SEVEN

Jessica Kincaid stood in shadow and she did not move.

Janson could not see what she had seen. Nor could he see whether he was in the sentry's field of vision she had stepped into. Without moving his head, he probed his surroundings through slitted eyes and decided that he was partly shielded by the three-foot-diameter trunk of a massive ironwood tree.

She stood still for so long that a shaft of sunlight that penetrated the canopy crept from the rough bark of the tree to the dull cloth of her pack and across her shoulder to the photon-absorbent camouflage paint on her face. Twenty minutes passed like two hours. Twenty more. Janson felt his limbs stiffen. His knees ached. His ankles locked. Gravity clutched the heavy pack on his back. Blood sank, drawn by gravity, pooling in his feet.

He imagined the outside of his body, his skin and clothing, as an unmoving shell and moved inside it, tensing and releasing muscle and sinew, clenching and unclenching, resisting the crush of inertia. He heard a faint rasping noise. What was it? He strained his ears. What was it? It rasped, again. Mechanical. Then a soft *click*. A weapon cocked? Not Jessica's. She hadn't budged. An old-fashioned revolver hammer clicking to full? His mind was forming pictures, telling stories. A rain-forest rebel cut off from the modern world. A rusty old gun. A grandfather's gift. Drawing a bead on Jessica? Again the rasp and *click*. A cigarette lighter? A disposable butane cigarette lighter? Janson smelled tobacco smoke. A puff of it drifted through the sunlight on a downward trajectory.

What they did next was Jessica's call. He could not see what she saw. Another drift of smoke. The sentry was not focusing, slipping out of his zone of attentiveness. They had to take advantage.

Tsk! in Janson's earpiece.

Kincaid signaling, but still not moving, which meant that she was telling Janson, *He might see me, but he can't see you. I can't move. You can. The smoke tells you where he is.*

Janson saw his route, a step back, a step closer to the ironwood, another up to it, glide around, and come up behind. Then what? Because Jessica was signaling even more by not acting. The sentry was smoking a cigarette. One hand occupied, eyes following the smoke, eyes half-closing as he drew the cigarette for another pleasurable drag. Nicotine and methane gases were dulling the edges of his awareness. It was an opportunity to strike—swivel the short barrel of her sound-suppressed MP5K and fire in a split second—but she was not striking. More than one sentry? Or a man alone, whose death would be noticed when he didn't report? Or the leading edge of a picket line bunched so close that others would hear the shot?

Janson stepped back, planting his foot carefully in case a numbed ankle or knee collapsed or locked up. Now close to the tree, now pressing the rough bark, now sliding around it, behind it, his field of vision opening up, broadening, his eyes sweeping carefully upward to the low branch or shooting platform from where the smoke was descending.

Something moved. A combat boot patched with duct tape arcing back and forth, the unconscious motion of tedium, a bored sentry swinging his foot like a pendulum. Janson continued edging around the ironwood until he could trace the line of the combat boot, to bunched camouflage cloth emerging from it, to the insurgent's shin and calf, to his knee, to the heavy automatic pistol in an improvised tactical rig made of black poly tarp strapped to his thigh, to the long barrel of the World War Two–era Russian machine gun lying across his lap.

Janson drew a knife.

The sentry's neck and face were obscured by leaves. His arms were bare, perspiration shining on his dark skin, but his chest was protected by a threadbare camouflage-patterned combat vest. If not bulletproof, it was still solid protection against a blade. Janson scanned the area around him. He was reasonably sure the man was alone. Anyone bored and stupid enough to be smoking would surely be talking if he had someone to talk to. The man took another deep drag and blew a smoke ring that descended toward Jessica.

Janson plotted a run straight at the man. Four steps, then up with the knife under his chin where the vest would do him no good at all. But to kill the sentry would be a last resort—or instant response if he suddenly spotted Jessica. Their best bet of getting into the camp and getting their hands on the doctor was to go in and out completely undetected. Killing a sentry would not serve, unless he left them no choice.

Suddenly the soldier jumped from the limb. He dropped the few feet to the forest floor, revealing the face of a bored teenager. Janson gripped his knife, waiting for Jessica to fire. But she did not move and an instant later Janson saw why. The kid had not seen them. He was slinging his machine gun over his shoulder and pawing at his fly. He urinated on the same tree he had jumped down from. When he was done he zipped up, turned on his heel, and headed up the path, moving in complete silence.

Janson found Jessica leaning against a tree and sucking on a water bottle, expressionless until he said, "Nice."

Her eyes lit. "I was never so glad to smell a cigarette in my life. Thought the son of a bitch would never move."

They stopped there and slept in alternating hour increments through the afternoon, standing watch for each other.

* * *

AT NIGHT JANSON and Kincaid were in their element, piercing the dark with panoramic digital sensor-fusion/enhanced night-vision goggles. A vast improvement over an early Air Force design, the $26,000 JF-Gen3 PSFENVG-Ds employed multiple image-intensifying tubes to give them command of the night with crisp vision ahead and nearly sixty degrees to either side.

Infrared enhancement made flesh-and-blood targets appear brighter than inanimate objects. The FFM sentry Janson spotted leaning on a tree looked shinier than the tree and the assault rifle cradled in his arms. Among the dark contours of boulders behind the sentry, the soldiers stationed as the sentry's backup glowed like copper flames.

Their panoramics were linked by radio. Kincaid, who was in the lead, again, was looking down, concentrating on silent passage over rough ground. Janson shared the sharp, green image that he saw by toggling a switch that opened a horizontally split screen in her goggles, displaying the danger ahead as well as the ground at her feet.

They stopped at a safe distance from the sentries and picked their way through a route around them.

The temperature had dropped to a comfortable lower sixties and Kincaid and Janson climbed at a good pace. They stumbled onto the charred wreckage of a helicopter. It had been there for a while. Vines were creeping over the tail rotor, which was eerily intact, but the odor of burnt rubber still hung in the humid air. Janson signaled a stop and cautiously scanned the treetops.

Now his screen split as Jessica shared her image of a machine-gun platform a hundred feet off the ground, right under the canopy. No flesh-and-blood bright spots. The gun was unmanned but ready, a heavy old Soviet model easily capable of downing a slow-moving helicopter lacking high-tech sensors. They passed another downed aircraft and another. Above each heap of charred wreckage was another treetop gun emplacement. The FFM did not screw around.

Tsk! sounded in Janson's earpiece, followed by a whispered, "What the hell is that?"

Janson heard it, too. A faint droning noise high overhead that once heard was not forgotten. He exchanged baffled lime-green glances with Jessica. "Can't be," she whispered.

Except both had heard it and drawn the same impossible but indisputable conclusion from the familiar sound. High in the night sky an unmanned Reaper hunter-killer combat drone, armed with Hellfire anti-armor missiles and laser-guided five-hundred-pound bombs, was circling the insurgent camp on Pico Clarence. Had President for Life Iboga somehow gotten his hands on the deadliest weapon in America's arsenal?

"Look!" Kincaid whispered.

Through their panoramics they saw a low ridge of volcanic stone, pocked with shallow caves. FFM sentries were running toward and diving into the caves. *They* believed it was a Reaper.

Janson tapped Jessica's shoulder. It was baffling but not their fight—at least not now—and definitely not their priority, which was to get inside the rebel camp, unobserved. He gestured for them to take advantage of the opportunity to move on through the space vacated by the sentries. The sound grew faint. By the time Janson and Kincaid were around the sentries, it had stopped.

Ten minutes later they heard another strange noise, different from the first, though also mechanical. They stopped and listened carefully. More vibration than sound, it resonated very faintly, in the far distance to the south, like the rumble of a freight train or of heavy trucks on a highway. But the only trains on Isle de Foree were narrow-gauge crop cars on the coffee plantations, and the rails Janson and Kincaid had crossed were rusty, indicating that wheels rolled on them only during the harvest. The nation's one highway, a short stretch twenty miles down island that connected the capital city of Porto Clarence to the President for Life Iboga International Airport, was way too far to hear.

A warm wind sprang up, rustling the forest canopy, and the rumble seemed to cease or was muffled. Janson and Kincaid forged onward and skirted some sentry posts and passed beneath numerous unmanned anti-helicopter machine-gun platforms. Then the panoramics began to register a strong glow ahead, which grew brighter, into a general flowering of light from hundreds of cook fires and lanterns. They were inside the picket lines, past the sentries, into the insurgent camp.

Any natural night vision possessed by the troops was blinded by their fires, while the panoramics' enhancement software adjusted instantly to changes in light levels. Janson and Kincaid moved surely, scoping safe routes toward the muffled buzz of a portable gasoline-powered generator. Electricity was a rarity in the primitive encampment, which meant that the generator was near the head-quarters and very likely whatever structure they were using for a hospital.

Tsk.

Janson stopped.

Kincaid had found it, the mouth of a large cave spilling steady white light into the dark. They had concluded earlier that the doctor would almost certainly sleep in the hospital to be near his patient and to make it easy for his captors to keep an eye on him. Janson and Kincaid worked their way toward it and sheltered in a clump of closely spaced trees. The night goggles showed little bright green dots running around the bark—ants feeding on something sticky.

From this angle they saw a second cave spilling the same steady glow of electric light. Headquarters or hospital? In which cave was the doctor and which contained the FFM leaders, who would be heavily armed?

Janson and Kincaid had reached a critical point in their operation. They had no desire to get in a shoot-out with the doctor's captors. Cross fires were indiscriminate and could get the man whose life they were attempting to save killed. Equally problematic was the effect killing the leadership would have on the revolution. While he was not interested in taking sides between the vicious Iboga and the insurgents who had slaughtered the crew of the *Amber Dawn*, it was clear to Janson that if there was a right side in the bloody civil war it was FFM, and he did not want to do anything to tilt the balance against them. Success would demand speed and stealth, in and out quickly and quietly.

The wind was growing stronger, which would help. Sleeping

men would not hear them over the constant rustle of millions of leaves. They waited, spelling watches. An hour before dawn, the lights in one cave went out.

"Bosses turning in," Janson whispered. "Give them a few minutes to fall asleep."

Ten minutes passed.

"All right, let's do it."

* * *

IT WAS NOT the first time that Terry Flannigan had awakened in dreamy disarray as a woman covered his mouth with her hand, pressed her lips to his ear, and whispered, "Be quiet." Husbands on business trips had a way of coming home early.

"We're getting you out of here," she whispered.

He'd heard that before, too. Into the bathroom and out the window. Or the guest room. Or, God help him, once in the closet, like in a *New Yorker* cartoon.

"Open your eyes," she said, "if you understand me."

Whatever groggy dream he'd been having came to a crashing halt when he saw the low rock ceiling of the FFM cave on Pico Clarence. A woman in commando gear was crouching over him, her face darkened with camo paint, her eyes intense.

"Who?" he whispered against her hand.

"Friends," she whispered, and Flannigan knew fear. No "friends" knew he was here. With Janet murdered, only her murderers knew he had been captured when they killed her and sank *Amber Dawn*.

"What friends?"

"ASC," she whispered, "your employer. We're taking you home— You awake? *Snap out of it!*"

ASC? What the hell was going on? How the hell did American

Synergy know he had been on the boat? He had doctored for oil companies long enough to respect and fear the enormous power they wielded in West Africa. He had seen what they were capable of. In remote places they were above whatever law existed. No way he could trust them.

Afraid she would see his confusion, Flannigan turned his face, only to see more death—a sentry sprawled on the stone floor. She raised her hand so he could speak again and he whispered, "Did you kill him? He was just a kid."

"Animal trank dart," she snapped. "Two cc's carfentanil citrate. *Get up!*"

Terry Flannigan's gaze shifted to the pool of light cast by a bulb over Ferdinand Poe's cot. He shook his head. "I can't leave him."

"What?"

"He's a mess. I'm the only doctor."

She rocked back on her heels and Flannigan got a better look at her. Skinnier than he usually went for, but a fine face and incredible lips. He had never seen eyes so focused, bright as ball bearings. She shot a glance across the cave, and a commando broad in the chest and light on his feet materialized at her side.

"He won't go," she whispered. "Won't leave his patient."

To Flannigan's astonishment, a smile crossed the guy's stern face. "I'll be damned," he said, and thrust out a powerful hand. "Pleasure to make your acquaintance, Doc."

"Can we take him with us?" Flannigan asked.

"No way," said the woman.

"They've got some lightweight stretchers, here," Flannigan persisted. "How many men do you have?"

"You're looking at it," said the woman.

"*Two* of you?"

Suddenly both looked sharply toward the mouth of the cave,

heads cocked like animals. A moment later he heard it, too, the hollow thudding sound of helicopters. In seconds they heard yells in the camp and pounding feet as the insurgents ran to their tree-top machine-gun emplacements.

"Three machines, maybe four," the man said.

Janson and Kincaid exchanged puzzled glances, hurried to the mouth of the cave, and peered out.

Paul Janson said, "Something's up."

"It's suicide to attack."

Already the machine guns farther out were chattering—quick, expert bursts—and Janson and Kincaid could picture the hail of heavy slugs shredding a helicopter's thin skin. Rocket fire *whooshed* and the rotor thudding changed timbre as the slow-moving helicopters shot back and tried to maneuver for advantage.

"Suicide," said Janson. "Unless—"

"It's a feint! Iboga's attacking on the ground."

They heard a tremendous explosion. A ball of fire crashed through the leaf canopy. A helicopter had blown up. A pillar of white smoke shot from the forest floor. The thudding noise grew more urgent. The guns fired longer bursts. A second explosion sent a shock wave through the canopy. It was followed by a moment of eerie silence. Then the silence was broken by a concerted roar of powerful engines and the clanking of steel tracks.

"Tanks!" said Janson. "The T-72s."

EIGHT

Heralded by the deafening roar of their 125mm main guns, tanks climbed the mountain firing four rounds a minute. High-explosive fragmentation projectiles cut broad swaths of blasted wood through the forest. Toppled trees ripped enormous gashes in the rain-forest canopy and crushed the encampment's makeshift shelters.

Surprise was total; the noise of the forty-ton armored monsters creeping into position to attack had been muffled by the rotor thud of the daring helicopter attack and the guns of the defenders. Machine guns churned from the steel hulls, raking the panicked FFM troops who were fleeing for their lives.

Janson gauged the range of the muzzle flashes through the trees to be less than a quarter mile. "We promised not to start a shooting war. So a rumble in the jungle comes to us."

"Run or fight," said Kincaid. "We have about ten seconds to make up our minds."

On their own, two operators trained in evasion and escape tactics could calculate the flow of battle and get away. The odds would shift against them if they took the doctor. If they took the doctor's patient, too, they would all die.

Flannigan darted up behind them. "Give me a gun."

"Do you know how to use one?"

"Hell no. It's for Minister Poe. He cannot face being captured again. He wants to go down fighting and save the last bullet for himself."

Janson and Kincaid shared a grim glance. Janson said, "The Russians export their crappiest tanks. 'Monkey models' with light armor, lousy sights, no infrared, no laser. And they carry their ammunition inside the crew compartment. Hit them right and the entire turret flies off like a jack-in-the-box."

"Otherwise they're still tanks?"

" 'Fraid so."

Kincaid said, "Your call."

Janson told Flannigan, "Tell your patient he will not be captured."

They opened their packs without another word and unlimbered the disposable single-shot preloaded Russian rocket launchers. Five RPG-22s and one more-advanced RPG-26.

"Take the 26," Janson told Kincaid. "You're better with it."

They headed down the hill toward the sound of the guns. Men were running past scrambling up the hill the other way, wide-eyed with shock. Acrid smoke swirled so thickly it blocked the early-morning sun. The ground was littered with rifles, helmets, even shoes thrown down by the stampeded troops.

An eighth of a mile from the firing, Jessica Kincaid spotted a tall tree to which wooden cross slats had been nailed as crude rungs that led up to one of the anti-helicopter machine-gun platforms.

She climbed with three of the thirty-inch launcher tubes slung across her back, a load that added twenty-five pounds to the MP5 submachine gun, M1911 pistol, spare magazines, knife, Kevlar helmet, ceramic vest, GPS, spare batteries, medical kit, knife, and water she was already carrying.

As she caught her breath on the platform, cannon fire brought down another clump of trees, which opened up a half-mile view of the tanks and a mass of ground troops behind them. A flash of yellow caught her eye. She found it in her binoculars and cursed that there had been no room for a real sniper gun on this incursion. The yellow was a scarf as big as a blanket wrapped around the head and neck of President for Life Iboga. The man was enormous. If she had her Knight's M110 the dictator would be dead and the tank attack would end.

Paul Janson sought a flanking position on the ground, slewing to one side, then racing ahead through the trees. Two hundred meters from the tanks he saw that the dark green armored behemoths had bogged down trying to cross a ravine, suggesting that the FFM camp was not as vulnerable in that direction as Iboga's troops had supposed.

Emboldened, FFM troops who had not fled rallied to take advantage of the temporary setback. They fired assault rifles from behind boulders and hurled hand grenades. One tank stopped moving as a torrent of lead breached its commander's vision slit. But the rest kept trying to climb the steep slope as the bullets bounced off armored hulls and the grenades fell short.

An insurgent stood up balancing an ancient RPG-7 on his shoulder. The heavy warhead protruded from a long, unwieldy launcher. As he tried to aim the weapon, a tank cut him in half with a sustained burst of machine-gun fire. Triggered by a dead hand, the rocket-propelled grenade flew over the tanks on a tail of white smoke and detonated in a tree. The backblast that roared behind the launcher tube threw an insurgent in the air and dropped him in a smouldering heap.

Jessica Kincaid laid two of her launchers, an RPG-22 and the RPG-26, on the shooting perch she had climbed to in the treetops and shouldered the second RPG-22. She reserved the superior 26 for her second shot. She would need the best she had after her first shot exposed her position. Eyes locked on the nearest tank, which was grinding over a rock ledge, she tugged the launcher's extension, which simultaneously lengthened the weapon to its full thirty-three and one-half inches and opened its front and rear covers. Then she raised the rear sight to cock it, found the tank, aimed for the seal between its turret and turret cavity, and fired.

The rocket's solid-fuel motor ignited and burned fully in a flash. The fin-stabilized rocket leaped from the smoothbore barrel and drove a two-and-a-half-pound high-explosive anti-tank warhead at Kincaid's target.

"Bull's-eye," she murmured under her breath.

It was a double explosion, the first burst at the bottom edge of the turret, the second an instant later as the ammunition inside the tank blew up, hurling the armored turret off the hull and onto the ground. Smoke billowed as if Kincaid's grenade had transformed the tank into a boiling pot.

She grabbed the RPG-26. The backblast had ignited the leaf canopy behind her, flagging her position. Every tank in the ravine tried to raise its main gun in her direction. But to elevate so high, they had to maneuver onto a slope. She cocked the 26—no time-wasting extension on the improved model, thank you, Russians—chose as her target a tank climbing a steep slope to draw a bead on her, and fired. She heard a flat cracking sound. Instead of screaming at the tank, the rocket misfired, jumped ten feet from the barrel, and tumbled to the forest floor.

"Fuck!"

The tank she had aimed at was traversing its main gun at her. She grabbed the remaining RPG-22 and jerked open the extension. Something exploded. The tank was suddenly spewing smoke. Its hatch opened and three men tumbled out, rolling on the ground to douse their burning clothes. Janson, she realized, had nailed it. But the fire in the trees behind her had drawn the attention of another tank.

"Get down from there," she heard him in her earpiece. She raised her sight and prayed this one wasn't another dud.

* * *

INSIDE THE T-72 three small men—none taller than five feet, four inches, could fit in the tiny space—teamed up to obliterate the RGP-armed insurgent in the tree who had already destroyed one of the tanks. The driver manipulated his tillers and gear sticks to force the machine up the side of the ravine. The commander guided the main gun and shouted the order to fire, twice. At the first command, the driver stomped his clutch to steady the beast. At the second, the gunner fired. The commander saw the flash of the insurgent's launcher. A HEAT projectile penetrated the armor plate with a burning jet of gas. There was a blinding light. Hot shell fragments ricocheted in the confined space like flying razors.

* * *

IN THE TREETOPS, the tank's 125mm shell screamed so close by Jessica Kincaid that a shock wave knocked her flat. Then the tank she had fired at exploded. She threw herself over the edge of the platform before another got the range, and climbed down the makeshift rungs as fast as she could.

As she hit the forest floor she heard Janson's voice in her earpiece, cold and deadly: "I believe I ordered you out of that tree."

"Yes, sir." She felt like a buck private chewed out by a full colonel.

"Pull another stunt like that and you'll be looking for a job."

"I thought I was a partner."

"Then you'll be looking for a partner," Janson shot back, and suddenly exploded in a degree of emotion she had never heard from him. "Jesus H! Jesse, you'll get yourself killed cowboying like that."

"Won't happen again, sir."

"Fall back to the cave; we've got to get out of here."

They ran convergent paths that brought them together at the hospital cave. Janson looked more himself than his voice had sounded on the radio, Kincaid thought, his usual cool, clear, alert, and focused like a blowtorch. "Iboga hid his presidential guard behind the tanks. They're coming up with all four feet."

"I saw him. Scary dude in a yellow scarf."

The FFM insurgents were falling back.

Inside the cave Kincaid and Janson found a dozen boys huddled around Ferdinand Poe's cot.

Paul Janson spoke in a loud, clear voice to rally Flannigan, Ferdinand Poe, and any of the kids who understood English: "Here's what we're going to do. We're going to put Minister Poe on a stretcher and spell each other carrying him, four at a time, two on each pole. The doctor will carry his medicine. You two boys—you and you—will carry water. This lady will lead," he said, indicating Jessica Kincaid with her MP5 cradled in her arms. "Follow her. I will cover our rear. Stick close together and we'll make it out of here. Quickly now, everyone, move!"

Flannigan supervised the shifting of the injured man from his cot to the stretcher, which was held by four of the largest boys.

Seconds after the ragtag caravan exited the cave and started climbing a narrow path farther up the mountain, one of the tanks
clanked into the clearing and fired its main gun into first the hospital, then the headquarters. Behind it double-timing squads of the
presidential guard raked the area with automatic weapons.

Janson, covering the rear and last out of the camp, looked
back and saw two FFM fighters spring up, aiming their unwieldy
RPG-7s at the tanks. Both fell in a hail of gunfire as they triggered
the weapons, but one landed a lucky grenade in the tank's vision
slit. The big machine veered into a massive boulder, grinding its
treads and spewing smoke.

But more tanks and hundreds more troops were pouring into
the clearing as Iboga's powerful force overran the rebel camp.
Janson saw Iboga himself, a dark-skinned three-hundred-pound
giant with a bright yellow scarf wrapped around his head like an
Arab kaffiyeh. Surrounded by his elite personal guard, signified
by yellow handkerchiefs knotted at their throats, he appeared to
Paul Janson to be the personification of the evil "big men" chiefs
who had destroyed African nation after African nation. A well-
placed shot could turn the tide of the battle. But the range, 150
meters, was extreme for his MP5, the dictator was shielded by
his tall guardsmen, and a missed shot would bring them streaming after Janson's charges, who had thus far not been spotted.
Too risky.

He ran up the trail after his people.

Jessica had them down on their bellies, crawling and dragging
Poe's stretcher along an exposed ridge that could be seen from
below. Janson waited until they had made it across before he followed, slithering low. He had just crossed the open space when a
loud cheer erupted from the chaos below. It was a roar of victory.
Janson looked down at the clearing and saw that the presidential

guard had captured a tall, thin man who he judged by the cheering was Ferdinand Poe's son Douglas Poe.

The cheers grew louder and louder as President for Life Iboga swaggered up to the prisoner. The dictator slapped his face. The thin man staggered. Soldiers yanked him upright and Iboga slapped him again. Then the dictator beckoned, and a pair of tanks clanked from the semicircle formation at the edge of the shattered forest, crossed the clearing, skirting the one the FFM fighter had set afire. Guided by Iboga's impatient gestures, they swiveled on their treads and faced off, gun to gun, leaving twenty feet between them.

Soldiers tied ropes to Douglas Poe's wrists, dragged him between the tanks, and yanked the ropes from either side, stretching his arms apart so that he stood as if crucified between the armored hulls. As the soldiers laughed, Iboga gestured for the tank drivers to move ahead, narrowing the space where the prisoner was held, creeping closer and closer until they pressed against his back and his chest. The laughter grew louder. Iboga whipped off his scarf and held it high over his head like a racetrack starter about to drop the flag.

Suddenly he looked up.

The taunting grin slid from his face.

NINE

Paul Janson heard the same distant sound they had heard last night, the growl of the Reaper. Iboga froze, scarf in the air, face locked on the sky. The hunter-killer combat drone had come back.

The soldiers and elite guard looked up, screaming, "Reaper! Reaper!"

Iboga whirled and ran, shoving men out of his way, racing through the armored semicircle formed by his victorious tanks. To Janson's amazement, the dictator's soldiers frantically gestured for the tanks to back away from Douglas Poe. They lifted him in the air and held him like a shield as if to show the lenses in the sky that if the Reaper fired its missiles it would kill him, too. The attempt was futile.

The ground shook. Thunder rippled. Iboga's tanks began to explode, one after another, in balls of fire. His soldiers' bodies and those of his guard who hadn't run after him were flung in the air.

The attack by the unseen, unmanned aerial gunships lasted less than thirty seconds. And when the smoke had cleared, every man left in the clearing, including Douglas Poe, was dead.

Paul Janson was stunned. Who but the Pentagon or the U.S. State Department could have unleashed the Reapers? Theoretically, the motive for involvement would have been West African oil. But in reality, Isle de Foree's corrupt government's wells and pipelines and refineries were decrepit, and the nation's oil reserves, like Nigeria's, were dwindling. Any potential new oil reserves were already spoken for in deepwater blocks off Angola, a thousand miles to the south. America embroiling herself in chaotic West African tribal wars seemed like a risky venture for little return. Unless, of course, Doug Case had lied when he claimed that the assignment to rescue the doctor had nothing to do with oil reserves.

If the Reapers weren't American, had some private entity somehow gained access to UAV technology? That did not seem possible. The heavily armed surveillance drone was the sharp end of an immensely complex weapon system dependent upon remote guidance via orbiting satellites. That was light-years beyond the abilities of a Nigeria or an Angola. It was hard to believe that even China could pull that off, yet, much less a private outfit.

Whatever it was, something—something else—was going down, some mission not apparent. Paul Janson vowed to find out what, because the Reaper gave whoever possessed it godlike power to observe and destroy.

* * *

BELOW IN THE clearing where the wreckage of Iboga's army smouldered, FFM fighters began venturing in from the forest, awed at their sudden, astonishing turn of fortune. They wandered among the bodies of the soldiers who moments earlier had been intent on exterminating them and gazed in wonderment at the twisted steel that remained of the tanks. A man picked up an assault rifle only to drop it, crying out, burned by metal too hot to touch. A man laughed and then they began to cheer their unexpected victory.

From the forest above Janson heard a second wave of shouts and cheering—boyish cries of glee—and he looked up to see the youngsters racing toward him down the path carrying Ferdinand Poe's stretcher. The rebel leader was conscious and propped up on one elbow, watching everything with burning eyes.

An anxious Terrence Flannigan ran alongside the stretcher, attempting without success to get his patient to lie back. They raced past Janson and down into the camp that they had fled moments earlier. Last to emerge from the trees above was Jessica Kincaid, MP5 at port arms.

"That looks even worse than it sounded," she breathed, casting disbelieving eyes on the wreckage below. "Bad day for the bad guys."

"Iboga got away."

"Minister Poe just told his bunch to storm Porto Clarence."

"That's the right move. Take the capital before Iboga regroups and end it now."

"What's *our* move?" she asked.

"Stick close to our doctor," said Janson. "Before a stray bullet saves ASC five million dollars."

* * *

"You will die on the way to Porto Clarence, Minister Poe," said Dr. Flannigan. "Please listen to reason."

"No man enters the capital before me," said Ferdinand Poe.

"You are leaking blood from every orifice. You have internal injuries. You cannot survive being carried twenty miles on a stretcher. Wait for your men to take the city and the airport so a helicopter can carry you to the hospital."

"*No man enters Porto Clarence before me!*" Poe sat up on the stretcher and tried to push the doctor away. But despite a spirit reinvigorated by the hope of impending victory, Poe's body was failing him. His round cheeks appeared to have collapsed from within. The deep hollows exaggerated the enormousness of his elephant ears and the length of his narrow nose, causing them to poke out of his head like cartoon appendages. His once-imposing crown of bristly dyed hair was matted to his perspiring skull.

Flannigan leaned closer to wipe blood from the corner of Poe's mouth. "The glory will kill you, sir."

"It is not for glory," said Ferdinand Poe. "It is for order."

Flannigan threw up his hands. "Talk sense to him!" he demanded of the commandos. By now he had named them in his mind. The woman was Annie Oakley for blasting Iboga's tanks. Her expressionless, impenetrable partner was The Wall. Flannigan still had no idea why ASC was paying them to take him "home" and still feared the worst, but The Wall exuded the sort of common sense that might persuade his critically ill patient to see reason.

The Wall disappointed Flannigan. "You're missing Minister Poe's point, Dr. Flannigan. He knows that the victors of his long and brutal war could burn the city to the ground if he's not there to restrain them personally."

And Annie Oakley chimed in, "Doctor, his fighters have been living in the woods for three years. He can't expect them to act like Boy Scouts unless he's there to read the riot act."

"Precisely," said Ferdinand Poe. "Only I can restrain the impulse to vengeance. Only I, because they have all seen *that*." He pointed

a trembling hand across the clearing where ten men were struggling to lift a two-ton gun tank turret that had blown off by the
Hellfires and crushed his son. "*That* gives me the moral right—the
example—to demand that they do not violate their fellow citizens,
that they do not throw our poor nation into even more horrendous
straits. This war must end today."

He gazed for a long moment as they levered the turret off his
son. Then he spoke softly. "Doctor, I appreciate your concern, and
professionalism. But in this case professional soldiers"—he nodded
at Janson and Kincaid—"even professionals who land on our island
for reasons not entirely clear, are better qualified to diagnose a military situation."

"I'm not diagnosing the situation, goddammit. I'm diagnosing
you."

"But I am not the patient, Doctor. Isle de Foree is the patient
and Isle de Foree is in critical condition—Stand aside, sir. I must
speak with my commanders." He gestured for Janson and Kincaid
to stay with him in the hospital cave.

Janson assessed the men who clustered around Poe's stretcher.
He had a dozen commanders who ranged from very young to very
old. They were steady, tested soldiers, revered Poe, and had done a
superb job of reforming their battered forces and rallying the men
streaming in from the forest. But none displayed the charisma of
their leader.

Poe addressed them in Portuguese. He spoke forcefully and
fired them up with a fist pointed at his son's body even as tears
of grief streamed down his face. When the army started down the
trail at a quick pace, with Poe's stretcher in the lead, he beckoned
Janson alongside.

"I've impressed upon my commanders the need to protect the
city from unnecessary destruction while capturing the Presidential

Palace. But it is not only for order that I rush into the capital. We must seize Iboga. He's looted the treasury, sent millions abroad. Without it we will start our new nationhood bankrupt. We cannot permit him to escape. Now I gather from the doctor that you and your associate are mercenaries paid to rescue him after he was kidnapped by what appeared to be a renegade faction of my movement. Is that correct?"

"Essentially, Minister Poe," Janson answered. This was no time to debate the fine line between mercenaries and security consultants.

"Judging by your ability to penetrate both the enemy lines and my lines, I assume that you and your associate are expert commandos."

"We *plan* such penetrations intensively and thoroughly," Janson answered, putting strong emphasis on the word "plan," for he saw that Poe was going to offer them the job of capturing Iboga and he did not want it. The cardinal rules of survival included no off-the-cuff operations, no decisions on horseback, no flying by the seat of the pants, no winging it. Besides, he and Jessica were on the edge of total exhaustion. Even were they fully rested, kick-the-door-in assault work was for younger, dumber types and he had already put that time in when he was younger and dumber. But mainly, he had taken a job and given his word to rescue the doctor, and abandoning the doctor in the middle of a shooting war was not his idea of rescue.

"We plan operations well ahead of time," he explained. "Our planning—all of our planning—is designed to maintain the advantage of presenting a small, unexpected, moving target."

"Small, unexpected, moving targets that destroy tanks?" Poe asked drily.

"We plan for a variety of events," Janson replied, as drily. "Listen, sir, I know what you want, but I cannot do it for you. Your own men know their city, know the palace, and are fully capable of grabbing Iboga."

"I fear this is easier said than done. Iboga is treacherous and deeply experienced in warfare. He fought in Angola. On both sides."

"Yours is an island, sir. I presume you've instructed your forces to seize the airport and the harbor. If no plane or boat can get out of here he is not going anywhere."

"Of course I've done that. Picked men are heading that way as we speak, and spies I've kept in the city will watch means of egress. But I know Iboga. He will have a plan and he will escape if he sees we are winning. I need your help. I am asking to hire you. I will pay you what you ask."

Janson shook his head. "You're a brave man, Minister Poe. I respect that. Here is what we can do for you: We can free up a dozen of your guard—who I imagine are your elite men. Correct?"

"Yes."

"Make them the hunters. We will escort and protect you personally. Guaranteed." He glanced at Jessica, who fired back, "Guaranteed!"

"I am not important," Poe protested. "It is not for me."

Janson said, "A war like yours in Isle de Foree is like chess. When the king is lost, the war is lost."

"I have no desire to be king. I am a democrat."

"In a war like yours," Janson repeated patiently, "it is the same thing. When the 'democrat' is lost, the war is lost. This is no time for false modesty, Minister Poe. There is no one who can save Isle de Foree but you, sir. We can help—for no charge, not a penny— by protecting you until your men take the city and arrest Iboga."

"Why would you do this?"

"I believe," Paul Janson answered sincerely, "that you are on the side of the angels."

"And you will incidentally protect the doctor," Poe shot back.

"I've already made that clear. The doctor is our obligation and responsibility. We have given our word to return him safe and sound."

* * *

As THE FFM pursued Iboga's forces it appeared, at first, that good fortune continued to smile on Ferdinand Poe. The FFM fighters who had been dispatched to the airport eight miles from Porto Clarence found it lightly defended by a demoralized unit that surrendered after a brief skirmish. No damage was done to the control tower and the hangars and little more than some bullet-pocked windows to the palatial President for Life Iboga International Passenger Terminal.

One of the nation's last helicopters—commanded by the formidable Patrice da Costa, Poe's spy inside the Iboga regime—swooped down to evacuate the injured patriot from the foot of Pico Clarence. Janson, Kincaid, and Flannigan accompanied Poe on the flight to the brand-new military wing of Porto Clarence's otherwise-crumbling Iboga Hospital that had been equipped to serve the dictator and his friends.

The hospital occupied prime real estate, with a view across the hazy harbor of the Presidential Palace, a red-roofed two-story white stucco building festooned with balconies, pocked with recently added air conditioners, and crowned by a tall, square bell tower. Palm trees shaded its lawns. A long pier thrust into the water.

Poe informed his doctors that he would not submit to any operation or treatment that rendered him unconscious until the battle was won. The only weakness he showed was a plea to Terrence Flannigan to remain at his side.

"I'm not that qualified in internal medicine, sir."

"But you were not given your job in his hospital by Iboga."

"Good point," said Jessica Kincaid. "He's right, Doc; you're the only one we can trust."

Terry Flannigan saw that he was not going anywhere just yet, though one way or another he knew he was not going anywhere *ever* with the commandos hired by ASC. Although Annie and The Wall never let him out of their sight. He bided his time and stuck close to the crazy old patriot who insisted on his bed being cranked up into a sitting position so that he could watch events unfold at the palace across the water.

Poe's presence seemed to have the effect the rebel leader had hoped for. Only thin, isolated pillars of smoke were rising from the city, and the scattered gunfire they heard sounded mostly like pistols. An hour from sunset, when there was still plenty of light in the sky, Iboga's personal flag, a yellow banner adorned with a red snake, was lowered from the pole atop the palace's tower.

Poe answered a cell phone. His face lit with pleasure. "Iboga is trapped," he announced to the room. "Alone.

"Don't kill him," he ordered into the phone. "We must learn where he put our money. Take him alive." Then he stared out the window at the pier and said to the American commandos, "You didn't want to chase Iboga. You're in the battle anyhow—box seats for the finale. Watch the pier. You'll see him running onto it in a moment."

Janson said quietly to Jessica, "War like Shakespeare wrote it. All the main players in the same room."

As predicted, Iboga retreated onto the pier, his bulk unmistakable, but running like a man fully accustomed to his girth and strong enough to carry it. Nor was he alone, but flanked by two men with machine guns who alternated spraying the pursuit and reloading fresh magazines from a seemingly inexhaustible supply grabbed easily from each other's rucksacks.

"Neat trick," said Jessica.

Suddenly one went down, shot. Now it was only Iboga and one guard who kept coolly firing behind them as they retreated farther and farther out on the pier. Janson scanned the harbor with binoculars, looking for a boat speeding to the rescue, but saw none. The shooting had driven everyone from the water. The Porto Clarence harbor was nearly empty from the deteriorating oil storage facility to the fishing docks and freight piers. The only ship that had not fled the harbor was a rust-stained Bulgarian passenger vessel stranded at the cruise ship terminal, Janson guessed, by the absence of tugboats to escort her to sea.

"Can I borrow your glasses?" asked Flannigan.

Janson passed them to the doctor, who focused clumsily on the running men.

"Recognize someone?"

"No," Flannigan answered hastily, and passed them back

Kincaid nudged Janson. "Aircraft."

It was a dot on the ocean horizon.

"They'll make mincemeat of a helicopter."

But the dot grew too rapidly to be a helicopter. In seconds they saw a jet fighter approaching at enormous speed. "Does the Africa Partnership Station have an aircraft carrier sailing with it?"

"Not that I heard of. Maybe it's coming down from Nigeria."

"They'll get quite a reception at the airport."

Traveling at six hundred miles an hour, the fighter was close enough in a few more seconds to reveal the distinctive drooping wings of a vertical/short takeoff and landing Harrier jump jet. Janson and Kincaid exchanged looks as the aircraft slowed abruptly from six hundred miles an hour and descended toward the pier on a trajectory that started steep and quickly became vertical.

"Iboga's ticket out?"

Unlike the familiar sight of a helicopter floating down in a landing, what the vertical/short takeoff and landing Harrier was doing looked impossible. A jet plane seen streaking through the sky was suddenly hanging in the air like a noisy Christmas ornament balanced on a thick jet of brown exhaust gases.

"But it's a single-seat fighter plane. They only have one seat."

"Trainers have two seats," said Janson. "Look at the size of that canopy."

Sturdy landing wheels emerged from the front and back of the fuselage and thin struts levered down from its wings like walking sticks. The sound of its engine straining to defy gravity thundered through the hospital's thick windows.

Ferdinand Poe snatched up his cell phone. "Stop him. Shoot him! Don't let him land."

A squad of soldiers burst from the palace firing machine guns.

"Lucky for them trainers aren't combat capable," said Kincaid.

"This one is," said Janson. He passed her the glasses. "Gatling cannon, port side."

The cannon spoke, even as the noise of the jump jet's engine spooled down from a thunder to a scream. Twenty-five-millimeter shells swept the pier of the men with machine guns. The jet landed hard and bounced. Its tail dropped, then bobbed up. The front half of the big canopy sprang open. A rope ladder fell to the pier.

"Should be interesting, one empty seat, two bad guys."

Iboga climbed the six rungs agilely and heaved his bulk into the front cockpit. The canopy closed. The engine thundered and the jump jet rose straight up on another column of brown exhaust, turning as it did until its nose faced the sea from where it had come. The column spewing vertically from its nozzles began to angle. Nose rising, the jet carrying the deposed dictator of Isle de Foree sped forward. In fifteen seconds, it was gone.

Jessica lowered the glasses. "Where's the guy who was with him?"

"Dove off the pier."

"Did you see any markings? I didn't."

"Just camo paint."

"So who sent Iboga his ticket out?"

"Same folks who sent the Reaper?"

"But the Reaper almost killed him."

"No, it didn't," said Janson. "Iboga ran way back behind the tanks, but he made a clear target wearing that yellow headdress. The Reaper's sensor operator could spot him easily on his video monitors. The pilot would have killed him if that was their mission—Look at poor Poe."

Ferdinand Poe was gaping at the empty space of sky where the jump jet had vanished, and Paul Janson saw all the hope and energy of his military victory drain out of the old man's wounded body.

Terry Flannigan laid a hand on his shoulder. "Time to rest, Minister Poe. You've done all you could. Your men are in control; the city stands safe."

It was hard to tell if Poe even heard him. But Poe did reach out and clasp ahold of Flannigan's hand. His eyes were already closed. His head sagged on his chest. Flannigan beckoned the nurses hovering at the door in crisply ironed and laundered white uniforms. They glided in and took charge, gently straightening the old man on his back and pulling sheets to his chin.

Flannigan turned to Janson. "I'll stay with him until we get some specialists in."

"From where?"

"Lisbon seems to be their connection to European medicine. Listen, I know you're supposed to deliver me to ASC, but it's going to have to wait. You can tell them for me, thanks for the rescue. And obviously I thank you, too, both of you."

* * *

TERRY FLANNIGAN OFFERED his hand, desperately trying to conceal his belief that not knowing who to trust, he would be wise to run for his life.

It worked, Flannigan saw. The commandos exchanged a look. Then each shook his hand and they left, Janson punching numbers into a miniature satellite telephone.

TEN

Mario Margarido, Ferdinand Poe's chief of staff, whom Janson had seen that morning in a flak vest bulging with AK-47 magazines, was waiting in the hall in a suit and tie. "We are grateful for all you did for Minister Poe."

"You're welcome," said Janson. "I wonder if you could arrange clearance for my plane to come in from Libreville? We want very much to go home."

"Please be our guest in Porto Clarence."

"Thank you. You are very kind, but it's been a long trip and we would like to sleep in our own beds."

Janson watched Mario Margarido ponder his request as it dawned on the man that the sudden acquisition of a nation gave him powers large and small. As the president's chief of staff, he could allow an airplane the right to land or he could close the skies. Heady stuff, the right to grant people permission to come and go.

"I wonder whether your airplane would have room for several of our agents stationed there to come join our celebration."

"It would be our pleasure." Janson smiled.

"Of course your plane is welcome to fly in from Libreville."

Janson raised Mike and Ed on the sat phone, and three hours later the Embraer touched down at the newly renamed Isle de Foree International Airport, where celebrants had pulled down every enormous letter that had spelled "President for Life Iboga."

"Leave your motors running," Janson called. "We're out of here, now."

They boarded and pulled the door shut and Janson said, "Go!"

"Seat belts, sir."

"Yeah, yeah, yeah. What's for dinner?"

"What do you think? Lobster."

"And?..."

Ed grinned proudly. "Texas dry-aged porterhouse steak, Angolan arugula, Gabon tomatoes, French bread, and Italian pastry. We traded lobsters with every charter pilot in Libreville. Even got champagne."

"We'll start on it as soon as we get a shower. I'm going first, Jesse. I'll be quick." He knew if he stopped moving he would fall asleep standing there. He shaved and showered quickly, luxuriating only briefly in soap and water, and stepped out to dress in slacks and an open shirt. "All yours."

Janson grabbed a phone and paced the small space. He called Zurich, Cape Town, and Tel Aviv and left succinct messages: "How can I get my hands on a jump jet?"

Trevor Suzman called back instantly from Cape Town, asking with a self-satisfied chuckle, "A two-seat trainer, perhaps?"

"I'm not surprised you already heard," Janson answered, smoothly flattering the deputy national commissioner of the South African Police Service, who was very proud of the fact that his duties overlapped, deeply, into foreign intelligence. "Did you happen to hear where it came from?"

"Only rumors."

"Care to share them with me?"

"No. For the simple reason that they are all nonsense. But I would remind you that the Harriers have a very short range. He couldn't have come from far."

"Nine coastal nations and a small ship are all within range," said Janson. "Tell me about those rumors."

"I'll know more tomorrow," said Suzman.

"I will call you back, tomorrow."

Janson kept pacing—wide awake now—driven by the bigger question: Who sent the Reaper? But he had no idea who in the world to telephone to ask how to get his hands on an attack drone. There were people he could try, of course, but the question itself would bring down all sorts of unwanted scrutiny.

The U.S. Air Force had fighting drones. The CIA had them. The Army and the Navy had them. Could one of those American services hire itself out to secretly intervene in the Isle de Foree war? He shivered at a sudden terrible thought. Did Cons Ops have the Reaper? What an unholy alliance that would be—spymasters with the hubris of gods made strong as gods.

He was forced to concede that tackling the Reaper question would take some careful thinking. No one who had acquired its power to destroy would give it up without a fight.

* * *

JESSE JOINED HIM at the table as Ed laid out the first course, cold lobster mayonnaise. "Thanks, Ed. I'll get the wine." Janson popped the cork and filled their glasses.

"Before we toast victory, a quick mea culpa."

Janson and Kincaid's mea culpa review of what went right and what went wrong was an operator's custom. Their Delta Force friends called it a hot wash, others called it a debriefing, or a wrap, but whatever the name, it was a way of rehashing an action in hopes of not making the same mistakes twice.

As was their custom, Kincaid went first: "We already know I stayed too long in the tree. Should have obeyed orders, because you were in a position to see what I couldn't."

Janson was still shaken by that and not in a forgiving mood. "You made me a promise when we hooked up. Remember?"

"I remember."

"What did you promise me?"

Kincaid glared back and answered between gritted teeth, "Quote: 'Teach me. I'll be the best student you ever had.'"

"And what did I say?"

"You said, 'Paul Janson's protégés have a nasty habit of getting killed.'"

"It's dangerous work. If I tell you to move, I mean move now."

"Yes, sir."

"Anything else?" Janson asked.

"That's it for now—Wait!" Her eyes widened. "Jesus, Paul, Iboga's shooter who dove off the pier? I missed it at the time—but he wasn't wearing a yellow scarf like the other presidential guards."

Janson pictured the two shooters swapping magazines. "I missed it, too. Wonder who he was? It was like he delivered Iboga to the Harrier and said, 'Okay, my job's done.'"

"Brass-balled dude diving into the enemy's harbor."

"Five'll get you ten he had a guy waiting with scuba gear."

"How about you, sir? Did The Machine make any screwups?"

Janson looked her in the eye. "Big one. My decision to push

toward the FFM camp in daylight was a near-fatal mistake. We should have waited to take advantage of our night gear. The only reason we didn't get shot by the sentry was that you spotted him and didn't let him spot you."

"Anything else?"

"I'm sure plenty will come to me in the morning—but for tonight, victory. The doctor rescued and, incidentally, a righteous revolution won."

Jessica Kincaid raised her glass and locked eyes with him. "To free doctors and free Foree!"

They touched glasses and sipped champagne.

"Nice. What is this?"

Janson unwound the towel around the bottle and showed her the label. "Mumm."

"Excellent."

They ate a little bit of the lobster, some salad, some bread, and a little bit of steak, a few sips of an Argentine Malbec, and every pastry on the plate. Ed cleared the dishes and closed the door to the front of the plane.

"Tired?" Jessica asked.

"Body yes, brain no. You?"

"Not right now. I'll probably crash for two days starting tomorrow.... Any bruises?"

"A few," said Janson. "... You?"

"Want to see them?"

"Oh, yes."

ELEVEN

The red-light district of Porto Clarence was near the cruise ship pier, a well-lit walk guarded by smiling policemen.

Terry Flannigan noticed that the only ship docked was a sea-beaten Bulgarian rust bucket with a big neon name board that read: "Varna Fantasy," Varna being the Black Sea port from where she sailed, Fantasy being Bulgaria's cruise line. So the Bulgarian tourists had had front-row seats to an African war and now were probably crowding the massage parlors. He had inquired of Minister Poe's new security chief where a gentleman might go for "some fun," and Patrice da Costa, who had spent the war spying in the city, had telephoned a warm introduction to a brothel the Bulgarians couldn't afford.

Flannigan was welcomed royally, told the night was on "Chief da Costa," and treated to a glass of wine while he watched a demonstration video of the staff hard at work. The HD preview was new in his experience but circumvented nicely the problem of choosing in front of all, which meant rejecting some to their faces. He chose a stocky blond Ukranian who looked a little bit like Janet Hatfield.

Face-to-face, he had to admit the resemblance was minimal, but he wasn't really going to be looking at her face, was he? In fact, he was probably going to keep his eyes closed. Or turn out the light. He did both. Then the damnedest thing happened. He couldn't get it up.

"This has never, ever happened to me before," he told the girl, who didn't seem to speak English but was very kind, so he felt a little less like a complete schmuck. It was good that she didn't understand English. In the dark he felt free to say, "This friend of mine got killed. And she was a good person. A lot better than me. But she was fun, too, sure of herself, and very, very steady. A girl to ride the river with, which is an admiring expression from where I come from. Funny thing was, it fit her doubly since she was a boat captain."

Funny thing, too, he felt tears streaming down his face.

Someone knocked at the door.

"It's paid for the night," he said, his voice cracking. "Go away."

But the girl turned on the light and pressed her ear to the door, then beckoned urgently. The old woman who ran the joint, who had sat with him while he watched the video, was whispering frantically. Flannigan opened the door.

"Dangerous man. Dangerous man. He's looking for you. I sent him away, but he didn't believe me that you weren't here. You must go."

Flannigan did not bother asking who the dangerous man was. This cinched what he had feared earlier. The soldier running with Iboga had indeed been Van Pelt, the rabid South African who had led the massacre on *Amber Dawn*.

Flannigan dressed, pressed money in the girl's hand, and let the madam guide him out a side door into a reeking alley. "Where will you go?" she whispered.

"Where I'll be welcomed with open arms."

He glanced into the street, saw the way was clear, and broke into a run toward the waterfront, sprinting as fast as he could, around a corner and onto the cruise ship pier. The *Varna Fantasy* had singled up her mooring lines in preparation to sail. The last lines were going slack as a tugboat pressed her against the pier and stevedores awaited the order to cast off.

A ship's officer stopped Flannigan at the top of the gangway.

Flannigan said, "Get the purser."

"He's sleeping."

"I guarantee you he'll be glad you woke him. He'll even thank you. If you don't, he'll fucking keelhaul you."

The purser appeared sleep lined and rumpled in a white jacket over his pajamas.

Flannigan said, "Good evening, sir. If your ship's doctor didn't jump ship here, he's probably disembarking at your next port of call, or the one after that. Correct?"

"What is it to you?" the purser asked warily.

"I am a physician. A trauma surgeon. I have additional specialties in coddling cruise ship passengers, healing crew of sexually transmitted diseases, and ensuring that your dining rooms don't serve dysentery. I have served on ships like yours for many years." He opened the waterproof wallet that never left his person, not in a world where paperwork was everything, and chose carefully from the contents. "Here is my passport and certificates and licenses to practice. Show me to my cabin."

Terry Flannigan knew that he did not have to advise the purser to leave his name off the manifest until the ship had left Isle de Foree waters. The purser, whose responsibilities included the health of two thousand passengers crammed into a small space, was not about to blow this unexpected stroke of luck by alerting the local authorities that a last-minute crew member was anxious to leave town secretly. Whatever the stranger might have done ashore, a qualified doctor was a priceless commodity.

PART TWO

Right from Wrong

Night

3°11′ S, 14°13′ W

Forty thousand feet above the South Atlantic Ocean

TWELVE

W hy don't we do this more often?" Jessica Kincaid whispered.

They always started slowly, like swimmers wading toward deep water in starlight. And they celebrated rituals: Inspection of Bruises. Healing Hands. Kiss to Make It Better. Now she lay on top of Paul Janson with her breasts pressed to his muscled chest, their lips brushing, legs intertwining, breath growing short, hearts racing.

The Embraer growled through the night sky. She thought Janson hadn't heard her over the drone of the engines. "Why—"

"Because my entire carcass would implode from an excess of pleasure?"

"No lies."

"What is the penalty for lying?"

"No evasions. Answer the question, Paul. Why don't we do this more often?"

"We're afraid," Janson whispered into her mouth. He cupped the back of her head with one hand and ran the other slowly down her spine.

"Of what?" she demanded, departing from his lips with a flick of her tongue to string kisses down his neck.

"We're afraid that one day one of us will come home from a job alone."

He had stolen a march on her. The hand behind her head had materialized between her thighs. "I'm not afraid," she whispered.

"Good. I wish I could say the same."

She crouched on her knees and straddled him. He rose to join her.

"Give me your hands," she said.

He held up both hands. With them balanced palm to palm she planted her feet on the bed and began to move. "I cannot believe we will ever be alone."

"At this moment," Janson gasped, "I'm inclined to agree with you."

"*Boss?*" Mike, the pilot, spoke on the intercom. "Awful sorry to bother you."

"What?" The cabin microphones were voice activated.

"Quintisha is calling on the sat phone. She says it's major."

* * *

QUINTISHA UPCHURCH WAS general operations manager for both CatsPaw Associates and the Phoenix Foundation. She was the only person in the world who could find Paul Janson anywhere, day or night.

"Switch it here, Mike, and turn off your end."

Breasts heaving, eyes blurring, Jessica stared down at Janson. "What the hell time is it? Doesn't that woman ever sleep?"

Janson said, "Hello, Quintisha."

"You didn't answer your sat phone, Mr. Janson." It occurred to Janson, not for the first time, that her honeyed, resonant voice combined the primness of a deacon's daughter with the steely resolve of a night court magistrate.

"Yes."

"Jessica didn't answer, either."

"I am under the impression that Ms. Kincaid is taking the evening off. What's up?"

"Douglas Case of American Synergy is in a state. He said to tell you, quote: 'The doctor flew the coop.' "

"*What?*"

"Mr. Case used extreme language demanding your private numbers. I hung up on him, of course, but as we're expecting five million dollars from ASC I thought it best to telephone the airplane."

Janson thought hard.

Quintisha Upchurch said, "We could use the five million, Mr. Janson. That airplane does not come cheaply."

"Tell Mr. Case I will deal with it." He spoke Mike's name. The voice recognition system routed him back to the cockpit. "Mike, have you passed your point of no return?"

The point of no return was not the middle of the ocean. Whether the Embraer could return to Africa or had to keep moving ahead to South America depended as much upon weight and wind resistance as distance already flown. It weighed less, thanks to burning off fuel, so it needed less power to maintain speed. Turning westerly headwinds into tailwinds would also allow Mike to fly with throttles pulled back. The math was complicated. Pilots like Mike did their "PNR" in their heads, minute by minute, as automatically as breathing.

"Twenty-nine minutes to point of no return."

"Hang a one-eighty. Back to Porto Clarence."

"One-eighty back to Porto Clarence—soon as I get clearance."

Jessica spoke up. "Mike? When you get clearance, be gentle."

"Say again?"

"Take it easy turning the airplane," said Janson. "We don't want anything falling off back here— Over and out."

They were still holding hands, palm to palm, and steadied each other when the Embraer banked.

"Don't you want to call your friend Doug?"

"Not before we know what happened."

"Which we won't know until we get to Porto Clarence."

"Which won't be for three hours."

"Time to reach a point of no return?"

"Time to reach several points of no return."

THIRTEEN

I'm afraid I was a bit short the other day with your Ms. Upchurch," Doug Case apologized on the sat phone.

"She understood you were under pressure," Janson said.

From the windows of the front room of Ferdinand Poe's hospital suite he could see the Presidential Palace across the Porto Clarence harbor and a broad gray-blue swath of the Atlantic Ocean to the east and north. Isle de Foree's flag—a gold, green, and black horizontal tricolor slashed by a diagonal band of red—had been raised in place of Iboga's yellow banner. It stirred spasmodically in the intermittent breeze.

That same breeze had cleared the usual equatorial sea haze.

Janson could see for miles. An enormous vessel was growing slowly larger on the northern horizon. He had been watching her for the past hour, while waiting for Doug Case to return his call. She was too slow to be a cruise ship or an oil tanker.

Doug Case said, "I've had time to cool down. It's not your fault the doctor lit out. Your check's been cut. We'll overnight it."

"Don't."

"What?"

"Hang on to it."

"What do you mean?"

"Send the check when we send the doctor."

"We're talking about five million bucks, Paul."

"But not ours, yet. Don't worry; we'll run him down."

He had nailed his first lead within minutes of landing at the airport. Poe's audacious spy, Patrice da Costa—joking that he was now "temporary security chief" of "temporary president Poe's temporary presidential guard"—took Janson to interview the madam of the brothel to which he had steered Flannigan the night before. The frightened woman acknowledged that the doctor had been there, although she did not know when he had left or where he had gone. In retrospect, Janson realized that Flannigan had not trusted him and had meant to run at the first opportunity.

"And when I do," Janson promised Doug Case, "I'll march him directly into your office."

Case said, "Don't worry about it. ASC did everything we could to help and you got him back to civilization safe and sound. If the man ran, that's his problem; he's on his own. I mean, we both did the right thing."

"Why did he run?"

Doug Case answered with a chuckle, "Turns out the doctor is something of a swordsman. It's very likely he was running from a pissed-off husband."

"In Porto Clarence or Houston?"

"Either or both, from what I've heard— Look, a medical beach bum like Flannigan is not the biggest loss. His type kicks around from job to job."

"From what I saw, he was thoroughly professional and totally committed to his patient."

"I'm not accusing him of being a drug addict or alcoholic banned from practicing in the civilized world. I'm just saying we'll get along without him. Let him go, Paul. We'll send a check. Fax an invoice when you get a chance."

"You'll get my invoice along with Dr. Flannigan," Janson retorted. His word, his credibility, and his professionalism were at stake. But he had another reason to keep the door open at ASC.

"If you insist," Case said dubiously. "But we're willing to call it a day."

"I insist. Though I could use a little help on your end."

"Shoot."

"Fill me in on everything you know about any clandestine service aiding the Free Foree Movement."

FOURTEEN

That's not something I'm up to speed on," Doug Case answered.

"You were in communication with their gunrunners."

"Well, people who knew their gunrunners."

"You were keeping tabs," Paul Janson persisted. "You must have heard something."

"You want hearsay?"

"I'm just getting started. I'll take anything."

"Why are you asking?"

Janson said, "Five million dollars is a lot of money. I intend to earn it."

"Mind me asking what does a clandestine outfit aiding the Free Foree Movement have to do with finding the doctor?"

"You're stalling me, Doug. What have you heard?"

Viscerally suspicious of his former government masters, Janson would not be surprised that an arm of one of the many U.S.

clandestine services had secretly aided the rebels in hopes of securing a potential stable oil supply. Maybe they'd caught wind of new unannounced discoveries. So it was not hard to imagine a covert U.S. outfit stepping out of the shadows to throw a little help FFM's way just to keep friendly relationships with potential winners.

But who arranged Iboga's escape was a larger question. Which was why Paul Janson was pulling every string he knew to pinpoint where the Harrier jump jet had come from. There weren't that many in existence. Less than a hundred. They were complicated machines all supposedly in the service of sovereign nations whose air forces could provide the advanced tech support and maintenance to keep them flying.

Of the players competing in the West African oil patch, China could have fielded a Harrier, perhaps launching and retrieving from a cargo ship. So could Nigeria. So, perhaps, Angola. And so, of course, could the U.S.

The vessel he had been watching draw near on a course that would take her past the island now clearly appeared to be a petroleum drill ship. Comparing her to an oil tanker crossing her wake—an ultralarge crude carrier—he guessed that the drill ship was close to a thousand feet long. The draw-works tower that thrust up from the middle of the ship looked fifty stories high. Was her arrival in Isle de Foree's waters a coincidence? Janson thought not. If his suspicion proved true, he would do whatever it took to undo ASC's treacherous schemes even as he pretended to still serve them. But he held hard to the hope that Doug Case was not lying to him.

"You told me," he said into his sat phone, "that this was not about petroleum."

Case laughed softly. "Well, let's say management made it clear that I was not permitted to be entirely forthcoming. Which I gather you guessed yourself."

"ASC being an oil company, the thought crossed my mind." Feigning dry humor, Janson listened for Case's voice to betray a lie.

"Paul, you're a man of many worlds, including the corporate world. You know damned well the chief of security is not in the policy loop. As I told your young lady, security chiefs are servants. We protect; we don't command."

"What's going on, Doug?"

"Can I presume that your phone is as secure as mine?"

"It's my own. What's going on?"

"I would really prefer to discuss this face-to-face in a swept room."

"I don't have time to come to Texas," said Janson.

"Okay. Here's the deal. Now and then, for many years—decades—American Synergy has helped small nations and their oil companies expand their reserves. I know what you're thinking: That's how oil companies seize control of foreign oil. Well, it doesn't work that way anymore. The producing nations are in the driver's seat, have been for years. What I'm talking about is essentially pro bono oil exploration that we do on occasion. It burnishes our image and makes friends in places where we might not be loved. Do you understand what I'm saying?"

"It sounds reasonable and it sounds like you're trying to do the right thing."

"We *are* doing the right thing."

"I'm surprised ASC's PR department doesn't flood the Internet with pop-ups advertising how nice and kind you are."

"Cynicism does not become you."

"Why keep it secret?"

"We explore quietly so our competitors don't take advantage and steam in with fleets of oil hunters. We hire subcontractors for the actual exploration that specialize in that sort of thing. Little guys you never heard of. Small independent outfits like Tullow—or like Tullow used to be, Tullow now being the poster child for independents that strike it rich."

Janson interrupted the digression. "What outfit is exploring for you?"

"I can't tell you. It's proprietary. In fact, I don't even know. In ASC's chain of command no one below Kingsman Helms knows who. There is a major 'Chinese Wall' between them and us, so we don't get accused of riding roughshod over the poor, downtrodden recipient of our largess."

"What happens if they find something good?"

"ASC is first in line to help the small nation harvest its discovery. It's only fair—don't forget these days the locals have the power to demand enormous royalties. We're working on tighter margins than we did in the bad old days."

"Does 'first in line' mean ASC gets exclusive development rights?"

"By doing good, we do good—but not just ASC. I mean, look, Paul. We're an American corporation with a responsibility to supply our country with stable sources of energy. In my book that's nothing to be ashamed of. Whatever the long-term future of energy, our country can't make good decisions if we're scrambling to keep the lights on."

"Were you doing good at Isle de Foree?" Janson asked, wondering, Good enough to persuade some clandestine echelon of the United States government to launch Reapers in service of an oil company?

"Let me put it this way: ASC just chartered the *Vulcan Queen*, a seventh-generation exploration drill ship that can sink two forty-thousand-foot wells in water three miles deep and keep her station while the wind is blowing sixty knots and seas are running forty feet. She's the first billion-dollar drill ship and we've dispatched her to Isle de Foree."

"Good answer, Doug."

"What do you mean?"

"You had me worried you were jerking me around."

"I'm not following you, Paul."

"I see her on the horizon."

"The ship? Already? Are you sure it's her?"

Janson said, "She looks like a floating Death Star."

"That's the *Vulcan Queen*."

"I wondered who sent her the day after the revolution."

"Now you know."

"But I still don't know which clandestine service supported the Free Foree Movement."

"Why just one?"

"What did you say?"

"It could be anyone. Ours, Chinese, Nigerian, South African. Anyone who wants oil."

"But no one knew about Isle de Foree's oil. Except ASC and your 'pro bono' subcontractors."

"ASC didn't *know*. We *hoped*. So why wouldn't others? I mean, what the hell does it cost to fund a ragtag rebel army? Compared to the value of making friends. If you dug deep enough you'd find that Ferdinand Poe was taking money from a half-dozen sources. Most of whom were also giving Iboga money. It's chump change compared to what it could yield. Where ASC was smart was spending the big bucks to explore. Now that he's won, who will Interim President Poe love more, the guys who paid him in machine guns—valuable as they were when the lead was flying—or the guys who set his new nation on the road to riches?"

"I'll ask him," said Paul Janson.

"Beg pardon?"

"We have a meeting scheduled."

"About what?"

Janson decided to answer Doug Case honestly. Give American Synergy Corporation's chief of global security something to ponder. "A job."

* * *

"You look better, Mr. President," said Janson.

"Acting President," Ferdinand Poe corrected him. The old man appeared frail but actually had some color in his cheeks. They'd given him a haircut and a shave and blue cotton pajamas and hooked him up to an intravenous feed. His eyes were a little dull— an effect of painkillers, Janson presumed, as was the slurring of Poe's words, though his voice was strong. He added, with a small smile, "After years in the bush, the healing effects of two nights' sleep in a real bed are not to be overestimated."

"I imagine that winning a revolution doesn't hurt, either," Janson replied.

Poe bridled. "We fought our revolution thirty-five years ago against Portugal," he said curtly. "Our war against Iboga was not a revolution; it was a defense of a democracy against a coup."

"I stand corrected," said Janson. The prickly response probably reflected Poe's realization that the nation he had wrested back from Iboga faced severe consequences from their long war.

Poe pointed out the window at the palace across the water. "It is an important distinction. You see that open square beside the Presidential Palace? Isle de Foree's revolution ignited on that patch of ground fifty years ago when the Portuguese landowners persuaded the army to attack demonstrators protesting working conditions on the plantations. You probably never heard of the massacre. Your Vietnam War was capturing the headlines and Portugal had already committed similar atrocities in Mozambique. Ours was 'old news.' But here on our island, the Porto Clarence Massacre initiated our sense of nationhood."

His gaze darkened with the memory. "The soldiers made the men, women, and children stand in separate lines. I was a teacher. The little boys were fascinated by the jets sweeping overhead, and the helicopters, how freely they maneuvered. Then they started firing their machine guns.

"People fled. The soldiers chased them in Jeeps and armored cars and drove them to jump from the seawall. I will never forget what my father said as he lay dying: 'Those who will benefit from this are the wealthy that already have plenty in their hand.'" Poe shook his head in disgust. "They slaughtered five hundred of us. The harbor filled with sharks feeding on the bodies. What did you want to see me about?"

"One who already has plenty in his hand."

"What does that mean?"

"Your chief of staff informed me that Iboga looted the treasury."

"Yes. It appears that over the past two years he moved millions and millions out of the country. Money we need desperately."

Janson said, "As I understand it, Isle de Foree will soon take in money from deepwater oil."

"Only if there are truly great reserves. And even then only after years of preparation, drilling, building infrastructure. Until and if the oil company pays royalties, we will have to eke by on signing bonuses."

Janson shook his head. Even if deepwater oil was discovered in economically recoverable quantities, it would be years before

Poe's impoverished island nation received royalties. " 'Eking by' will hardly help you rebuild."

"I am aware of that," Poe said grimly. "The bankers are offering loans against future oil rents."

"But to borrow when you need to borrow," Janson said, "is to hold the beggar's bowl."

"We are aware of that, too. Nor are we unmindful of the 'resource curse.' A rising tide of oil money will drown a democracy unless we strictly manage it. We can't do that if we form the habit of borrowing against it. Yet how else do we replace the money Iboga took?"

"Would you like me to get it back?"

Paul Janson's noncommittal expression concealed enormous excitement. Any hunt for Iboga would be by its nature an investigation of who had sent the Harrier jump jet to rescue the dictator. It might even lead Janson to whoever had sent Reapers to the battle. Ferdinand Poe turned angry eyes on him. "You know I asked your help before to capture Iboga and you refused. This all could have been averted if only you had helped."

"Under those same circumstances I would refuse again," Janson replied. "Circumstances have changed. Now I have time to plan, time to go about it meticulously."

"But it would take forever. Liberia is still hunting Taylor's loot. Nearly ten years, now, they've found nothing in his name."

"Liberia's Taylor was in power for a long time. He systematically stole and took bribes and kickbacks over many years. Your Iboga was in power for a little over two years. And there was no great influx of foreign investment money to steal. My company has access to accountants who specialize in this sort of recovery."

Ferdinard Poe was suddenly impatient. "I propose paying you five percent of whatever you recover of Iboga's loot."

Janson's pulse quickened further. The original job of rescuing the doctor had bloomed into an astonishing opportunity. Five percent of even a poor nation's treasury would swell the Phoenix Foundation's coffers and vastly increase its reach. And that kind of money would allow him to pick and choose CatsPaw jobs for years to come. He hesitated only long enough to make Poe wonder whether he would demand more. Then he moved to close the deal. "Plus expenses. Understand that they could be considerable. We will require reimbursement on a weekly basis."

"Done."

"Not so fast. There is one other proviso."

Ferdinand Poe registered Paul Janson's profound change of expression. The amiable negotiator suddenly wore the face of an unyielding warrior. "What proviso?" Poe asked warily.

"I went to Black Sand Prison this morning," Janson said.

"To what purpose?"

"Mario Margarido made the arrangements so I could interview the wives Iboga left behind to learn how he arranged his escape."

"Were you anticipating that I would ask you to hunt him?"

"Professional interest," Janson answered. "It behooves me to keep up with the methods of people like Iboga."

"Were his wives helpful?"

"Marginally," was all Janson would reveal.

"What is this 'proviso'?"

"I don't do renditions." Never again.

"I do not understand you, Mr. Janson."

"I will not return the dictator to Isle de Foree to be tortured."

Ferdinand Poe sat up straighter in his bed. "There is no torture anymore on Isle de Foree," he said staunchly. "At Black Sand you must have seen my edict banning torture—my first edict since democracy's victory. No doubt Iboga's officer corps are chortling in their cells at my 'weakness'—even as they plot schemes to return him to power. But *not* slaughtering dangerous men as a precaution is the price a free country must pay to remain free."

"Your edict was duct-taped to the front gate," said Janson. "And those of Iboga's inner circle I saw were being treated humanely."

"Then why won't you return Iboga for trial? A fair trial, I assure you."

"Unfortunately, copies of your edict did not make their way to every dungeon in the prison."

"What do you mean?"

"I found Iboga's head wife spread-eagled naked on a stone floor. She was manacled hand and foot."

"That is what she did to our women."

"When I reminded the jailor about your edict, he told me, 'Acting President Poe ordered no more beating. But she doesn't know that and she remembers what she did to our women. Let her skin crawl in anticipation.' Then he pointed at the whips hanging on the wall and he asked me, 'Where do you think those whips came from? The Red Cross?' "

"One can't control everything," said Poe. "By the time you capture Iboga, I will have put the prison in proper order."

Janson said, "My forensic accountants will run down the money. But I will hand Iboga himself over to the International Criminal Court in The Hague."

"You don't believe me?"

"I believe your intent," Janson replied with a warm smile that would have done the wiliest diplomat proud. "But you have an entire nation to put in order and it will be a while before you can 'control' everything."

"No," said Poe. "Iboga will string the court along for years."

Janson said, "In researching the original job of rescuing Dr. Flannigan I happened to learn quite a bit about you, sir. I admire you. You're a practical man. You attended the London School of Economics to master English because mastery of English would help you promote the cause of Isle de Foree in a world where English speakers wielded power. And you're a brave man. You are the kind of man that people need to serve and protect them. But there are limits to what practicality and courage can achieve in the midst of chaos. You'll have enough on your plate without having to resist your own people's desire to take vengeance on Iboga. And before you say it is none of my business, capturing him will make him my business."

"All right!" said Ferdinand Poe. "Clearly you will not budge. Give him to the World Court, if you must."

"I must."

"Now *I* set a condition: If Iboga ever manages to trick his jailors and escape from The Hague, you promise to find him again before he comes back to retake Isle de Foree."

"Count on it," said Janson.

FIFTEEN

37°35′20.66″ N, 0°58′59.79″ W
Cartagena, Spain

P ut her on the ground, guys," Janson told his pilots. "Jesse's
gotta beat the doctor into Cartagena."

Seen from six thousand feet, cutting a long V wake
through a placid Mediterranean Sea, the *Varna Fantasy* gleamed
pristinely white in the morning sun.

They were standing behind the pilots, looking out the wind-
shields over Ed's and Mike's shoulders as CatsPaw Associates'
Embraer 650 banked in a wide turn around the *Varna Fantasy* and
headed for the coast. At the rocky edge of the blue-green sea they
crossed over Cartagena, Spain, the Bulgarian cruise liner's next
port of call.

Janson grew uncharacteristically talkative, which indicated to
Kincaid that he was about to hide something from her. Cartagena,

he told her, cut an uncommonly deep and sheltered indentation in a difficult stretch of Mediterranean coast that had made it a welcome harbor for three thousand years. Phoenician navigators and merchants had anchored in its blue-green waters, as had colonists from Carthage, Roman conquerors, and Spanish warships.

"The Romans left behind stone roads, theaters, and played-out silver mines. The Spanish erected fortresses on the headlands and breakwaters below and surrounded the waterfront with freight piers, shipyards, and factories. In our more peaceful, prosperous times they built that long mole to dock cruise ships."

"Care to tell me where you're going?" she asked.

"Not sure, yet," was all he would answer. He pulled disappearing acts now and then, though not as often as he used to.

As they descended toward the nearest airport, a sleepy general aviation field outside the town of Murcia, Jessica Kincaid asked Mike if she could sit in the first officer's seat for the landing.

"Negative. Sorry, Jesse, but it's a short runway and a nasty crosswind. I might need Ed's reflexes."

Kincaid elbowed Ed and said, "I have faster reflexes than this old guy."

"Yeah, but Ed's been practicing for thirty years. Next time. Don't worry; you'll get more landings."

Her red rental Audi was waiting on the private aviation apron.

"Good luck with the doc," Janson told her. "If he gives you any trouble, you've got Freddy Ramirez standing by in Madrid."

Freddy Ramirez was a former CSID Spanish intelligence operator. He had learned his trade battling Cuba's aggressive Directorate of Intelligence, which trafficked in cocaine and repeatedly attempted to penetrate CSID. Like Janson, Freddy had gone private. His Protocolo de Seguridad was well connected wherever Freddy Ramirez had followed the trail of Cuban coke, and Janson counted on him in Central America and Miami, Spain itself, France, and Italy.

Kincaid said, "I think I can handle one doctor. If he's aboard." *Varna Fantasy* had sailed the night the doctor disappeared from Porto Clarence, but he was not listed on either the passenger or crew manifest filed with Isle de Foree Customs and Immigration.

* * *

THE EMBRAER WAS thundering back into the sky before Kincaid cleared the airport gate. It took off into the westerly wind and quickly swooped north and possibly east, she thought, but by then it was climbing out of sight.

Foot to the firewall brought her into Cartagena as the tugboats were easing the *Varna Fantasy* past the outer breakwater. Kincaid battled tourist traffic through the narrow streets of the old walled city and pulled onto the cruise ship pier after the ship had crossed the harbor and tied up. Shuttle buses were waiting and sightseers queued eagerly at the gangway, anxious to get ashore after back-to-back three-day passages from Porto Clarence to Dakar, Senegal, and from Dakar to Cartagena.

Jessica Kincaid drove around the buses and found a parking space by the yacht marina that was sheltered by the pier. She had made it just in time. The bus drivers were stubbing out cigarettes and starting their engines. The ship loomed above the dock. Passengers were leaning over the rail gawking at the city that faced the harbor with a wall of cream-colored eight- and ten-story apartment buildings. Green plazas and palm trees stood between the buildings and the water.

Kincaid heard a sharp whistle and spotted the source through her open sunroof. She had noticed the boat rigger standing at the very top of a tall sailboat mast as she drove in—an athletic race-yacht gorilla in white T-shirt and shorts, his face shaded from the fierce sun by a visor and blue-iridium polarized sunglasses. He was working alone without a belaying line, which meant that instead of another crewman winching him up, he had climbed a halyard using *étriers* attached to rope ascenders. Standing in the stirrup-like *étriers*, he was at eye level with the passengers waiting to disembark from the *Varna Fantasy*. He flashed teeth in a hello-blond-foreign-tourist-ladies grin. The ladies snapped his picture with their cell phones.

The passengers began trooping down the gangway.

Kincaid watched every face. It was not difficult. There were more women than men, and most of the men were older than the doctor. She presumed the crew could disembark last. And when they had all boarded the buses, she had not seen him. There was a second gangway aft, a working route that touched the pier behind a chain-link fence and led into the terminal building. That would be for the crew.

The rigger gave her a whistle as she got out of the car, legs flashing from cool linen shorts. In her role as a carefree tourist she returned a thanks-for-the-compliment wave. She walked into the terminal building and approached the Fantasy Line's booth and engaged the women working there in a mix of English, French, and Spanish.

* * *

HADRIAN VAN PELT had been standing for hours in his Petzl rope ascenders atop the one-hundred-foot mast of the racing sloop, pretending to lubricate the masthead sheaves and change a burned-out anchor light. From this high up he could see over the cruise ship to the headlands that embraced the Spanish port, and beyond the headlands the blue-green water of the Mediterranean. Directly beneath him, beside the Real Club Nautico de Regattas, was the cruise ship pier where the passengers had trooped off the *Varna Fantasy* and boarded shuttle buses to the Old City.

He reasoned that ship's crew had to wait until the passengers disembarked, but he was taking no chances the doctor might disembark with them. Van Pelt still could not figure out how he had missed Flannigan when the ship docked in Dakar. This stop in the Mediterranean was his next opportunity, and he intended to finish the job here.

Then, seconds ago, movement under him had caught his eye. From the row of cars parked beside the boat slips a slim woman had stepped out of a red Audi. She was wearing retro cat's-eye sunglasses. The open visor that shaded her face did not cover her spiky brown hair. When he had whistled, she returned a noncommittal wave, locked her car, and hurried into the terminal.

Van Pelt clamped his gloves around the wire forestay and kicked out of his rope ascenders. He launched himself into the air, plummeted in a controlled slide down the slanting forestay, and landed as lightly as a much smaller man would. Then he vaulted off the sailboat onto the concrete pier and headed for the woman's car.

He had last seen her in Porto Clarence, Isle de Foree. American, he had figured, judging by the I-own-the-world thrust of her shoulders. She had been sitting in a café, in animated conversation with the old woman who owned Isle de Foree's priciest whorehouse.

Hadrian Van Pelt could wonder if it was a big coincidence. Or he could wonder whether she, too, had tracked Dr. Terry Flannigan to Cartagena, Spain, the *Varna Fantasy*'s next port of call after Dakar. But why wonder when he could ask her?

He knelt beside the Audi as if to tighten a running-shoe lace, opened his tool pouch, activated an electronic scanner that read key codes—a Czech-built instrument that cost more than the car—and popped her door locks. He climbed in like he owned it, looked to ensure that no one was watching, and squeezed himself onto the floor of the backseat.

Van Pelt did not doubt that a professional with her wits about her would spot him in the back as she opened the door. But a professional would also recognize the snub nose of the bullpup-configured Micro TAR-21 assault rifle protruding from his tool pouch. She would see that she had no choice but to obey his order to get in and drive before he drilled a hole in her head with the silenced weapon.

* * *

AFTER ATTEMPTING TO answer Jessica Kincaid's questions and accepting small bribes sufficient to treat themselves to a nice lunch—an amount that Janson had taught her could buy a lot of information—the women at the Fantasy Lines counter began glancing at the clock.

Kincaid thanked them for their time and stepped out into the sun again.

"Fuck!" she muttered under her breath.

There was no Dr. Terrence Flannigan aboard the ship, she had learned. The women had actually telephoned the ship for her and confirmed that. The ship's doctor was a Senegalese, enjoying a free cruise vacation, which meant that somehow Terry Flannigan had given Kincaid the slip at Dakar. Or had never been on the damned boat in the first place.

Now what?

The pier was deserted. All the buses were gone. Midday, midweek, the sailboats crammed side by side in the marina were empty. Nothing moved but indicators tracking the wind on their mastheads and some generator turbines spinning lazily. The blue-green water was barely riffled by the weak remnants of the morning breeze. Across the harbor, smoke rose straight from a distant chimney. The fortresses on the rocky promontories that guarded the narrow mouth to the sea baked in the sun.

It appeared that the only people left working in the Spanish city were waiters serving lunch to the rest. Even the good-looking rigger had called it a morning and abandoned his perch on the mast.

Lunch. Then out of here.

She hurried to her car.

SIXTEEN

Jessica Kincaid stopped six feet from the Audi and opened her handbag. She took out a Marlboro box, opened it, shook her head in disgust, crumbled it in her hand, turned on her heel, and walked back to the terminal building, pausing at the door to drop the crumpled box in a trash receptacle.

The terminal was air-conditioned, pleasantly cool, encouraging passengers to linger at the many shops. Like the Fantasy Line desk, most of the shops had closed for lunch. Those open were virtually empty today, but for bored clerks.

Kincaid headed for the ladies' room. She heard a hand drier roaring inside. Good. No need to go in. She veered across the echoing lobby into the drugstore and bought a box of Marlboros and a cigarette lighter, then asked the woman at the checkout register for an instant cold pack. She found it among the ACE bandages and braces for sprained wrists and paid for the cold pack and a Spanish newspaper. Then she went to the ladies' room. The woman who had been drying her hands was just leaving.

"*Perdón.*"

"*No hay problema.*"

Kincaid checked that all the stalls were empty and that she was alone, wadded a piece of newsprint into the sink drain to act as a stopper, and filled the sink halfway with cold water. Ignoring the instructions not to open the cold pack, printed in five languages, she tore it apart and poured its ammonium nitrate crystals into the water to dissolve them. She soaked a sheet of newspaper in the solution, let the excess drip, and held it in front of the hand drier. The wet paper tore easily, so the drier blew it apart in her hands. She tried again, got the trick of it standing farther back from the warm air flow, and dried it completely. Dry, it was even more fragile, threatening to crumble in her fingers. To prevent that, she laid it on a sheet of dry newsprint and then she folded them tightly into a rectangle a foot long, an inch wide, and half an inch thick.

She put it in her bag, strode quickly from the ladies' room, across the lobby and out to the pier. She walked slowly to her car, while looking around like a tourist, opening the Marlboro box, pocketing the sealing string of cellophane, tamping the tobacco down on her free hand, pocketing the inner foil, and tapping loose a cigarette.

She saw no one watching from any of the boats in the slips. None of the parked cars seemed to have an occupant. No one seemed to be peering down at her from the ship, though they could be.

She scoped the area as she would if she were installing Lambda Team. She would put marksmen in the palm trees nearest the center, marksmen on the roofs of the buildings behind them, a marksman in a stalled truck on the overpass. For her own position

she would take the lighthouse that marked the channel around the
outer breakwater. A long shot with the water effects and sea breeze
to adjust for, but the hit would be hers.

If there were snipers, she would be dead by now. If there were
snipers, there would be no heavy guy hiding in her car, making it
sit a hair lower on its springs.

She was a woman; he could be a scum rapist. But damned
few rapists could break into a locked Audi without setting off the
alarm. And the fact that the Audi was still where she had parked
it confirmed that whoever was inside was not trying to steal it. He
was waiting for her.

She had noticed something else, subconsciously, as she walked
out of the terminal, a discrepancy that hadn't fully registered but
had heightened her awareness: The rigger who had been atop the
sailboat mast had left his rope ascenders attached to the halyard
he had climbed. To retrieve them he would have to climb back up
with another set, which made no sense unless he'd had a reason to
come down real quick, such as to break into her car.

It had to be about the doctor. Dr. Flannigan was the only reason
she was in Cartagena. The guy in her Audi had to be an operator
who had come to meet the *Varna Fantasy* for the same reason.
Somehow he must have connected her to the doctor.

Woman or not, she could not call the cops. Janson Rules: no innocents in the cross fire. She had to assume that the operator was
a professional. The poor cops would never know what hit them.

She stepped closer to the car, put the cigarette between her lips,
shielded the lighter by turning her back to the wind, still looking
for the guy's partners. If he had them, they were invisible. The marina was thick with boats. They could be watching from inside one
of the cabins.

She gazed around the marina like a visitor reluctant to leave a pretty place. Still holding the lighter, she pretended a lazy drag on the Marlboro and walked along the edge of the pier, gazing down into the cockpits of several sailboats as if admiring the polished chrome and varnished brightwork or dreaming of sailing away. She hadn't had a cigarette since she was sixteen and the hardest part was not coughing on the toxins.

She spotted things she could use in the cockpit of the boat the rigger had been working on. She turned around and stepped closer to the car. She crouched in a swift, sure motion, slipped the folded rectangle of ammonium nitrate–impregnated newspaper under the car, thumbed the lighter, touched the flame to the newspaper, and rose as quickly.

She got ten feet away before the smoke bomb ignited.

The Audi suddenly disappeared in a whirlwind of thick white smoke. Kincaid jumped down into the sailboat's cockpit and scrambled back to the pier carrying a Halotron fire extinguisher and a six-foot-long boat hook.

The rigger was a big man. It took him a moment to untangle himself from the backseat. He threw open the back door on the passenger side and stumbled out coughing in the acrid smoke.

Kincaid dropped the boat hook.

She shouted, "Fire! Fire!"—staging a quick-thinking-passerby performance for the benefit of potential witnesses—and aimed the extinguisher at his face. He had removed his sunglasses and even as she blasted him with the pressurized heat-absorbing liquid she recognized him as the commando who had conducted the brilliant rearguard action that enabled President for Life Iboga to escape from Isle de Foree.

He was just as cool here, a highly trained, lightning-fast operator who, despite being half-blinded by the smoke bomb and the sweet-ether-smelling stream of Halotron stinging his eyes, whipped a

Tavor Micro TAR-21 assault rifle from his tool pouch and thumbed the fire selector level to fully automatic mode.

Kincaid knew instantly what he was going to do. Taken by surprise, unable to see who was attacking him and how many they were, he would spin in a circle and pull the trigger, spew the entire 30-round shot magazine in a rapid burst of deadly fire, slam a fresh magazine from his bag into the weapon, and gun down anyone still standing, whether attacker or innocent bystander.

Kincaid dropped the fire extinguisher and scooped the boat hook off the concrete. The hook end consisted of two blunt studs for pushing off, which were rounded to minimize the risk of tearing sailcloth; the hook for snaring lines was similarly rounded and curved back toward the handle. The pole was made of aluminum sheathed with vinyl. It was too light to stagger as big a man as she was facing or even knock the gun out of his hands.

Kincaid hurled it like a javelin.

She aimed for his eyes.

He was amazingly fast, with the reflexes of a cobra and the fighting instincts of a Spanish bull. He raised a big hand to block the boat hook, brushing it slightly off-course, and turned away. The hook missed his eye but bashed his temple. The stunning blow would have dropped most men. It hardly slowed him. But Kincaid had achieved her first goal of keeping his finger off the trigger.

He lunged at her.

He outweighed her by a hundred pounds. He spread his long arms to bear-hug her between his empty hand and the gun. He was thinking he could smother her with his weight, a common football-clod mistake. Kincaid backpedaled and drew from the sheath hidden under her compact shoulder bag a carbon-fiber scalpel.

She slid the razor-edged blade inside the crook of his elbow.

She ripped it the length of his forearm. He kept coming and Kincaid kept slicing, down his wrist and through the heel of his hand. As his hand opened convulsively, releasing the gun, she continued cutting, crossing his palm, opening the flesh from his elbow to his fingers.

The Micro TAR-21 fell to the pavement. It was made of plastic and bounced. Kincaid caught it on the hop. Backing away before he could grab her, bobbling the weapon around to point the business end his way, she tucked it close to her body, rotated the selector lever to semiautomatic, and demanded, "Who the hell are you?"

He raised his bloody arm. His face had gone chalk white with shock, but it was contorted with rage. He pointed a red dripping finger at her face. "You are dead meat."

"*Me?* I'm not bleeding like a stuck pig. I'm holding the gun." She aimed it at his knee. "Who are you?"

"Fuck you," he retorted. If the shock and awe she had already blitzed him with would not make him answer her, the fear of her shooting him in the leg wouldn't, either. Kincaid went at his ego instead, tearing into it with the same ferocity with which she had slashed his arm.

"Fuck me? Fuck you. Where'd you learn to fight? Kindergarten? Nobody taught you to lead with bone? You shoulda blocked me with your radius. You made me a present of your soft side."

It worked. Crouching there dripping blood like a wet-behind-the-ears recruit, he had to prove to the 130-pound woman who had taken him out that he was important. He spit out a word that sounded like, "Sar."

"Sar?" she shouted back. "What the fuck is sar?"

"I'm sar. You're dead meat."

"Yeah, yeah, yeah, you already told me that. What is sar?" She gestured again with the gun.

He glanced past her toward the terminal and relief crossed his face. "People. Go ahead and shoot."

Kincaid was already watching them from the corner of her eye. Middle-aged couples strolling her way, still distant, but drawing closer. Too far away to hear the sound-suppressed Tavor, but they would certainly hear him scream. He used the distraction to whirl in a swift, smooth motion and dive straight off the pier exactly as he had done at Porto Clarence. He speared the water with barely a splash, slick as a dolphin.

Kincaid raced after him. This time he wouldn't have anyone stationed under the pier to help him escape. She balanced on the edge, eyes sweeping the surface for his bubbles to see where to propel herself into the water, soles clenched to push off the concrete rim. The Tavor was waterproof. She could put a slug in him underwater if she could get close enough. There! She dug in her feet to push off hard. Suddenly she heard Paul Janson's voice in her head. Loud, like the boss was sitting on her shoulder.

Never get in the wrong fight.

She had no business rassling an operator his size in the water, not a powerful swimmer who speared the surface without a splash. He'd use his superior weight and strength to drag her under like a raccoon drowning a coonhound.

The couples were closer, exclaiming. They had seen him dive or they saw the smoke. She was still holding the TAR-21, tucking it tight to her body. She slid it under the nearest car, scooped her handbag off the pavement, and palmed her knife into its sheath. Then she picked up the fire extinguisher and made a show of spraying the last tendrils of smoke under the Audi.

They came running as fast as they could in holiday sandals, shouting in Spanish, gesticulating wildly. Kincaid gesticulated back, pretended not to understand Spanish, pulled out her keys, climbed in the car, smiling. *"Gracias, gracias."*

She started the motor, lowered the window to clasp the nearest woman's hand. *"Gracias.* Thank you. I'm okay." She made eye contact, squeezed the plump, sweaty hand reassuringly, waved a casual *adios* to the rest of them, and drove off the pier, following the signs on the Paseo de Alfonso XII that would take her to the AP-7 Autopista del Mediterráneo and out of here, hoping she had jollied them out of calling the cops.

She saw a million Traffic Group patrol cars on the limited-access toll road and a ton of radar traps. She stuck to the 120-kilometer limit and none took notice of the Audi. Home free. No one had called the cops.

Halfway to Valencia she pulled into a busy rest stop. Hungry as always after a fight, she piled a cafeteria tray high with asparagus, artichokes, mushrooms, and sardines and wolfed them down while texting Janson.

Doc jumped ship mayb Dakar.

She paused to reflect. The M-TAR-21 assault rifle, "Micro" as it was, was still a mighty big gun to wave around in public. There were two reasons a professional would risk carrying it: Its high rate of fire on automatic made it a deadly defense weapon in the event the operator had to fight his way out of a jam, but it was also extremely accurate and extremely quiet, the perfect rifle to single-shot Flannigan from the sailboat mast as he stepped off the ship.

In other words, she resumed texting Janson,

Porto C diver hunting doc to terminate.

She went back for dessert, chose two dishes of flan and a double espresso. Returning to her table, she sent another message:

PC diver dove again. Unit called ?sar? Iboga friend—doc enemy.

She spooned up the flan and stirred sugar into the espresso. Then she thumbed into her phone:

?Next?

SEVENTEEN

Where next, Boss?" Mike asked.

The Rolls-Royces were whining down to stop as Ed parked the Embraer outside Jet Aviation's fixed base operation terminal in Zurich, Switzerland.

"Leave the aircraft here and have it serviced. You guys fly home commercial. Catch up on your sleep."

"Home? Wouldn't mind seeing the house, mow the lawn."

"Spray the roses," said Ed. "Pat the cat—when do you want us back?"

"Quintisha will find you."

Janson's pilots knew better than to ask where he was going.

All week Paul Janson had been calling in markers from former friends and foes from his long years at Consular Operations. Spies, bankers, state ministers, criminals, and law officers owed him favors and often their lives. Ironically—and very conveniently—there was much overlap between the CatsPaw Associates corporate security consulting business and the Phoenix Foundation. His two organizations fueled each other.

The family of experts Janson had gathered served both sides, often unknowingly.

The information miners, the eyes and ears who brought him word of a derelict agent, also alerted him to paying jobs and dug up information to perform those missions. The money managers who held the IRS at bay and kept the nonprofit side both solvent and legitimate could move cash and dispense payments where needed. Facilitators, specialized operators, computer wizards, and hackers, all were put to work on various aspects of the hunt for Iboga, Iboga's rescuers, and the elusive doctor whom Janson was starting to think of, ruefully, as Fleet-Footed Flannigan.

The CatsPaw Associates machine was operating at full bore. Results, however, were disappointing. The accountants were making some progress on where Iboga had hidden Isle de Foree's millions. But in a fruitless week of polling the clandestine world Janson's people had found nothing about who had dispatched the Harrier jump jet that rescued Iboga and nothing about where the dictator had gone.

The freelance researchers coordinated by the home office had pointed out what Janson already knew: In a world that contained more than one hundred thousand "superrich" fortunes of over $30 million, plenty of individuals could afford to buy an elderly Harrier. And complex aircraft support systems were not necessary if they intended to fly it only once and ditch it in the sea when they were done with it.

An intriguing hint came from a recording in the Gulf of Guinea Maritime Security database of a radio exchange that had occurred the night before Iboga's defeat on Pico Clarence. Supertanker watch officers hailing each other as their vessels passed close in the dark a hundred miles off Gabon were interrupted by a thunderous noise. One officer, who had served in the Royal Navy, identified the never-forgotten sound of a Harrier storming down to a vertical landing. On their radars they spotted a large ship, a freighter or another tanker, on which a Harrier could have landed. But the ship showed no lights and did not answer their calls.

Janson speculated that if the Harrier had night-fighting capability it could have joined the ship by flying offshore from Gabon, a former French colony. That ship could have steamed within Harrier range of Isle de Force when Iboga made his escape the following afternoon. Janson ordered CatsPaw to canvas aviation officials in Gabon. But the fact was the nation had many remote airstrips where the Harrier could have jumped off after flying in from Angola or Congo, coming and going in complete secrecy.

So while the CatsPaw Associates and Phoenix Foundation machines continued to grind away and Jessica Kincaid hunted for the doctor, it was time for "the boss" to disappear. Time to go back to what he did best, alone.

He had Jet Aviation's limo run him over to the main passenger terminal. He wandered around the terminal until he felt comfortably un-followed. Then he boarded the train to Zurich, where he roamed the underground shops of the Hauptbahnhof. Only when he was absolutely sure he was not being followed did he leave the train station. From the station plaza he rode the escalator up to the Bahnhofstrasse and cut through a neighborhood of narrow, tree-lined side streets.

He crossed a shallow branch of the Limmat on the Gessner Bridge and onto Lagerstrasse. Lagerstrasse paralleled the enormous railroad cut that brought the sleek trains into the center of the city. Four blocks on, he entered the lobby of a low-rise commercial building beside the tracks, climbed the stairs to the third floor, and knocked at the door of a freight-forwarding business.

In the outer reception room he gave his name.

This gained him admittance to an inner reception room.

An iris scan confirmed that he was expected.

A receptionist led him to a back office where the floor vibrated at a fine pitch set by the trains whisking past the building. A clerk wordlessly handed him a Tyvek polyethylene envelope and left Janson alone, closing the door behind him. Janson locked it.

He dumped the contents of the envelope on a bare table and carefully examined the paper and plastic that supported a legend he had not used for several years. The identity package for security-services executive "Adam Kurzweil" was so meticulously assembled that the crisp new Canadian passport was accompanied by its expired predecessor, which Janson recalled he had last used to enter Hungary. The new one had the latest radio frequency identification chip issue encoded with Kurzweil's particulars and a biometric profile designed to slide Janson past the scanners. It was a reminder, not that he needed it, that in the post-9/11 decades when transportation security employed ever more sophisticated digital technology, one had to pay for the best countermeasures to stay ahead of the game. Happily, the best was still found in this nondescript building on Lagerstrasse.

He emptied his wallet into the Swiss Post Priority envelope they had supplied, and addressed it to a cell phone shop on the nearby Uetlibergstrasse. A CatsPaw Associates private shell corporation owned a nonparticipating interest in numerous such shops in Europe and Asia. The investments bought the key codes to their front doors, mail drops, and exclusive access to safes in their cellars.

He refilled his wallet with the new passport, driver's license, medical insurance cards, credit cards, dog-eared family photo-graphs, and business cards—both Adam Kurzweil's, which were expensively embossed, and several that Kurzweil would have re-ceived from sales prospects.

He walked back to the train station, posted the envelope, bought an expensive carry-on shoulder bag, two changes of clothing, a tan raincoat, and a windbreaker. He left the station and boarded a tram. He got off at the Stampenbachplotz stop and walked to the Hotel InterContinental. He left his distinctive raincoat in the men's room and walked out into the streets, where he eventually hailed a taxi to a residential neighborhood. He walked some more, removed his necktie, folded it and his suit jacket into his shoulder bag, put on the windbreaker, and rode a tram to the industrial Oer-likon quarter.

He walked from the Oerlikon tram station out of the central dis-trict of shops and cafés, passed factories old and new, and at the end of a cobblestone alley knocked on a windowless steel door. He stepped back and unzipped his windbreaker to let the cameras have a good look. To his surprise, the door was opened personally by the man he had come to see.

Neal Kruger was tall and tanning-bed bronzed, with thick curly hair turning gray and the slightly quizzical expression of a hand-some lifeguard or ski bum shocked to discover he had stumbled into middle age.

"Hello, Neal."

The weapons dealer clasped Janson's hand, pulled him inside, and hugged him hard. "Too long, my friend. How are you?"

"Very, very well," said Paul Janson. "You look like you're prospering."

"The United Nations' failure to impose world peace continues to stoke the human desire to accumulate arms. I am, indeed, pros-pering."

"Since when do you open your own front door?"

"It is a luxury to feel so secure that I don't need armed men to welcome old friends."

"You're taking a damned fool chance," said Janson.

"A luxury by definition is an indulgence."

"You'll get yourself killed. Or snatched."

"There are four concealed cameras over the alley."

"I saw them. And the gas port. It would not be easy to take you, but not impossible."

"Will I get a bill for security advice?"

Janson did not smile back. "You should be more careful. If not for you, for your wife and son."

"She left me. She took the boy."

"I'm sorry." That explained the lapse. "Then the advice is on the house. There's no protecting a man who doesn't give a damn."

Kruger led him inside. His office was a mess. He had laid out a tray of bread and cheese on his desk and opened a bottle of Cote de Rhone. Janson sipped sparingly, though he dove into the cheese, having not eaten since early morning. They traded information on old friends and then Janson got to the point. "Any luck with the jump jet?"

Kruger nodded. "Twelve old T.10 Harrier two-seaters from the nineties were updated to a T.12 capability to train pilots for the Brits' GR.9 fleet. Marvelous aircraft. Fully combat capable. Even night fighting. Now they're being replaced by the F-35B Lightning II Joint Strike Fighter, which means that for a while there were a dozen vertical-slash-short takeoff and landing two-seaters for sale around the world. Nine of them are currently serving the Spanish and the Turks. The Nigerians managed to crash two of them, after which they put the third back on the market."

"Who bought it?"

"A fellow I know who deals with mercenaries."

"*French* mercenaries?"

Kruger shot Janson an admiring glance. "Why come to me for answers you already know?"

"Not this time," said Janson. "It's just that..."

"It's just that what?"

Janson hesitated only a moment. His instinct to conceal was tempered by the knowledge that Neal Kruger lived on information. Any information Janson gave the arms dealer would cause him to return the favor, though at the risk that he would trade on it with others. Janson said, "I interviewed two of Iboga's wives."

"How many does he have?"

"They caught three of them. God knows how many others escaped into the bush. Illiterate peasant girls. Little older than children really. Anyway, they both said the same thing when I asked about how Iboga got away: 'The French, the French.' It was like a chant or a prayer. I doubt they know where France is, but they were parroting what Iboga kept saying near the end: 'The French will save me. The French will save me.' It was pretty clear he had arrangements with someone. Now you're telling me that a Harrier jump jet ended up in the hands of a merchant who deals with the French."

"It hardly sounds like the French government. They muck about in their former colonies like the Ivory Coast, or Senegal. But Isle de Foree was Portuguese."

Janson agreed. "Have you heard of a freelance outfit called Sar?"

"Sar? No. What is it?"

"They might have been who sent the jump jet. Or they supplied operators on the ground for whoever did. And it appears they do assassinations."

"That's a crowded field."

Janson swirled the wine in his glass, eyed the ruby color against the light. He was glad he had come personally instead of continuing with Kruger on the phone. The phone couldn't show the disorderliness of a man's office or provide such a window on his state of mind. Kruger would become increasingly less useful unless Janson could help him change the course of his life.

"Why did she leave?" He recalled a younger, athletic woman with a warm smile, a ripe body, and erotic eyes that rarely left Kruger's face.

"She said I took her for granted."

"Any chance of getting her back?"

Kruger shook his head. "In my experience, when you lose your glow in the eyes of a woman it does not rekindle. . . . She was right. Sort of. I didn't mean to take her for granted. But I was working harder than ever. Traveling more. Hugely distracted."

"By what?"

"Drones. Everyone wants them. Few have them."

"Like Predators? Reapers?"

"The smaller stuff. The Israelis are making some amazing machines. The Chinese are trying. Russians, of course."

"With Reaper capability?"

"Small rockets, perhaps. Not the big stuff."

"Take out tanks?"

"No, no, no. But they'll make short work of a terrorist in an SUV. Or a parliamentary rival in a Mercedes. Guidance is the big problem. If you don't have your own cloud of satellites like the U.S., you're juggling rented satellite space with all the discombobulation that can breed, not to mention deeply compromised security. A drone can be a big disappointment if an enemy hacker redirects it back at you."

"Have you ever heard of a Reaper or a Predator in private hands?"

"A real one? No way."

"It would have to be government, wouldn't it?" Janson asked. "*United States* government."

* * *

JANSON CAUGHT THE tram at the Oerlikon station and was back at the Hauptbahnhof minutes later. He took an overnight train to Belgrade and had breakfast with a Serbian militia contractor, a former army officer who had built a business supplying brilliantly trained bodyguards capable of offensive operations.

But the Serb knew nothing. The trip to Belgrade was a waste of time. Other than Neal Kruger's speculation about some sort of "French Connection." Paul Janson was no closer to discovering the source of the jump jet, no closer to picking up the trail of the escaped Iboga.

He took a ramshackle taxi to the airport, not sure what next, thinking maybe Paris. On the way, scanning the *New York Times* on his cell, he caught a lucky break—an unexpected opportunity to call in a valuable debt. Instead of flying to Paris, he boarded a Turkish Airlines flight to Baghdad.

EIGHTEEN

The haughty sheik arguing with Club Electric's bouncers was demanding to keep his guns, Janson's translator told him.

"Now what is he yelling?"

If he could not keep his guns, the sheik insisted that his bodyguards keep theirs.

Club Electric's bouncers were unimpressed. All patrons of Baghdad's premier nightclub checked their guns at the door. No exceptions.

It was hot, 114 degrees, hours after dark. Janson's translator kept glancing up the street that paralleled the Tigris River, as if wondering which of the Hummers, Land Rovers, and Cadillac Escalades approaching the valet parkers was hauling a car bomb. Patrons lined up behind them looked as anxious to get inside the blast walls.

The sheik surrendered at last.

Janson exchanged the automatic he had purchased on the way in from the airport for a plastic claim check. Bouncers whispering into walkie-talkies ushered him through Kevlar-reinforced doors. He paused at the top of the stairs to let a group of Iraqis catch up with them and slipped inconspicuously among them. They descended switchback flights of green-lighted Lucite steps into a cavernous, windowless room pulsing with Arab music. Hundreds of prosperous men in shirtsleeves were drinking Pepsi-Cola, smoking water pipes, and watching soccer on flat-screen TVs.

"The joint is jumpin'," he told his translator, flummoxing the earnest young student. In fact, the blast walls, the zigzagged stairs designed to baffle the impact of an explosion, and the absence of window glass made for a relaxing atmosphere.

He told the translator to wait in the roped-off area set aside for bodyguards.

"How will you understand, sir?"

Traveling in Adam Kurzweil mode, the normally reticent Paul Janson conducted himself more openly. The Canadian security-services executive appeared sure of himself, forthcoming, brash, and even boastful. "The owner of Club Electric," he explained, "speaks English."

The translator was in awe. The new Club Electric was the hottest nightclub between Vienna and Mumbai. Janson might well have claimed kinship with Iraq's prime minister, whom Janson had already spotted in a far corner of the big room eating dinner with the mayor of Baghdad. "You *know* Michel Sarkis?"

"When I knew 'Michel,' he was 'Mike.' Wait over there, please. I'll call you when I need you."

Sarkis, a stocky Lebanese with jet-black hair, was table-hopping. Janson drifted through the big room, tracking Sarkis to a table of Iraqi businessmen and German bankers near where the mayor and prime minister were dining. The club owner stood bouncing from foot to foot, smiling and brimming with energy, bantering in French-accented English.

"From where am I?" he replied to one of the German bankers. "The answer is as complex as any international affair. *Conceived* 1975 in Beirut the night the civil war broke out. *Born* on the high seas crossing to America. What ship? The SS *France*, of course. The last truly elegant liner ever built. She bred in me a taste for beauty and pleasure."

In fact, the *France* make her final westbound crossing in 1974. But Janson had no need to challenge Sarkis on the small stuff.

"*Then* Greenwich, Beverly Hills, Manhattan, and Paree. *Always* Paree."

Janson passed close behind him and whispered so only the nightclub owner could hear, "What about Florida?"

Sarkis whirled around. "*Bonjour!*" he cried, a welcoming smile and widespread arms failing to mask the panic in his eyes. Janson was not surprised that Sarkis didn't recognize him.

"Sarasota, Florida, Mike. When you have a minute I'll be out on the deck."

"I'm very busy, sir; let me buy you a drink and—"

"How's the Lamborghini running?"

Sarkis's smile went rigid. "I'll meet you on the deck."

Janson followed the neon palm tree arrows that pointed the way through blast walls to the outdoor deck that overlooked the Tigris and the city lights. Few patrons braved the heat. The waiters were wilting. The river was low. Janson smelled burning plastic, oil, and sewage.

He chose a spot on the railing just beyond the glow of the red, white, and blue Pespi display coolers and stood with his back to the water. Sarkis kept him waiting ten minutes, as if sending a message that he was a fleet-footed survivor who had already recovered from the shock of Janson's blast from the past.

"How's the Lamborghini running?" Janson asked again.

"Sold it to a Russian," Sarkis answered brusquely. "What's up?" Out of earshot of his elite Iraqi customers, Sarkis sounded like an American who had grown up in Danbury, Connecticut, dropped out of state college, and used his smiling good looks to sell Florida vacation condos to well-fixed widows.

Janson answered, "What's up is that you are rich and well connected and can help me buy a Harrier jump jet."

Interestingly, Sarkis did not deny it. All he said was, "Why would I help you?"

"Gratitude for saving your life. Or terror that I know enough about your life to destroy it."

"I don't know you. I don't know why you think that Sarasota is somehow important to me."

"It was a while back," said Janson. "I've followed your career since with admiration."

"To blackmail me?"

"Only to call in a marker."

"How much?"

"Not money. Information. Actually, let me amend that. I want truthful information."

Sarkis snapped his fingers. Two bouncers hurried toward them.

Paul Janson said, "Imagine a hot night on the Florida 'Suncoast.' Envision a good-looking college dropout in his twenties. He's wearing the two most valuable things he owns: a white linen suit one of his girlfriends gave him and an expensive watch from his refugee parents' Danbury, Connecticut, jewelry store. He has a French accent he can turn on and off because at home Mom and Dad spoke French, their language back in Lebanon.

"Picture him charming old ladies into buying Sarasota condos. His commissions are small and he has to kick back a bunch to his manager. He's living hand to mouth, money all around him, none of it his. He's aching for a break. And here's the thing I admire about this kid: He is ready to seize it if it comes his way. And that night it does."

Sarkis looked at Janson. He had a look of queasy fascination on his handsome face. "Go on!"

"Call off the muscle."

Sarkis banished the hovering bouncers with a gesture. "Go on!"

Before Janson could speak the lights went out. The entire city was suddenly dark. The reflections on the water vanished. The sky was too murky to admit the stars. Baghdad's notoriously embattled electrical grid had died again.

"Ten seconds," said Sarkis. *"Go on."*

The deck shook. Diesel generators rumbled to life, and Club Electric was ablaze in light again, though still surrounded by the dark. "Best generators the American taxpayers' money could buy," said Sarkis. "Haliburton left them at the airport. Still in their crates. Go on."

"Sarasota Film Festival. A thousand people drive inland to a party thrown by a Realtor attempting to sell million-dollar condos in a swamp too many miles from the beach. The dropout in the white linen suit is hoping for a commission, but nothing's selling and he leaves early, just as the party is beginning to wind down, figuring he'll drive out of the swamp ahead of the traffic jam. But when he tries to claim his car, he discovers that the valet parking system has completely broken.

"The car parkers are drunk. The boss has run for it. They stopped tagging the keys and the keys are piled in a huge heap. A thousand people are about to attempt to collect their cars. A hundred are already there shouting, 'Where's my keys?' The locals are worrying about their Mercedes and Range Rovers and Aston Martins, and the tourists are trying to remember what color was the rental they got at the airport.

"The dropout thinks quick. He collars the one parking attendant not drunk but terrified, and he waves his last two hundred dollars under the kid's nose: 'Find the keys to my yellow Lamborghini and the dough is yours.'

"The attendant finds the keys, and the guy in the white suit with the expensive watch and the French accent drives away in a two-hundred-thousand-dollar automobile thinking he's going to blast straight across the country—do not stop for girlfriend, do not look back—all the way to Beverly Hills, California, where rich women are kind to young Frenchmen in Lamborghinis."

Sarkis stared at Janson. "Then what happened?"

"The kind of twist he couldn't make up, except that's the way life works, sometimes. The guy who owns the Lamborghini is a terrible, terrible person."

"And chases him?"

"Was the guy who caught you the owner of the car?" Janson asked.

Sarkis's eyes got even bigger. "Wait a minute! Was that you?"

"That was me and you never knew it until now, but I saved your life."

Sarkis looked across the river where other generator-driven light clusters were popped up around the city like white fireworks. He said, as if describing a half-remembered dream, "Somehow you passed me in a stupid Honda and cut me off."

"The Honda was customized. I knew how to drive fast. You didn't."

"You shined a light in my eyes. You asked to see my license. I thought you were a cop. But you didn't ask for my registration. Then you took my keys and told me not to move. It was dark. I couldn't see for sure, but I thought you were lying down under the car."

"I was removing a radio-triggered explosive device so it wouldn't blow your front wheel off and flip you into a swamp at eighty miles an hour."

Sarkis digested that quickly. "An explosive device that you had attached?"

"Correct."

"Why?"

"The owner was a terrible person. You were innocent. At least by comparison."

"How did you know it was me, not him, driving?"

"I didn't. I picked up the Lamborghini on the side road out of that development and followed, waiting for the right moment to blow the wheel. He had to be going fast, which you were, safely clear of other drivers, and next to water or some kind of drop-off he wouldn't survive. When we reached such a spot and I was just about to key the signal, I realized something was off. The Lamborghini was all over the road. But the owner was not such a clumsy driver. Which meant the driver I was following was probably not the person I was supposed to, uh, kill."

"You gave me back my license. You gave me the keys. You said, 'Disappear. Get out of the state and don't come back.' You asked if I needed money. I said, 'Yeah.' You gave me a wad of twenties and hundreds— How did you know about Danbury and my parents?"

"I took your name off your license. You struck me as a guy who was going places—bent places—and I figured you'd come in handy some night. I checked you out and have kept track of you ever since. This morning I saw your picture in an article about Club Electric."

"And tonight's the night?"

"Tonight's the night, Mike."

"Mind me asking—"

"You've had your questions. Listen up. I need your help. You know everybody in Baghdad and everybody in Beirut, and everybody in Dubai. And more people than you should know in Kabul."

"I own a nightclub. I know my patrons."

Janson showed his teeth. "Don't waste my time, Mike. I know who you are and what you've done."

"The Lamborghini was years ago. I was a kid."

"The Lamborghini was the beginning. You want to hear a story about Tehran? No? How about Kandahar. You're still a U.S. citizen. They'll hunt you to the ends of the earth."

"I didn't do anything in Kandahar anybody else didn't do."

"Mike, I don't care. I'm not judge and jury. But I want what I want. And I'm not leaving Baghdad until you find for me a freelance outfit, possibly French, that can field a Harrier jump jet."

NINETEEN

Two days later, Janson texted Jessica Kincaid a heads-up.

Not sar. SR. Securité Referral. Bad-guy rescue squad.
Watch self. SR lethal.

He left Baghdad on an Austrian Airlines flight to Vienna.

A name was golden. A huge step forward. Securité Referral was
an outfit that might or might not exist. It might or might not be
French. If it did exist, it apparently served a unique clientele, dictators about to be toppled. Michel Sarkis claimed that he had no
idea nor the means to find out who they were or where they were
or how they ran their business, and Janson believed him.

Needless to say, Securité Referral did not maintain a Web site
for dictators. Janson guessed they solicited their business by con-
tacting their clients directly before they were needed. Convincing
an autocrat he was about to be overthrown was tricky stuff, as such

men would react violently to intimations of failure. But the smart ones who had planned ahead would be amenable to hearing out a rescue scheme. Such men would have sent fortunes abroad for just such an event, and such men would be very lucrative clients. No one ever went broke presiding over the collapse of an empire.

With a name to trace, Janson was ready to wheel out the big guns.

Striding through the new Skylink Terminal corridors to connect with another Austrian Airlines flight to Tel Aviv, he got an urgent text from Jessica. It was the first he had heard from her since she had reported in detail on their secure sat line her encounter with the "diver" and the weird conclusion that they were not the only ones the doctor was running from.

> Doc mayb Cape Town. Can u intro SA security?

Janson sat-phoned Trevor Suzman, deputy national commissioner of the South African Police Service, to arrange a helpful welcome.

"And what do I get in return for this generosity?" Suzman asked.

"Interesting company."

He texted the contact number Suzman gave him back to Jessica.

* * *

At Ben Gurion Airport, a brusque Israeli immigration officer with the face of a teenager and the close-cropped hair of recent military service scrutinized Janson's Canadian passport. He waited calmly, maintaining a neutral expression. Security-services executive Adam Kurzweil was in their computers from previous visits. Unless there had been a monumental screwup with Kurzweil's renewed passport, he would be welcomed as a free-spending out-fitter of corporate security departments and private militias who did business with Israel's enormous arms industry.

The officer asked to see the stub of his boarding pass.

Janson turned it over.

The officer typed on his keyboard, stared at his monitor, and abruptly wandered away, carrying Janson's passport and boarding pass. This was fairly typical behavior on the part of officials at Ben Gurion Airport, and he could expect to be left standing awhile and/or even be grilled in an interview room about his background and his contacts in Israel.

It would turn into a problem, however, in the duplication lab that the Mossad, the Israel espionage service, maintained in the bowels of the airport. The Mossad was equipped not only to in-spect the veracity of a document but also to clone it. The joke, a bad joke, would be an Israeli operator penetrating another nation under the cover of a forgery of Janson's forged passport. Worse, no joke at all, would be the Mossad technicians discovering flaws in the document in the course of copying it.

The security cameras sprinkled in the ceiling were trained on the lines of the travelers awaiting entry and on each and every immigration desk. Janson let an expression of irritation cloud his face. He looked around impatiently and after a while longer began drumming his fingers on the desk, the picture of a busy man who, while he understood the need for security, was getting fed up. A full ten minutes passed. The lines behind him grew longer with this desk out of commission. Finally, the official returned with a superior, a woman about thirty who ordered Janson to follow her to an interview room. His passport was not in sight.

She sat behind a computer on a plain desk. He could not see the monitor, nor was there a chair for him. She typed and stared at the monitor. Janson studied her face: nice ears and nose, high tanned forehead, hair scrunched back tightly, mouth hard, eyes bleak. Central Casting, he thought, send me an unpleasant functionary.

"It's been a while since you visited Israel, Mr. Kurzweil," she said, addressing the monitor.

Janson said, "I'd have returned sooner, but my back surgeon ordered me to lift nothing heavier than a wineglass and it took considerable postoperative therapy before I could carry my bag." It was hanging from his shoulder and had been searched repeatedly.

"And that is your only bag?" She looked offended by Kurzweil's expensive lightweight parachute fabric trimmed with calfskin.

"I travel only with carry-on," Janson answered, adding with a smile, "It gives the baggage security people less to worry about."

The smile had no effect. "And what is your business on this visit?"

"Shopping."

"For what?"

"Before I answer that, I wish to respectfully inform you that the government of Canada has followed the lead of the British Foreign Office and advised its citizens not to surrender travel documents to Israeli airport officials unless it is absolutely necessary."

"It is absolutely necessary," she shot back. "I repeat: What is your business on this visit?"

Janson spoke quietly. No one won a shouting match with an Israeli. That went triple for officials at Ben Gurion Airport. Nonetheless, he put an edge in his voice. "I do not want to hear of a passport identical to mine being carried by a member of a hit squad who resembles my photograph gunning for a Hamas leader."

"If you are referring to an incident in Dubai distorted by the media, you are laboring under a common misconception."

Israeli espionage could be very, very good or unbelievably clumsy. Most of the time the Mossad enjoyed quiet successes, but now and then it perpetrated clownish excesses, like sending twenty operators to murder one terrorist while allowing themselves to be caught for YouTube on security camera videos.

"Please return my passport."

To Janson's relief, the interviewer slid it out from under her keyboard and placed it on the desk in front of her. At least they weren't cloning it while she stalled him. But she wasn't exactly handing it back. She said, "What are you shopping for?"

"Submachine guns, light machine guns, and pistols."

"For your government?"

"For my clients."

"Who are?"

Tradecraft said, *Trust your legend*. As Paul Janson he'd be smooth. Adam Kurzweil was not smooth. Janson was unflappable. Kurzweil was a prickly son of a bitch. He reversed a heart-slowing exercise to speed it up. His face grew red.

"You're out of line, lady, and you know it. You know who I am. You know I've come here before to conduct business. You're jerking my chain for the hell of it."

"Mr. Kurzweil, in the course of executing my responsibilities I can make your life considerably more unpleasant than a 'jerked chain.'"

Janson raised his voice. "As if times weren't tough enough already, Israel Weapon Industries faces fresh competition from China's Norinco. Norinco wants my business, not to mention Serbian, Turkish, and Brazilian start-ups, who could teach even *your* factories a thing or two about bribery. IWI can make your life unpleasant, too. Not to mention your entire career."

She stood abruptly, cold gaze fixed at a point in the middle of his forehead. "Welcome to Israel, Mr. Kurzweil." She stamped an entry permit, instead of the passport—a routine dodge that allowed a businessman to enter the Arab nations that denied entry to those who had visited Israel.

He pocketed the Kurzweil passport. Then he surprised her with a warm Janson smile and a white lie of the sort that extinguished burning bridges: "Thank you. And may I say that if my schedule weren't entirely booked I would invite you to dinner."

A return smile made a hard mouth pretty. "If I weren't married, I might accept."

They shook hands. Janson rented a car and drove a short way from the airport to a high-end assisted-living complex in the Tel Aviv suburb of Nordiya. In the Mediterranean sunlight on a perfect June day it was a beautiful setting. Lush gardens and stands of palm trees surrounded cream-colored stucco apartment buildings that were crowned with red tile roofs and softened by waterfalls. A lavish clubhouse with flower boxes in its windows sprawled around a gigantic outdoor swimming pool.

Israel's former Mossad operators could not ordinarily afford to end their days in the company of wealthily retired expatriate doctors, lawyers, and businessmen. But Miles Donner had more than his civil service pension to draw on, having worked his whole life under the cover of being a highly paid London-based travel photographer.

To Paul Janson, Miles Donner was "The Titan."

"Better for a spy to be known for his failures than his successes," Donner had taught Janson when Janson was in his twenties and Donner was sixty-five. "Best not to be known at all."

No one had ever taught Janson more. No one knew as many secrets. Secrets came to Miles Donner and stuck to him like burrs on an aimlessly wandering sheep. But he was the original wolf under the sheepskin and had never spent an aimless moment in his long career serving Israel.

He had not looked like a titan, not with his soft face. Janson recalled sensitive features, full lips, warm eyes, and the easy, aloof manners of a middle-aged English gentleman who had prospered in the law or medicine. "Better to be underestimated than feared. Be soft. Surprise them with hard."

The sight of a now-frail Donner struggling to his feet to greet him in the nursing home foyer stunned Janson. It had never occurred to him that time would diminish such a man. Oddly, though, Donner appeared less soft in frail old age, as if he no longer had the strength to conceal his nature. He was eighty-five, with wisps of white hair edging his bald dome, big ears, and an old man's prominent nose. He wore glasses, now, black frame glasses. But he watched the way he always had, as if through two sets of eyes, one warm and smiling, the other, barely visible, focused like searchlights on his subject's deepest thoughts.

"I have a surprise for you," he said, in his upper-crust English accent. "Come along." He disdained the elevator and walked unsteadily to the stairs. Janson instinctively went ahead to catch him if he fell. Donner noticed but did not remark on it. They walked slowly to the far end of the enormous swimming pool. At a table set off to one side in the shade of a cluster of palm trees sat two more men from Janson's past. Grandig was younger than Miles, a vigorous seventy. Zwi Weintraub had to be at least ninety-five and looked it from his pinched cheeks to the oxygen tubes in his nostrils.

"Young Saul," he greeted Janson. "You don't look a day over eighty."

"And you look like you could give Methuselah a run for his money." Janson took Weintraub's tiny hand in his. "How are you, sir?"

"I've stopped buying oxygen bottles in bulk."

Grandig shook hands with a fist still hard. "And how am I, thank you for asking? Fine if I could trade in my skeleton. Or at least the aches."

"Don't start with the organ recitals," Miles said with a benign smile. "Paul, when you telephoned that you had questions, I thought, who better to answer them than the Stern Gang?"

"I didn't know they were still in business."

"You thought we were dead," cackled Weintraub. "We're not; we just look that way." And Grandig said, gesturing at the opulent surroundings, "Who could resist an invitation to spend even one hour in Miles's splendid quarters?"

Janson had met them when he was a freshly recruited, probationary Consular Operations officer posted to the U.S. embassy in Jerusalem. He was supposed to liaise with the Mossad. But the CIA, habitually at war with the State Department's Cons Ops, had skillfully undermined him, whispering to key Israelis that Janson's mission was to spy on the Mossad. The Mossad shoved him out of the way by assigning him to a marginalized unit of older men who had lost a power struggle within the Israeli spy agency.

They had nicknamed him "The Kid," the only time in his life Janson had been called that, having grown into a man's body by age fourteen. But in the presence of Zionist veterans who had fought the British and the Arabs on the battlefield, outfoxed them in Israel's spy wars, and hunted Al Fatah and Black September terrorists to the death, Janson had felt very much "The Kid." Interestingly, he had discovered there was no Israeli word, Hebrew or Yiddish, to express that American phrase for a young man invited into a circle of older practitioners; but the native-born Israeli sabras and even English Miles had grown up on American movies and peppered their speech with screenplay slang.

Janson had realized the second he reported that he had been knocked out of the loop. Weintraub, their commander, had been seventy-five years old. Of their so-called field agents, Donner was nearly sixty-five, and Grandig, the youngest, was pushing fifty. They knew they were out of the loop.

"Welcome to the Stern Gang," they had greeted him, explaining that the original Stern Gang had been a radical branch of the Irgun during World War Two, frequently jailed by the British and shunned by their fellow Zionists as too radical. Avraham Stern himself had ended up shot.

"You've pissed someone off for sure, young Janson," Weintraub had said.

"Or scared the hell out of them," Miles ventured. "Either way, you had better get used to Siberia."

Janson had pulled every one of the few strings he had in those days to try to get out of it, but to no avail. He was liaison to the Stern Gang and would be for his entire time in Israel if the CIA had any say in the matter, and they did.

Donner, old Weintraub, and Grandig had treated him kindly. It was easy to see that the young American was going stir-crazy, and they invited him on excursions to "come shooting" at a military firing range. Janson was Army Ranger trained already and had received early doses of Cons Ops instruction. But there were assassin gun tricks he hadn't known yet. Similarly, when the old men arranged for him to work out with close-combat instructors the Jewish Krav Maga techniques had opened him to huge new possibilities in hand-to-hand fighting. To see his grandfatherly comrades in action was a revelation that still served him.

Would he like to see the Mossad's explosives school? They had accompanied him there repeatedly, admitted with a wink and a grin by young officers deeply loyal to their former bosses. They took him to "the kitchen," where Mossad scientists concocted antidotes for exotic poisons. And to "the paperworks," where passports, visas, and credit cards were fabricated.

Janson had been grateful. He would have gone nuts without the excursions. Only gradually had it dawned on him that he was not being taught so much as tested.

He said so.

Donner didn't blink an eye. "You've passed with flying colors," he replied. "How would you like to join a rogue operation?"

"What kind of rogue operation?"

"Less Shakespeare's 'sweet little rogue' than savage-elephant rogue."

"Without my bosses at State knowing?"

"Without any bosses knowing."

"Not even the Mossad."

"Especially the Mossad."

"You guys are almost retired. I'm just starting out. Why would I risk my entire future on a rogue operation?"

"Shall we take a walk?"

Donner and Weintraub took him on a long hike in the desert. Deep in the Negev, far from anywhere, without a house or road in sight, the British-born spy and the old sabra commando had taken turns patting him down for a wire. They did it without apology.

It occurred to Janson that they didn't completely trust their friend Grandig. "What's going on?" he asked.

"We are faced with a problem. You can help us."

"What kind of problem?" asked Janson.

"A South African problem."

Back then the white South Africa dictatorship was vigorously defending apartheid but losing to the African National Congress and world opinion. After suppressing the black majority for generations, it was only a matter of time before the pariah regime went under. Janson had fixed his mentor—for Miles was surely that by now, more than any he had had—with an inquiring gaze and told him that he was familiar with the rumors about Israeli–South African collaboration and had always assumed them to be overblown.

Donner had replied, "Israel would not have an arms industry if we hadn't had South Africa as our main customer."

"How can a Jewish nation fought for by the survivors of the genocide of the Nazi Holocaust deal with a police state that invented apartheid—which is no better than another form of state-sponsored oppression?"

"The South Africans saved us."

"President Vorster was a Nazi. Botha wasn't much better."

Miles waggled his hand in a yes-no gesture. "Regardless of your opinion of those gentlemen—and I believe the world will discover that F. W. de Klerk is cut of different cloth—white South African gold and white South African diamonds paid for Israel to develop our high-tech weapons. We had the scientists. They had the means."

"But black—"

Miles cut him off harshly. "At the end of the day, my young friend, we discover what will we do to save ourselves."

"What will we do to advance ourselves?"

The Titan had laughed. "There is the paradox. You say to save ourselves we must advance ourselves. Very American—full of moral hope—until you run into the paradox. First we must save ourselves or there will be nothing to advance."

Janson had heard that same argument on various issues in the State Department. His reactions—and people's reactions to his reactions—sometimes made him feel like a preacher at an orgy. It would take him years to become more supple, but even then a hard edge on his deepest beliefs made it impossible to succumb fully to compromise. Or, he supposed, had left him brittle.

"What does this have to do with me?"

"Among the weapons Israel developed is an atomic bomb."

"I know that. I am young, not ignorant."

"Young and aggressive."

"Aggression is a fine quality in an operator," said Weintraub.

"Not when he waves it like a flag," Donner had snapped back with uncharacteristically visible passion that young Janson had felt aimed straight at him. In that moment he understood that The Titan believed that Paul Janson possessed the intellect and personality, as well as the physical gifts, to be taught to excel in the highest ranks of the clandestine world.

Janson knew that his superiors in the State Department did not doubt that Israel had the atom bomb. It had been widely assumed. Israel had been very clever about maintaining it as a threat to their enemies, without riling their friends who were trying to prevent nuclear proliferation.

"Nuclear deterrent by implication," Janson said. "But I hadn't realized South Africa's role. How did this happen?"

"Back in the seventies, we traded pounds of rare tritium for tons of South African yellowcake uranium."

Uranium for fissionable material, tritium to boost its impact.

"All right. Israel needed yellowcake to build its bomb. What did South Africa want with tritium?"

"To make their bomb."

That had rocked Paul Janson to the core. "South Africa has a nuclear bomb?"

"Six of them, actually."

"But they are insane."

"Actually, they are not. They've decided to destroy their nuclear weapons."

"That's a huge relief, if true. Are you sure it's true?"

"They are taking the most sensible course. They see the handwriting on the wall. They know they won't be in power for long. So they will destroy their nuclear bombs rather than let them fall into the hands of the blacks, who they don't trust to use them responsibly."

"Score another for bigotry and hatred."

"Unfortunately, it's not unanimous. Their most radical army general wants to keep the bombs to use them against the blacks."

"That's the sort of insanity I'd expect."

"General Klopper is only one man. But he is powerful, beloved of the far right wing of the National Party, the die-hard Apartheidists, and the Broderbon, and commands the loyalty of his elite commando groups. Nor is there any reasoning with him. Hans Klopper is obsessed by fear and hatred of black Africa."

"If Israel gave South Africa the bomb, then the Mossad has to stop him."

"Mossad doesn't want to hear about it," Donner shot back.

"They have to hear about it. It's their job to stop him."

"The Mossad," Weintraub had explained with an air of weary patience, "nurtured the relationship with South Africa. Initiated it. Without the Mossad, there would have been no relationship. The Mossad has a huge stake in the relationship and the resultant personal connections. Therefore, they simply *hope* that clearer heads will prevail and the six nuclear bombs will magically disappear."

Donner stepped in. "Unfortunately, it will not play out that way unless this officer is stopped." He had looked Janson full in the face. "That is our rogue operation. Will you help?"

"Help you how?" Janson had asked.

"Kill the bastard. We can't get close to him. We're too well known, by the Mossad and by our counterparts in South Africa. But you are a stranger."

They code-named Janson "Saul."

The operation itself they named biblically, in the Mossad tradition, "Operation Sword Fall." Janson had protested. He had read the Old Testament to prepare for his posting to Jerusalem, and knew that facing capture by Philistines, Saul had fallen on his own sword.

They meant the other Saul, the Stern Gang laughed. The one who became a Christian and built the Catholic Church. "Paul before he went native," Donner had joked.

Still, the mission they laid out verged on the suicidal.

The best thing about it was that no one would ever know. Not the U.S. State Department, not Consular Operations, not the CIA, not the South African Security Service, not even the Mossad. The Stern Gang used their still-formidable connections within the Mossad to fill the blank weeks in Janson's record with tantalizing hints of Janson's participation in a top-secret operation in Iraq. To this day that legend had stuck and Paul Janson's first killing was still a secret. Not even Jessica knew.

*　*　*

JANSON MADE HIS pitch to the retired spies while they sipped tea at the shaded end of the swimming pool. Donner's and Grandig's tea was iced and sprinkled with mint leaves, old Weintraub's hot in a glass and sucked through a sugar cube.

Janson described in colorful and precise detail the Harrier rescue of President for Life Iboga and how he had subsequently learned that the commando who had escorted the dictator aboard the jump jet with blazing guns claimed to be with an outfit called Securité Referral. They listened closely, intrigued by the boldness of the operation and its flawless execution. "A brave man, this diver," Grandig said of the commando.

"He handled himself well," Janson admitted.

"A dangerous combination. What are the chances of turning him to your side in this matter?"

"They were slim when he was trying to kill a man I'm being paid to keep alive. Now they're nonexistent, since he came up short tangling with one of my people."

"Fascinating."

"Here's something even more fascinating." He told them about the Reaper intervening in the climactic battle on Pico Clarence. When he finished, they were sitting forward in their chairs and exchanging incredulous glances.

"You lead an interesting life, Saul."

But when Janson asked Donner, Weintraub, and Grandig to use their contacts around the world to identify Securité Referral, they resisted. He was not surprised. He had expected to find them old and cautious and deep in the grip of habits of discretion. But primarily, Janson knew, the old patriots were asking themselves the question they had always asked: Is it good for Israel?

Their resistance took the form of pooh-poohing their ability to help.

"Who do we know anymore at our age?" asked Grandig, the youngest.

"*Your* age?" Weintraub echoed disdainfully. "Everyone *I* know is dead."

"I was not thinking so much of you as your acolytes," said Janson. "Your protégés hold key intelligence and security positions in various parts of the world."

"Our protégés aren't getting any younger, either."

"Then *their* protégés," Janson coaxed. "Gentlemen, I am fully aware that few men have contacts like yours. Poll your people for me. The name Securité Referral is bound to ring some bells."

They stared into their empty glasses.

He looked at Miles, who had been listening silently. Miles had taught him, "If you have something to say, don't until you know what you want its effect to be." Now Miles said, "Two phrases you will not hear often in Israel, my friend: 'Excuse me.' And, 'Thank you.' "

Janson squared his shoulders. "I don't expect thanks. I do believe I have earned the right to ask a favor as small as this."

"Maybe we owe you," Weintraub grumped. "Maybe we don't. Sword Fall was not exactly a one-man operation."

"One man got close enough to do the job," Janson said grimly. "He's come back to collect."

Weintraub shrugged his scrawny shoulders. "Who loves the bill collector?"

Janson saw that he had succeeded in maneuvering them into a position where none were comfortable.

Finally, Grandig raised a new objection: "What sort of bill collector would demand that we risk our friends' cover asking them questions?"

Janson glanced again at Miles Donner. The English Jew winked, acknowledging that Grandig had given Janson the opening he was working toward. Janson pulled a plastic sack from his shoulder bag and upended it. The contents clattered on the table. "Go phones. With prepaid SIM cards. No one will know who called who."

"Who sold you these untraceable prepaid minutes?" asked Grandig. "The phone shop at Ben Gurion Airport otherwise known as Mossad-dot-com?"

"With Subscriber Identity Modules programmed by Shin Bet," Weintraub chimed in, "so the security agency can eavesdrop on the people we call?"

"No, I paid cash in Sadr City. As soon as your protégés tell me where Iboga's jump jet went and who runs Securité Referral, you are welcome to protect your friends by swallowing the SIM cards."

TWENTY

Three days later Janson was still in Israel. The old men were slow. Weintraub napped between telephone calls and insisted on being driven home to spend each night in his modest flat on the far side of Tel Aviv. Grandig camped on Donner's couch. Janson dozed in an armchair during the very few hours that Donner himself would actually sleep. Slow as the old men were, they stuck to it, at first honoring their obligation to Janson but soon caught up in the chase, making call after call overseas to younger men and women in the field. As Donner explained on the drive back from delivering Weintraub to his flat, "Retirement is a spectator sport. But it is more satisfying to do than to watch. They won't thank you, but they are happy you gave them a job."

"Are you happy I gave you a job?"

"It is always a pleasure to watch an old acquaintance in action."

Like a photograph coming into focus as pixels hardened on a monitor, an image of Securité Referral formed around bits and pieces garnered from scores of queries. The details resembled what Janson had already seen in action on the palace pier in Porto Clarence. Securité Referral did exist. The outfit appeared to have been organized by a tight-knit group of renegade clandestine officers with the express purpose of providing safe havens in rogue and criminal states for deposed rulers and war criminals and the fortunes spirited out of their countries.

It appeared to be a new operation, which would explain why few had heard of it. The old men's telephone calls revealed two rescues before Iboga: the exfiltration under the noses of the DEA of a Colombian drug lord about to be extradited to the U.S. and the rescue of a Kyrgyzstan general who had reigned over the ex-Soviet vassal state just long enough to steal $10 billion. Securité Referral had established a niche business rescuing what international prosecutors called politically exposed persons.

"Sounds like a sort of anti–Phoenix Foundation," Kincaid drawled when he filled her in on the telephone. "Providing a fresh opportunity for bad guys to be really bad."

"I'll admit it sounds a little cartoonish."

"The Klingons of corporate security?"

"Except that we've seen them operate."

"Porto Clarence was mighty slick," Jessica agreed.

Janson said, "Think about what happens if that Kyrgyzstan general gets back in power. Or they rescue some Balkan warlord who ends up controlling a rogue state like Croatia. All of a sudden Securité Referral will be operating under the wing of a sovereign nation."

The names of a few top operators surfaced, the sort of ethically unrestrained specialists Janson would expect to be recruited by a freewheeling outfit that answered only to itself: Emil Bloch, a highly skilled French mercenary he knew only by reputation; Dimon, a Serbian computer wizard; Viorets, a Russian foreign intelligence service officer who slid smoothly between official duties for the SVR and private work for Gazprom and LUKOIL. There were some more French, and a deadly Corsican—Andria Giudicelli. Grandig had run into Giudicelli twenty years ago in France, while thwarting an attempt to burn EL AL's Paris office. No politics, he said, Giudicelli was loyal to the highest bidder.

Nothing emerged about Securité Referral's leader. Then a protégé of Miles relayed rumors of a South African mercenary who had engineered with Emil Bloch the assassination of a Russian exile hiding in Switzerland. Kruger in Zurich told Janson he had heard of the assassination, had heard nothing about Emil Bloch, but had heard rumors of a South African.

Jessica Kincaid had judged by his accent that the guy she tangled with in Cartagena was South African. And Janson recalled that Ferdinand Poe had at one time had South African mercenaries running guns to his camp.

Janson telephoned Poe's chief of security, Patrice da Costa.

"Hadrian Van Pelt," da Costa answered. "Traitorous bastard."

"What do you know about him?"

"I never saw him. I was in Porto Clarence. But I gather he wormed his way into Douglas Poe's trust when President Poe was in Black Sand— May I tell Acting President Poe that you are closing in on Iboga?"

"So far we have reports that Iboga has been sighted in Russia, Romania, the Ukraine, and Croatia and on the French island of Corsica. Either he's traveling a lot or more likely we're just catching rumors."

"Iboga is a very large, very black, very frightening-looking African, with ritual scars on his face and a crazed gleam in his eye," said da Costa. "One would think he stands out. Even when he isn't wearing a yellow headdress."

"One would think," Janson agreed mildly. He liked da Costa but was disinclined to explain to a client's underling that a planet housing five billion people offered many places to hide for a well-heeled fugitive protected by professionals who had a major stake in his future—a future that Securité Referral must know could include seizing control of oil-rich Isle de Foree if they could keep Iboga alive and free long enough to launch the counterattack that Ferdinand Poe feared.

Janson passed the name Hadrian Van Pelt to Freddy Ramirez in Madrid.

Freddy got back to him within the hour, deeply embarrassed.

"Sorry about this, but we screwed up. The Catalan police took a guy to the hospital they found passed out in Barcelona. We missed it. Barcelona's a long, long way from Cartagena. His passport said 'Hadrian Van Pelt.'"

"What did he pass out of?"

"Blood loss. It took ninety stitches to close up his arm."

That's my girl, thought Janson. "Where is he?"

"Snuck out of the hospital. Stole a Mercedes which they found in Madrid. My friend at Immigration tells me a dude his size with his arm in a sling flew to London under the name Vealon, Brud Vealon, and changed planes to Cape Town, South Africa."

Where Jesse was now, Janson thought uneasily.

"Do we have anything on Van Pelt and Vealon?"

"Nothing on Vealon. There was a South African Olympic swimmer named Van Pelt. Common name down there, but from your description sounds like the same guy. He was disqualified from the Athens games for doping. Research can't find a word about him since 2004."

Janson texted Kincaid a heads-up that "the diver," likely named either Hadrian Van Pelt or Brud Vealon, was headed her way. He telephoned Suzman in Cape Town to ask for his help in shadowing Hadrian Van Pelt. Suzman knew the name not only as a disgraced athlete but also as a mercenary soldier. "Fell off my radar years ago."

"What did you think it meant when he fell off?"

Janson heard shrugged shoulders in Suzman's answer. "I never paid it any mind. I assumed he got shot in the Congo or someplace."

Exactly what someone like Van Pelt would want government security officers to assume, if he was moving up to something as big as Securité Referral.

* * *

IN THE BACKSEAT of Miles's car that evening, Zwi Weintraub, who was snuffling on his oxygen, suddenly awakened. "You see the pattern?"

"What pattern?"

"Referral's operators are all self-starters. Men who can run an operation are in the field. They do their own work. The workers are the leaders; the leaders are the workers."

"You mean there's no headman?"

"Any one of them is capable of being the headman."

"All chiefs, no Indians?" asked Donner. "How do they keep from killing each other?"

"A good question," said Weintraub, closing his eyes again. "Perhaps they've found a method to alter human nature."

"A pact," said Paul Janson. "They've sworn to band together against anyone who tries to take control."

"A confederation of musketeers." Miles Donner smiled. "All for one and one for all."

* * *

JESSE TELEPHONED FROM Cape Town. "Got your text. 'Fraid I'll miss the diver. I'm in a cab to the airport." She was hoping to catch a plane to Johannesburg, where she would transfer to a long-haul Qantas flight to Sydney. "Where I think the doc is."

"How'd he get all the way to Australia?"

"Jumped ship with the *Varna Fantasy*'s purser's wife, dumped her in Cape Town, hooked up with a Qantas flight attendant named Mildred. Mildred got him comped onto a flight to Sydney. He's either the horniest bastard on the planet or running scared. The purser's wife thinks he's running scared. Of course the poor thing has to tell herself something to explain the fix she's in."

"Good job."

"I feel like a divorce lawyer's gumshoe."

An hour later Miles Donner awakened Janson from a catnap with a grim face. "They're shutting us down."

"Who?"

"Shin Bet."

Israel's security agency had been alerted to heavy overseas phone traffic emanating from Nordiya, Miles reported. "I was given advance warning by an old friend."

"Just from some extra calls? There are thousands of expats living in this area, calling home to London and New York. Our calls couldn't have made a blip Shin Bet would notice."

"Of course not."

"Then what happened?" Janson asked, sensing the answer even as he spoke.

Miles said, "I suspect that somewhere in Europe some friend of Securité Referral tipped Shin Bet about all the questions."

"But why would Shin Bet—"

"They're doing their job. They've been alerted to unusual traffic. They have to act. Internal security is their responsibility. Securité Referral knows that, of course."

"Securité Referral is hitting back. Destroy the phones."

"I already have," said Miles. "The operation is terminated. Get out of Israel while you can. I've arranged for a chap to drive you to the airport. Hurry, my friend. The car is at the service entrance."

"Lie down on the floor until we reach the highway," the driver told him as Janson emerged from rows of black plastic garbage bags outside the facility's kitchen.

"An ignominious retreat," Janson said to Donner as they shook hands good-bye.

The old man winked. "Be known by your failures."

* * *

JANSON WAS STANDING in line at Ben Gurion waiting to buy a ticket to Paris when Suzman called back from Cape Town. "Your boy's come and gone. Never left the airport. Changed planes for Sydney. Which is, I believe, where your 'interesting company' just boarded a flight to."

"Is there any way you could stop him?" Janson asked.

"Not without shooting down a commercial airliner. He connected in Johannesburg with the SAA flight to Perth."

"You said Sydney."

"He missed the direct Sydney connection. He'll have to change in Perth to get across Australia."

Janson could not raise Kincaid on the telephone. He left messages but got no replies. He texted her a warning that Van Pelt would probably arrive in Sydney several hours after her. And again, he did not hear back.

Cursing that he didn't have the Embraer close at hand, he hunted frantically for the fastest flight to Australia. Sydney was nine thousand miles from Israel. He had to change planes in Bangkok. With the layover, the trip would take nearly twenty-four hours. Kincaid would land in Sydney with Van Pelt close behind, ten hours before Janson caught up.

He held fast to the mantra *she is predator, not prey*.

PART THREE

Blind Side

35°18′29″ S, 149°07′28″ E
Canberra, Australia

TWENTY-ONE

Dr. Terry Flannigan reckoned he had less than a day before the people trying to kill him caught up in Canberra. They'd already tracked him from Dakar to South Africa and certainly by now the Qantas flight to Sydney. Back-tracing him to Mildred, they would discover that the flight attendant had gotten him a package trip to Australia's capital including his hotel and this morning's guided tour of Parliament House.

He had to do something fast, but he didn't know what.

A sweet little blonde gave him a shy eye as they trooped off the bus. She looked fresh faced as a country schoolteacher. Flannigan guessed she had recently broken up with a lousy boyfriend and had signed onto this package tour by herself to recover; now she was lonely and feeling brave. But how could she help him stay alive? Even if she smuggled him home to some godforsaken Outback kangaroo ranch, how long would it take them to catch up?

He stuck close to the group as they were herded into the parliament. Inside he felt the most secure he had in two weeks, guarded by fit-looking Parliamentary Security Service officers with radios. Not supercommandos like The Wall and Annie Oakley, but backed up by Federal Police and the Australian Army.

When they were led into the Senate Chamber itself, he relaxed and began to enjoy himself. Then an excellent brunette Green Party senator noticed him noticing her from the public galley. She was single. He saw no wedding ring. Besides, married ladies in public life didn't hook up with strange men in public places and Madame Senator was definitely sending hookup signals.

The session ended on a speech she delivered with wit and passion: "Australia should be a nation deeper than just a coal mine for China." At that point she climbed up into the public gallery and dismissed their guide to lead the group herself. This act of hands-on egalitarian democracy blew the minds of his fellow tourists and gave a frightened Terry Flannigan an excellent idea for how to save his life.

Those fit-looking Parliamentary Security Service officers with radios were responsible for the personal safety of their lovely legislator. Surely they would extend protection to her new friend when he was in her presence.

Politicians were difficult—being equal parts exhibitionist and narcissistic—but fortunately he knew how to handle them, having had a long on-and-off thing with a Texas congresswoman. The trick was never to show you liked them. The second you showed a politician that you liked her, she was looking for the next one to like her. *Look at me. Aren't I wonderful? Think so? Good-bye.*

So, having made definitive eye contact, now when the comely senator smiled his way he looked away. Which only made her smile harder. It was like taking advantage of fish in a barrel, but people were trying to kill him, after all, so he really had to do what he had to do.

The senator invited the entire group on a private tour, which included a stroll through the office of the prime minister. Then she quietly invited Flannigan to join her for lunch in the Members' dining room. Her people peeled him deftly loose from the group headed for lunch in the cafeteria. As they did, the sweet little blonde, who saw exactly what was going down, slipped a folded piece of paper into his pocket with her cell phone number and the information that she would be in Canberra for the rest of the week.

Admiring how fully the senator filled her skirt as she walked ahead to tell her staff that she would be tied up for the afternoon, Terry Flannigan recalled Sigmund Freud's famous question: "What do women want?"

Write this on your notepad, Dr. Freud: *I am fifteen pounds overweight, losing hair and gaining jowls, with a roving, if not predatory, eye that should warn any woman with a brain to steer clear, but for some reason, bless their hearts, they want me. I am not saying I deserve it, but I am grateful.*

* * *

DANIEL, A STURDILY built former U.S. Navy SEAL intelligence officer, resigned his commission after three tours in Iraq to quadruple his salary with a private security contractor. He was disdained by regular military as a showboat and overpaid hired gun, and his last memory of Baghdad was of leading a State Department convoy at high speed through narrow streets.

He had awakened with a titanium plate in his skull a month later on the coast of Cornwall, England, in the Phoenix Foundation wing of a Methodist nursing home. The security contractor had gone out of business. Phoenix had paid the therapy and shrink bills, and when Daniel had felt capable of making his way in the world he fled to the Mediterranean island of Corsica and opened a dive shop for tourists.

Today he was back in Cornwall, visiting a buddy, Rafe, who hadn't been as lucky. Rafe, a former British officer, was still stuck in rehab. Daniel had bumped into another private contractor buddy, Ian the Brit, a tattooed bodybuilder who was living in England and visited Rafe regularly. The three men were bound together, as Ian put it, "by one bloody big bang."

The facility in which Phoenix rented its wing served what the Brits called the healthy demented, people who had lost their minds to Alzheimer's and ischemic strokes but were still capable of walking. It was a pretty place built in a Roman villa style that embraced the sun. Even when the sea breeze was too cool to venture outside, the sunlight brightened the public rooms clustered around three sides of a courtyard that opened to the south.

Elderly ladies dressed for an excursion were gathering outside the dining room, remarking that the restaurant appeared to be doing a brisk business today and inquiring how soon the bus would leave for Exeter. That such a vehicle was as fictional as the restaurant only became apparent when the staff opened the dining room doors and the residents took their accustomed chairs for lunch.

"You never see old blokes in this place," said Ian.

"Men die young," said Daniel.

They were standing in the doorway watching the old ladies because Rafe had started crying and a counselor was trying to talk him down. Daniel and Ian looked back to Rafe's room, where a salty wind made white curtains flap in the sunlight. Their eyes met and slid apart. Rafe was a mess. They'd been sketching maps of the shoot-out, kinda going through how the insurgents' fire had channeled them straight into the mother of all improvised explosive devices, when Rafe started crying.

This was Daniel's first visit to the poor bastard, and he was thinking he could not wait to get the hell home. He knew that on many levels he was personally so distant he might as well be living on Mars, but at least he was out. And Ian was getting better, too, since he "graduated," driving an intercity bus between Birmingham and London, hoping to meet a girl.

Out of nowhere Daniel heard himself saying, "We kept Coalition officials alive while Iraqi officials were the star attraction at a turkey shoot."

"Coalition paid better," Ian replied gloomily.

"I read," said Daniel, "that an IED blast changes how your brain works, if you're close as Rafe was."

"We weren't that far, either."

"But Rafe was closer." Rafe had been leaning off the running board at ninety miles an hour firing warning bursts at civilian vehicles when the lead car detonated the IED. "It screws up your prefrontal cortex. That's the part that makes you who you are. Rafe was a happy guy, before."

Ian's expression said he could not bear to talk about Rafe's prefrontal cortex, which could have been his prefrontal cortex. He changed the subject, with a bitter smile.

"You know what the Old Man calls us?"

"What?" Daniel asked with sudden interest. The "Old Man" from Phoenix had dropped in once while Daniel was still in rehab. If the Old Man asked him to lead a convoy into Hell, Daniel would ask only if there was time to suit up or were they going in naked.

"I heard him tell the head doc."

"What did he call us?"

"Banished Children of Mammon."

"Did he really?"

"I didn't get what he meant," said Ian.

"It means contractors like you and me and poor Rafe get no vets hospital, no pension, no health care."

"I know that. And I know 'banished.' What the fuck is Mammon?"

"Money. We did it for the money and now we get zip."

Ian nodded. "Yeah, I get that. 'Mammon' means 'money'? How come?"

"Like a money god."

"So we prayed to the fucker and got our asses in a sling."

Daniel was surprised to feel his face break into a smile. "Exactly . . . You hear anything on the Old Man?" he asked.

"He was putting feelers out the other day. He's looking for Iboga."

"Who's that?"

"Don't you watch the news?"

"I don't watch the news," said Daniel. "I don't read the papers. I don't surf the Internet. If I walk by TV in the airport, I look the other way. Whatever is going on out there, I don't give a flying fuck. Who's Iboga? Why's the Old Man hunting him?"

"He was an African dictator who stole the country's money when the insurgents kicked him out. The Old Man must have hired on to get it back."

"African? What does he look like?"

"Big black bastard weighs twenty-five stone at least."

"Give it to me in pounds."

"Three hundred."

"Does he sharpen his teeth?"

Ian looked at Daniel. "Why do you ask?"

"I seen him."

"Go on!"

"I did. Didn't get a good look, but how many three-hundred-pound guys are black with pointy teeth?"

"Where?"

"Corsica. Where I live."

"What, he's just walking around Corsica?"

"No, he's holed up with a crew on Capo Corso. Up north. I seen him last week at Bastia, where the ferries come in from Nice and Marseille."

"If you didn't get a good look, how do you know his teeth are sharpened?"

"A guy who was closer told me. They got off a yacht, piled into SUVs, and convoyed north."

"Why are you saying they're holed up?"

"The locals were saying they were like a crew hiding out or setting up a job. The locals are into that shit, so they keep track of the competition. Corsica's a wild place."

"Tell me again what you're doing there?"

"I'm down in Porto-Vecchio, way down south. Other end of the island."

"Mind me asking what you're setting up?"

"Nothing. I got a dive shop for the tourists."

"Really?" asked Ian. "Was that expensive, to set up a dive shop?"

"No big deal. I always saved my money. No way I was going to get treated like garbage and come out of it poor. Hey, you should come down sometime. I got room in my house. Beautiful water. Beautiful fish. Beautiful girls. Nice people, Corsicans, long as you don't piss 'em off. Don't fuck with them and they'll give you the shirt off their back."

"Excuse me, young man," said a small voice.

The two big men looked down at a tiny white-haired woman carrying a handbag on her arm.

"Yes, ma'am?"

"Is this where we get the bus to Exeter?"

"No, ma'am," said Daniel. "It's back there in the restaurant, where they're serving your lunch."

* * *

QUINTISHA UPCHURCH ANSWERED her "graduates'" line, the phone number that was given to the growing flock of Janson's saved. Calls came in for help and to help. She could tell by the tone of the voice which it would be. This was a "to help" call, and she recognized the British Midland accent as belonging to a boy named Ian.

"Ms. Upchurch, if you were in communication with Mr. Janson, you might mention that a certain former president for life was spotted in Corsica. Up north on Capo Corso."

Quintisha Upchurch promised to pass it on.

The professional qualities that had convinced Paul Janson that she was the woman to administer CatsPaw and Phoenix included a habit of discretion grounded on innate reticence. She would never dream of mentioning that Daniel, the rough American with whom Ian had been discussing Iboga in a Cornwall nursing home, had telephoned her minutes earlier with the same message. Or that since similar messages were flooding in from widely scattered parts of the globe, she would first shunt them through the research person assigned to collate and vet before they were passed to the boss.

* * *

IN THE PRIVACY of a First Class sleeping pod, Paul Janson worked the airline phone. His first priority was to drastically reduce his flying time to Sydney. He called a general in the Royal Thai Air Force. Their conversation got off to a bad start.

"I recall that you were against me," said the general, a fighter pilot who had risen quickly in the ranks thanks to excellent connections and ordinary skills enhanced by extraordinary bravery.

"You recall," Janson replied bluntly, "that I determined you were the lesser of two evils."

"What do you want?"

"Recompense for that action."

"Why?"

"You profited by it. You're an active serving general. The other guy is dead."

Thai Chinese, like all overseas Chinese, were not the sort to pontificate about honor and respect. They weren't like Pakistanis and Afghans, proud of "honor killings," or Italian Mafia clinging to their secret societies and *omertà*. But these children of the Chinese diaspora who peopled the merchant class of Southeast Asia practiced a code of honor no less strong for their reserve. As strangers in strange lands, they divided the world into two categories. Strangers were by definition enemies. People they knew were friends. What Janson had always admired most was the fluidity—once they knew you, once you had done business or traded favors or shared a kindness or taken their side, you were a friend.

After a long silence, the general asked, "What do you need?"

"The fastest jet in Bangkok capable of flying four thousand, six hundred, and eighty-five miles to Sydney ahead of my commercial connection."

"That's all?"

Janson could not tell whether the general was being sarcastic. But they both knew he could have asked for so much more than a fast long-haul jet. Janson thanked him warmly. The debt was settled. That which was needed most was most valuable.

Janson left urgent messages with a contact in Sydney who

worked undercover for the Australian Crime Commission, thinking he could look out for Jessica at the airport. While Janson waited for a response, he followed up on the SR names. Bloch, the French mercenary, was believed to be in a Congo jail. Dimon, the Serbian computer wizard, was reported active in the Ukraine. Viorets, the Russian, was currently on leave from the SVR, and the Corsican Andria Giudicelli had been seen days earlier in Rome. Van Pelt, Janson already knew, was headed for Sydney.

Iboga, who had supposedly left a trail through Russia, the Ukraine, Romania, and Croatia, had now been seen simultaneously on the French island of Corsica and in Harare, the capital of Zimbabwe, which were six thousand miles apart.

Janson closed his eyes and tried to sleep. He was wondering what light, if any, the doctor might shed on ASC and Kingsman Helms's schemes in Isle de Foree. He was really no closer to Iboga than when he took the job from Poe. He *had* learned SR existed and must have fielded the Harrier jump jet, but not enough more to do anyone any good. He knew nothing yet about who had launched the Reaper attack. And so far he hadn't added a single dollar to the Phoenix Foundation's treasury. Five percent of zip recovered loot was zip.

He gave up on sleep and telephoned the forensic accountant leading the Iboga money hunt. They'd had some success, some indications of accounts in Switzerland and Croatia. "These days," the accountant warned Janson, "Zagreb's a tougher nut than Zurich."

"Can we get to the dough?"

"At this point," she said, "we're still in locating mode."

When the airliner began its descent into Bangkok, Janson dialed Quintisha Upchurch. "Have you heard from Ms. Kincaid?"

"No, Mr. Janson. I've left messages."

Janson heard a familiar loud noise in the background and

smiled despite his concern. The blatting roar of a compression-release "Jake" brake slowing a forty-ton eighteen-wheel Peterbilt 379EXHD told him that Quintisha was in CatsPaw's rolling "home office," a Brinks armored tractor-trailer driven by her husband.

Jessica had named Quintisha's husband "the single scariest dude I have ever laid eyes on." A former Force Recon Marine officer and a deeply troubled vet until he married Quintisha, Rick Rice drove the interstates delivering Brinks bulk shipments of credit cards, precious metals, and casino tokens. The tractor's cab was bullet-proofed and fitted with gun ports, but as Jessica had noted, "When the driver looks like he's *hoping* you'll try to rob him, folks tend to go rob something else."

Guarded by her husband and always on the move as they criss-crossed the United States, Quintisha administered CatsPaw and Phoenix from the phones and computers in the Peterbilt's stand-up sleeper. On Sundays, they parked the truck in VFW lots. Rick would hoist some beers with the vets while Quintisha, an ordained deacon, would take herself to the nearest African Methodist Epis-copal church and sing in the choir, teach Bible study, or preach a sermon. Sunday supper would be at the home of some local police chief or a highway patrolman who had served under Rick in the Gulf War, Iraq, or Afghanistan.

"I was about to telephone you, Mr. Janson. A couple of your young men report sighting Iboga in Corsica."

"Who? Daniel?"

"Yes. And Ian, in England."

Janson called Protocolo de Seguridad's HQ in Madrid. "Freddy, can you tap any Coriscans?"

"Does it matter if they're on the run?"

"They have to be able to go back to Corsica."

"That eliminates most of them." Freddy pondered a moment. "I'll find a couple."

"There's a chance Iboga's hiding up in Capo Corso. See what you can find out."

* * *

"ARE YOU AWARE that you are bleeding?" asked the civilian fuck-head in the South African Airways seat next to Hadrian Van Pelt.

Beads of blood were popping from the stitches in his forearm. Ninety red dots, one for each stitch, had spread until they joined their neighbors, soaking the bandage and oozing through his shirt-sleeve. He should have worn red. Or he shouldn't keep squeezing a hard rubber ball, rhythmically as a heartbeat. But he was obsessed by a weird fear that the muscles in his right arm would shrink like beef biltong if he didn't work them. That's what the bitch had done to him. It was crazy how bad it was bugging him. He had been wounded, before. No big deal. It went with the business. But he couldn't shake the feeling that she had exposed the flesh of his arm like a slab of dried meat.

"I say, sir. Are you aware you're bleeding?"

"Yes, I am aware I am bleeding," he answered in measured tones so the fuckhead didn't summon the flight attendants, who might signal the air security agent pretending to be a businessman in the back row of the Business Class cabin. "I was in an automobile ac-cident."

The fuckhead reached for the call button. "Shall I summon help?"

"No, thank you," Van Pelt said, adding a cool smile to shut the fuckhead up. "It's not as bad as it looks. My doctor changed the dressing just before I boarded the plane."

He picked up the handset in his armrest and checked yet again for text messages. At last!

> Arrangements complete. We'll have her waiting for you in Sydney.

Awesome. Van Pelt's hard mouth parted in an anticipatory smile. But a second text message was anything but excellent. The American hired by Ferdinand Poe to hunt Iboga was changing planes in Bangkok, from a commercial flight to a faster aircraft provided by the Royal Thai Air Force.

Van Pelt placed an urgent voice call to the SR *camarade* who was functioning as facilitator on the Isle de Foree project. The *animateur de groupe*, as the Frenchies put it, pretended to be an NGO administrator directing a rice shipment to starving Pakistanis while his phone swept for eavesdroppers. When it finished, he said, "Clear."

Van Pelt said, "Charter me the fastest jet in Perth....Why? Because if you don't, he's going to get to Sydney ahead of me."

TWENTY-TWO

Jessica Kincaid received no messages from Paul Janson and no replies to her calls and texts when she changed planes at Johannesburg. She left more messages, then popped an Ambien and slept for eight excellent hours over the Indian Ocean. When she awoke, she flicked her phone on for a moment to surreptitiously check messages and still found none. Strange. She ran a credit card through the airliner's handset to text Janson.

She had her finger on the button and was one millisecond from pressing Send when she remembered that in Spain the diver had somehow broken into her locked Audi without setting off the alarm. "Hadrian Van Pelt" or "Brud Vealon" likely had access to hot electronics. She put down the airline phone. Then she picked up her Iridium 9555 G and eyed it speculatively.

Assume the worst.

Her sat phone had been hacked.

At the moment, it didn't matter how.

Assume the worst, again. If her phone was hacked, then when she had called Paul's, whatever virus or bug the hacker put in hers had migrated into Janson's. The messages she left for Janson could have been captured by Securité Referral. Maybe SR couldn't crack the encryption. Maybe they could.

Using the Qantas handset, Kincaid dialed a distress number she knew by heart. Back when she had worked for Consular Operations, if she suspected that her phone or laptop had been tapped or hacked the procedure was to telephone a secure subbasement in the State Department's Truman Building where high-tech guys with tool belts would try to help. When you were working with Janson, the procedure was similar, though who picked up the phone or where they were was anyone's guess.

CatsPaw, the Phoenix Foundation, and the eponymous Janson Associates were more virtual than physical. Brick-and-mortar headquarters were expensive, distracting, and vulnerable. Employees in them were identifiable and exposed to attack at work, on their way to work, and in their own homes. Rather than maintain—and have to defend—a fortress, Janson used the Internet and the Web to link independent contractors into a organization that had no physical existence.

Kincaid had never met the expert she was telephoning and knew him only by his number. What distinguished him from his State Department counterpart was his independence. It was unlikely he wore a security badge—government or private—and was jockeying for a closer parking space in a vast employee lot. As the phone rang, she pictured a skinny long-haired guy in a windowless room humming with computer cooling fans and illuminated by walls of backlit monitors. He might work alone or he might work with other geeks who looked like him. He could be in a suburban tech park in Silicon Valley or Beverly, Massachusetts, or the Czech Republic.

* * *

JERRY'S SPORTSMAN'S PARADISE, a bar in a New Jersey strip mall off Route 17, was a fifteen-minute drive from the expensive bedroom communities of Saddle River, Ho-Ho-Kus, and Wyckoff. Of the twelve patrons watching football reruns and horse races on the flat-screens midafternoon on a weekday, four were unemployed, three were retired, and five were engaged in the business of suburban housebreaking—three as thieves, one as a fence of stolen jewelry, and the fifth as a steerer who had an uncannily unerring ability to tell the thieves whose house was unoccupied.

The housebreakers knew him as Morton, an unassuming white guy with the beginnings of a potbelly, a pasty–always-indoors complexion, a very expensive leather jacket, and a gray porkpie hat. He was not often at Jerry's, showing up once or twice a month, but his information was good as gold. He sat at the corner of the bar, where he could see the room, smiling faintly.

Morton was smiling because he liked what he was hearing through his iPod buds, which connected to a mini-dish amplifier. At the far end of the bar a thief he had dealt with before was putting a new dude hip to Morton's talents.

"If Morton tells you the home owner has gone to St. Barts and the housekeeper takes Monday off, then the guy's in St. Barts and the housekeeper ain't there on Monday."

"How does he know?"

"Fuck knows. But he knows."

"Maybe he's psychic."

"Whatever, he's good at it. Check him out."

The new dude walked down to Morton's end of the bar. Morton pretended to turn off his iPod. "Hey, buddy. What's up?"

"I hear sometimes you have information."

"Sometimes," said Morton, who had already satisfied himself that the thief wasn't a cop by eavesdropping on a cell phone conversation the guy had earlier with his wife about picking up their kid from soccer practice.

"I hear it's good."

"It's gold," said Morton. "Gold is expensive. Twenty-five percent."

"Can you give me an idea where you get it?"

Morton looked at him. Did this jerk really think he was going to explain that geotags embedded in the smart phones of rich fools who posted photos on Twitter gave away home addresses and vacation locations, not to mention a picture gallery of unattended swag worth stealing? Or did he think that Morton was going to confess that he, the best computer hacker in the world, was a "white-hat" do-gooder who protected corporations from criminal "black-hat" and "gray-hat" hackers—except when sometimes he came down to Jerry's Sportsman's Paradise to pick up a couple of extra bucks, stick it to some rich bastards, and get off on hanging with lowlifes good geeks weren't supposed to know?

"No," said Morton. "I cannot share such an idea with you."

The guy wasn't stupid enough to be surprised. He shifted gears and asked a different stupid question: "I hear that it won't cost me anything until I put it to use."

Morton looked him in the eye. "You don't pay me until you've sold whatever you've got that my information enabled you to get."

"Yeah?" he asked in a tone that said, *What's the scam?* "What makes you so sure I'd pay you, ever?"

"Self-interest," said Morton. "You will pay me because you will want another tip— Excuse me a sec."

One of five cell and sat phones tucked in a row of custom-tailored pockets in the lining of his leather jacket was vibrating.

He checked the screen. SITA SATELLITE AIRCOM. Someone calling from an airliner telephone. And that was all. Not who they were, what plane they were on, where they were going. Just somebody who flipped over their in-seat handset, ran their credit card through it, and punched in Morton's number, which SITA's OnAir service routed through a satellite to vibrate his phone. Not as much as he wanted to know, but they did have his number.

"Hang on a minute; I have to take this," he said to the thief, hurried out to the parking lot, which contained the sort of recently detailed, certified preowned Audis and BMWs you could cruise a bedroom community in without drawing the attention of the police.

"Tell me why I shouldn't hang up."

"CatsPaw," said a woman.

"Go ahead," he said, trying not to sound too eager. CatsPaw meant money. A lot more money than walking the wild side with house thieves.

"Has my sat phone been compromised?"

"Give me the number."

She did. He said, "Turn your phone on, ringer off. Call me back using the airplane phone in five minutes."

The thief had stepped out the door to smoke a cigarette. "Hey, what about—"

"Later."

Morton got into his unassuming Honda, locked the doors, Wi-Fied into a large computer under the backseat, and punched up her number. When she called in five minutes he said, "They scored you big-time, sweetheart."

She muttered something that sounded like, "Fuck."

He waited a second for the usual indignant *How did they hack into my phone?* At that point he would explain that since he hadn't been there he could only guess that they got her by walking alongside her in the airport terminal with a powerful transmitter disguised as a laptop or sitting next to her in the lounge or even on the plane. Unless they simply "borrowed" her phone for a minute when she left it lying around, which, being CatsPaw, she probably hadn't. Instead of asking a dumb question, she asked the only pertinent one: "When did it happen?"

"Twelve hours ago," he answered, which would tell her where it had happened. "Do you remember how to upload your SIM card?"

"Yes," she said in a pissed-off voice that made that single syllable sound like, *Fuck, yes, who the hell do you think you're talking to here?*

"Upload immediately to this number." He gave her a number. "Okay, turn your sat phone off. Turn it on again in ten minutes. Wait five minutes, then call me back on the AIRCOM phone."

He got another *yes*. Hey, not his fault she got hacked.

He found the routing drone they had slipped onto the SIM card. It was a sophisticated East Europe jobbie that redirected her voice and text signals to some number in Bucharest. Oddly, it also blocked her communications; the usual way was to let the messages through; that way the target wouldn't know she was hacked and would keep sending more messages to spy on. He wiped the drone and uploaded the contents of her SIM card back to her otherwise intact.

First thing she wanted to know when he told her the sat phone was now clean was, "What did it do to the guy's phone I've been calling?"

"His is clean as a whistle."

"How do you know it didn't give his the virus?"

"I know because he called a half hour ahead of you with the same sort of problem and I checked it for him."

"He called before I did?" Now she sounded pissed off she'd come in second.

"Yeah. He was hip to the issue."

"Fuck! Did it give the hackers his number when I called him?"

"Well, yeah. If we're talking about the same guy. About whom I can tell you nothing, just like I can't tell nobody nothing about you, because I don't know nothing."

"Did you change his number?"

"Well, yeah. Like I'm going to change yours."

"How do I know how to call him?"

"The old number will ring through. If he wants to answer you, he will."

"Okay. I got that. What about these people who hacked me? Were they able to see where he is?"

"Only if he was dumb enough not to disable his GPS when he answered their call."

"He's not."

"I didn't think so," said Morton, "but let me give you some advice."

"What?"

Why am I doing this? he wondered. The answer was, he could not help himself. Deep down—way deep down—he was a white hat.

"What advice?"

"Don't call him from where you're at now. For all you know, whoever hacked you twelve hours ago could be on the same plane you're on."

"Thanks for the help."

"Pleasure doing business with you."

Morton returned his phone to its slot in his jacket, chose another, and called his mother. Thankfully, the machine answered.

He left a message that he would not be home for supper. Then he drove to New York City to find an expensive woman to celebrate earning in two twenty-minute sessions of private security consultation more than top IT guys earned in a month.

Hours later, avidly watching his reflection in a mirror over a king-size bed, Morton suddenly remembered the routing drone's odd feature of blocking the woman's calls when it passed them on to Bucharest. He probably should have mentioned it to her. But she would figure it out in the end, Morton supposed.

* * *

HURRYING FROM THE arrivals gate, looking for the first place she could call Janson without getting arrested for violating the rule posted on huge signs that you couldn't use a mobile phone in a security area, Kincaid paid close attention to the crowds streaming off their planes. Had one of them hacked her in the Johannesburg airport?

She got through Immigration and past Customs.

Finally, in an exit corridor that led to the terminal hall, she called Janson. And wouldn't you know it, the goddamned phone dropped the call. As she redialed she noticed other people were staring perplexedly at their phones and poking buttons as if they, too, were losing calls. She looked at her screen.

"No Service."

She felt the skin prickle on the back of her neck.

She looked around to see who was jamming the signals. Passengers, tired from the long international flights, were all carrying and rolling bags big enough to conceal electronic blocking devices. She slowed down and watched the faces of the people she had been tracking since she went by Customs. Businessmen and -women, tourists, homecoming Aussies with backpacks, families, two look-alike tall, stocky blondes, sisters, each dragging a yellow-haired kid.

Ahead the corridor opened wider and Kincaid could see people lined behind ropes hopefully gazing to greet their loved ones. She slowed more and let people overtake her. One of the blondes went ahead with both kids. The other was bumping into Kincaid, making excuse-me gestures as she jammed a pistol into her side and whispered in a nasal Australian accent, "It's wearing a can, doll. No one will hear."

Kincaid saw a sound suppressor screwed onto a Beretta, a quiet weapon to begin with.

"Hollow points. No blood, either. The bullet won't leave your liver."

TWENTY-THREE

Jessica Kincaid ground her teeth. They nailed her good. She never saw it coming.

Now who was the football clod?

Forget it.

New Game.

How did the woman get a gun into the secure area? Had to have an accomplice among the security officers, who would be watching closely for Kincaid to resist. No way she could fight back, not here. There were people all around and security cameras everywhere. The Australian was holding the Beretta with reasonable competence, but she looked jumpy, nervous enough to be unpredictable. If Kincaid screwed up taking the gun away from her, some bleary-eyed yawning travelers would end up with hollow-point expanding slugs tearing through their lungs.

"Keep walking!"

Kincaid had slowed to gauge the reaction. Very jumpy. A rogue cop, she thought. The woman had been or still was a cop, moonlighting. That would explain getting the gun through Security. And the case of nerves. Knowing her face could be recognized on security cameras or that she could bump into officers she was acquainted with, she had to have some kind of plausible story but damned well didn't want to have to use it.

Kincaid picked up speed, though only slightly. "You got me," she said. "Take it easy. Just tell me what you want me to do."

"Walk ahead of me. Follow the signs to the car park."

She had a van in the parking lot with no windows in back. Two more women were waiting inside. It smelled like they'd been drinking wine. The back cargo door was locked by steel bolts, and there were no side doors. A translucent sunroof let in light from the overhead street lamps, but it was not the kind that opened.

The woman at the wheel—the other "sister," who must have handed off the kids to somebody—started the engine as soon as they got the doors locked. The third woman was a heavyset grinning maniac with a cocaine blizzard in her eyes, a prison matron's mean mouth, and a pistol in her waistband.

They pinned Kincaid's wrists behind her with a disposable nylon double lock flex-cuff—more cop stuff—and took her phone and her bag and shoved her into the cargo area, which was covered with a musty carpet. Blondie, the woman who had nailed her in the terminal, stole her gold bracelet and put it on. Kincaid pegged her as the leader of the trio. Cokie took the ring Janson had given her in Amsterdam, which pissed her off. The thievery was more confirmation of what she suspected. They were locals for hire—a crew of rogue cops and crooks who usually robbed pimps and drug dealers. Who had hired them to snatch her? Who but Securité Referral?

Blondie felt the slot under Kincaid's bag and appeared surprised not to find a knife. Through airport security? Did she think Kincaid was nuts? But they did know to look for it. Proof positive they were working for the diver. Kincaid shifted internal gears in an urgent attempt to dampen panic. She knew she could not master panic, no one could, but Cons Ops had taught her ways to go around it, by concentrating step-by-step on questions and answers that might guide her toward action.

Clearly, she and Janson had underestimated Securité Referral's reach. But what was this, revenge? The thought of being delivered, handcuffed, to the South African mercenary whom she had taken down and humiliated threatened to redline the panic.

What about the doctor? Wasn't the doctor what Van Pelt wanted? But her capture was about both the doctor and revenge, she feared. That Van Pelt was hunting Dr. Flannigan didn't mean he couldn't spare an hour to give her a long and terrible death.

The only good news Kincaid could cling to was that the women were happy with her expensive bracelet and beautiful ring and didn't bother stealing her cheap Swatch. They couldn't see her hands behind her back. She worked her fingers past the cuff and pressed the Swatch's stem to switch on her GPS asset-tracking signal that would allow Janson to track her location on Google Maps—God bless the Internet and the CatsPaw hard geeks and soft geeks who had tweaked a device originally marketed to parents to spy on their teenagers.

Wouldn't it be nice if Janson was near enough to help? Wouldn't it be nice if he otherwise arranged for a local CatsPaw contractor to help? Before the miniature device's tiny battery ran down in two hours? Wouldn't it be nice if pigs could fly?

The van was moving fast on a highway. She saw signs through the windshield for the Sydney Central Business District and the Harbour Bridge to North Sydney. "Where are we driving?" she asked.

"Luna Park," called Sister at the steering wheel.

"What's Luna Park?"

"Amusement park."

"Haunted houses," Cokie said. "Scary stuff." She leaned close, leering at Kincaid, breathing wine in her face, mocking her fear.

Kincaid twisted her shoulder as though to relieve the stress on her pinioned arms. Her blouse puckered open in front, revealing glimpses of her breasts lit by the lamps arching over the road and oncoming headlights. Cokie wet her lips and glanced at the front of the speeding van. When she saw that Blondie had moved next to the driver, she plunged her hand into Kincaid's blouse.

She slipped inside Kincaid's bra and caressed her nipple. Kincaid tried to prepare herself for pain by separating thought from flesh, exiling her mind to a fog-shrouded beach where invisible breakers rumbled on the sand. Cokie positioned her thumb and index fingers like a pair of pliers.

* * *

PAUL JANSON DROVE a rental Volkswagen Golf out of Sydney Airport, fearing that he would never see Jessica Kincaid again. Despite the speed of the Thai jet, a privately registered craft that was allowed to land as a general aviation corporate plane, he had arrived moments too late to catch up with her before she had cleared Immigration. Suddenly his Iridium phone vibrated. It was not a phone call vibration but a distinctive on-off, on-off pattern. He stood on the brake and pulled onto the shoulder to read the screen.

Up came a miniature Google Map. His heart soared when he saw that it displayed the same airport highway he was on. A red dot that represented the current position of Jessica Kincaid's Swatch was blinking fifteen miles ahead of him, nearing the Sydney Harbour Bridge.

Janson floored the rental and tore back onto the road, weaving through light traffic.

All that the blinking red dot indicated for sure was that Kincaid's fake Swatch was in a moving vehicle. It might be on her wrist. She might still be alive. Or it might be on the wrist of someone who had killed her after she activated the concealed GPS. Even if it was her, its battery life was short. It could stop signaling her position at any moment. But after twenty-four hours of no communication— and the undeniable evidence that Securité Referral had hacked her phone—it was a million times better than knowing nothing at all, and he homed in on it with hope and cool deliberation.

His was not the only vehicle breaking the speed limit at this late hour. He tucked the rental tight behind a big Mercedes, betting it would draw the highway patrol's attention first. If not, if they came after him, they were welcome to follow until he caught up with her. Then they were welcome to help or get out of his way.

He glanced at the Iridium. The red dot had disappeared. The signal had faded, the battery dying or no longer strong enough to transmit from a location shielded by metal. He switched to direct mode, instructing the software to scan for intermittent signals that were too weak to power the light on the map continuously but possibly strong enough to spit out bursts of the map coordinates if only for a second at a time.

* * *

SLOWLY, SADISTICALLY COKIE dug her fingers deep into Jessica Kincaid's breast. She gasped and allowed herself to whimper until she heard Cokie's own breath quicken with vicious desire. Then Kincaid bit down hard and sank her teeth into the fleshy mound at the base of the woman's thumb.

Cokie screamed. She jerked her hand away and slapped Kincaid in the face. Kincaid kicked her, further enraging Cokie, who hauled off and punched her with all her considerable strength. It hurt like hell and spun Kincaid around so hard that she caromed off the wall of the van and fell backward against her tormentor.

"What are you doing?" yelled Blondie. "Get away from her!"

Cokie punched Kincaid again. Kincaid tumbled like a rag doll against the back of the van. She'd have a black eye and a bitch of a headache, soon.

Six feet away, Cokie was boasting, "That'll teach her to bite."

Blondie was not so easily fooled. "Where's your pistol?"

Kincaid tucked her cuffed wrists under her hips. To rack the Beretta Tomcat's slide, much less cock, aim, and shoot, she had to drag her hands around from behind her back, which meant getting them all the way under her feet. She crunched herself into as tight a ball as she could. But she couldn't get around her feet while holding the gun.

Cokie reached into her waistband. "Right here— Shit!"

Kincaid let go of the gun and frantically tugged her wrists under her heels. They hung up on the rubber of her shoes. She pulled with all her strength, tearing skin.

"You dumb dyke!" Blondie shouted, reaching into her windbreaker.

"Her word, not mine," said Kincaid. "Hands up, girls."

Her hands were still cuffed and blood from her wrists was making the Beretta slippery. But the gun was in front of her now, and she was up on one knee, braced against the back door. She racked a round into the chamber and flicked off the safety. "Up! Up! Up!— *You* keep driving. Both hands on the wheel where I can see them."

Sister hesitated, looking back for orders from Blondie.

Kincaid fired a shot into the floor. It made an earsplitting *crack* in the enclosed space.

Sister's hands flew to the top of the wheel. Blondie put hers in the air. But Cokie acted like she was above all this and fumbled clumsily for the automatic she carried in her shoulder holster. Kincaid whipped the stubby barrel toward the woman's forehead.

Blondie saw that Kincaid would not hesitate to pull the trigger.

"No!" Blondie screamed. She threw herself on Cokie, pinning her down and shielding her with her body. "Don't hurt her," she pleaded. "Please don't shoot."

"Tell her to put it down."

"I'm not putting it down!" Cokie screamed. "She can't tell me to put it down."

Blondie elbowed Cokie in the mouth and grabbed the gun, which she had dragged halfway out of its holster.

"Drop it! I'll shoot you both."

Blondie shoved it across the floor toward Kincaid and showed empty hands. "It's cool. It's cool. No one's shooting. Just don't—"

"Sister at the wheel! Toss me your weapon."

A big police-issue Glock slid past Blondie to where Kincaid crouched.

"And your backup! Don't make a mistake; it'll be your last."

Sister reached down slowly. An ankle gun came sliding back.

"Your gun with the can!" Kincaid shouted at Blondie.

The silenced Beretta slid across the carpet.

"Where's your backup?"

"Ankle."

"Give it!"

A Jetfire skipped past Kincaid.

"Cut this cuff!— You keep driving. Both hands!"

Blondie reached very slowly toward a pocket, saying, "I've got the cutter here. I'm just pulling it out, carefully."

Kincaid recognized the manufacturer's snipping device. "Come closer. Tell your friend not to move. Stop there! Extend your arm. Other hand behind your head. Cut it."

The special tool snipped through the plastic and its metal core. "Drop it."

Kincaid slid their weapons behind her.

"You! Driving! Pull off the road and stop on the shoulder. Nice and easy. Turn on your blinkers. Do *not* move your hands from the top of the wheel."

As the van slowed to a stop, Kincaid picked up the clipper and cut the remains of the cuffs off her wrists.

Blondie said, "The highway patrol will stop to investigate."

"Love to meet them," Kincaid lied. In fact, the last thing she wanted was interference by the highway patrol.

"Who sicced you on me?"

"South African guy."

"Describe him!"

"I never saw him. He called on the phone. My phone showed an overseas number and he sounded South African."

"I'm going to ask an important question. I already know the answer. Lie to me and I'll shoot your friend." Kincaid leveled the barrel at Cokie's head. "What did he tell you to look for?"

"A knife in your bag."

"Where in my bag?"

"Underneath. A slot in the bottom."

"Good answer—here's a harder one: How'd he know to call you?"

"I don't know."

"You're asking me to believe that you kidnapped me for a complete stranger. Say good-bye to your friend."

"No! No. He got my number from people who know me."

"Know you as what?"

"I'm a cop."

"No kidding. What people? Who are these people?"

"You know." Blondie shrugged. "Mafia."

"Mafia?" Kincaid asked. How the hell big was Securité Referral? "You at the wheel, hands on top!— What do you mean, mafia? Italian?"

"Local. Sydney. Just one of the Calabrian clans. They have a coke franchise."

"Are they connected in Europe?"

"They bring stuff in, but it's fragmented—very loose, each clan on its own."

"So the South African knows local Calabrian mafia who know you can be bought?"

"Correct."

"Where are you supposed to hand me over to him?"

"Luna Park."

"You already said. Where in Luna Park?"

"Camper van in the car park."

"With cuffs!" screamed Cokie. "And plastic tie clippy things. He's going to tie you up and do you proper, you bitch."

Kincaid put ice in her voice. "My outfit has a rule: No innocents get shot. But none of you are innocent. *Shut her up!*"

Blondie grabbed Cokie's hand and tried to quiet her.

"What?" Cokie yelled. "You taking her side?"

Blondie took Cokie's round cheeks in both hands and tried to make eye contact. "Please don't be crazy. Just this once."

"I'm not crazy!"

"Please?"

"She can't make me—"

"She'll kill you. I don't want that to happen," Blondie pleaded.

"Fuck her. Fuck all—"

Blondie threw a headlock on Cokie and clamped her free hand over her mouth. Cokie tried to bite her. Blondie squeezed harder and Cokie stopped struggling.

"Driver!" shouted Kincaid. "How long to Luna Park?"

"Ten minutes. Just over the bridge."

Kincaid could see the lights of the bridge through the windshield. They speckled a giant blue arc in the sky. "Get going!"

"Where?"

"Luna Park!"

TWENTY-FOUR

Luna Park?" Blondie echoed incredulously.

Kincaid fired another shot in the floor. *"Go!"*

The van lurched into the light traffic and accelerated to highway speed. Kincaid studied "Sister" in the rearview mirror. Cop or not, she was wearing the cowed expression of someone who was going to do what she was told and hope things got better. Kincaid turned her attention to the leader.

"Hold on to your friend."

"I'm holding her."

Blondie, too, was sufficiently cowed to behave herself. But having bullied and broken her down, now Kincaid had to build her back up. She had to make Blondie strong enough to help her nail Securité Referral to the wall.

"Okay, girls. How are we going to get out of this?"

"What do you mean?" Blondie asked warily.

"The South African is trying to kill me. You've broken every law

in Australia trying to help him kill me. But you're a police officer—
I should be more specific. You are a *stupid* police officer. Incredi-
bly stupid. But you still have a leg up over civilians. So how are we
going to get me safely out of here and you guys not in jail for the
rest of your lives?"

"Good question," said Blondie, her face lighting with hope.

"What is your name?" Kincaid asked. "Just your first name. I'm
not ratting you out unless you force me to."

"Mary."

"Okay, Mary. Who's at the wheel?"

"Doris."

"Doris, you're doing fine up there. Stay at the speed limit. Mary,
your excited friend here, whose head you're doing an excellent job
of holding, what's her name?"

"Everybody calls her Mikie."

"Fuck you!" yelled Mikie.

"Nice to meet you, too, Mikie. Okay, Mary, let's go to work.
Whose camper van is it?"

"I don't know."

Kincaid pretended to be patient as she asked, "What does it look
like?"

"Toyota Hilux, white box, blue cab."

"What is a Toyota Hilux?"

"A four-berth camper on a Toyota truck."

"Beds to screw you on!" Mikie screamed.

Kincaid said, "Give me back my phone— Careful reaching in
your bag, Mary.... Thank you. And my bracelet... Thank you."
Switching the gun smoothly from hand to hand, her eyes never
leaving the three women in front of her, she put on her bracelet
and pocketed her phone.

"And my bag."

Mary found it on the floor behind the passenger seat and tossed it where Kincaid indicated.

"And my ring."

"No fucking way!" yelled Mikie.

Kincaid gestured with the gun. Mary tightened her grip on Mikie's neck. Mikie yanked the ring off her finger and twisted around to throw it out the driver's window. Kincaid cracked her wrist with the gun barrel. Mikie screamed in pain, and Kincaid caught the ring falling from her hand. The gun barrel stayed on target as Kincaid slipped the ring Janson gave her back on her finger.

"So how are we going to get out of this?" she repeated.

"I don't know. I don't know," Mary said.

"You said you're a cop, right? What rank?"

"Detective sergeant."

"Even better. What about Doris? You're a cop, too, Doris, aren't you?"

"Yeah," came the tight-lipped reply.

"What rank?"

"Senior constable."

"How about Mikie?"

"No fucking way," said Mikie.

"Didn't think so. Okay, Mary, you're a detective sergeant and Doris is a senior constable. Why don't you arrest the South African?"

"*Arrest?* Are you having me on? Too many questions, when I march him into the station."

"Did I tell you to march him into the station?"

* * *

"33°51′08″ S, 151°12′38″ E" read Janson's Iridium screen. He had lost Jessica Kincaid's GPS asset tracking signal as the battery grew weak. Suddenly it was back, spitting out the coordinates of the Swatch's location.

Google Earth showed her Swatch smack in the middle of the Sydney Harbour Bridge.

He saw the bridge a quarter mile ahead, a dark arch like the humpback of a symmetrical stegosaurus. There was movement on top, just under where the flags flew. Tourists shackled to a safety line on the famous guided Bridge Climb—climbing the arch, silhouetted against the glowing clouds, plodding up the slope like prisoners of war.

Then the GPS coordinates faded from the screen, her battery dying again, or the device blocked.

* * *

"STOP THE VEHICLE!" Kincaid ordered. A very good idea was falling apart even before they entered Luna Park's garage.

"What's wrong?" said Doris.

"Read the sign."

It was suspended over the driveway, a white board held by chains.

MAXIMUM VEHICLE HEIGHT 1.9 METRES

"We're not that high."

"A camper on a truck is. He can't fit in there. Who told him he could?"

"Mikie."

"Who else?..." Kincaid thought hard. "Turn around, Doris. Head back where the road went under the bridge approach. We'll cruise the area. He's got to be waiting nearby."

They circled for five minutes. All of a sudden Mary reached reflexively toward her belt.

"Is that your phone?"

"Yeah. It's on vibrate."

"Check if it's him."

She turned the phone so Kincaid could see the screen. "BLOCKED."

"Answer it. If it's him, tell him we're waiting where the road goes under the highway to the bridge—see down there by those stairs, Doris?"

Doris steered the van toward the steps, which were barricaded with sawhorses and signs that the walkway was closed for the ongoing bridge upgrade and renovation. Walkers were directed to the bike path.

"Tell him we're down there, Mary. Make him come to you."

"Hello?" said Mary, listened a moment, and nodded to Kincaid. "Yeah, sorry about that. We're here.... Yeah, I know you can't fit. We're parked down the road at the bottom of the steps to the bridge.... No. Past the tow truck garage— No, there's no one around. The stairs are closed for the upgrade. It's cool. It'll just take a second to put her in your vehicle." She turned off the phone. "Five minutes."

"How good are you two? This guy is really tough."

"We need our guns back," said Mary.

"Sure."

Watching the Australian detective's eyes, Kincaid popped the magazines out of their police pistols, cleared the chambers, emptied the magazines, put them back, and tossed the pistols to them. "He's strong enough to break your disposable cuffs. Got steel?"

"Yeah."

Kincaid could see that both women were hunkering down into

themselves, preparing for action—tough street cops pumping up for a bust. Excellent. Bent as hairpins, but still good at their job.

"Cuff him hand and foot. Throw him in the back of the camper. Chain him to something he can't break loose. I'll take him from there."

"And you'll just let us go?"

"If you don't screw up."

"What about the money he's supposed to pay us?" asked Mikie.

"Mikie. Come here. I want to show you something."

"What?"

"Put your hands behind you. Come closer. Look at this." Kincaid rapped her hard on the temple with the Tomcat, and Mikie collapsed in a silent heap.

"What did you do that for?" Mary cried.

"So she can't try to screw it up to get me killed."

"Good move," said Doris.

"Here he comes."

Kincaid watched from inside the van, through the open window on the driver's side, as the two cops executed a thoroughly professional takedown. They waited until Van Pelt stepped out of the camper's cab. Then flashed their badges and drew their weapons.

Caught flat-footed in what Kincaid assumed Van Pelt must be guessing was some sort of police sting, the big South African did not resist. He turned around as the cops ordered with the resigned expression of a man who knew that expensive attorneys would shortly rally to his defense and placed his big hands on the hood of the Toyota. Doris kicked his feet apart, without getting too close, and covered him with her empty pistol. Mary patted him down. She removed a gun from a belly holster and another from the small of his back. More evidence, Kincaid thought, of SR's long reach.

Moments after passing through airport security, the operative had gotten fully equipped.

Kincaid raised her own weapon now that Mary had a loaded gun in her hand. But the Australian detective continued the procedure as if this were an ordinary arrest. She clamped a cuff on Van Pelt's left wrist and told him to bring his hands together. Van Pelt obeyed, sliding his bandaged right arm across the hood. But just when the cops felt safe was the most dangerous moment.

Kincaid yelled, "Heads-up!"

The South African mercenary exploded into motion, straightening up and swinging both arms wide, knocking both women to the ground and lunging for his guns, which had fallen to the pavement.

Kincaid fired through the open window. But Van Pelt was still in motion and the Tomcat lay too small in her hand to shoot accurately at any distance. The slug fanned Van Pelt's face. Startled by lead flying from an unexpected direction, he jumped back from reaching for his own guns, grabbed one of the Glocks that the cops had dropped, and dove behind the camper. In the seconds it took Kincaid to get out of the van, the Securité Referral operative leaped the sawhorses and bounded up the stairs to the Harbour Bridge.

TWENTY-FIVE

Kincaid vaulted the barricade and chased after Van Pelt, two steps at a time.

When Cons Ops used to bring her in to master-class the pick of the new agents, she always warned the women that they faced one real disadvantage: "We may be faster than men," she told them, "and more observant, but we're shorter." Here it was with a vengeance.

The SR agent was a foot taller than she and in just as good condition. Kincaid climbed two steps at a time. Van Pelt pulled ahead in bounds of three and four as if she were standing still. She couldn't see him when she got to the top of the stairs and found herself on a lit pedestrian walkway enclosed by a high mesh fence topped by three strands of barbed wire to stop suicide jumpers.

Kincaid climbed onto the handrail to see farther. It was nearly bright as day. The bridge deck and the stone pylons that bracketed the arch were floodlit. Architecture lights rimmed the enormous steel truss as it curved into the night sky, powerful lamps illuminated huge flags at the top of the arch, and low-hanging clouds reflected the glow of the city's buildings on both sides of the harbor. She clung to the mesh fence and searched the 150-foot-wide deck. Traffic was scant. A smattering of cars and trucks sped by on six lanes of highway. A train rumbled along one of two railroad lines. Cyclists flickered on the bike path, and she saw a second enclosed pedestrian path on the far side, which, unlike the one she was on, was open to walkers. The fence was high. Van Pelt was probably still on this footpath. But in which direction was he running? Across the water to the Central Business District or—

There!

In a splash of lamplight in front of the pylon where the arch started to span the harbor, he was running toward the water. She jumped down and ran after him.

Her view along the normally straight footpath was blocked by the construction work and he repeatedly disappeared behind sheds, work platforms, and stacks of material. There! She saw him again. But it was hopeless; he was still drawing ahead. The Central Business District was only a mile across the water. Once he reached the stairs on the other side, he would vanish into the city while she was still pounding across the bridge.

All of a sudden, he stopped. Kincaid put on a burst of speed, swiftly halving the distance between them. She saw ahead of him a blue flasher. It was right on the pedestrian path. Police? Van Pelt seemed to think so. He jumped onto the fence and started climbing the wire mesh.

At the top, where the mesh started to curve inward under two rows of barbed wire, he gripped the wire between the barbs. Then he swung his feet high in the air like a trapeze artist, flipped himself upright, and landed on the wire. Pinwheeling his arms to catch his balance two hundred feet above the black water, the South African pulled himself onto the girder above him and disappeared inside the massive steel web of ties, struts, plates, and flanges riveted into countless triangles that joined to form the trusses that shaped the arch.

Kincaid saw that the flashing light drawing nearer was a two-man police bicycle patrol. She had an instant to act before they saw her. She climbed up the fence as Van Pelt had, jumped for the top strand of wire, gripped between the barbs and flipped herself skyward as he had, got her feet under her, and used the wire's springiness to bounce in a long jump to the girder.

She caught the edge with her fingers. The steel was freshly painted, slippery as a stack of plastic bags, and she lost her grip and started to fall backward. A sheet metal sign warned people not to climb on the bridge. She grabbed it. It sliced into her fingers. She gripped hard and pulled herself onto the girder.

It was oddly quiet inside the maze of steel, and much darker. What faint light there was came from beams and shafts that penetrated the openings between struts and plates and cast huge shadows.

Suddenly she heard Van Pelt high above her, pounding on metal steps. He had found an interior staircase that zigzagged up into the web. Kincaid located it and went up after him. The flights of steps were narrow. Here and there they ended at the foot of a steel ladder, which in turn joined at the next level another flight of steps.

Kincaid was guessing that Van Pelt thought she was another cop, the Aussies' backup. And if he believed he had been caught in a sting he had to assume that there were cops everywhere. At least it looked that way. He wasn't even wasting time looking back. The longer he thought that way, the better. He was in for a surprise when he saw who she was. His second surprise would be discovering that he was carrying an empty gun.

She heard his feet pounding the metal.

The stairs were so narrow that her smaller size was now an advantage. She could climb faster than he could. She heard him cry out in pain. He must have banged his head on a projecting step or one of the many knobs of steel projecting from the girder. She grazed one herself as she ran from one flight to the next, but she couldn't slow down or he would escape.

Her eyes were adjusting to the light. Or perhaps more light penetrated as she climbed and the structure grew more airy. The top of a flight revealed another ladder. She climbed it, raced up another flight of stairs, and rounded a tight corner bounded by massive plates of riveted steel. Van Pelt was standing in it, facing the top of the stairs. He had his left arm pressed against his torso, in the classic shooter stance protecting vital organs. In his right hand he was aiming the Glock at Kincaid's face.

She pawed for the gun she had pocketed in order to climb with both hands.

He pulled the trigger twice.

"Bring bullets next time, asshole."

Van Pelt got over the shock of firing an empty pistol instantly. "You think you can stop me with that?" He lunged at her.

"Kneecapping'll do it," Kincaid said, trying to steady the little gun in hands that were wet again with blood from her wrists and firing twice at his knee. She heard him cry out, but he slung his empty weapon underarm in her face. It caromed off her skull as she ducked, slicing her scalp. Before she could fire again he had bolted around the next corner and was pounding the next stairs.

She knew she had hit him, but not in the knee or he wouldn't be running like that. She slipped on something wet and fell hard. Righting herself on the steps, she felt the wet she had slipped on. Sticky blood—his this time. He wouldn't get far.

The stairs and ladders stopped with no warning. She looked up, saw the glowing sky, saw the moving silhouette of Van Pelt climbing hand over hand up an improvised ladder of triangular cutouts in the girders. There was a sudden lull in the wind that whistled through the steel, and she could hear his laboring breath. But he was climbing fast, undaunted by whatever wound she had dealt him, and she saw no clear shot through the steel.

Pocketing the gun again, she felt for hand- and toeholds in the openings between the ties and struts that formed the panel he was climbing and started up after him. Something stung her eyes. His blood was dripping down on her, she thought at first. But no, her own blood was trickling from her scalp. She tried to brush it away with her sleeve and kept climbing, her breath coming short from exertion.

She heard voices. Numerous voices. Was she hallucinating? It sounded like people calling to each other. Not cops, not pursuit, but people having fun. Maybe she *was* hallucinating. Her head hurt and she was sure as hell breathing hard, slipping into oxygen deficit, climbing hand over hand, foot over foot, like Spider-Man, minus the spidey juice that made him stronger than humans. Chill! Stay with this!

She concentrated on the endless task of lifting leaden arms and legs in a steady rhythm while trying to stay alert for another ambush. She had to remember to look up. High above her, Van Pelt appeared to be emerging from water. He had reached the top. He was climbing out of the steel into the air. She heard the voices, again—frightened now, shouts, a cry of pain, and then the pounding of Van Pelt running again.

She reached the top. She swung herself up off the girder onto a narrow windswept catwalk. The slope of the arch curved down behind her. People yelled. She turned and looked up and saw the arch still curving higher into the sky. The people were between her and the summit—a crowd of eight in identical jumpsuits. They wore radio headsets and were tethered to a cable beside the catwalk. Bridge climbers, she realized.

The Sydney Bridge Climb was advertised on the plane and in the airport. Groups of tourists were escorted to the top of the bridge to enjoy the stunning view and have their pictures taken above the beautiful city. Two of them were slumped unconscious on the catwalk, laid out by Van Pelt. He had broken past them and was racing toward the top.

A girl saw Kincaid and screamed.

"There's another one!"

Kincaid ran straight at them, pointed to the side she was going to pass, and ordered in a shout louder than the wind, *"Disperse!"*

The tourists shrank from the sight of a determined woman with blood streaming down her face. She blasted past them.

She saw Van Pelt fifty feet ahead, running like the wind.

The bastard was home free, running fast and easy, untroubled by his wound, and again taking advantage of being so much faster than she. A second climbing party suddenly materialized ahead of him, between him and the crest. The leader was shouting into a walkie-talkie. Without hesitating, Van Pelt jumped from the catwalk to the girders that traversed the bridge and ran, balancing himself hundreds of feet over the roadway and train tracks, racing across them to the opposite arch.

Kincaid followed. Her heart soared. She had better balance. She could run faster on the girders. In fact, the faster she ran the better her balance—as long as she didn't miss a step and plunge a foot through a hole in the steel. He was picking his way more slowly, tiring, limping, stiffening up like a man afraid of falling. She was only twenty feet behind when the SR mercenary reached the far arch and scrambled onto its catwalk. His way was clear. There was nothing between him and the summit and when he crested it and started down he would go even faster. Kincaid reached the catwalk, scrambled over the rail, and ran after him.

A lone figure appeared at the top of the arch.

Kincaid blinked, gasping for breath, half-blinded by her own blood, thoroughly confused. The tourists' voices had been weirdly hallucinatory. What she thought she saw now was even stranger. Hunched over a mobile phone, peering myopically through wire reading glasses at the yellow glow of a Google Map, the lone figure looked like a bridge climber who had somehow gotten lost, untethered from his group at the top of the bridge 450 feet above Sydney Harbour. He looked up from his phone at the sound of their pounding feet and removed his reading glasses as if to take a better look at the enormous Van Pelt charging the narrow catwalk straight at him. He slipped his glasses into his pocket, put his phone in another, and stood up straight.

"Janson!" The sight of his innocent specs and the span of his shoulders sent an invigorating blast of adrenaline through her arms and legs. No way she would let Paul Janson beat her to the catch. Kincaid summoned her last reserves for a final burst of speed to tackle Van Pelt's ankles.

Van Pelt thrust his right shoulder forward like a battering ram. A loud yell stormed from his lips, a feral howl of destruction. He hurled his left hand in a pile driver blow with all his running weight behind it.

Paul Janson slid inside the arc of the mercenary's fist, and Kincaid knew she had lost the race. But she had to admit that the traditional prizefighter punch that her partner chose from his close-combat arsenal was a thing of awesome beauty. With a synchronized explosion of footwork, hip pivot, and body momentum, the hand that had pocketed his mobile phone closed into a fist and flew with precisely directed energy. Quick as flame, smooth as oil, it traveled the shortest possible distance to strike the running man's jaw with the audible crunch of a meat cleaver and lifted him over the guardrail and into thin air.

The SR mercenary fell with a scream of astonishment.

Plunging toward the water far below, wheeling through the beams of light that decorated the arch and illuminated the highways on the deck, buffeted by the wind and drifting like a kite, Hadrian Van Pelt took a full seven seconds to fall 450 feet.

Doubled over, Kincaid gasped, "I almost had him."

* * *

PAUL JANSON LAUGHED, giddy with relief to have her back safe. "What in hell did you think you would do with him when you caught him? He outweighed you by a hundred pounds."

"His gun was empty— Sweet Jesus, look at that son of a bitch!"

As Van Pelt's falling body dropped through the last band of light, they saw him twist around and turn a somersault in the air. With his arms held high and his feet pointed down, he knifed cleanly into the black water

Janson grabbed his phone, switched off the Google Map, and touched Redial.

"...Me again. A man just jumped off the Harbour Bridge, dead center. He cut the water clean with his feet, so he could have survived.... Tall, blond hair, broad shoulders, right arm in a bandage. Confirmation would be appreciated."

He told Kincaid, "My friend with the Australian Crime Commission says sharks came back when Sydney cleaned up the pollution. Your boy just jumped into a harbor full of bulls and great whites."

"Poor sharks."

"There's the harbor patrol."

"Good. This time I want to see a body."

Blue flashing lights were setting out from both North and South Sydney shores and racing toward the center of the mile-wide strait between Milsons Point and the Central Business District. Janson handed Kincaid a mini water bottle from his windbreaker. As she gulped gratefully, he spit on a handkerchief and wiped the blood from her face.

"Ditch that gun in case we run into the cops."

Kincaid threw Mikie's Tomcat into the harbor. "Where to?"

"Canberra. My friend on the commission traced Dr. Flannigan to a package tour. I have people watching his hotel."

They walked down the arch, side by side, bumping shoulders like a couple heading home from a late-night date.

"Paul?"

Janson leaned close to hear her over the wind. "What is it?"

"Don't you think that SR is going to way too much trouble for revenge? They had a whole program in place to nail me. Plus, what they did to our phones? No professional wastes that kind of energy on payback."

"They could be doing it for the money. What if someone hired SR to hunt us?"

"Who?"

"Whoever hired SR to hunt the doctor."

"Why?"

Janson had been weighing that question since Securité Referral had hacked their phones. "Clearly, we've threatened somebody."

"We've been hired to capture Iboga. That threatens Iboga and SR."

"Yes, but Iboga hasn't the assets to hound us."

"SR sure as hell has."

"Yes, but what if SR is essentially what they appear to be—hired guns doing a job?"

"Like us."

"In essence," Janson agreed. "We're paid by Ferdinand Poe to capture Iboga and we're paid by ASC to rescue the doctor. SR is paid by somebody to protect Iboga and kill the doctor."

"Are you thinking we threatened the same people the doctor did?"

"I'm thinking what I've been thinking all along. We can kill two birds with one stone when we grab the doctor. Even if he doesn't know who is hunting him, Dr. Flannigan must have a good guess why. We can work it back to who."

TWENTY-SIX

I rented a bicycle," the blonde told Terry Flannigan when he called her cell phone. She had a breathless little-girl voice and she sounded very excited. She had actually gasped like a teenager when she heard his voice. "Canberra's the most wonderful city for riding a bike. I've been riding every day. But I had a feeling you would call today, so I put a picnic in my basket."

"I'm not exactly in bike shape," Flannigan admitted freely. He was a firm believer in warning young women not to expect a lot when he took his shirt off.

"There aren't any hills. Just flat, wonderful paths. They go all around the lakes and miles and miles out into the countryside. There are private spots where you can lie in the grass all by yourself."

"I used to ride bikes," he said, hoping her picnic included a blanket. "Where do I rent?"

She told him where and gave him directions to pedal along the lake to a more private place they could meet, as if understanding and not minding that his thing with the senator might be longer term than a picnic.

Flannigan took a taxi from the senator's charming flat in a row of town houses—she was chairing a committee hearing until late afternoon—and walked down a short slope into the park to the rental place where they gave him a bike, a helmet, and a map.

It turned out to be true that one did not forget how to ride a bike. After a wobbly hundred yards, he was pedaling along just fine. The spot she said she'd meet him was only a half mile away, and by then he was actually enjoying himself. The pleasure of the warm sun, the crisp breeze, the truly attractive park with its sparkling lakes, lawn, and trees and the delicious sight of numerous good-looking women pedaling bicycles in short skirts and tight jeans ceased abruptly when he turned onto a path that ran closer to the water.

Out of nowhere, swooping down like wolves, Annie Oakley and The Wall blocked his way. They put firm hands on him before he could run. The Wall didn't seem quite so big out of his jungle fatigues but was big enough to make mincemeat of him. Little Annie looked like she'd been in a bar fight, with sunglasses over a black eye, a Band-Aid parting her hair, and raw scrapes on her wrists.

"Don't be afraid," she said. "We're on your side."

"I'm not afraid," he lied. He was so scared his face felt cold, as if the blood had drained from it.

The Wall noticed and said soothingly, "We are not the ones trying to kill you. We will protect you."

That would be wonderful news, if he was fool enough to believe them. "How did you find me?"

"Your fellow tourists noticed the senator take a shine to you."

"What do you want?"

"We want to deliver you safe and sound to ASC headquarters in Houston. As soon as your employer sees that you are alive and well, you'll be free to go. No one will hurt you."

"Either you're lying to me," Flannigan said, "or someone is lying to you."

"What do you mean?" asked the woman.

"I don't work for ASC."

The two of them exchanged looks.

"I haven't worked for them in five years."

The woman said, "That is not true. You were aboard *Amber Dawn* when the FFM rebels attacked."

"Well, that answers that," said Flannigan, feeling a tentative glimmer of hope.

"What do you mean?"

"Now I know that you two aren't lying."

The man stepped closer. "Can you explain— By the way, Doctor, we've been through a bunch together, but we've never exchanged names. We know you're Terry. I'm Paul. This is Jesse."

Paul thrust out his hand. Flannigan took it and saw a degree of warmth in Janson's watchful eyes.

"You *were* on the boat, weren't you?"

"I was on the boat. But ASC didn't *know* I was on the boat."

"*What?*" The looks they exchanged this time were like clashing laser beams.

"No one knew I was on the boat."

"What are you saying?" Jesse snapped. "You stowed away?"

"I hitched a ride. I had a little trouble in Port Harcourt. I had to get out of town. *Amber Dawn*'s captain was a friend of mine. She smuggled me aboard and hid me in her cabin. No one knew I was on the boat."

"No one?"

"She'd have been fired. It was strictly against company policy."

"Why didn't you tell us earlier?"

"They killed everybody on the boat. How could I trust you? How could I trust anybody?"

A bicycle bell chimed merrily. Flannigan looked up the path from the lake. There was his little friend, even prettier than he remembered and frighteningly young. Wondering how dirty an old man Jesse and Paul thought he was, he said, "Can you excuse me a second? I'll be right back. A lady I have to say hello to."

They shot sharp glances at the blonde, took in the picnic basket attached to her handlebars and her shy smile. "Wait," said Paul, moving between him and the girl.

Jesse walked over to her and smiled. "Hello. We are responsible for that gentleman's safety. Would you mind if I frisked you for weapons?"

"Weapons? Is he all right?"

"He's fine. We're just making sure that he stays that way. This will just take a moment, with your permission."

Kincaid checked her clothing, with gentle apologies, and the picnic in her basket. The forks and knives were plastic disposables. Kincaid nodded to Janson. Janson told Flannigan, "You're going to have to ask her for a rain check, Terry."

* * *

"You're a woman," Janson said to Kincaid while they watched the doctor explaining the situation just out of earshot.

"Yes, I am, Paul."

"Can you explain how a guy who looks like that has women falling all over him? The purser's wife, the flight attendant, the senator, not to mention the poor tugboat captain. And now this little knockout. Okay, she's a hick kid, but a woman like the senator should know better, don't you think? I mean do you find him attractive?"

"Depends upon what you mean by 'attractive.' "

"Attractive enough to run off with the guy."

"Watch how he talks to her. It's like his eyes, his ears, every pore is with her—appreciating her. When a guy like him wants to be with a woman he's totally there."

"So women want concentration?"

"It's in short supply—but there's something else likable about Terry. Way underneath, he's solid. And kind of sad— *What?*"

Paul Janson exploded into motion.

TWENTY-SEVEN

Kincaid whirled after him. Janson had moved so swiftly that he was on top of the couple in an instant, chopping with his open hand, breaking the girl's wrist before she could stab Flannigan again with the stiletto she had pulled from the bike's hollow handlebar.

Kincaid smashed her cheekbone below her helmet with her elbow as she raced past Janson, frantically searching for the assassin's backup. It would be a sniper. In a tree in the gardens seven hundred meters across the lake. Or by the museum on a spit of land jutting parallel to the one they were on. Paul knew that and was dragging Terry to the ground, hauling him behind the thin cover of a bush, and shouting at nearby walkers and bikers, "Get down on the ground. Get down!"

Kincaid saw a flash on the roof of the museum—sun on a scope, nine hundred meters.

"Roof!" Pointing to the sniper's position, diving to the grass, she rolled toward Janson. They pulled Flannigan behind the brow of a low mound. The rifle fired, unheard. A slug thunked into the mound. Earth flew in their faces.

"How many?"

"One, so far."

Less than five seconds had passed since Janson spotted the stiletto. The assassin was trying to mount her bicycle, but she was staggering from the impact of Kincaid's elbow and in shock from her broken wrist. The bicycle got away from her and fell over. She tried to run. Suddenly the airholes of her helmet spewed blood as a rifle bullet dissolved her skull.

Janson and Kincaid traded looks. Stabbing Flannigan would have been the killers' plan B, if they had not intervened. Plan A would have been the girl luring Flannigan into the sniper's sights. And now, before abandoning weapons and melting into the museum crowd, the sniper had killed the injured backup assassin so she could not talk.

Janson dialed 000.

"Ambulance. Lake Burley Griffin. Garryowen Drive. Across the lake from the National Museum. Stab wound."

"Tell 'em not to bother," Flannigan whispered. His face was white, his lips blue

"You'll be fine."

"Don't bullshit a surgeon—she got my celiac artery. I have about two minutes.

"Listen, you gotta know this—*Amber Dawn* was disguised as an OSV. They Rube Goldberged a secret exploration vessel. The people shot by the rebels weren't roustabouts. They were petroleum explorers."

"What did they find?"

"They threw their computers and transmitters overboard—like

they were done uploading confirmation data and keeping it secret. Christ, I can't believe this is happening to me." He shook his head. "No way rebels accidentally did the oil company a favor, keeping the discovery secret by killing everybody. They were *sent* to kill 'em."

So much, thought Janson, for Doug Case's story about burnishing ASC's image with pro bono exploration for downtrodden nations. ASC had been exploring solely for itself behind a scrim of independent contractors.

"That's why I thought they'd sent you to kill me. They were afraid I knew about the discovery— Hey, little Annie?"

"Me? What, Terry?"

"Annie— What's your name? Oh, right, Jesse. Honey, I'm gone. I wonder if I could hold your hand? No offense, Paul, but I'd rather go out with a girl."

Jessica Kincaid took Terry Flannigan's hand in one of hers and laid her other hand on his brow. "Take it easy, Terry. You'll be okay. Hear the ambulance? They're coming."

"Good-bye, Annie...." His eyes closed. Sirens grew loud.

"Terry," said Janson. "*Terry!* The guy who helped Iboga board the jump jet? You thought you recognized him."

"He led the rebel unit that attacked the boat."

How many sides was SR on?

"Take care of yourself, Jesse."

Kincaid laid Flannigan's hand across his chest, took the other, which had fallen to his side, and crossed it over the first. "Jesus H, Paul, did we fuck up."

"If it was not a random attack, how did the rebels in a speedboat locate that one small OSV fifty miles from Isle de Foree on a foggy night?"

"This poor silly bastard was on to something. And we missed it. I missed it. I missed her goddamned knife."

"Coincidence? The first blip on their radar led them to a victim that just happened to be *Amber Dawn* throwing computers overboard?"

"Terry told me at the hospital that he gave up regular practice because amputations really got him. He said he'd lie awake afterward, wondering should he have done it different."

Janson barely heard her. "Radar alone could not guide them to precisely that one boat. Unless someone attached a tracking device before *Amber Dawn* sailed from Nigeria. What if they signaled *Amber Dawn*'s coordinates traced by the scientists' encrypted satellite uploads?"

Kincaid rubbed her eyes. "You tell me, Mr. Machine."

"Whoever received the uploads could have betrayed the scientists who transmitted them—an ice-blooded way to ensure that no one on the boat would reveal the discovery."

"Doug Case lied to you about Terry Flannigan working for ASC."

"Apparently so."

"So how can you believe Case's story that gunrunners told him Terry had been kidnapped?"

TWENTY-EIGHT

Rest assured, President Poe," said Kingsman Helms. "American Synergy Corporation's Petroleum Division doesn't want a 'BP' in Isle de Foreen waters any more than you do."

"Acting President," Ferdinand Poe corrected him.

He was one tough old bird, Helms thought, considering that he had been tortured nearly to death only a month earlier. Helms had expected to call on a trembling old man in his hospital suite. Instead, Poe had received him in his working office adjacent to the ceremonial "throne room" in the Isle de Force's Presidential Palace, where President for Life Iboga used to accept ASC bribes.

"I've asked repeatedly," said Poe, "for detailed contingency plans in the event of blowouts, pipeline breaks, tanker collisions, and groundings. I have received from ASC standard boilerplate responses riddled with gobbledygook pseudo-science that would embarrass even BP. In fact, one of my bright young aides informs me that parts of it appear plagiarized from discredited BP safety filings."

Helms ran a powerful athlete's hand through his wavy blond hair. Whoever back in Houston had prepared the latest report on Poe's condition could consider himself fired. A perfunctory courtesy call by the president of the Petroleum Division on the president of this pissant island—a ceremonial state visit as it were—was devolving into a goddamned Spanish Inquisition.

"Mr. President—"

"Acting President!"

"Sir. You have my word that our latest, updated disaster contingency plans will be emailed to your petroleum minister by tomorrow morning."

"Thank you. Now let's get down to business."

"I beg you pardon, Mr.— Sir. What business?"

"At the moment, we have an oil lease agreement—Isle de Foree and American Synergy Corporation."

"At the moment?" Helms countered.

"The terms of our current agreement are excessively generous to American Synergy."

"We have an agreement that gives ASC exclusive exploration rights for five years," Kingsman Helms replied coldly. It was time to take off the gloves. If Poe wanted an Inquisition he would get one that would make the Spanish Inquisition seem benign.

"We have a further agreement that ASC retains development rights of all reserves that ASC discovers in these five years. Remember that we are not drilling for 'easy oil' in Isle de Foree's ultradeep waters. Our up-front investment is huge. We are taking geological risks, engineering risks, and capital risks. If we are so fortunate as to drill down to a 'commercial discovery,' we will have earned our additional agreements that give ASC the exclusive right to develop a petroleum accessing and processing infrastructure on Isle de Foree and in her waters. In other words, Mr. Acting President, if we find it, we own it, and you get royalties."

"It is the royalties that are troublesome," Poe shot back. "Our percentage is too low and the means of auditing payments are opaque. In other words, Mr. President of ASC Petroleum Division, the agreement is not fair."

"Surely you would not prefer to do business with extractors that have the scruples of China or Russia?"

Poe refused to rise to that bait. He said, "The Free Foree Movement accepted your terms at a time of desperate weakness. We appreciate the help you gave us at the time. But the situation has changed. We are no longer hiding in the jungle."

"Are you threatening to renege?"

"Nations don't renege. They renegotiate."

Helms smiled. "I am glad to hear you speak of nations, as there are more than one involved."

"What other nations are involved?"

"Nigeria is the strongest that comes to mind. When Isle de Foree broke away from Equatorial Guinea and became an independent nation, weren't you backed by Nigeria?"

"That was many years ago. Nigeria imposed onerous oil-sharing deals on Isle de Foree in exchange for support—and Nigeria supported Iboga to protect those deals." Poe glared angrily.

Helms interrupted before Poe could accuse ASC of playing both ends against the middle by supporting Iboga until they were sure the dictator had lost the war. "Nonetheless. You developed your existing fields in partnership with Nigeria."

"Inshore!" Poe protested. "Inshore. Nowhere near the deepwater blocks that ASC is exploring for us."

"Nigeria could easily claim that the fields that ASC is investing in so heavily to explore are on the toe thrust of the Porto Clarence fields. Nigerians are a grabby bunch. I wouldn't be surprised if they argue that the Porto Clarence fields are a structural trend connected to the Niger Delta itself."

"Nonsense. Our new fields would be hundreds of miles from the Niger Delta."

"Seabed disputes are as much about geology as distance. But the sense or nonsense of the argument would be worked out in treaty negotiations. Failing that, the issue would move to the Chamber for Maritime Delimitation Disputes of the International Tribunal for the Law of the Sea and then the Seabed Disputes Chamber— or is it the other way around? Seabed Disputes first. I can never remember. The lawyers can work it out."

"Isle de Foree does not have time for a protracted legal battle with Nigeria. Whoever we permit to explore for us will continue to."

"If you violate the international court orders to cease drilling and exploring until the dispute is resolved, I guarantee you that Nigeria will invade first and answer the world's questions later."

Ferdinand Poe rubbed his mouth, as if to prevent a doubt from passing his lips.

"And I wouldn't be surprised if Gabon piled on to see what they could grab," Kingsman Helms said, rising to his full height. "Mr. Acting President, we have a deal. ASC stands by its deals. We hope you do, because if you don't, Isle de Foree will be the partner that ends up alone."

Ferdinand Poe stood painfully from his chair. "Our nation—this island—has the minutest window open for the shortest instant. In this moment, we can speed the clock ahead of the past. We can erase the final memories of colonialism. We can blot out the memory of terror that Iboga visited on our people. We can use this gift found under the sea to build a homeland that welcomes prosperity, decency, and peace. In other words, Mr. Helms, I will resist your schemes with every breath in my body. This ruinous, larcenous contract will stand on my dead body. We will renegotiate it. Or break it."

Kingsman Helms turned on his heel and walked out of Poe's office. Margarido, Poe's chief of staff, was standing in the hall and looked at him inquiringly. "I trust you had a good meeting, Mr. Helms?"

"An excellent meeting. Always a pleasure doing business in Isle de Foree—Excuse me; I have a call."

He took out his satellite phone.

Mario Margarido went into Poe's office. "Well?"

Poe was slumped behind his desk, his mouth working. He looked up wearily. "When I agreed to oil lease terms with American Synergy in exchange for their support in our war against Iboga, I truly believed that liberating our country from that monster would make Isle de Foree a better home for our people. I had a dream that I could be like another Nelson Mandela—free our nation and then step back and let the young build her anew. You warned me at the time that I was making a deal with the Devil."

The chief of staff smiled, hoping to calm Poe, and said, "It was my job to be your Devil's Advocate."

"I explained how desperately we needed the help and you agreed. But it never occurred to me how determined the Devil is to remain the Devil."

"What happened?"

"I asked for fairer terms."

"And?"

"He told me to go to hell."

"That doesn't mean you have to."

"He made it very clear he would embroil us with the Nigerians."

"Yes, I wondered about that— So what do we do?"

"Same thing we did with Iboga. Resist."

"Do you really want to wage war, again? So soon?"

Ferdinand Poe stood up and limped to a window that overlooked the seawall. He collected his thoughts. Then he repeated to his old comrade the essence of what he had told the oilman from Texas.

"Yes, I am ready to resist, again, if I must." Poe turned around and faced Margarido. "And you, my friend?"

Mario Margarido bowed his head. "I would be a liar to say I was anxious to. But surely you don't have to ask."

* * *

KINGMAN HELMS TOOK his telephone outside. His Sikorsky VIP S-76C++ was waiting on the windswept terrace that served as the palace helipad. He twirled his hand in the air, gesturing impatiently for the pilots to crank her up, and bounded up the boarding steps.

"Out of here. Now."

"Where to, Mr. Helms?"

"*Vulcan Queen.*"

The ultraluxury helicopter lifted off immediately. Its so-called Silencer cabin and QUIETZONE gearbox made it quiet enough to talk on the phone, but when Helms saw that it was Doug Case calling from an airplane he did not bother to answer. Fuck him.

The helicopter swept seaward, thundering low over the Black Sand Prison. Last time Helms had been in Porto Clarence, the prison had been full of Ferdinand Poe's allies. Now the rebels were dancing in the streets and President for Life Iboga's officer corps were festering inside. There, thought Helms, was Poe's Achilles' heel. If Poe had a brain in his head he would shoot the whole bunch. Like most fools, Poe picked the wrong fights. Instead of killing the army officers who truly meant him harm, he wanted to slug it out with American Synergy over some misguided issue of principle.

Twenty minutes later, fifty miles to the south, when Helms could see the *Vulcan Queen*'s immense double drill tower his phone rang again. The Buddha. The CEO and chairman of the board of American Synergy calling from Houston. Helms answered hastily. "Yes, sir. How are you today?"

"How are things in Isle de Foree?"

"Poe wants to renegotiate. I told him we'd fight him."

"Will he fight back?"

"I'm not sure, sir. But I'm afraid it looks like he might."

The Buddha said, "For the sake of your division of the American Synergy Corporation, you better hope like hell that he doesn't," and hung up.

"Fuck!" Helms threw his phone on the chair beside his. He jumped up and stared over the pilots' shoulders at the *Vulcan Queen* growing large beneath him. Ordinarily, the sight of the thousand-foot Vulcan-class drill ship bristling with derricks and deck cranes filled his heart. *Vulcan Queen* was a completely self-contained explorer capable of steaming to the deepest imaginable oil fields in the world at fifteen knots and drilling two exploratory wells simultaneously in stormy seas when she got there. Satellite-directed one-hundred-ton tunnel thrusters and eight rotating propulsion pods could hold her in position as tightly as if she were welded to the distant sea bottom. Manned by two hundred employees and sending remote submersibles to forage miles below, the drill ship was in her complexity and her mission a thing of powerful beauty, and Kingsman Helms felt all of the pride of the captain of the ship. More, he thought. More like a king in his castle or the admiral of a battle fleet. *Vulcan Queen*'s mere captain worked for him. He could always fire the captain. Which, of course, was what the Buddha had just told him could be done to him, the mere president of one mere division of the American Synergy Corporation. His phone rang. Case again. Helms was too angry to pretend he didn't hate the cripple's guts.

"It would have been goddamned helpful had I been informed that doddering old President Poe is fully capable of reaming out a goddamned regiment."

"Acting President Poe," said Doug Case.

"Don't fuck with me, Case."

"Had you informed me you were calling on Acting President Poe, I would have filled you in with an up-to-the-minute dossier."

"You should have known I was calling on him."

"I do not spy on branch presidents," Case replied blandly, making "branch presidents" sound like shopping mall bank managers. "When they inform me of their travel plans, I inform them exactly what's waiting for them. In minute, accurate detail."

"What are you calling about?"

"Paul Janson says come to Singapore."

"I'm not going to Singapore. You deal with him."

"I already tried. Janson said, and I quote, 'Bring Helms. Tell him I'll blow this thing sky-high if he doesn't get his ass to Singapore in twenty-four hours.' What 'thing' would this be, Kingsman?"

"I don't know."

"The man seems to think he has you by the short hairs. Anything to do with the fact that Dr. Terrence Flannigan was stabbed to death last week?"

"Have you paid Janson, yet?"

"He wouldn't take the money," answered Case. "I stay at the American Club in Singapore. Shall I book you a room?"

TWENTY-NINE

The city-state of Singapore, an equatorial island at the southern end of the Malacca Strait, was as hot and humid as Isle de Foree. But there were no mountains to escape to, only air-conditioned shopping malls. Singapore was flat, with a few low hills, and the city, which occupied much of the island, was densely populated. Development had erased the jungle; streams flowed in concrete ditches between high-rise apartment buildings and glittering hotels; swamps had been drained and dredged to serve commercial shipping with a concrete shoreline. The port was enormous, a transhipment colossus with one foot in the Indian Ocean and the other in the South Pacific.

"*Namaste,*" Paul Janson greeted the Gurkha security officers guarding the entrance to the American Club with a folding-stock Remington shotgun, a Heckler & Koch MP5, pistols, and *khukuri* knives. *I bow to the God in you.*

He was glad to see good men getting paying work, but they had to wonder, as he did, whether their employment was overkill: Gurkhas were the fiercest, best-trained fighters in the world and Singapore the safest of nations. Janson's own club up the street, the Tanglin, whose members were the elite Chinese, Malays, Indians, and English who ran Singapore, made do with doormen who kept the taxis from cluttering the driveway.

Doug Case had left word at the front desk that he was waiting in the Union Bar. It was decorated like a sports bar with a big TV. Janson assumed that homesick American businessmen huddled here Saturday afternoons. It was quiet this morning and Case had the place to himself. He had backed his wheelchair into a corner.

"Welcome to the exotic Orient. May I order you a cheeseburger and fries?"

"Where's Kingsman Helms?"

"Running late. He'll be here any minute. Good flight?"

"On time," said Janson, sitting where he could watch the door. He had dressed for the climate in linen shirt and trousers with a jacket draped over his arm. Case wore a bespoke tropical suit of ultralight 300 wool.

"Where's Ms. Kincaid?"

"Traveling."

"I'm disappointed. I was looking forward to laying eyes on her again."

"She asked you a good question last time: How did you know that the doctor had been kidnapped? You answered that the gunrunners told you."

"Correct."

"Still your answer?"

Case had hazel eyes. They offered up a glint of steel. "Why wouldn't it be? What's up, Paul? What's eating you?"

"Did the gunrunners mention what the *Amber Dawn* was doing south of Isle de Foree?"

"Not that I recall. Delivering or picking up something, I presume. That's what service boats do. If you're interested, I'm sure it's in the company records."

"I'll wait for Helms. Maybe he knows. How long did Terry Flannigan work for ASC?"

"There's Helms!"

The tall blond executive bustled into the bar and crossed the room in several long strides. "What," he demanded of Paul Janson, "were you going to 'blow sky-high' if I didn't travel halfway around the world to humor you?"

"How long did Terry Flannigan work for ASC?"

Kingsman Helms sank into a chair and said, "You could have asked that on the telephone."

"I don't think you would have answered it on the telephone. How long did Terry Flannigan work for ASC?"

"Briefly."

Janson looked at Doug Case. Had Doug known? Hard to tell.

"What do you mean, briefly?"

"He was let go for schtupping some VP's wife."

"I don't understand. Why'd you hire me to save him if he no longer worked for ASC?"

"He had been one of our own. And he was taken from one of our boats. It was agreed that it would be good for company morale to see even a former employee rescued."

"There's a lot of fear in foreign oil patches," Case chimed in. "It's hard to get top people to work in them."

Janson kept his focus on Helms. "What was the *Amber Dawn* doing south of Isle de Foree the night it sank?"

"That's another I could have answered on the telephone. You're batting two for two."

"What was the offshore service vessel doing south of Isle de Foree where there were no oil rigs to service?"

"The *Amber Dawn* was completing a secret three-D seismic program for the Isle de Foree deepwater blocks. We had contracted a small Dutch company to conduct a seismic acquisition project, and they jury-rigged the *Amber Dawn* as a streamer three-D seismic vessel."

A surreptitious glance at Doug Case revealed a minute widening of the corporate security chief's eyes.

Janson asked, "Why didn't you just send a real one? What was the big secret?"

"I told you about our pro bono contractors two weeks ago," Case interrupted.

"You did not tell me *Amber Dawn* served an independent subcontractor."

Case leveled an angry gaze at Kingsman Helms. "Apparently that loop was above my pay level."

Janson said, "Why don't we hear Mr. Helms's version of the truth?"

Helms shrugged. "The truth is, secrecy is bred in the bone in the oil business. Has been from the start. We're selling a mysterious commodity. How much oil there appears to be at any given time dictates price, from the gas pump all the way back to reserves imagined in the ground."

"And how much you'll pay the nation that owns that ground?"

"I see where you're going with this and you are dead wrong. It's not like we were hoodwinking Ferdinand Poe."

"It's not? Who were you hoodwinking?"

"Our rivals. Other oil companies. But primarily the Chinese. It behooves us when we're guessing and hoping for a big find to keep it secret until we know for sure. Keep in mind, we are looking for oil where we are not likely to find it. But we never know. The petrological world is full of surprises."

"You're not *guessing* what's in the Isle de Foree deepwater blocks. You know already."

Helms shook his head. "I wouldn't go so far as to say that. I'll admit—in confidence—we've got reason to hope. But nothing is in the bag."

Paul Janson said, "It was enough in the bag for ASC to support both sides of the Isle de Foree civil war."

Kingsman Helms did not deny the accusation. Instead, he looked Paul Janson straight in the face and said, "The problem with the supply side of oil is a problem of accessing the resources in the ground. But a purely logistic problem becomes a political problem when governments claim access."

"That's a common corporate complaint."

"Complaining is useless until a corporation admits that governments force us to make choices in order to access the product our customers require."

"What choices did ASC make to drill for Isle de Foree's oil?"

"Survival choices," Helms answered blandly. "We at ASC are on our own in an increasingly competitive and contentious world. Gone are the days that the mere existence of American military might covered our back. We're a global corporation, but big as we are, we compete with companies that are fronts for the Chinese and Russian governments. They're not afraid of us anymore."

Helms fell silent.

Janson asked, "What survival choices did you make?"

"Everywhere we explore, the American Synergy Corporation is whipsawed between anarchistic locals and rapacious Chinese.

ASC has no choice but to cover our own back. If our government won't lead us—and I assure you they won't—we will lead the government. They don't mind taxing us, but they won't protect us. Since our government won't level the playing field, then ASC must meet the Chinese head-on by doing what we have to do to level the playing field."

"In other words, if the U.S. government won't help ASC, ASC will help itself."

"Without apology!" Helms shot back. "It's a new world, Janson. It's passed you by."

"Dr. Flannigan told me as much."

Kingsman Helms smiled patiently, as if humoring Janson. "What did the good doctor tell you?"

"He told me that ASC did not know he was aboard the *Amber Dawn*. That's why he fled. He thought you sent us to kill him."

Kingsman Helms just stared. "That is ridiculous. The man was a lunatic."

"He told me that *Amber Dawn* was secretly exploring for oil."

"I already admitted that to you."

"Two minutes ago. But since the doctor was killed, I've spoken with people who were in the rebel camp. It seems that the FFM fighters who murdered her crew were executed by Ferdinand Poe's son as punishment for going rogue."

"The least they deserved."

"But they swore with their dying breath they had been *ordered* to murder the crew."

"That's as bloody and contradictory a story as daily events in the Niger Delta."

"But if it is also a true story," said Paul Janson, "then the question is, if the FFM fighters were tricked into murdering your crew, who set them up?"

"Who's to know?" Helms shrugged. "Poe's son died in the final battle and our doctor was assassinated in Australia—on your watch. And now, if you're done telling dead men's tales, I'm going to bed. I've been flying all night."

"Sleep tight," said Doug Case.

Kingsman Helms strolled out of the Union Bar without another word.

Paul Janson said, "Doug, you look surprised."

"I never heard it laid out quite that way before."

It struck Janson that the last time he had seen Doug Case genuinely surprised—the only time—was in Ogden, Utah, when he kicked a Glock 34 out of his hand before Doug could shoot him. He studied Doug's face, trying to read him. "You weren't surprised that Flannigan no longer worked for ASC."

"I learned it recently."

"After you hired CatsPaw?"

"After."

"What about *Amber Dawn*'s mission?"

"That came as fucking news."

"No wonder you don't look happy."

Doug stared. Then he said, "Stop me if I'm wrong, but Helms essentially said, 'No witness, no crime.'"

"That's how I heard it—Hold on; he's back."

Helms rushed into the bar. "Almost forgot. Janson, we're cutting CatsPaw a check for a million dollars. You didn't exactly rescue the doctor in the end, but you tried hard. Fair enough?"

"Fair enough," said Janson.

Again, Doug Case looked surprised. Janson explained, "It will help with expenses."

Helms grinned. "Good. That way you won't feel obliged to overcharge next time we hire you."

"Wouldn't dream of it." Janson smiled back.

Helms said, "I wouldn't want you to take what I said about the new world the wrong way."

"Passing me by?"

"I may have stated it too forcefully. I'm passionate on the subject of the future. I learned when I was seven years old that leadership is not about now, it's about then. Not about the present, but the future."

"That's a big lesson at seven."

"I observed a failure of leadership when my dad took me to Greenan Oldsmobile to pick up a new car. Remember that little Olds called a Cutlass?"

"Inspired by an oil crisis." Janson nodded.

"Dad was real excited. He ordered it specially built from all the best options in the brochure, including a powerful new V-six that Oldsmobile had borrowed from the new Cadillac. We get in for a test drive with old Harry Greenan—a cagey New England Yankee. Harry gets all tight-lipped and he grumps, 'They won't build any more of these.'

"My dad asked why not: 'Wonderful car, feel this ride. Quiet, smooth, fast as heck.'

"Old Harry says, 'But you bought a big car for little-car money.'

"It was like my father had disturbed the social order, the way things had always been done. Instead of selling the blazes out of it, Olds took all the options out of the brochure. To buy such a good car you had to spend more money on a German or Japanese import.

"Oldsmobile Cutlass had been the biggest-selling car in America. Sales plummeted. Now they're out of business. It taught me that leadership is not about now; it's about the future. The future was smiling on Oldsmobile and they turned around and looked at the past. I vowed I would never make that mistake."

He turned on his heel and left.

Janson waited until he was sure Helms wasn't coming back again and said to Doug Case, "You were listening like you knew the punch line."

"Last time it was a Pontiac."

"Tell me, what did you mean, you never heard it laid out that way? Never heard what laid out that way?"

"The global corporation as buccaneer. Don't you love Helms's 'They don't mind taxing us, but they won't protect us'?"

"Gives him a lot of latitude."

"Total." Case covered his face with his hands. After a while he spread his fingers and stared between them "A million people work in U.S. intelligence. Right?"

"Give or take."

"Do you think there's room for another?"

"What do you mean?"

"I mean, do you suppose that with my credentials and your help explaining my checkered past I could go back to government service?"

"*What?*" said Janson. Now he was the one surprised. "What do you mean?"

"I'm thinking of going back to serving my country."

"And kiss good-bye flying First Class in six-thousand-dollar suits?"

"That's just stuff. I don't care about stuff. I never have— Don't get me wrong; I love my 'superchair.'" He patted the wheelchair's controls-studded arms with deep affection. "You have no idea what it means to bop around so freely when you can't. But I'll bet the Phoenix Foundation would keep me in wheelchairs if I weren't earning ASC bucks."

Janson nodded. "Count on it. Are you seriously considering leaving ASC?"

"Yes."

"Mind me asking how long you've been thinking about it?"

"Never considered it until ten minutes ago."

"Why?"

"It's a new world, like Helms said. But not one I particularly like. Our government, most governments, at least the democratic governments, are completely distracted by their new main job—propping up collapsing economies. They'll be coping with going broke for decades. That leaves a huge power vacuum. Global corporations are jumping in with all four feet."

"We've seen this building," said Janson.

"Yeah, but you and I came up in simpler times. Rogue government agencies were our villains. Bureaucrats with agendas using us like tin soldiers. Now governments are fading. The shift of wealth in our country from ordinary folks to rich people—and internationally from us to China—puts the globals in the driver's seat. I see a world coming real soon where rogue corporations are more dangerous than rogue government agencies."

Janson nodded, silently pondering a far more sinister threat: How long before rogue global corporations partnered with rogue government agencies? How long before a covert agency helped a global corporation hire mercenaries like Securité Referral to dispatch a Harrier jump jet? How long before ASC and Cons Ops swung a deal to call in a Reaper drone missile attack? If they hadn't already.

"Why don't we go next door?"

"What's next door?" asked Case.

"The Tanglin Club. We can get a better lunch than here, talk about your plans."

It was a short walk in the Singapore heat, but even Doug riding his electric chair was perspiring when they reached the cool sanctuary of the Tanglin's lobby.

"Fancy or pub?" asked Janson.

Case peered longingly into the formal Churchill Room with its plush banquettes and tables set with linen, silver, and crystal. "Pub. Something tells me I better get used to scaling down."

Janson led the way to the Tavern Bar.

Dark beams, framed prints of dogs and horses, foxhunt horns hanging from the ceiling, and a crowded bar of dedicated drinkers all spoke "England." Janson chose a table near the buffet. Chinese waiters and Malay busboys whisked away a captain's chair to make room for Case. Janson sat diagonally from him so they could speak quietly. Case looked around at the men and women arriving for lunch while Janson ordered beers.

"Heck of an ethnic mix. Like a Singapore remake of a Hollywood World War Two bomber crew."

"Old Singapore saying: Money doesn't hate."

"Money for sure. These folks look like they own the city. How'd you wangle a membership?"

"A friend put me up. . . . I have to tell you, Doug, your 'global corporation as buccaneer' is very troubling."

Case laughed. He seemed to be pulling back from their earlier intimacy and Janson regretted the change of venue. He had thought that Case would unburden himself more over lunch; now Janson realized he should have kept pressing him when he was in the mood at the American Club. He had to work him back to that mood.

"What's funny?" he asked.

"You're one yourself," said Case.

"One what?"

"A rogue. Aren't you bypassing governments with your Phoenix Foundation? Or do 'Janson Rules' give you a pass."

"They give me a clear eye."

"Yeah, right. But I find as I get older I'm less clear about so much. Then something like this comes along and I don't know what the hell to do."

"Like what comes along? Global buccaneers pushing government out of their way?"

The laughter left Case's face. He nodded grimly. "If it's true that ASC killed its own people to keep the reserve discovery secret until the war was resolved, then they're already doing it."

Janson nodded back. "If true, then we were both used."

"Don't I know it. They used me to use you to rescue the doctor so someone else could kill him."

"Who would that someone be?"

"How would I know?"

"You're ASC security chief."

Doug Case said, "Hiring killers isn't part of my job description." He shrugged, adding, "At least not yet. If they hired killers, then there must be someone else in the corporation doing that—an unofficial security guy I never met. 'Cause I sure as hell didn't hire any assassins."

"Who would they hire?"

"The world is full of reliable killers."

Janson asked the big question and watched Doug's reaction: "Do you know people at Securité Referral?"

"No. What's that?"

"Outfit I ran into."

Case looked at Janson expectantly. But it was clear that Janson did not regard this lunch as a mutual intelligence-sharing event. "Care to fill me in on them?"

"Not today."

Case shrugged, again. "Anyway, this kind of stuff has me thinking it's time for me to make a move."

"Worth thinking about," Janson agreed.

"I've thought about it." He looked around. Then he placed his hand emphatically on the wooden tabletop. "I'm leaving the fuckers."

Janson seized the opening: "Why not hang with them for a while?"

"What the fuck for? These bastards are perverting my world— You know, for the first time I sort of get what you must have felt when you started Phoenix."

"It's a big move you're talking about. A complete life changer."

"Maybe I can't change the whole world, but I can try and fix my world."

"Figuring out *where* to go will take some time. Then we'll have to put out feelers for a new job. Until you find out *where* you want to serve why don't you hang with ASC for a while longer?"

"And do what?"

"Keep an eye on things."

Doug Case gave Paul Janson a look that mingled astonished disbelief with deep admiration. "Work for you?"

"You'd be your own boss. Just stay in touch."

"You're asking me to be your mole inside ASC."

THIRTY

Stay in touch."

"Got a number I can call?"

"Quintisha Upchurch will patch you through."

"Wait a minute. Let's be clear. Information mole? Or active mole? Do you want me to spy? Or do you want me to do stuff?"

Janson said, "No offense, but considering how they've kept you out of the loops, you'd have to be pretty damned active to come up with anything spectacular."

"What's your idea of spectacular?"

"Did you send the Reapers that defeated Iboga's tank attack?"

"Paul, I am not that high up the food chain."

"Who at ASC is? Helms?"

"I don't know."

"The Buddha?"

"Could be."

"Can you find out?"

"What makes you think I haven't been trying to? It's a huge question. But I'm no closer than when I started asking."

"You know how to get ahold of me."

"Paul, what are you up to?"

Paul Janson stood up from the table. "I already signed for lunch. There's great Asian dishes at the buffet. Can you get back to the American Club on your own?"

"I got to Singapore from Houston on my own. I think I can make it back to the American Club. Where are you going?"

"Europe."

* * *

JANSON SPENT THE rest of the day on the telephone in his room upstairs at the Tanglin.

Late in the evening he went out to the airport and boarded the overnight Singapore Airlines flight to London, arriving at six o'clock in the morning Greenwich Mean Time. He passed through Immigration and Customs on his own passport and wandered Terminal 5 until he was sure he had not been followed. Suddenly he plunged into the long tunnels that connected to the Heathrow Express.

The airport train raced past highway rush-hour traffic into Paddington Station.

Janson checked again that he had no one in his wake and took a taxi across Hyde Park. He hopped out at Exhibition Road and walked circuitously to a cobblestone mews in Ennismore Gardens where he rapped a bronze griffin-shaped knocker on a sturdy black door. While he waited for sounds of stirring inside the house, he heard the echo of ironshod hooves of horses of the Household Cavalry clattering from Knightsbridge Barracks.

A tall, full-bodied woman in a sky-blue silk dressing gown threw open the door. She had shiny black skin, a regal stance, and enormous bright eyes. Her hair had been hastily stuffed under a turban that matched her dressing gown. Her full lips twitched in a smile.

"Have you any bloody idea what time it is?"

"Hoping I'm not too early for coffee."

"Breakfast, too, I suppose?"

"I'll cook the breakfast."

"Anything else?"

"Information."

"Janson, there was a time you would have jumped at 'anything else' before you asked for information."

"You're too exquisite to be rushed," said Janson, "and I am in a major rush. May I come in?"

"Princess" Mimi was the daughter of a piratical Lagos property developer who made millions erecting international hotels and luxury condos on prime public land deeded over to him by his cronies in Nigeria's government. Mimi herself was not a crook. But Mimi lived very comfortably in the house in Ennismore Gardens that would be her father's place of exile the inevitable day he had to flee prosecutors or, far more likely, the chaos of Nigeria imploding in corruption and civil war.

Among the lovers she chose to bless briefly were top men in Nigeria's army and oil ministry. She had a great gift for friendship; men she dropped still squired her around London's best restaurants and still boasted of their accomplishments, hoping to win her back, which made her a font of the sort of gossip and rumor that usually turned out to be fact. Ironically, she maintained in her larcenous father's future safe house a salon for Nigeria expatriates of every persuasion. Out-of-favor politicians, banished journalists, and revolutionaries with prices on their heads argued politics in her drawing room, vastly expanding Mimi's knowledge of West African schemes and machinations. From Lagos to Cape Town, if it happened in Africa, Princess Mimi knew it first.

"I heard you were in Angola," she remarked as she poured coffee in her immaculate tiled kitchen, which overlooked the communal gardens behind the house.

"Passing through."

"Did you enjoy the seafood?"

"Enormously."

"Do no secrets ever pass your lips?"

Janson got off the kitchen stool, stood to his full height, and kissed her on the mouth. "Not today."

"You kiss like a man in love with another woman."

"I kiss like a man in a rush. Mimi, I need help. You can give it to me. And you can help me even more if no one knows we've spoken."

Mimi smiled. "My lips will be sealed the instant you leave. What do you want?"

"Could we start with the Nigeria–Isle de Foree connection?"

"The military connection or the oil connection?"

"I thought they were the same."

Mimi smiled again. "I am testing your depth of knowledge."

She picked up a telephone, carried it out the door into the garden, and spoke rapidly. When she came back indoors she said, "I invited a couple of boys to come straight over to brunch. Do you still cook omelets?"

Janson started warming a pan on her huge AGA range and broke a dozen eggs into a bowl.

"What else?" she asked.

"Iboga. Is he possibly hiding in Nigeria?"

"Impossible. He would be brought to book. No one would protect him."

"Not even the army?"

"Iboga is toxic. Nigeria has got enough image problems on the continent without sheltering bloodthirsty dictators. We've not yet recovered from our own. And may never."

"Do people you know talk about where he might be?"

"Just talk. Sightings here and there. He's not exactly nondescript."

Janson smiled and gave her a story she would like to repeat. "An MI5 chap once told me that back when Idi Amin fled Uganda he was spotted in Saudi Arabia by a satellite."

"Iboga is fatter than Amin. And satellites are more technologically advanced today."

"What sightings have you heard about?"

"France. Romania. Bulgaria. Croatia. Russia."

"Where in Russia?"

Mimi shrugged. Her dressing gown slipped off a round shoulder.

"How about Corsica?" Janson asked.

Mimi nodded. "I heard Corsica."

"Really?"

"Just the other day, from a fellow down there on holiday. He didn't actually see him, but he heard mention."

"Where?"

Mimi shrugged again. "He was yachting. So I suppose by the sea."

"Do you know about Securité Referral?"

"No. What is it?"

"Sort of a freelance union of rogue covert agents."

"Drug smuggling?"

"Anything that makes money, I gather."

Mimi warmed oil in a pan and began sautéing whole tomatoes. Janson grated cheese and sliced bread for toast. The guests arrived,

Everest Orhii, a thin, middle-aged Nigerian in a worn blue suit and open shirt, and Pedro Menezes, a former oil minister of Isle de Foree, who was better dressed and looked extremely prosperous. Janson nodded his thanks to Mimi and murmured, "Pretty impressive on short notice."

"You already knew I was impressive," said Mimi. "Or you wouldn't have come here."

Minister Menezes gazed hungrily at the omelet Janson was dividing. Everest Orhii, the Nigerian, tore gratefully into the portion Mimi passed across the kitchen table. Both men, it turned out, were in exile, the Nigerian scraping by to spend money for lawyers in hopes of someday returning to Lagos. The Isle de Foreen was hoping to bribe his way back to Porto Clarence. Orhii had worked in the Nigerian oil ministry, though at a lower level than Menezes was at in Isle de Foree.

They each had cell phones, which were constantly ringing. Each would jump from the table, shout, "Olá!" or, "Orhii here!" and rush out to the garden for a private conversation.

"Before the civil war," Menezes told Janson, "Isle de Foree resisted jointly exploring deepwater blocks with Nigeria."

"Even though Nigeria was supporting Iboga?" asked Janson.

"The policy was initiated well before Iboga. The Nigerians had taken advantage years earlier when we were desperate. The shallow-water agreements were not fair."

"No," said Orhii, returning from the garden and redraping his napkin across his flat belly. "It was not that the agreements were not fair."

"Then what?" demanded Menezes.

Orhii swallowed a slab of toast in two bites. "Isle de Foreens dislike Nigerians. They accuse us of being overbearing. It is reflexively typical of small nations to dislike big nations. As many nations hate America, so many hate Nigeria."

"To have Nigeria as a neighbor is to sleep with a hippopotamus."

"My nation and your island are separated by two hundred miles of open gulf."

"Hippos can swim."

"They all say we are pushy!" Everest Orhii shouted. "They say that we push ahead of the line and take all we want."

Pedro Menezes's phone rang and he rushed out to the garden.

Orhii motioned Janson closer. "If you want to know about petroleum exploration in the deepwater blocks, ask Everest about the bribes he took from GRA."

"What is GRA?"

Orhii shrugged. "I don't know. Sadly, they never visited my office. I suspect they dealt directly with my superiors, however."

"Mimi?"

Mimi shook her head. "Not on my radar. Ask Pedro. He's happy to talk. He's so bored in London. He wants to go home and be oil minister again, but that will never happen. Ferdinand Poe will allow only the war veterans in his cabinet."

Mimi carried her phone out to the garden, passing Pedro Menezes on his way in.

"What is GRA?" Janson asked when Isle de Foree's ex–oil minister took his chair and addressed the remains of his omelet.

"Oh, them." Menezes smiled. "Haven't heard from them in years. Though why would I, stuck in London?"

"What are they?"

"Very generous."

"What do you mean?"

"What he means," interrupted Everest Orhii, "is that GRA paid him plenty to allow them secret access to explore deep waters south of the fields Isle de Foree was supposed to share with Nigeria."

"There was no connection," Menezes retorted disdainfully. "No Nigerian rights."

"The geology is incontrovertible. It's the same patch."

"The geology is as clear as the history and our sovereignty. They are our waters and our sea bottom. Not Nigeria's!"

"It would never stand up in court."

"It doesn't have to, now."

"You ripped us off."

Janson laid a big hand on each man's arm and said, "Gentlemen, what do the initials 'GRA' stand for?"

"Ground Resource Access," answered Menezes. "I believe."

"Believe?" snorted Everest Orhii. "You must know who gave you all that money."

"Their business cards read: 'Ground Resource Access.' I never found it listed on any exchange, however, or in any professional society."

"Ground Resource Access?" Days earlier Janson had listened to Kingsman Helms say, "The problem with the supply side of oil is a problem of accessing the resources in the ground." Coincidence? But, as Janson had told Helms, he had heard it from other oilmen. Common nomenclature.

"Was it an American company?" he asked.

"I don't know."

"Were the people you dealt with American?" he asked patiently.

"The man who called on me appeared to be American."

"What did he look like?"

"Rather like you. Fit, like a former soldier."

"Could he have been a soldier?" asked Janson, thinking perhaps GRA was a front company for a U.S. covert service.

Menezes shrugged.

"Do you recall whether his card read 'Limited' or 'Incorporated'?"

" 'Inc.' He was American. No doubt about that."

"And when was this?"

"Four years ago."

Someone was taking the long view of Kingsman Helms's assertion that "a purely logistic problem becomes a political problem when governments claim access."

Mimi returned. Janson gave her a shadow of a nod. Time to move along. He had learned all he could here. CatsPaw's freelancers could research the name.

"Finish your breakfast, my friends," said Mimi. "Thank you so much for coming."

In minutes she had them firmly out the door. "They weren't much help, were they?"

"Every bit helps. Thank you." He glanced at his watch.

"Don't rush off," said Mimi.

"I have a full schedule."

"But I have another guest for you."

"Who?"

"An angry policeman."

Janson stifled the impulse to leave. Mimi was gaming him, but with a smile that suggested she had something special in mind. "What do you mean?"

"He is a Frenchman. He held a very high position in security. He ran afoul of the French president, who was not known for treating his officers kindly. He was demoted, unfairly."

"Are you thinking he knows something about Sécurite Referral?"

"No— I mean for all I know he might, but that's not why I telephoned him."

"Then what?"

"Guess where he held his high-security post?"

"Princess!"

"Corsica."

Janson smiled back at her beaming face. "Bless you, Mimi."

"He'll be here in an hour. Would you like a shower or something? You've been on a plane all night."

"A shower would be terrific."

* * *

DOMINIQUE ONDINE HAD served most of his career on the island of Corsica, a French province, where he had battled national separatists, Union Corse mafia, and the contentious clans that warred over slights, insults, and long-simmering feuds. He was a pale-skinned man who appeared to have worked mostly indoors or at night.

"My life I give my country. My life is snatched from me by a politician."

It was still not noon, but Dominique Ondine had had several cognacs by the smell of him. Mimi poured him another, which he gripped tightly in a thick fist with scarred knuckles. Janson nursed his as they spoke across Mimi's table, which was now laden with a hamper's worth of cheese, bread, and sausages that the nearby Harrods Food Hall had wheeled to her house in a pram.

"Madam Princess informs me that you are traveling to Corsica."

"Yes, I'm meeting up with an associate there."

"I hope for your sake you are not in the business of developing property."

"Why is that?"

"Corsica teeters on the brink of anarchy. The nationalist movement protests ever more vehemently against 'colonization' by rich tourists. They hate developers seizing beachfront property for hotels."

"That shouldn't be a problem. I'm a corporate security consultant."

Ondine raised a bushy eyebrow, blinked through a haze of cognac, and gave Paul Janson a closer look. Shaved, showered, and wearing a crisp blue dress shirt borrowed from Mimi's collection, the American with the pleasant demeanor had struck the Frenchman as a banker, physician, or lawyer on a London vacation. Now Ondine wondered.

"Arson and dynamite," he told Janson, "are the Corsican's weapons of choice. Vendetta his 'court of law.' Corsicans are a people who look in, not out. Such an attitude complicates the task of guaranteeing security for outsiders who annoy them. You'll have your hands full."

Janson answered casually, although with earlier Iboga sightings neither as credible nor as current as the ex-SEAL Daniel's, he was already working up a legend to cover an operation on the island. Jessica Kincaid was there already, doing recon and feeding information back to CatsPaw. Freddy Ramirez's Protocolo de Seguridad was recruiting an exfiltration force. Quintisha Upchurch was marshaling intermediaries to lease helicopters, boats, and a freighter.

"Fortunately," Janson told Dominique Ondine, "we have contracted only to guarantee the legitimacy of foreign investors. Their physical safety falls to others."

"I don't understand."

"Your government, the French government, desires not to run afoul of EU laws against money laundering. It is my job to vet potential investors in development projects that have French government support. In other words, if a drug smuggler wants to put his illegal profits into a Corsican beachfront hotel he will fail to pass scrutiny and his money will not be allowed into the project."

"Ah. You're more of an accountant."

"Precisely," said Janson, putting on his wire-rimmed glasses.

"I repeat: Corsica teeters on the brink. If the separatists attack and you happen to be among those sipping champagne in a millionaire's holiday palace at Punta d'Oro, angry Corsicans may not honor the distinction."

"Thank you for the warning." Janson raised his glass and inclined it toward Ondine. "I will avoid the bubbly and stick to honest cognac."

Ondine smiled at last.

"Tell me," Janson asked. "In your experience, which Princess Mimi assures me is broad and deep, have you come upon an organization named Securité Referral?"

"*Non.*" Ondine cut a length of sausage, slapped it on a chunk of bread, and chewed mightily. Janson noticed Mimi's bright eyes zero in on the Frenchman. He's lying, Janson thought.

"Does the name Emil Bloch ring a bell? Possibly one of their people."

"There was a mercenary named Bloch," said Ondine. "A former Legionnaire."

"But you've not heard his name in connection with Securité Referral?"

"*Non!*"

"Another I have heard mentioned in connection with Securité Referral is a Corsican. Andria Giudicelli."

"*Merde.*" Ondine looked like he would spit on the floor if he weren't in Mimi's kitchen.

"You know him?"

"Know him? I arrested him twenty years ago."

"On what charge?"

"Corsican recycling."

"I beg your pardon? Recycling?"

A smile twitched Ondine's lips. "'Recycling is what Corsicans call arson. He burned down a rival's factory. His friends broke him out of prison and he fled. Hasn't been on Corsica since."

"Could he have joined up with Securité Referral?"

"I don't know what Securité Referral is, so how could I answer that?"

"Did I understand correctly that you are retired?" Janson asked.

Ondine finished chewing and wiped his hands on a napkin. "I do occasionally what you do—consult. It is better than sitting around."

Janson gave him a Janson Associates card. "I wonder if I might have your card so I could call on your services."

"But of course." Ondine produced a card and stood up from the table. "*Merci*, Princess. Pleasure to make your acquaintance, Mr. Janson."

"I hope to call you soon," said Janson. They shook hands.

Mimi saw the Frenchman to the door and came back. Janson was shrugging into his jacket.

"Where are you going?"

"As I told the man, Corsica."

"He lied about Securité Referral."

"I believe so."

"Why?"

"Either he's heard of it and fears it or he works for it. From what I've seen, he's the type they look for: sharp, professional, connected, and on the edge. On the other hand, he's a bit over the hill."

"Why didn't you question him further?"

"Because he would not expect such questioning from an 'accounting fellow.' "

"But you will follow up?"

Janson kissed her on the cheek. "You have been wonderful. As always."

THIRTY-ONE

A fire-gutted hotel was the first sight to greet Paul Janson as he steered a motor yacht he had chartered in nearby Sardinia into Porto-Vecchio, a sailing and tourist town that occupied a deep indentation in the rocky southeast coast of Corsica. Shattered windows gaping like dead eyes, walls blackened by smoke, the burned-out twelve-story tower stood grim sentinel over the gleaming boats that crowded the inner harbor. Spray paint graffiti reading "*Resistenza!*" and "*Corse pour Corsicans*" left no doubt how the fire had ignited.

He left the yacht in charge of its captain and walked into the town, watching the narrow streets and sidewalks in the reflections of luxury shop windows, trading imperceptible nods with the muscular proprietor of a dive shop, and stopping briefly at the speedboat dock of a company that offered parasail rides. As he left the waterfront, he paused to look at the hotel. Workmen boarding up the ground-floor windows were banging industriously with hammers and nails, but the cleaners removing the graffiti were trading conspiratorial grins and not scrubbing very hard.

Janson hailed a taxi. It took him up into the hills, through tiny villages, past quarries, olive groves, and empty houses. The French language on bilingual road signs had been painted over and he saw "Corsican National Liberation Front" scrawled on a house that had its roof blown off. SR could do worse than hide Iboga here; restive islanders were not the sort to inform the police about a man on the run.

Janson got out of the taxi at a village café in an ancient stone building and asked the driver to come back in an hour. A patio shaded by a canopy presented views in two directions, turquoise water, east, and rugged mountains to the west. He could see the harbor far, far below opening into the Tyrrhenian Sea, the hundred-mile stretch of water between Corsica and Italy, and up a narrow road switch-backing down from the mountains. Scents of lavender and myrtle wafted off the sun-baked brushy land. The café was nearly empty midafternoon, and Janson had the patio to himself. He ordered a *quatre fromage* pizza and a glass of Ajaccio rosé and was just finishing the soft, oiled crust and peppery wine when he heard the high-pitched rasp of a powerful machine driven to the max.

Down the mountain road flew a red Ducati 848 sportbike.

One guess, Janson thought grimly, who was driving at that break-neck pace, though he could not help admiring her skill. Boots, knees, and thighs married tightly to the machine, torso levering independently, Kincaid was reading the bends in the narrow road, braking ahead of the corners, throttling early to maximize the engine's gyroscopic and load-transfer effects, and accelerating smoothly out of them. But formidable skills aside, Janson knew she was pushing the limits of physics and luck. One mistake would flip her fatally end over end into the brush, and he had to wonder whether the near-suicidal speed meant that Kincaid was still so freaked out by the Australia catastrophe that she was pushing herself too hard to make up for it.

The Ducati whipped out of the final turn, throttle blipping a series of high-rev downshifts, braked hard, and stopped in front of the café. Kincaid, clad boot to helmet in black deerskin and festooned with high-power Swarovski field glasses and a Canon digital camera with a foot-long lens, heaved the bike onto its centerstand and swaggered onto the patio. A dog-eared copy of the British Ornithologists' Union's *Birds of Corsica* tossed on the table adjoining Janson's explained the surveillance gear.

She removed her helmet, spiked her fingers through her hair, and glanced at Janson—one single tourist appraising another. Janson played his role with an expression of sincere interest. She ordered a pizza and a glass of wine, mimicking the local u Corsu dialect well enough to elicit an appreciative smile from the café's waitress.

When they were alone on the patio, Kincaid said, "Stop looking at me like that. I'm all right, just lettin' off steam."

"Glad to hear it, and deeply relieved that they've suspended Newton's Law of Gravity—so what do you think of Corsica?"

"Corsica's like down home. I thought I was back in Red Creek with all their feudin' 'n' fightin'. Of course, if you're not agin' 'em, folks are as nice as nice can be. Specially out in the mountains. Beautiful mountains. Wow. Then you come around a bend in the road and there's this turquoise-blue ocean jumping up at you and white sand beaches as far as you can see. Might be fun to come back sometime, when we're not working."

"Hard to picture you sitting still on a beach."

"I meant rock climbing."

"Is Iboga here?"

"Looks that way. But he's moving around a lot." She opened her bird guide to a blank "Notes" page and hurriedly sketched a map of Corsica. The island, a hundred miles long and fifty wide, looked like a hand closed in a fist with the index finger pointing north. "They started him up here on Capo Corso. Freddy thinks they came in from Italy by boat. Then they seemed to move him down into these mountains down the middle. But I lost them. Now Freddy's guys think he's on this private peninsula near Vallicone. That's here, up the coast from Porto-Vecchio. Freddy's absolutely convinced that's where he's at."

"Why?"

"It's a damn fortress."

THIRTY-TWO

Jessica Kincaid flipped the page in her bird guide and drew a
map of the peninsula thrusting into the Tyrrhenian Sea.

"Fifty-foot cliffs all around, so we can't come on a boat,
nowhere to land. Might do it in a little inflatable into a tiny crack of
a fishing cove—though we'd need a fisherman to guide us in—then
climb the cliffs. But how do we get him down without a damned
derrick? Can't helicopter in—they got radar."

"Radar?"

"Whoever is there is scared the locals think they're resort developers. So if it is SR, it's kinda ironic that they're hiding Iboga
on an island that is a powder keg where all outsiders are suspect. Rumor has it SR is developing the peninsula into a gigantic
resort. They have pissed off Corsican separatists, Union Corse
mafia, the poor fishermen they ousted, and the ecologists, who
tend to get pretty violent in France. I hear they've declared war
on the French government and the superrich. From what I've

seen I don't blame them—this is the kind of place money destroys."

"What you're saying is no one in the government is stopping whoever owns the peninsula from defending themselves."

"They can hold off an army, but just in case, they also have their own helicopter with long-range tanks. So if they are SR and they do have Iboga, they could make it easy to France or Italy if they had to run for it."

"What about the road?"

"Not without tanks." She drew a line up the spine of the peninsula. "This is the only road. They got it enfiladed here and here, with stone guardhouses. I scoped out a Dushka in the one nearest the main road."

"A Dushka? Looks like they're taking the separatists pretty seriously." The DShK ("Dushka") was a .50-caliber heavy machine gun capable of wreaking fatal destruction on any military target in the air or on the ground, short of a tank.

"I'll bet SR thinks the separatists pose a bigger threat than little old you and me. Anyway, the machine guns tipped it for Freddy."

"It fits SR's way of doing things," Janson agreed. "Strong position, but ready to jump."

Kincaid planted a finger on the southeast coast. "They can jump anywhere from here. Across the Strait of Bonifacio is Sardinia, where you chartered your boat. How long did it take you?"

"Twenty minutes to cross the strait. A couple of hours to here."

"Sardinia belongs to Italy. SR seems plenty comfortable crossing borders. Maybe they're going there next. Ten, fifteen ships a day pass through the strait. They could put Iboga on one of them. Or they could settle into that Vallicone peninsula, or come down here to Porto-Vecchio. Look at those boats down in the harbor."

Hundreds of motor yachts and bluewater sailboats packed the

harbor, moored cheek by jowl in the many marinas. Several ships stood by the outer piers. Seagoing ferries were arriving from Naples and Marseille.

"They could stash Iboga on one of those big-bucks yachts—take him anywhere in the Mediterranean. Which one is yours?"

"The little hundred-footer at the end of that long row of big ones."

"Yeah, well, you can see this is the big-bucks hangout for rich Europeans."

"Iboga's rich."

"I'm thinking maybe they've been headed here all along, just being cagey about it. There's like gated estates in the hills and giant yachts in the harbor. There's a bunch of privately owned islands off Bonifacio, including at least one everybody says belongs to the Mafia. If you're going to ground in luxury, this is the spot."

Over the turquoise Tyrrhenian Sea came the rumble of heavy engines. Janson spotted the familiar high-wing silhouettes of a fleet of camouflage-green turboprop C-160 Transalls approaching the coast at two thousand feet.

"French Foreign Legion," Kincaid explained. "Deuxième Régiment Étranger des Parachutistes has rapid-intervention units barracked up north at Calvi."

An orange smoke flare began burning on the beach. Kincaid scoped it with her field glasses.

"It's an exercise. There's brass observing."

As they watched, the airborne Legionnaires jumped, spreading behind the planes in tight formation. They plummeted nearly to the ground. Seconds after they opened their parachutes, they hit the sand.

"Very nice," said Janson.

Kincaid passed him her field glasses. "Look how they bunch on the beach."

The paratroopers were free of their chutes and aiming assault rifles at their objective—a truck on top of which stood a sergeant glaring at his hand. Janson couldn't see it, but he knew it had to be a stop watch.

" 'Hard Training—Easy War,' " said Kincaid. "Legion motto."

"Where'd you hear that?"

"I had a glass of wine with their colonel."

"Really? ..." He looked at her. "Did the colonel express an opinion about the Vallicone peninsula?"

"I did not think Iboga was a subject to raise with a French officer."

"Roger that," said Janson. He checked his watch and stared at the maps Kincaid had drawn.

She said, "I've got Freddy and his boys holding the fort at Vallicone—awaiting the word from you."

"I've got helicopters on call and fast boats on a freighter standing by in the Bonifacio Strait. What I don't have is proof Iboga is on that peninsula."

Kincaid tapped her map. "To me, these machine guns say Iboga's there. So do the radar and the helicopters. We have to hit them fast, before they move him."

"If we raid the peninsula and he's not there, we end up in a shooting war with some outfit that feels strongly enough about its security to mount machine guns, radar, and helicopters."

"We can't just sit around while they whisk him out from under our noses."

"I want to know more before I commit to a raid that could turn into an ugly mistake."

"We have to do something."

"We'll start by getting you out of that leather. Go down to Porto-Vecchio and buy some clothes."

"It's a Eurotrash town. The shops only sell slutwear."

"Slutwear will be most appropriate."

"Come again?" Kincaid asked with a dangerous glint in her eye.

Janson opened his wallet and showed her an engraved invitation.

"The Ministry of Economic Affairs, Industry and Employment and Agence Développement Economique de la Corse request the pleasure of Janson Associates' company at a champagne reception for investors in a hotel and condo consortium."

"Where'd you get that?"

"Friend in Paris. There'll be deep-pockets developers and a bunch of French business elite. Someone ought to have the lowdown on a valuable piece of real estate like Vallicone peninsula. We'll do our act and nail down some intelligence we can count on."

"Which act?"

"Rich old corporate security consultant hired to protect Agence Développement Economique de la Corse from criminals who launder money through legitimate projects—accompanied by trophy girlfriend masquerading as personal assistant."

"Which part do you play?"

"Meet me at the yacht. It's called *Tax Free*."

Kincaid nodded, still impatient, but liking the new challenge. "Where's the plane?" she asked.

Janson looked at his watch again. "Ed and Mike should be taking off from Zurich just about now," he assured her. "They'll be landing at Figari Airport in two hours." He knew she wasn't asking about the Embraer. She meant where was her favorite rifle?

* * *

JANSON COMMANDEERED *Tax Free*'s flying bridge to make phone calls. High above the water, the outside steering station on the roof of the motor yacht's wheelhouse offered a view of the crowded marina, Porto-Vecchio's harbor, and the sun-washed houses of the town, and privacy from the crew scrubbing decks, polishing chrome, varnishing brightwork, and vacuuming carpets.

Quintisha Upchurch reported that everything he had requisitioned was in place. "Including the decoy, though I must say the Russians were really prickly about it. It would have been easier to get one of your arms dealers to sell us a real one."

Janson confirmed names, numbers, and details, and she closed by saying, "Mr. Case called. He said to tell you he had been 'underground' and that you would know what he meant."

"Thank you, Quintisha, talk to you soon."

Janson returned Case's call eagerly. "Underground" would be Doug's jokey code for "mole."

"What's up?" he asked when Case answered.

Case said, "I'm not sure what this means, but Kingsman Helms has been badmouthing the hell out of Acting President Poe. I get the impression he's raising sentiment in the company against him."

"To what purpose?" asked Janson.

"You're asking me to guess?"

"You're in ASC's Houston HQ," said Janson. "I am not."

"My best guess? Helms is laying the groundwork to turn ASC against Poe."

"To what end?"

"Backing a replacement."

"Interesting," said Janson. "That will bear some thinking. How are things otherwise?"

"Personally, I'm itching to get out of here."

"Hang in there," said Janson. "Let all this play out. Any luck with the Reaper connection?"

"No. And I'm not expecting any. It would be a personal connection—strictly one-to-one—retired officer in private work paying a ton of dough or promising a brilliant future to a serving officer."

"That is obvious," said Janson. "Keep poking. What do you know about GRA?"

"Rings a bell. Sort of. Can't place it. What does it stand for?"

"Ground Resource Access."

"That's oil talk."

"Yes, but could it be a company name?"

"Who knows?"

"I'm asking you."

"I'll get back to you on that. Where are you?"

"London. But call Quintisha. I'm probably heading out of here."

"Talk to you."

* * *

DOUG CASE SAID good-bye to Paul Janson and hung up smiling.

Cons Ops had trained them how to lie. Glibly. Effortlessly. There wasn't a lie detector or voice analyzer invented they couldn't fox. He had been one of the best. Janson, per usual, *the* best. So damned good that Doug Case was half-inclined to believe that Janson really was in London—even though he knew beyond any doubt that Paul Janson was in Porto Vecchio on the island of Corsica.

THIRTY-THREE

Jessica Kincaid stalked into *Tax Free*'s salon wearing six-inch spike heels and white vintage Capri pants low on her hips. The iridescent clutch in her hand was barely big enough to hold a cell phone and a knife, and it was a mystery to Janson how a silk handkerchief had been reengineered as a halter top.

"How do I look?"

"Young enough to be carded by a responsible bartender— Wait a minute! No, you don't. Where are your muffin tops?"

Kincaid cast a wintery eye at the bared swell of her hips. "I don't have muffin tops."

"But teenagers do. You don't look chubby enough to pass for my teenage girlfriend."

"Russian girls are the main competition for rich dudes in this town. We ain't gonna see no muffin tops at that party."

As they started to leave, Janson's phone rang.

"One second. This guy's returning my call." He said hello, listened briefly, and covered the phone.

"What's up?" asked Kincaid.

"Did you tell me that Van Pelt was wearing shorts when you tangled with him in Cartagena?"

"He was pretending he was a boat bum."

"Did he have a tattoo on his leg?"

"No. Why?"

"Sydney Harbour Patrol found a shark-bit leg. But it had a tattoo, a big snake wrapped around his leg."

"Jesus H ... Going up the leg? Or down?"

"You know, I didn't ask."

"Either way, it's not his."

"Then it's possible your boy's still in business."

* * *

THE RECEPTION WAS held on a four-hundred-foot mega-yacht— *Main Chance* of Hong Kong—moored stern-to at the marina's outermost pier. A ballroom opened onto a vast deck, on which most of the hundred guests had gathered, since the evening was warm and the sky clear and the band inside too loud. The intense evening sun illuminated the stone and stucco houses on the surrounding hills, a startlingly pretty sight marred by the blackened remains of the burned out hotel.

As Janson had expected, he was not the only man at the party accompanied by a young girlfriend, publicist, or personal assistant. They accepted champagne from a passing waitress wearing even less than Kincaid, pretended to sip it, and went to work. Kincaid acted as roper, catching the attention of deeply tanned middle-aged men wearing gold, Janson stepping in to introduce themselves as, "Paul Janson, Janson Associates—my colleague Ms. Kincaid." When the men spoke only French, Janson let Kincaid translate, although he usually understood most of what they were saying.

The fire-gutted building offered an easy opening and the words "security consultant" were greeted by remarks along the lines of, "You'll be busy here, you can see," and, "They've got this overly green attitude in Corsica about the coastline."

Janson and Kincaid heard complaints from some about the scarcity of opportunity: "Corsicans hate selling property. They think without a house they're not a Corsican." Others reveled in the value such scarcity produced. Nonetheless, "housing prices," they were told repeatedly, "are still cheaper than the Riviera."

Jessica swooped into a scrum of rich old men draped in jewelry and engaged them in conversation. Janson cruised some more and was told several times that the market was starting to take off.

"Big villas run a million to two million euros on Corsica. Double that here in Porto-Vecchio."

"Now's the time to swing a big deal," a transplanted Atlanta, Georgia, developer assured him.

Jessica snagged an elderly Frenchman. Suntanned and covered in age spots, he had yellow teeth, a pound of gold around his neck, and a four-carat emerald dangling from his left ear.

"Monsieur Lebris," she told Janson, "is under the impression that you are my father."

Janson returned Lebris's curt nod and told Kincaid, "Monsieur Lebris is *hoping* I am your father."

"Monsieur Lebris invests in land around Vallicone."

"Wonderful," said Janson. "Please use your excellent French to tell him that I said that several of our clients have expressed interest in that area. Too bad the peninsula is not for sale."

Kincaid translated.

Lebris shook his head emphatically and replied in a torrent of French too rapid for Janson to understand.

"What did he say?"

"The peninsula is not necessarily not for sale. It is currently under a short-term lease and the owners, an 'ancient' family in Paris, just might sell for the right price."

"Rented?"

"Rented fits SR's pattern," Kincaid observed quietly to Janson. "Keep moving. They're gypsies. No fixed base. Just like us."

Lebris spit a sudden oath and pointed angrily at the shore. A gang of agile separatists was draping a huge sail from the roof of the burned-out hotel. Dripping letters of red paint spelled:

RESISTENZA!

CORSE POUR CORSICANS

ÉTRANGÈRE ALLER LOIN

FLNC

The party fell silent, but for the beat of the band inside the ballroom. Lebris cursed, "*Terroriste!*," rushed to the railing, and shook his fist.

" 'Foreigners, get lost!' " Jessica translated. "FLNC is the Corsican National Liberation Front."

"I like their style. These people could be a big help."

"For a diversion?"

"If we can find a way to do it without getting them shot."

"They seem capable of looking out for themselves." Three masked men were rappelling rapidly down the side of the building like professional mountaineers. Swiftly responding squads of gendarmerie and agents of the Direction de la Surveillance du Territoire found the narrow streets blocked by a trio of abandoned trucks. In the confusion a jet-black cigarette boat roared up to the jetty. The separatists leaped aboard and the high-speed craft raced toward the darkening east, leaving patrol boats in its wake.

Kincaid said, "A big fire would do the job. The Legion colonel told me that the brush is so flammable that his trainees are only allowed to dry-fire their rifles."

"A French cop told me arson is Corsica's national pastime. Any thoughts about wangling an introduction to FLNC? I doubt your friend the colonel is on friendly terms with any arsonists."

Kincaid looked around the deck. The guests had turned their backs on the burned-out hotel and the party had resumed as if nothing had happened. "Doubt these folks know any."

Janson glanced at the gangway up which guests were still arriving and got a surprise. "Speaking of the devil."

"Where?"

Janson directed her attention across the deck. "The pale Frenchman."

"The one who looks rich or the one who looks like a cop?"

"Ex-cop," said Janson. "I met him in London. Dominique Ondine."

"What's he doing here?"

"I don't know. He was head of security here until he got transferred for pissing off the president of France."

Ondine glided through the party with the self-assurance of a man carrying a warrant and a gun.

"What does he want?" asked Kincaid. "Money?"

"Let's hope so."

They exchanged nods across the crowd as Ondine drew near. He looked Jessica up and down, glanced at the other scantily clad young women, and said to Janson, "I see you've adopted the local custom."

"My associate Ms. Kincaid," said Janson.

Ondine bowed over Kincaid's hand. "Mademoiselle."

Janson said, "I didn't expect to see you so soon."

"I imagine you didn't."

"Are you looking for work?" he asked, explaining to Kincaid, "Monsieur Ondine is a private security consultant."

"Like you," said Ondine.

"Forensic accounting?" asked Kincaid.

The Frenchman smiled. He had not been drinking cognac, not today, thought Janson. "Nothing so intellectual," said Ondine. "More the sort of security that involves weapons."

"Not our thing," said Janson.

"Mr. Janson, I've reconsidered your question about Securité Referral."

"Why?" asked Janson, watching him carefully, while Kincaid scoped the party for Ondine's backup.

"Why? If there is such an animal as an honest policeman, it is I."

Paul Janson told Dominique Ondine, "I want to know why a man who calls himself 'an honest policeman'—and is a *retired* honest policeman at that—followed me all the way to Corsica at his own expense."

Dominique Ondine indicated the burned-out hotel with the red-lettered protest sail flapping from the roof. "The fire was last week. Only the latest incident. Empty villas have been shot up, their owners' Mercedes bombed while they're away, their boats sunk."

"You told me that in London. Corsica's a powder keg. Separatists, Union Corse mafia, poor fishermen, and environmentalists. Not Securité Referral."

"To be sure," Ondine agreed. "Arson and vendetta are endemic in Corsica. Corsicans routinely take matters into their own hands."

"You told me that in London, too. You also told me that you had never heard of SR. May I ask you again? Is Securité Referral a Corsican organization?"

"*Non.*"

"Then what is the connection? You're baffling me, Monsieur Ondine."

"Securité Referral thrives under such lawlessness."

Janson and Kincaid exchanged smiles visible only to them. SR thrived among the lawless? So did CatsPaw.

"Continue, monsieur," Janson said brusquely. "What do you want from me?"

"Work. The consulting business is slow."

"Can you give me information that will help me fight Securité Referral?"

"Do accountants fight?" Ondine smiled.

"Don't get cute," said Kincaid.

Ondine looked at her sharply. Kincaid stared back.

The Frenchman dropped his gaze. "I cannot give you such information."

"Can't or won't?" asked Janson.

"I cannot. I do not know it. But if I could, I would not. I am not inclined to suicide."

"At least we agree that you know of them."

"A little. Securité Referral is international, but it was conceived by French intelligence officers—servants of their country turned criminal—who learned their trade spying in Russia. Now it is everyone— Russians, Serbs, Croats, Africans, Chinese. That is all I can tell you."

"There is something else you can do for me."

"Name it."

Janson nodded at the burned-out hotel. "Do you see the sign they hung from the roof?"

"Of course."

"By midnight tonight, I want a secure meeting with the operators who hung that sign."

"You're not serious. The separatists are my enemies. As a policeman I hunted them."

"You better believe he's serious," said Kincaid. "If you work for us, when you see a job that needs doing you do it. This meeting job needs doing. You're the man. Set up the meeting."

Ondine swallowed hard. "What may I offer them to come?"

"Money."

"How much?"

"One million euros."

Ondine gasped. "One million euros to come to a meeting?"

"No. One million if they do the job."

"What job?"

"The job they'll learn about at the meeting."

"What is my cut?"

"Ten percent finder's fee. After they do the job."

"I will do my best."

"Midnight," said Janson.

"And when we leave this party," said Kincaid, "tell those two cops moonlighting as waiters not to follow us."

THIRTY-FOUR

The only problem with heroin was getting it. With a consistent supply it was a very fine drug. Snort it and nothing ever hurt, particularly when a man's brain spun every day of his life like a turbine, always at full speed, consuming his mind and soul and spirit faster than Abrams battle tanks burned kerosene. Heroin put the brakes on for a moment, long enough to recharge and come out swinging. It helped not to have an addictive nature and it was vital to understand that only losers shot up with needles. Many in the veterans hospital spiraled down from lesser drugs into heroin. He had ascended.

It was night. Almost.

Doug Case had been talking nonstop on his sat phone since the sun was high in the sky. Seated in his wheelchair, staring out his office window at the sea of electric lights that the vast, powerful city of Houston spread from horizon to horizon, he felt neither pain nor anxiety but increasingly in charge of what had started out as a bad situation.

His phone rang. He answered, saying, "Did you get the plane?"

"C-160 Transall twin-engine turboprop."

"What color?"

"Well, there's a little problem with that. It's camo, like you asked, but blue."

"I told you camo green."

"Yeah, but—"

"Camo green! I don't care how you do it. Paint it or get another one. Camo green. Standing by tomorrow."

Case stabbed END. He weighed the relaxing prospect of doing a line or two against the possibility of nodding off at a crucial moment. He decided not to. Drugs were not addictive. Losers were.

He endured ten full minutes of quiet and was sick of the lack of action when his phone finally rang again. He guessed who it was before he checked the screen and was right. The Voice. Clockwork, every five days. He doubted that the caller recognized his own pattern.

"Hello, Strange Voice," Case answered. "How are you tonight? If it is night where you are."

"You sound very chipper, Douglas. How are you?"

The caller's voice was disguised. The sound emitted by his telephone was digitally morphed by a voice transformation system originally developed for psychological warfare and to fool voiceprint ID systems. Case recalled it from his early days at Cons Ops. Digitization, miniaturization, new understanding of articulatory position, and software advances from VTS1 to VTS14.8 had improved it mightily. It enabled the caller to change timbre, transpose pitch, add confusing vibrato and tremolo—even capture and synthesize signals to generate impersonations. The Voice could sound like a robot. He could sound like a little girl. He could sound like Jon Stewart or Hillary Clinton. Tonight he sounded like a cross between Stewart and WALL•E.

The Voice's phone line was secure. It revealed nothing to Case about his identity or where he was calling from. Nor, Case presumed, did the caller necessarily know where he was, such was the anonymity of cells and sat phones. The difference was that if The Voice asked for Case's location he would reveal it immediately. While Case would not dream of asking where the caller was.

Case presumed the caller was from within the American Synergy Corporation, high in management—one of the vipers, most likely—or on the board of directors, or the mysterious Buddha himself. Though he could be from outside the corporation, he had a very clear concept of what was going on inside it. Case had received his first call two years ago. "You were the most talented covert officer ever to serve your country," The Voice had flattered him. "Serve me and be rewarded."

Their relationship had already made Case the wealthiest man he knew and, he suspected, a man with a golden future if he stayed loyal, obedient, useful, and discreet.

"I *am* chipper, thank you, sir. What can I do for you?"

"I want a member of Ferdinand Poe's circle replaced."

"By whom?"

"First create the vacancy."

"When?"

"Soon. Be prepared."

"Who?"

The Voice named Ferdinand Poe's chief of staff, Mario Margarido.

The steady Margarido was the glue that held Ferdinand Poe's

ramshackle new government together while it struggled to repair infrastructure and right the economy of the war-torn island. With Margarido suddenly gone, the acting president's only strength left would be his spy turned security chief, Patrice da Costa, and his own formidable will. Case wondered if The Voice was planning a coup. To ask would be presumptuous. Better to remain loyal, useful, obedient, and discreet.

"Do you have any preference how Margarido is removed?"

"It would be best not to have him machine-gunned in public."

Case recognized the studied sort of dry sense of humor calculated to flatter the knowledgeable listener on his sophistication and to pass on additional information without saying it aloud

"Beyond that limitation, use your best judgement. The least suspicion the better, but a soupçon of doubt will keep others guessing."

It sounded very much like a coup. "I'll take care of it. As soon as you want it done."

"I will give you word when the time comes. Will you farm it out to SR?"

Case hesitated. "I'm not sure. Events have sped up. Surprisingly."

"Do you sense a problem with SR?"

This time Case did not hesitate. There was a fine line between obedience and partnership. Trust spawned partnership, and whoever The Voice was, Case's long-term hope was to become his partner. Money was one thing—a fine thing—but power was another on a whole higher scale. Case answered honestly, admitting his worst fear about contracting Securité Referral to perform black work.

"My original impression of SR was that of a criminal cartel of top-notch ex-operatives who accept the value of submitting to an independent, stand-alone operation that answers only to itself."

In the interest of stoking an atmosphere of partnership, Doug Case paused to let The Voice lead their conversation. The Voice jumped right in with a second dose of dry humor.

"Qualities that only the best corporations demand. They sound wonderful. What's the problem?"

"My one worry was that they might see Isle de Foree as a transit base for South American drugs smuggled to Europe. Would they seize the opportunity to create a narco-state?"

"A natural concern. Nonstate actors are certainly the future. Launch a fleet of retired 727s to fly the Atlantic between Latin America and Isle de Foree, transit cocaine and weapons to West Africa, then across the Sahara into Europe. It's only a matter of time until organized crime claims a nation."

"But I expected that once ASC took control of Isle de Foree we'd have no trouble stopping SR from acting."

"Eliminating competition is a perk, shall we say, of dominating a sovereign nation. He who dominates first wins. What has changed?"

"SR has changed. They're more ambitious."

"Or did you underestimate them?" The Voice, Case knew from their conversations, could wield language like a knife between the ribs.

"Frankly, I did underestimate SR. I failed to ask how SR happened to be on the scene, already. I thought they were just supplying mercenary trainers."

"When," demanded The Voice, "did you realize that you had underestimated them?"

"When they rescued Iboga."

"I was under the impression that we—that you—had hired

SR to rescue Iboga. I thought that was rather slick on your part."

"I wish I could take credit for the rescue. But I cannot. It's clear now that SR convinced Iboga ahead of time that he might need rescuing. And it is clear, too, that SR has all along seen Iboga as their best bet to own Isle de Foree. They rescued him to reinstall him in a future coup."

"I am beginning to understand," the Voice said, "why you sense a problem with Securité Referral."

"I'm afraid they smell the potential of Isle de Foree's petroleum reserve."

"Goddamned right they do! Did it ever occur to you that SR took the *Amber Dawn* job to keep the reserve discovery quiet for them, too?"

"Belatedly, sir."

"Oil is a hell of a lot more valuable than drugs. Oil is the foundation of a legitimate state. Narcocracies are pariah nations, shunned, sanctioned, preached against. But no sovereign nation that exports oil will ever be treated like a pariah. No matter how much so-called legitimate states bitch and complain to the United Nations."

Doug Case did not reply. He could only hope at this juncture that silence would work his will.

The Voice said, "If you engage SR to take out Poe's chief of staff, SR will know ahead of time the precise moment they'd have the best shot of taking over."

"From under our noses," Case agreed, seizing the opportunity to inject the word "our."

"The last thing we want is a goddamned coup we didn't organize. You better engage someone else to remove the chief of staff."

"You're absolutely right, sir," said Case.

By playing it straight, by admitting his mistakes, by allowing, encouraging, goading The Voice to parade a superior intellect, Case had won a "we."

"I presume that a former covert officer with your background who has maintained his contacts has another crew in mind."

"Standing by."

THIRTY-FIVE

A hundred feet above the Tyrrhenian Sea on a moonless night Paul Janson could not see the cable that tethered his parachute to the RIB churning toward the Vallicone peninsula, nor could he see the rubber boat itself, though he could see the frothy white propeller wash spewed by its muffled engine.

Daniel, the former SEAL, was driving. The Corsican helping Daniel steer around the rocks, Adolfo, was a fisherman who was wearing patched blue jeans, ragged sneakers, and the first expensive, brand-new garment he had owned in his life, a light-absorbent Gore-Tex windbreaker black as midnight, a gift from CatsPaw Associates. Adolfo knew where the rocks lay just below the waves, making him currently the most valuable of the twenty men Janson had recruited to snatch Iboga from Securité Referral.

Janson no longer doubted that Iboga was holed up on the peninsula. Nationalist separatists already plotting an attack in the mistaken belief that the new residents were building a gated resort had reported at yesterday's midnight meeting that they had seen Isle de Foree's deposed president for life angrily pacing the grounds of the main house. *Sanglier gigantesque*, they had described him. A giant wild boar.

Janson kept his attack plan simple: a classic razzle-dazzle to give the SR operators guarding Iboga a strong motive to retreat, first by destroying their outer defenses—the machine-gun positions blocking the road—next by taking away their ability to escape with Iboga, their helicopter, and finally, before they hunkered down to fight like cornered rats, by puting terror in their hearts so they would scatter, deserting Iboga in a chaotic every-man-for-himself rout.

The passenger harness dangling beside Janson held a deep wicker basket that carried his weapons: a pump shotgun; a beautiful old matte-black Bushmaster rented from the Porto-Vecchio family of Union Corse; and two rocket propelled grenade launchers supplied by Neal Kruger's man on the island.

A soft *tsk* in Janson's headset told him Kincaid was in position with the outer blockhouse in her sights, waiting for the first explosion.

* * *

At the point where the Vallicone peninsula began its mile-long perpendicular thrust from the shore into the sea, two strong Corsicans dragged a large black duffel bag through the dense brush, stirring aromas of lavender, rosemary, and thyme from snapping twigs. They navigated in the dark by keeping the rumble of breaking waves to their left and the stiff offshore wind in their faces and prayed that the noise of wind and sea would prevent the guards with their .50-caliber machine guns from hearing them.

These two Corsicans were familiar with every hectare of the

quarter-mile-wide peninsula, from these fields to the higher ground at the seaward end where the main house, outbuildings, and broad lawns perched on the cliffs. Born and raised nearby, they had poached game on the peninsula since they were boys with the same shotguns they had strapped to their backs. When, at a distance of three hundred meters, they saw the faint silhouette of the first stone hut that guarded the single-track road, they unzipped their duffel bag and spread out the contents: a high-capacity gasoline-powered air pump and a large sheet of plastic fabric that looked like the makings of a tent but was in fact an inflatable decoy.

* * *

"Go!" JANSON SAID into his lip mike.

Daniel opened the throttle and the RIB increased speed. Janson felt the parachute rise higher, whisking him above the loom of the land. He tugged the elevator lines attached to the lifting slots in back of the canopy and it shot up another hundred feet.

He pulled his panoramic digital sensor fusion/enhanced night-vision goggles over his eyes. The surface of the peninsula appeared green, the radar dome a dull circle, the house and the helicopter darker. He saw a flicker of tiny bright figures—the infrared enhancement of flesh and blood.

SR fighters were running from the house to the helicopter.

Janson found it hard to believe that Securité Referral's radar was sensitive enough to detect the almost nonexistent targets presented by the parasail and his body. More likely, a guard had stepped outside the house and heard the RIB's motor. But whatever it was had raised the alarm.

Janson drew a grenade launcher from the basket beside him.

Choppier seas near the cliffs were rocking the boat and jerking the towline. The parachute shook. He targeted the helicopter and fired. The flash from the fiery rocket motor ignition reflected on the thirty-foot canopy of parachute cloth above his head. The high-explosive fragmentation warhead dropped short of the helicopter and exploded on the ground.

He had missed a direct hit and could only hope that the flying fragments of shrapnel that scattered the fighters had put some serious holes in the helicopter. Janson dropped the empty launcher into the sea and grabbed the second. The SR fighters stopped running, scanned the sky, having been alerted by the flash, and started firing pistols and bullpup rifles in his direction.

* * *

THE CORSICANS IN charge of inflating the decoy did not hesitate when they heard Janson's first grenade, though now came the dangerous part, starting the noisy gas-powered air pump. They positioned the exhaust pipe facing away from the blockhouse, stood in front of it to further muffle the racket, crossed themselves, loosened their shotguns, and jerked the start cord.

The motor started on the first pull. It didn't sound as loud as they had feared and the plastic began to inflate. In seconds, it ballooned into the massive shape of a full-size T-90 battle tank. Invented by the Russian Army to confuse enemy reconnaissance satellites and intelligence operators on the ground, the decoy's plastic fabric was impregnated with chemicals that reflected targets to both radar and thermal-imaging devices.

They felt in the dark for the tie-downs and knotted them around shrubs before the wind could pick the thing up and blow it away. When the Corsicans were sure they had it securely tied down, they slithered away through the brush, putting as much distance as they could between themselves and the balloon.

* * *

THE SERB MERCENARIES guarding Securité Referral's first block-house had no radar repeater in their position, but they had thermal imaging and night glasses and a night scope for their Dushka.

What they saw three hundred meters out in the dark was the chilling silhouette of a Russian T-90 battle tank complete with a 135mm smoothbore cannon jutting from its turret. Lesser men would have run for their lives. These were Serbs with long years of bloody history behind them, and while they knew it would ulti-mately prove futile, if not lethal, they opened fire with the forlorn hope of a lucky shot penetrating a view slit.

A blizzard of armor-piercing half-inch bullets crossed the maquis and tore through the balloon. To the Serbs' astonishment, the "tank" jumped in the air, sagged weirdly, and then collapsed flat on the ground. For a second they couldn't believe their eyes. Then, through their night glasses, they saw plastic flapping in the wind.

"Balloon!"

"Balloon!"

They started laughing but quickly sobered. Someone was out there, someone who would pay dearly. They dragged their machine gun out of the confines of the stone hut so they could pivot the barrel in every direction and began traversing the dark.

* * *

"THANK YOU, GENTLEMEN," whispered Jessica Kincaid.

At five hundred meters a child could disable the machine gun with her Knight's sniper rifle braced on a bipod. She sighted in on the Dushka's feed mechanism and touched her trigger. The Serbs jumped like circus clowns and looked everywhere at once for the source of the sudden change in their situation. To be positive that she had reduced the machine gun to scrap metal, Kincaid fired again, destroying its dual triggers.

By now, the Serbs knew they were in the sights of a sharp-shooter.

Brave, but not fools, they ran inside the stone blockhouse.

Kincaid ran, too. Scooping up the fifteen-pound Knight's, glassing the rough ground through her panoramic goggles, she charged full speed deep into the peninsula, hunting for SR's second machine gun.

* * *

PAUL JANSON TRIGGERED his second grenade. The rocket ignition lit him up again, but before the SR men could concentrate their fire the grenade spiraled into the helicopter. It exploded, thunderously. The shock wave lifted the parachute several feet and blew out all the windows in the house. Janson immediately grabbed the Bushmaster and the shotgun and pounded the quick release on his harness.

As he fell, he jerked the rip cord of a landing chute strapped to his back. It popped open; he steered as far as he could from the SR men who could see his new chute by the light of the fireball consuming the helicopter.

* * *

KINCAID STRUGGLED THROUGH thorny brush to the top of a low rise. When she spotted the second blockhouse, a stone hut similar to the first, she flung herself flat and planted the Knight's bipod. She flipped back her goggles and got the blockhouse in her sights, but before she could acquire the DShK itself, it acquired her and the once-heard, never-forgotten earsplitting din of a stream of .50-caliber bullets was bracketing her head.

"Fuck!"

Alerted by the explosions and the roar of their sister gun up the road, the SR gunners must have been looking for whoever had started the battle to blunder into their field of fire. She slid backward down the rise, dragging the Knight's with her, and tore madly to the right even as the Dushka got the range and gouged holes in the ground where she'd been one second before.

She knew two ways to deal with them. One would be to leave the Knight's and advance through the brush with pistol and knife. But that would take way too long. She had to find a new shooting position, fast. Bursts of small-caliber gunfire in the distance told her that Janson had his hands full at the house. And silence behind told her that the Corsican contingents were sensibly waiting for the all clear.

She pulled on her panoramics again and inspected the lay of the land. It was less flat than at the beginning of the peninsula and offered more shooting positions, but each of those would be visible to the men manning the Dushka. She kept crawling to the right, taking care not to shake tall bushes that the machine gunners could see. A tree, one of the very few, appeared in her vision. She slithered to it and got the Knight's in approximate position before she raised her head to look around it.

A burst of fire cut the tree in half, hurling splinters and dropping the top to the ground. Son of a bitch! Of course they were watching the tree nearest her last position, waiting for a dumb football clod like her to crawl to it. This time she stayed where she was, counting the twenty seconds it would take to crawl with the gun to the next likely position. Then she eased the Knight's muzzle under the fallen trunk, swiftly found the Dushka in her scope, and fired once, smashing the machine gun's bolt chamber.

She had to hand it to the SR guys. They had balls. With their weapon blown out of commission, both came charging into the brush, fixing to hunt her down. They were well trained, too. They spread apart, a smart by-the-book tactic to put a sniper at a disadvantage. Forced to slew the rifle from side to side to acquire widely separated targets in the night scope, she might miss both. They came fast, leaping through the brush, the taller one pulling ahead.

Kincaid shot the one behind him first. That bought her precious seconds. Before the leader realized that the man behind him had fallen and dove for cover, she found him in her crosshairs.

* * *

TSK! SHARP IN Kincaid's earpiece.

"What."

"I could use a hand."

That was the closest Janson had ever come to asking her for help.

"Would you settle for the French Foreign Legion?" she asked.

"As soon as the road is clear."

"It's clear."

"Good girl! Bring 'em on."

* * *

A LOW-SLUNG SHERPA 4x4 personnel carrier raced up the peninsula's narrow road, closely trailed by a heavy Renault TRM 10000

6x6 truck swaying on the bends. The convoy stopped in sight of the house where the burning helicopter cast garish light on trampled gardens and shattered windows.

A bullet-headed sergeant leaped from the Sherpa bellowing orders. The Renault's canvas sides flew open. Squads wearing green berets, drab fatigues, and jump boots piled out of both vehicles and fixed bayonets to FAMAS-1 rifles.

Some of the mercenaries defending the building had encountered the fearsome Legionnaires of the Deuxième Régiment Étranger des Parachutistes rapid-intervention unit in North Africa and the Ivory Coast—an experience none wished to repeat. Those few threw their guns out the windows. The rest protested angrily in a polyglot chorus of French, Russian, Chinese, Afrikaner, and English, "Fight, you cowards."

"You couldn't pay me enough," said a big Australian who stepped through the bullet-riddled front door with his hands in the air.

A Russian raised a pistol and took deliberate aim at his back.

A Chinese smashed the pistol to the floor with his assault rifle, breaking the Russian's arm.

* * *

THE SR TROOPS guarding Iboga had been disarmed and herded into the Renault before they heard the distant wail of police sirens on the mainland. They exchanged puzzled glances when their captors splashed gasoline on the high grass and brush downwind of the house, ignited it with a thermal grenade, and cheered like banshees. But only when they threw their berets into the jagged flames did the SR men realize that they had been taken by a gang of separatists, displaced fishermen, Union Corse, thieves, ecologists, and arsonists disguised as the French Foreign Legion.

* * *

Jessica Kincaid was sprinting up the road when she saw the fire coming her way. The brush was dry and the sea wind strong, fanning the fire into twin walls of flame divided by the narrow road. She saw immediately that it was moving too fast to outrun. She poured her water bottle on her sleeve, breathed through the wet cloth, clutched her Knight's close, and ran between the fiery walls.

She burst through the last of it, coughing and gagging, straight into the powerful arms of Freddy Ramirez, who smothered the flames on her backpack with his gloves. "You okay?"

"Terrific. Where's Janson?"

"In the house. Tell him the hoist is rigged."

She found Janson rummaging through the arsenal the SR had left behind in the house's library. "Ran out of grenades. You all right?"

"Woulda been nice if someone told me burning the place down was part of the plan."

"Sorry about that. The Corsicans got caught up in the moment."

"Where's Iboga?"

"Barricaded in the wine cellar with the senior Securité Referral guy. Just spoke to Ondine. We have about ten minutes to get him down to the boat before the gendarmerie rustle up a helicopter."

He snatched up a stun grenade and led her down the stairs to a stone-walled basement. The wine cellar was behind an oaken door. Splintery holes pocked the wood. "He shoots when you talk to him," Janson explained. *"President Iboga!"*

A slug tore through the wood and smacked into the opposite wall.

"Who's shooting? Iboga or the SR guy?"

"Hard to tell."

Kincaid called, "Iboga!" A woman's voice was not expected.

"Who is there?" Iboga's voice was deep, guttural, and slurred. "Who are you? What is going on?"

"He sounds drunk."

"He's in a wine cellar."

"Who? Who? Speak, woman!"

Kincaid shouted back, "We're not exactly friends. But we guarantee you safe passage to the World Court in The Hague!"

Janson and Kincaid flung themselves back as another slug splintered the door. Janson handed Kincaid the stun grenade, leveled his Bushmaster at the knob, and flicked the fire selector to AUTO. But before he could blast the lock, they heard angry shouts inside, then another gunshot, which didn't penetrate the door, then a heavy thud.

"They're fighting," said Kincaid.

"We need him alive or Isle de Foree will never see their money. Ready!"

"Go!"

Janson triggered the full 20-shot magazine into the lock. Even with the suppressor, the noise was deafening in the confined space. Kincaid kicked the door. It sagged open and she whipped her arm back to underhand the stun grenade.

"Hold it!" said Janson.

Two men were struggling on the stone floor, Iboga, the three hundred-pound giant, on top, with his hands on the throat of the man under him and his sharpened teeth tearing at his face. Iboga's opponent was pounding him with powerful blows to his belly and groin. They appeared evenly matched in ferocity and combat skills and it was hard to tell who would win. Iboga's superior weight was offset by his age. He appeared to be fifty or so, while the powerful man under him was less than thirty.

"Look at his arm," said Janson.

Kincaid saw the bandage and breathed an astonished, "Jesus H."
She drew her pistol and jammed the barrel to his head. "Fight's
over, Van Pelt. Break it up."

Janson pressed the Bushmaster to Iboga's head. "Let go!"

The two separated violently, Iboga backhanding Van Pelt's nose
as he loosened his grip on the mercenary's throat, Van Pelt rolling
out from under with a boot to Iboga's groin that doubled the former
dictator into a fetal crouch, gasping for breath.

Janson flipped Iboga on his belly, swiftly cuffed his hands behind his back, and hauled him to his feet. "We're outta here."

"Stop!" said Van Pelt. Blood was streaming from his cheek.

Janson said, "Try to follow us, you're a dead man." He pulled a
second set of steel cuffs from his windbreaker and tossed them to
Kincaid. "Lock him to that," Janson said, pointing at a massive iron
ring in the floor and covering him with the Bushmaster.

Van Pelt jerked his hands away. Kincaid moved like lightning,
slapping one cuff around Van Pelt's ankle and the other to the ring.
Van Pelt's eyes slid toward a pistol he or Iboga had dropped in their
fight. Kincaid kicked it out of Van Pelt's reach.

Van Pelt pointed a finger in her face. He was trembling with
rage. "I'm warning you. Don't cross SR."

"You're warning me? You're warning *me*!"

"*Jess!*"

"Right. We're outta here. Come on, President for Life. We're going for a boat ride."

"I'm warning you!" Van Pelt screamed.

"Warn the French police," Janson said. "They'll be here any
minute."

"I know who you are," said Van Pelt.

"No, you don't," Janson said, herding Iboga out the door. The former dictator was limping and half doubled over, still gasping.

"*I know who you are!*"

"You *think* you know me. You don't."

"I know about the do-gooding."

Janson paused in the doorway. "What?"

Van Pelt said, "Iboga is my client. Return him to me immediately."

Kincaid pushed back into the cellar, eyes hot, nostrils flaring. "And if we don't?"

"Secure Iboga," Janson ordered softly. "Pat him down. He's got a ton of pockets in that bush jacket. Confiscate everything— weapons, phone, money, passport—everything on his person. I'll take care of this. . . . Do it!"

"Yes, sir." She backed out the door.

"Answer her question," said Janson. "If we don't return your client? What will you do? Report us to the police? Press charges for delivering a bloodthirsty dictator to the World Court to stand trial for crimes against humanity? Go ahead. We'll be long gone. You'll still be nailed to the floor."

Hadrian Van Pelt stood to his full height. His bloodied face was tight with rage, but it was controlled rage. "I give you one final warning," he said with deep conviction. "If you do not return Securité Referral's client this minute, we will hound you to the ends of the earth. You will stare over your shoulders for the rest of your lives. You will be so busy struggling to stay alive that you will never do a do-gooding job again."

"Who will lead this hounding? You?"

"Believe me."

"I believe you," said Paul Janson. "You leave me no choice."

He picked up the fallen pistol and aimed it at Van Pelt's head.

Van Pelt laughed at him. "A do-gooder would pull the trigger on a man chained to the floor?"

"Twice."

Van Pelt stopped laughing. His lips turned white. "Twice?"

"As assassins are trained to," said Paul Janson. He did it so fast that the two shots sounded almost like one.

PART FOUR

Ambush

Evening
29°45' N, 95°22' W
Houston, Texas

THIRTY-SIX

Doug Case was leading "Chair Night" at the Phoenix Boys Shelter his halfway house for teenage gangbangers crippled in gunfights—on the south side of Houston when his cell phone buzzed with the one call he would never block, even when he was visiting the kids. The Voice was calling, sooner than five days, breaking pattern. Events must be coming to a head if even the cool, dispassionate, wise, and cynical Voice was getting anxious.

"Guys, I'm really sorry," Case apologized. "I gotta take this call. Who's going to fill in for me?"

He chose two from the eager hands and watched the kids proudly as he backed his own chair toward the door. Those who had already earned their superchairs presented the new kid who had earned his by painstakingly learning to master the multiple controls with the fingers of one hand. The other had been paralyzed along with his spine in a gun battle the kid had lost defending a crack-cocaine business in an abandoned house on Higgins Street.

A male nurse lifted the shrunken form, which was all that remained of a hefty teenager, out of his ordinary chair and placed him in his customized super.

Case wheeled out to the foyer. There was an armed guard at the front desk and wire mesh on the small windows to discourage attacks by gangstas not yet crippled from the shoot-outs they had fought in backyards of the Sunnyside neighborhood. Case glanced through the window at his black Escalade idling at the curb. His driver was sitting at the wheel with a pistol in his hand.

Case parked his chair in front of a glass case displaying trophies that Phoenix shelter boys had won in qualifying events for the Paralympics, wheelchair basketball, wheelchair fencing, wheelchair tennis, power lifting, judo, and archery.

"George," he called to the guard.

"Yes sir, Mr. Case."

"Still indulging in your coffin nails?"

George grinned. " 'Fraid so."

"Why don't you step outside and have a smoke. I'll cover for you."

George stepped out eagerly.

Case answered the vibrating phone: "Hello, Strange Voice."

"Took your time picking up."

"I had to create some privacy. Sorry."

"How are you making out with Paul Janson?"

This was a happy subject and Case answered, "Janson bought it hook, line, and sinker."

"He really believes that you're quitting ASC?"

"Better than that."

"How so?"

"Janson believes I switched sides. He thinks I'm now his mole inside ASC."

"Mole?" Digitally distorted, the caller's laughter squeaked like a slipping fan belt. "Where'd he get that idea?"

"I let him recruit me."

The Voice laughed harder. "Well done! Very, very well done, Douglas. You are a man after my own heart."

"I'll take that as high praise, sir."

"What does he want of his mole?"

"Nothing specific, so far," Case lied. "General observations."

"Let me offer you a word to the wise."

"Please do," Case answered hastily. All the distortion in the digital spectrum could not muffle the suddenly icy tone of threat.

"Don't get so caught up in your performance that you come to believe it."

"I won't."

"What makes you so sure? Paul Janson is a man who can offer a broad array of temptations."

"I'm not mole material."

The Voice was not convinced. "Don't get so caught up that you believe that becoming mole material would be in your interest. It would not be in your interest. It would lead to unbearable pain and suffering."

Case was enraged that anyone would dare to threaten him. If he could, he would reach through the phone and crush the life out of The Voice. But when Case looked at his reflection in the trophy case, he saw a man in a chair. The poor devil mirrored back a crumbling smile of remorse and regret. The days of crushing the life out of men who challenged him were gone forever. Savagery these days would be of the mind.

As he shook with thwarted anger, it took all his strength to force himself to answer mildly, "Not to worry. I know who butters my bread. And I am grateful."

"I'll be in touch."

They rang off.

Case gazed inquiringly at his reflection.

The threat was not characteristic. The Voice had never threatened him so openly. Even when the mysterious caller had risked his first overture, he had never tried to control Case by sowing terror. He had a funny feeling—a gut feeling born of a lifetime of plots and counterplots—that The Voice had inadvertently revealed that he was deep inside ASC, not outside. Inside and very, very high up. Why else would he be so paranoid that Case might betray ASC's strategy to Paul Janson?

Then a funnier feeling hit Case. Was the revelation not inadvertent, but deliberate? Was The Voice subtly signaling that he trusted Douglas Case more than ever by revealing more about himself? Were they nearing the time when they would deal face-to-face as equals?

There was a way to find out.

Case made two quick calls, then stared into the trophy case, waiting for his phone to ring. It did. The Voice.

"Yes, sir."

"I've just received word that Iboga was snatched from Securité Referral."

The glass trophy case reflected a wide smile. "As I predicted, SR has proved to be a disappointment."

"But we've lost Iboga just when we need him most."

"I would not call Iboga lost," Doug Case replied with another smile for his reflection.

"What the hell would you call him?"

"Temporarily misplaced."

"You sound damned sure of yourself."

"I am in this instance, sir. Please don't worry."

"Don't you think you should get yourself to Isle de Foree ASAP?"

"I already have an ASC Gulfstream gassing up at Hobby Airport. I'll be aboard in twenty minutes."

"I think you should go in force."

"I've already beefed up security on the *Vulcan Queen*."

"As a precaution?"

Doug Case went for broke.

It was time to claim his rightful role. Before the coup.

"Not a precaution. In *anticipation* of when you ask me to remove Chief of Staff Mario Margarido."

The distorted voice made a noise that was probably a chuckle. "I admire you, Douglas. You do stay on top of things."

"Thank you."

"Are you ready to remove Margarido?"

"Of course, as I promised. Everything is set."

"Do it!"

"Consider it done."

"And when you get to Isle de Foree?"

"Yes, sir?"

"Do everything in your power to support Kingsman Helms."

That came as fast and final as a red-hot sword in the gut.

Case ran the possibilities: The Voice was Kingsman Helms himself, ensuring Case's support. Or The Voice was the Buddha, who had chosen Helms as his successor. Or the Voice was an outsider, a board member or a rival who wanted his man Helms in charge of ASC.

A sword in the gut any way Case looked at it.

"Douglas, are you still there?"

"I will do everything in my power to support Kingsman Helms."

"Excellent. I knew I could count on you."

THIRTY-SEVEN

Dawn
39°55′ N, 09°41′ E
Tortoli Airport, Sardinia, 820 miles south-southeast of The Hague

I boga was seasick. He had gotten queasy in the RIB during the short run through the surf from the cliffs of the Vallicone peninsula to the cigarette boat waiting offshore. On the cigarette, he had groaned loudly and drunkenly as it sped him to the freighter cruising the Strait of Bonifacio. Hoisted aboard in a cargo net, the dictator proceeded to vomit wine on the deck.

In the bright light of the ship's galley, which smelled of grease and coffee, Janson and Kincaid inspected every item that Kincaid had taken from the dictator. A thick, new lizard skin travel wallet contained authentic-looking French, Russian, and Nigerian passports, an international driver's license, and Visa and American

Express credit cards in the name of N. Kwame Johnson. There was a gold money clip full of euros, an old-fashioned Zippo cigarette lighter, the latest iPhone with a treasure trove of contact numbers, a beautifully crafted French shepherd's folding knife, a gold and diamond Rolex watch, a plastic Baggie of loose pills, including oxycodone, aspirin, and Viagra, and several mini-Baggies, each holding a half a gram of a black powder, which Janson assumed was Iboga's namesake hallucinogen extracted from the Tabernanthe iboga rainforest shrub. He uplinked the data on the iPhone SIM card to the forensic accountants, along with the credit card numbers and passport numbers, with instructions to pass on to Research anything that did not serve their hunt for the money.

Iboga was too seasick to interrogate, shaking with dry heaves. Janson knelt beside him, coaxing him to drink water so as not to become dangerously dehydrated. There would be time on the plane to talk about the money. And more time, if necessary, parked on a runway in friendly territory.

Off the east coast of Sardinia, they lowered him into another RIB to slip ashore at Tortoli Airport. The RIB motored quietly through the last wisps of night, steered by Daniel. Iboga retched over the side.

"God punishes in mysterious ways," Janson told Kincaid.

They were seated on the inflated tubes where they joined to form the bow. She couldn't see his expression in the dark, but she heard a faint grin in his voice that relieved her deeply. This was the first he had spoken other than to issue quiet orders since they had left Corsica the night before. "How are you?"

"Hanging in there."

"Like you told him, Paul. He gave you no choice."

"Doesn't mean I enjoyed it."

Kincaid took his hand. There was a softness to it that always surprised her. "Janson Rules," she said. " 'No killing anyone who doesn't try to kill us.' He would have killed you and killed everything you hope for."

"Still didn't enjoy it. But thanks for the thought."

"Don't blow me off! It's not a goddamned *thought*. I'm trying to screw your head back on straight."

"Well, thanks for the head screwing. I mean it. Thank you." He patted her arm distractedly, dialed his cell phone, shielding the light in his palm, listened to it ring, and hung up. "Still can't raise the boys."

Ed and Mike had reported earlier in the night that they had landed the Embraer at Tortoli Airport and parked as out of the way as they could. It was a tiny field outside the town of Tortoli—trees around the control tower, in Ed's words—that handled a couple of tourist charters a day. The single runway ran from a bare-bones terminal to the beach, which the RIB was approaching. With the prevailing wind from the east, the Embraer had descended over the hills and would take off over the water, which meant hiking six thousand feet from the beach dragging Iboga in the dark.

They heard him retching into the gentle surf.

"Good thing we brought the dolly."

The rubber boat ground ashore on the sand. Daniel helped them shoulder Iboga across the beach and went back for the dolly. They strapped him to it standing up. Its fat pneumatic tires rolled easily on the asphalt runway.

"Good job," Janson told Daniel, shaking his hand.

"Get home safe."

Each gripping a handle, Janson and Kincaid started rolling Iboga toward the distant control tower, which was invisible against the dark hills behind it. Janson flipped down his panoramics. There it was, a squat structure in a clump of trees. Parked near it was a plane—not the Embraer. Its engines were wing mounted. Hauling on the dolly handle, jogging beside Kincaid, he scanned the area around the buildings. There was the Embraer, showing no lights of course but pointed straight down the runway, with its door open for them and boarding stairs extended.

"I see the plane."

The night glass's infrared enhancement showed the bright bulge of the big Rolls-Royces on its tail. They appeared brighter than the buildings and the other plane, which meant that Ed and Mike had the engines warm, ready to take off in a flash.

Iboga stopped groaning. As was common with seasickness, the restorative effect of being on dry land was rapid. Suddenly he spoke.

"Where take?"

"Holland. The Hague. International Court."

"I pay bribe. Let me go."

"How much?" asked Janson, without slackening pace.

"Ten million euros."

"Where are you going to get ten million dollars?" Kincaid asked scornfully.

"I get."

"Hundred million," said Janson.

"Seventy," Iboga shot back. And Janson felt his hopes soar. Iboga was bargaining like a man who had no doubt he could raise the money. Nor did he sound concerned by the amount, as if he could easily afford it and have plenty, the lion's share, left for himself. Unless he was scamming them, angling to distract them, looking for a chance to break away.

"Where?" Kincaid demanded. "How do we get the money?"

"You take me. I get."

"Where?"

"First you say yes. And you give me back my stuff."

"I'm not saying yes until you tell me where. And I'm damned sure not giving you anything back until I have the seventy million in my hands."

After a moment of rolling in silence, Iboga caved. "Zagreb."

Zagreb made sense, thought Janson. Zagreb was the capital of Croatia, among the most corrupt countries in eastern Europe, the kind of nation where transnational criminal organizations like Securité Referral could play a powerful role. He imagined the enormous kickback SR would have received from the Croatian bank, and even the government itself, for steering Iboga's stolen money to them.

Suddenly Kincaid whispered, "What's that?"

Janson heard it, too, from behind them, the rumble of heavy engines, approaching from the sea. He flipped up the panoramics. The control tower had grown visible in the predawn light.

"Turboprops."

The aircraft engines rumbled overhead and faded toward the hills. Then they heard the plane turn around and the sound grew louder.

"Descending."

The tower windows were dark, the field closed for the night. Whoever was approaching was coming in without air controller assistance. Janson and Kincaid picked up the pace so as not to be exposed in the landing lights. They followed the plane by its sound. Suddenly they saw its profile silhouetted against the graying sky, a high-wing, twin-engine transporter.

"Weird," said Janson.

Kincaid agreed. It looked like a C-160 Transall, the twin-engine turboprop that they had seen flown by the Deuxième Régiment

Étranger des Parachutistes rapid-intervention units exercising in Corisca. It came down fast and skillfully. Landing lights blazed on at the last second, revealing a camo-green fuselage. The massive tricycle landing gear absorbed the impact. Propellers reversed with a roar and the Transall slowed so quickly that it was able to turn around in less than a third of the runway. With another roar, it came straight at them, landing lights aglare.

"What?" yelled Iboga, blinking, struggling to shield his eyes with his trussed hands. Janson and Kincaid had already flipped down their night gear, which neutralized the glare.

When they saw the rear cargo door spilling paratroopers onto the tarmac, they had only seconds to escape. But that would mean abandoning their prisoner and drawing fire at Ed and Mike on the Embraer.

"It's the goddamned French Foreign Legion."

"This is Italy. They can't come here."

"Looks like no one told them."

A stentorian voice amplified by a bullhorn bellowed French.

"He's saying, 'Hands in the air.' "

"I got that." They raised their hands. "Now what's he saying?"

"Uhhmm ... 'We arrest Iboga ... taken illegally from France.' "

Two soldiers ran up, grabbed the dolly's handgrips, and wheeled Iboga to the Transall.

"Here come the cops."

An Italian police car squealed around the terminal, past the control tower, and raced onto the runway with flashing blue lights. Two Carabiniere officers jumped out, straightened their black tunics, and swaggered toward the Transall. A French paratrooper stepped forward and fired a long, loud burst with his assault rifle. Bullets whistled past the police and blew out all the windows in their patrol car.

Kincaid said, "Since when does the French Army issue AK-47s?"

A second burst over their heads sent the Italians running into the dark.

Janson counted paratroopers. "That Transall holds eighty. I see ten."

"They're not Legionnaires. They're as phony as ours were. Jesus, who the hell are they?"

"Just hope they keep the act up and don't strafe us. Those AKs aren't phony."

"And just let them take Iboga?"

"We'll follow them," said Janson, with little hope. "If they don't shoot our tires out."

The gunmen in paratroop gear unstrapped Iboga from the dolly and helped him up the Transall's steps.

At the top, the wary-looking Iboga suddenly broke into a grin so broad that it showed his pointed teeth.

"What is going on?" said Kincaid. "He looks happy as hell."

"Wait," said Janson. "It's going to get worse."

One of the phony Legionnaires presented Iboga with a bright yellow scarf, his signature Arab kaffiyeh. Iboga gathered it around his enormous skull. For a long moment he stood proud as a king. Then he gestured imperiously for the trooper to shoot Janson and Kincaid, who were still holding their hands in the air.

The trooper did not pull the trigger but with help of the others urged Iboga into the transport. He argued and kept pointing at Janson and Kincaid. It took four strong men to shove Iboga in the door. To Janson's surprise, the last man up the ramp did not strafe the Embraer's landing gear with his assault rifle. Instead, he threw a mock salute as the airplane started rolling down the runway, and pulled the door shut.

Janson vaulted up the Embraer's steps, with Kincaid right behind him.

"Fire 'em up, boys! Follow that plane—*Oh, God!*"

Ed's and Mike's seat belts held their bodies in the pilot and co-pilot chairs. Their throats had been cut and the cockpit stank of blood.

THIRTY-EIGHT

Vicious, senseless..." Kincaid's voice was cracking, her mouth trembling. "Why didn't they just kill us instead?"

"Ed and Mike were easier to kill."

There were times, Janson thought, that he was ashamed to be a human being. These two men, these gentle men, so precise in their skills, so quietly proud of the partnership they forged daily with the elegantly engineered Embraer, so ready to whisk Janson anywhere in the world, to change course without hesitation, to be always loyally at his service, to risk their licenses to play fast and loose to serve him, did not deserve to be murdered.

"Senseless," Kincaid repeated. "They're just pilots. They're not— Oh, God, they were always so nice to me."

Not quite senseless, thought Janson. There was purpose behind the murders. The phony Legionnaires had left him and Kincaid holding the bag, stuck on the ground, on foreign soil, with two dead men to account for. They would be tied down for weeks explaining to the Italian authorities. Under Italian law they could be held without charges for two years.

He was heartsick. The inner circle of CatsPaw and Phoenix was small, very small. His family. Jesse, Quintisha, his pilots. He stared out the windshield. How many miles had Ed and Mike looked through it taking him places he had to go? The Embraer was pointed east down the runway. The sky was brightening over the sea. The Carabiniere would be radioing reinforcements.

"I'll get towels and blankets," he said. "We'll lay them out aft."

Kincaid followed him to the back of the plane, stumbling like a woman wrenched from sleep. They got blankets and towels from the linen locker and hurried forward, Janson moving with increasing urgency. He stopped to retract the stairs and lock the door. He found Jessica on her hands and knees in the cockpit, toweling blood off the deck. They wrapped Ed and Mike as best they could in the blankets, carried them aft, and strapped them into the fold-down bunks.

"Iboga looked surprised. He didn't expect to be rescued."

"Yeah, I saw that. Fucking SR."

"These guys weren't necessarily SR. SR would have shot everyone in sight. Cops, us."

"They did Ed and Mike."

"They did the bare minimum to leave you and me holding the bag so the Italians will hunt us instead of them. We can spend a year in Italy. Or we can try and get out of here so we can track down Iboga and his money."

"And get who did this to Ed and Mike?"

"Have you been practicing takeoffs on the simulator?"

She tore her eyes from the shrouded bodies. "Yeah, Ed set it up. Mike sat in with me."

"How'd you do?"

"Aced it. Second try."

Janson said, "It's been a while since I've flown and I expect you're better at it than I am."

"Not saying much."

"I'll lay smoke. You get us out of here."

* * *

KINCAID WIPED MIKE'S blood off the left-hand chair, climbed in, and adjusted it forward so she could reach the rudder pedals. Ed had taped a card to the throttle on which he had written "V_1 114" and "V_R 130."

V_1 was her all-important takeoff-decision speed, which Ed had based on the weight of the aircraft, the length of the runway, the temperature, and the speed of the wind. It told Kincaid that she had until the fifty-thousand-pound jet plane was hurtling at 114 knots—130 miles per hour—to decide *not* to take off. If she lost an engine slower than that she had to abort. Above 114 knots, she had to try to take off. She showed Janson the bud that Ed had set on the airspeed indicator at 114 knots. It would be Janson's job, as the one not flying the ship, to call out, "V_1." At V_R, rotation speed—which Ed had written as "130 knots"—Janson would simply call out, "Rotate," so Kincaid would know when to draw back on the control yoke to elevate the nosewheel off the runway.

Janson climbed into the co-pilot chair, slipped on the headset, and turned his attention to the electronics. "Laying smoke" meant using the Embraer's defensive aid suite to make Air Traffic Control think that the twin-engine passenger jet was either elsewhere or nowhere at all.

But first he switched off the transponder, which replied to radar queries from ground control and other airplanes. Then he shut down the AFIRS (Automated Flight Information Reporting System) air-to-ground data link service that had recently replaced the antiquated "black box" onboard flight data recorder. Now they would leave no electronically enhanced trail in the sky.

He checked the flight plan in the computer. Ed had filed for The Hague, Holland, eight hundred miles to the north. That was now out the window.

"We'll hang a right, shoot low and fast as we can down the coast past Sardinia and out of Italian territory into Mediterranean Free Flight Airspace."

"Let's see if I can get off the ground, first."

Kincaid touched the left-hand engine master switch, then the start lever. Number One engine's compressor started cranking on battery power. Janson watched her eyes flicker between controls and monitors. The Embraer's automatic engine start sequencer made it slightly similar to starting a car in that she did not have to decide when the turbine was spinning fast enough to introduce fuel and when to ignite it. The engine caught immediately. She let it spool up as she used its generator to crank the Number Two engine's compressor. Number Two was balky. The sequencer refused to ignite the fuel.

Janson saw flashing lights through the branches of the trees around the control tower. "If we're going we better go now."

Number Two engine hadn't fired yet, but without hesitating Kincaid released the brakes and throttled Number One. The plane began rolling. A police car careened around the control tower. The driver started to pull in front of the moving Embraer. The sudden howl of Number Two engine finally churning to life made him think better about it and the car veered away. The FADEC (Full Authority Digital Engine Control) speed synchronized Number Two revolutions with Number One.

"The good news," Kincaid muttered, testing flaps, slats, and rudder, "is Ed and Mike had her ready to fly. They did their checklist and kept the motors warm. We're going to find out how warm. The other good news is idle to takeoff thrust spool-up time is quick on these Rolls-Royces."

"What's the bad news?"

"It's a short runway. I have to turn around and go back to the beginning."

Janson nodded reluctant agreement. The plane had taxied several hundred meters already and the sea at the end of the runway looked remarkably close in the early light. Kincaid turned the nosewheel, pivoted the plane 180 degrees in its own length, and steered back at the police car. Janson flicked on the powerful landing lights, blinding the police. The police car careened out of Janson and Kincaid's way and scurried behind the terminal.

At the beginning of the runway Kincaid pivoted the plane again, set the brakes, and smoothly slid the throttles forward until they clicked into the indent marked: "TOGA" (takeoff/go-around). The engines screamed as they spooled up toward takeoff power. The plane began to shudder. Kincaid reached for the brake release. She paused to check that the engines were turning at the same speed. It was not necessary, Janson knew, as the sequence synchronized them automatically, but she had picked up habits of caution from Mike and Ed, whose flying careers predated automation.

Kincaid released the brakes.

Nine tons of thrust shoved the Embraer forward. Janson felt the chair press hard into his back. Already the ground was moving fast beside them. The airspeed indicator numbers rolled like a slot machine. Janson watched anxiously for the little bud that marked 114 knots. The Embraer felt heavy on its tires, rumbling over the worn tarmac. The beach was racing at the windshield, the surf bloodred as the sun broke the horizon. His hand, unbidden, inched toward the landing gear switch.

"Not yet," Kincaid said coolly.

"V_1," said Janson.

They were committed.

Janson watched for VR. At last, 130 knots indicated airspeed.

"Rotate."

Kincaid hauled back on the control yoke. "Here we go, my friend."

The Embraer rotated, raising its nose centimeters before the tires hit the beach and canting the wings to an angle to the wind that gave them lift. The main gearwheels swirled a rooster tail of sand and surf. But now the wings were carrying the Embraer and the engines thrust the ship to safety speed.

"Gear up."

* * *

JANSON IGNORED REPEATED radio hails from Italian Air Traffic Control.

"Take her back down to the deck," he told Kincaid. Ground radar antennas, going round and round, could track them three hundred miles from land. They had to fly under the radar.

"A hundred feet suit you?" Proud of her takeoff, she had high color in her cheeks and fire in her eyes.

"Try not to hit any boats."

They streaked south, ten miles off the coast, two hundred feet above the waves, startling fishermen and yacht captains.

Janson was hoping that the early hour, territorial jealousies, and general confusion would make Air Traffic Control hesitate before requesting the Italian Air Force to scramble Panavia Tornado interceptors. Time to ratchet up the chaos: He typed a private code on the co-pilot's keyboard that unlocked alternate transponder options. The transponder was supposed to identify the Embraer and reveal their flight plan and their altitude when queried by ATC radar. The alternates—violating every civil aviation rule in the world—would answer ATC radar queries with false data about a phantom Embraer flying an illusionary flight plan.

In twenty minutes they rounded the southern tip of Sardinia and angled westward into the Mediterranean. "Up," said Janson.

Kincaid set the auto throttle and autopilot for climb-out and asked, "Above or below one-eight-oh?"

Flying above eighteen thousand feet mandated instrument flight rules.

"Above," said Janson, placing a heavy bet on their false transponder signals and EUROCONTROL's latest experiment with a Mediterranean Free Flight scheme that allowed aircraft flying the lightly trafficked airspace above the sea between Europe and North Africa to manage their own separation instead of maneuvering at the specific orders of Air Traffic Control. Permission to fly as an "autonomous aircraft," not being required to report every move, should make it easier to disappear.

He was hoping, too, that the situation on the ground at Tortoli was so confusing that the police might not have distinguished the fake French Foreign Legion Transall from the Embraer. The Italian police at Tortoli Airport whose vehicle was shot to pieces would have already reported a French Foreign Legion Transall C-160 with French markings.

The sky was blue and empty in every direction, the rising sun behind them and a vast stretch of the Mediterranean ahead. But this was still Europe of the European Union, where it seemed that half the adult citizens worked for one regulatory agency or another.

And Janson could do little about that but pray the Italian government would spend the next three hours expressing outrage to the French through diplomatic channels, time to get past the Strait of Gibraltar and out over the high seas of the Atlantic Ocean.

"Where are we going?"

"The only place I can think of that will take us in without questions is Isle de Foree. How are you doing on fuel?"

"Ed and Mike topped off in Rome, but it won't get us near Isle de Foree."

The first officer's Multifunction Control Display Unit confirmed they hadn't the fuel. Janson played with the functions to put together a flight plan. "Figure two thousand miles to the Canary Islands if we can get past Gibraltar."

"Big if."

The narrow choke point between the coasts of Spain and Morocco was guarded by Spanish, Moroccan, U.S., and British military bases.

"As long as no one is really hunting us I can fake our way through. It's not like trying to sneak up the English Channel dodging fleets of transatlantic jets leaving and arriving in northern Europe. So we fuel up in the Canaries and then clear sailing three thousand, six hundred miles on a dogleg around the bulge of Africa to Isle de Foree."

"Thirty-six hundred miles is pushing it. When we flew up to the Mediterranean, Mike was practically tacking into crosswinds."

"If it looks hairy, we can take our chances in Praia or Dakar, but I'd rather not. Freddy's people can help us in the Canaries, but we don't have any special friends in the Cape Verde Islands or Senegal."

Janson tapped in another private code that revealed the chaff and flare operating manual. He regarded the Embraer's chaff and flare dispenser hidden under the fuselage as an absolute last resort.

The main purpose of electronic countermeasures was to trick enemy missiles—which was not the case here. There was no way a high-end business jet was going to tangle with fighter planes. The task Janson required was to confuse ATC radar and, worst case, failing that, to confuse air force fighter jets sent up to intercept the unidentified target. But before they deployed electronic countermeasures, the best chance was to remain unidentifiable by leaving the transponder off. Which meant keeping a sharp eye peeled for other aircraft on a collision course, unlikely as it was in lightly trafficked skies.

"Something tells me you might be right that those fake Legionnaires weren't SR," said Kincaid. "But that was a slick operation to launch on such short notice. It was almost as if someone expected us to snatch Iboga from SR."

"Set up by someone who didn't want him to stand trial in The Hague," Janson agreed. "Who could include the Nigerian Directorate of Military Intelligence, the mysterious GRA, and American Synergy Corporation."

"Maybe you should ask your friend Doug."

"Not quite yet."

Janson used his sat phone to call CatsPaw Research. "GRA? What have you found?"

"Nothing. No such company exists on the record."

"Are they possibly a subsidiary of American Synergy Corp.?"

"That was one of my thoughts. I found no connection to ASC."

Janson thought hard. "Are they possibly a government front? A CIA front or ..." He let the thought lie between their telephones and the researcher finished it for him, "Cons Ops?"

"Well?"

"Could be. But there is no record. No paper trail. And certainly no digital trail."

"The only piece of paper I know of was a business card."

"What did it look like?"

"I didn't see it. I was told about it. How would you like a trip to London?"

"Could I fly Business Class?"

"You can fly Business Class. Look up a fellow named Pedro Menezes. He's a former oil minister of Isle de Foree. He says he took money from GRA."

Kincaid reached across and tapped his arm. "The *Amber Dawn*. Didn't somebody say it was owned by the Dutch?"

Janson said into the phone, "Look into a Dutch connection. Ask Mr. Menezes about Dutch independents."

They rang off.

Kincaid reached over and tapped again. Urgently. "Paul!"

"What?"

"Where are his cigarettes?"

"Whose?"

"Iboga's cigarettes. He had a lighter, but no cigarettes. No cigars."

"Maybe he smoked the drug."

"No, you eat ibogaine. You don't smoke it."

They looked at each other in astonished disbelief. What had they both missed? "Where's his stuff?"

"My backpack."

Janson scrambled for her backpack and found the mesh bag inside that contained the items she had taken from Iboga. He plucked out the Zippo cigarette lighter and brought it to the first officer's chair. It looked like a lighter. The brand "Zippo" was stamped on the bottom of the case, with a flame dotting the letter *i*. He opened it. Inside, it looked like a lighter, with a rough steel wheel and a blackened wick. He held it to his nose. It smelled of lighter fluid. He flicked the wheel. To Janson's disappointment, a spark flew from the flint and the wick ignited. He blew out the flame, pulled the mechanism out of the case, and turned it over. There was the cotton wool that absorbed the fluid with a screw head. He unscrewed it. Out fell a normal flint. He opened his pocketknife to an awl blade, snagged the cotton wool, and pulled it out. He looked inside the case. The interior was empty. He squeezed the cotton wool.

"Aha."

He spread it on Ed's keyboard and peeled the fibers off something hard inside and held it up for Kincaid to see. "What is this, a key? It looks like a key to a safe."

Kincaid gave him a pitying look she reserved for covert operators who began their careers in the twentieth century. "Janson, it's not a *key*. It's a flash drive that looks like a key. You hang it on your key chain."

Janson stuck the flash drive inside the nearest USB port and looked at Ed's screen. "Numbers. Routing numbers. A list of them." He called CatsPaw's forensic accountant on his Iridium. "Try these," he said, and read them off.

She called back in minutes. "Four banks in Zagreb."

"Can you get into them?"

"Whose rules do you want to play by?"

"Corrupt dictator rules."

"We can try to get in with the help of a certain third party to whom we've already hinted that a million-euro gratuity might be authorized."

"Consider it authorized," said Janson.

* * *

As THEY APPROACHED the Strait of Gibraltar at an altitude of forty-two thousand feet, Janson switched off the Embraer's radar so as not to broadcast their presence, leaving them dependent entirely on what their own eyeballs could perceive beyond the Embraer's blind spots astern. He was searching the sky when suddenly a Royal Moroccan Air Force Mirage F1 rocketed up from Casablanca Air Base Number 4.

It would have nailed them for sure if Janson hadn't glimpsed an early flash of sun on its swept wings. His hand had been poised over the flare switch since they drew within two hundred miles of Gibraltar, and he pressed it instantly. The chaff and flare nacelle departed the Embraer with a sharp bang. Moments after it ejected, its internal rocket fired and it flew astern, putting miles between it and the Embraer before it exploded open like a flower, scattering reflective chaff and burning hot points designed to show up on the Mirage's acquisition suite as myriad targets.

"Up or down?" asked Kincaid.

Janson debating diving to the deck again, versus the attention that maneuver would draw before they made it under the radar. "Up. Fast."

Kincaid fire-walled it west.

Perplexed and angry controllers queried them on the radio with swiftly increasing urgency. Janson ignored those who spoke fluent English and bullshitted the rest. Five minutes passed slowly. Had the Mirage given up? Or was it coming back for them? He cast his eyes in every direction he could see, praying that the immense blue sky would not be split by the silver dart of a warplane.

At last it looked like they had escaped notice. The Mirage had given up. Nor did additional interceptors appear in the windshield. Ahead and to either side all they could see was the blue North

Atlantic Ocean. Eleven hundred miles to the southwest lay the Canary Islands, two and a half hours' flying time.

Kincaid confirmed that the autopilot had the course, stood up, and stretched.

"Mike would have been proud of his pupil," Janson told her.

"If they were SR, I don't understand why they didn't kill us. Iboga sure as hell wanted them to."

"Maybe Iboga wasn't calling their tune. That was as much a capture as a rescue."

"You mean to take his dough? But they had him weeks before we took him. If they wanted his money they could have forced it out of him."

Janson's sat phone chimed the bell-like note that indicated Quintisha Upchurch was calling. "Yes, Quintisha."

"Acting President Ferdinand Poe would like to speak with you, urgently."

Janson called Poe. The old man answered in a voice high-pitched and anxious. "Do you have Iboga?" he shouted.

"I did, Mr. Acting President. I'm afraid I lost him. I'm working at getting him back."

"I told you he would escape."

"Yes, I know and—"

"You don't understand. They killed Mario Margarido."

"Who killed him?"

"Who knows," Poe said, adding bitterly, "He supposedly drowned in his swimming pool."

"Where is Chief of Security da Costa?"

"I don't know."

"I will be there in thirteen hours."

"Iboga is coming back. I know it."

"I will be there ahead of him. I guarantee it."

THIRTY-NINE

Janson telephoned Doug Case. "Anything new underground?"

"I wouldn't know. I'm forty thousand feet *above* ground on a company jet drinking champagne and thirty-year-old Bordeaux and eating beef Wellington."

"You'll miss that luxury in your new government job."

"It was great the first hour; now all the guys and the too-few gals are text messaging their kids at home. Folks don't know how to party anymore."

"Where are you headed?"

"Isle de Foree. We've got a big media shindig aboard the *Vulcan Queen*. Where are you?"

"Italy."

"Italy? What are you doing in Italy?"

"Talking my way out of a jam. What's the media thing about?"

"It was supposed to be a public signing of ASC's exploration agreement with Ferdinand Poe—ASC and the new acting presi-

dent shaking hands for the world to see. Only I just heard that
Mario Margarido died. God knows what monkey wrench that will
throw into it. Mario was pretty much the voice of sanity in the
rebel regime— Listen, I gotta go. I got calls stacked up."

"Doug. Any new information on GRA?"

"Ground Resource Access? No."

Janson put down the phone and looked across the engine control pedestal at Kincaid. "How's old friend Doug?" she asked.

"Closemouthed," answered Janson. "Why don't you get some
shut-eye? I'll babysit the autopilot while I make some calls."

"I'm not that tired."

"I need you rested."

"What's up?"

"Can you land this plane in the Canaries, take off again the second we refuel, and land it again on Isle de Foree?"

"I just aced a takeoff. Any luck, I can ace another. They're ten
times simpler than landings: push straight down the runway, rotate
on the right speed. But landings, if you get too slow, you under-
shoot; too fast, you might overshoot. The plane wants to keep on
flying unless a wind shift punts you sideways or a wind sheer drops
you like a rock. What I'm telling you, Janson, there's a reason Mike
never let me land her myself. Twice will be pushing my luck."

"How'd you do on the simulator?"

"Two out of three."

"So you're getting better."

"Why do you ask?"

"It's going to be tough finding a pilot we can trust to join us in
the Canaries on short notice. Besides, with all the crap I've added
to the plane, the most we can carry without burning too much fuel
to make Isle de Foree is eight people and gear, including the pilot."

"So?"

"I'd rather put the additional weight into another shooter than a pilot who can't do anything but fly. Particularly if I can't find one I can believe in."

"We're going to war?"

"Add it up. Poe's chief of staff drowned in his swimming pool. American Synergy Corporation brass are heading to Isle de Foree for a 'media event.' And Iboga is loose because I blew it. I'm obliged to fight him when he shows up in Isle de Foree."

"It's the kind of war you hate: off-the-cuff; decisions on horseback; flying by the seat of your pants; winging it."

"It wasn't your screwup. You are not obliged to fight it."

"You're right about one thing."

"What's that?"

"I better get some sleep." She stood up. "Your airplane."

Janson slid into the left-hand seat. "Got it," he said. "Sleep fast."

* * *

WHENEVER MIKE, A former Naval aviator, would touch his wheels to the ground early on the landing strip as if replicating the carrier landings of his youth, he warned Jessica Kincaid never to try the stunt. There was simply too much danger of landing short.

She let two thousand feet of tarmac on the southeast coast of the Canary Island of Fuerteventura race under her tires to be sure she had the runway made before she pulled the power back clear to idle. The Embraer dropped hard, bounced, and swerved. The swerve was a deadly invitation to overcorrect. But she steadied the beast with a race car driver's sure hands, confident that the eleven-thousand-foot runway built for 747s packed with tourists gave her a mile more run-out room than she needed.

Things went as well at the terminal. Freddy Ramirez's employees at Protocolo de Seguridad had worked miracles with the airport's general aviation assistant operations manager. Money changed hands, and the Embraer was refueled and ready to fly even before Freddy himself drove up to the boarding stairs in a windowless airport security van with four men carrying trombone, double bass, keyboard, and guitar cases. Uncommonly fit-looking for middle-aged musicians, they turned out to be retired Spanish Navy Special Operations Unit officers.

Freddy Ramirez apologized for having come up short one shooter. Janson acknowledged the scant lead time, told him not to worry about it, as the weight of one less man would translate to a few more miles of fuel, and thanked him warmly for rushing directly from the action in Corsica.

As expected, no trustworthy pilot had been found.

Kincaid calculated her V_1 and rotate speeds—both higher owing to the comfortingly longer runway and the weight of the passengers and their weapons—and got cleared for takeoff using the Embraer's legitimate November-Eight-Two-Two-Romeo-Papa call sign and a flight plan filed for Praia, Cape Verde Islands. Both transponder and AFIRS (Automated Flight Information Reporting System) operated normally until Janson disabled them in international airspace over the open ocean three hundred miles south of the Canaries and west of Africa, out of ground-based radar range.

Janson continued working his phone. He spoke with the arms merchant Hagopian in Paris; Dr. Hagopian's half-Portuguese, half-Angolan agent in Luanda; Neal Kruger, whom he tracked down to Cape Town, where he claimed to be "on holiday"; and Agostinho Kiluanji and Augustus Heinz, the "Double A" gunrunners whose agent was desperate to get back into Hagopian's good graces after forcing Janson to catch up with the freighter in a helicopter. After repeated attempts, he finally made contact with the pilots who owned LibreLift in Port-Gentil, Gabon.

"All right, that's the last of them," he told Kincaid, satisfied that he had made every contact he could for the moment yet sharply aware that not all would bear fruit on such short notice. "We're good to go."

"Catch some sleep. You look a hundred years old."

Janson closed his eyes on a bunk across the narrow aisle from Ed's and Mike's shrouded bodies. As Doug had reminded him in Houston, "Devoted followers have a habit of getting killed in our line of work."

Whatever happened to Janson Rules? He should have taken better care of Mike and Ed. Weren't Janson Rules about innocent civilians? He should have warned his pilots that Paul Janson's good works put them at risk of dying for the paradox of atoning for violence with violence. Were the murders of Ed and Mike "punishment" for his murdering Hadrian Van Pelt? How would he make amends for this?

"You look worse," said a weary Kincaid, when he relieved her on the flight deck.

"How we doing on gas?"

She reported good news. The Flight Management System, which was monitoring fuel burn and the latest winds, had found a fuel-saving route above the jet stream that would allow them to fly direct to Isle de Foree.

"Good job."

Janson sat in the first officer chair. Then, keeping one eye on the autopilot, he went online to learn everything he could about Vulcan-class drill ships.

FORTY

B usy night in Porto Clarence," Jessica Kincaid noted as she taxied the Embraer back from a landing on Isle de Foree International Airport's short, windswept runway that had turned every man on board pale.

Janson scanned the field for aircraft Iboga might have come in on.

It *was* busy. Janson's had been the only plane on the tarmac when he flew out after taking the job to capture the dictator. Tonight, three gold and white American Synergy Corporation Gulfstreams were parked at the lavish terminal Iboga had built to honor his regime. A euroAtlantic Airways Boeing 777 was getting ready to depart and a TAAG Angola Airlines 737 was taxiing toward the runway. The presence of scheduled passenger planes indicated to Janson that Ferdinand Poe had persuaded the airlines that Isle de Foree was sufficiently stable to resume commercial service to Lisbon and Luanda, which was no small achievement.

He saw a brand-new S-76D helicopter in gold and white ASC

livery lift off. Another was boarding a line of men in shirtsleeves with carry-on luggage. Assuming that they were ASC company men being ferried offshore to the *Vulcan Queen* drill ship for the "media shindig," Janson looked for Doug Case's wheelchair, but didn't see him. Maybe out with the first load.

The Isle de Foreen immigration officer who had cleared the Embraer when they were last here greeted Janson warmly. Janson asked where he might find Chief of Security da Costa.

"You just missed him. He's boarding the Lisbon flight."

"Da Costa's leaving?" Now, with Iboga on the loose? "The Lisbon plane's still on the ground. I have to see him."

"Come! Run! Perhaps we can catch him. We'll deal with the paperwork later."

The immigration officer led Janson into the terminal, where the emptiness of the vast building suggested that the commercial flights were not yet carrying many passengers. Lights were on everywhere, but few of the counters were manned and the travelers lined up at the gate to the euroAtlantic Lisbon flight were but a handful.

"There!"

Janson crossed the space at a dead run.

Da Costa, who was carrying a blazer over his arm and pulling a small wheeled bag, looked stunned to see him. "What are you doing, here, Mr. Janson?"

"Where are you going?" Janson asked.

"Lisbon. Holiday, actually."

Janson said, "I understand that Chief of Staff Margarido passed away."

"Tragic. So young."

"Isn't it an odd time for you to leave on holiday, with President Poe's chief of staff suddenly dead?"

Da Costa answered with a bland smile and a blithe, "This is a long-planned trip. Farewell."

"Are you aware that Iboga could be coming back?"

"I'm aware that you did not catch him. Farewell, Janson. I must go."

"Give me a parting gift," asked Janson.

"A gift?" Da Costa looked at him curiously. "I am not a wealthy man, Janson."

"Not a bribe. A gift that might make you feel a little better about leaving now of all times."

"What gift?"

"Before you leave for Lisbon, order Poe's presidential guard to form up at the palace."

"I can't do that. They're on maneuvers in the interior."

"No one is guarding the palace?"

"A few remain."

"Then please order them to give me clearance to land a helicopter at the palace."

Instead of asking Janson why, da Costa took out his cell phone. He looked relieved for a chance to help. "I can do that for you. How is the helicopter marked?"

"LibreLift. Gabon 'TR' prefix to the registration number."

Da Costa spoke briskly into his phone. Then he told Janson, "It is done."

"Thank you. Are you sure you don't want to postpone your holiday?"

Da Costa looked Janson in the face. A muscle was twitching in his cheek. "I survived as a spy in Iboga's stronghold by trusting my instincts. My instincts now tell me to board what could be the last flight to Lisbon. Please don't look at me with such disdain. It is not easy to turn your back."

"I know," said Janson. "It's almost as hard as *not* turning your back."

Da Costa flushed red. He spoke in a whisper. "The people who bribed me to leave think I did it for the money. I did it for my life. It's over, here. Iboga will rule. I would be a dead man to stay."

"Who gave you the money?"

Da Costa walked away. Nearly to the gate, he stopped and headed back.

Janson met him halfway. "Change your mind?"

"No," said da Costa. "But here is another gift. If I were you, I would read the flight status video display."

Janson's eyes shot to the nearest monitor. One more flight was scheduled tonight, an arrival from Angola. TAAG Angola Airlines 224 from Luanda, which had been originally scheduled for 2100, nine o'clock, was marked "Late" and was now rescheduled to arrive at midnight.

The security chief's pained smile told Janson all he had to know. Friends of Iboga, who was half-Angolan and a veteran of Angola's civil wars, had helped the deposed dictator board that flight so he could return to Isle de Foree.

* * *

THEY TOOK TAXIS to the Presidential Palace, two to accommodate the Spanish shooters' instrument cases, one for Janson and Kincaid and their bags.

"First time I ever took a cab to war," she muttered. "Where did everyone go? The streets are empty."

The palace itself was as surreally quiet. A single uniformed guard with an assault rifle and a pistol on his hip waved them inside and handed Janson a grease-stained business card that read: "LibreLift."

Janson sent Kincaid to speak with the anorexic French pilot and found Acting President Ferdinand Poe in his office with several elderly men and a boy of fourteen. Poe wore a white linen suit, his comrades their jungle fatigues. All were armed. Poe himself had a compact FN P90 on his desk with a stack of spare magazines, an incongruous sight until one recalled that less than a month ago Poe had been defending a rebel camp in the caves of Pico Clarence.

"Where is my army?" Poe echoed Janson's question bitterly. "Some units are on abruptly scheduled so-called 'maneuvers,' along with my guard. Several others are in their barracks, waiting to see what happens."

"Are they neutral?"

"For the moment. They fear Iboga more than me. They won't risk angering him until they see which way the wind blows, and it won't take much longer to see that it is blowing in my face."

"Where are Iboga's officers?"

Poe surprised him. "In Black Sand Prison, where they belong."

"Still in prison? Who's keeping them there?"

"My few loyal men hold the prison."

"Well, that's a damned good beginning," said Janson. "As long as they're locked up they can't turn the army against you."

"I fear that when Iboga arrives he will arrive in enough force to take the prison and free his officers. They will rally his former troops. When that happens it will be all over but the killing."

"I'm afraid he's on an Angola Airlines flight. He'll be in Porto Clarence by midnight."

"Goddamn Angolans! They probably held the plane for Iboga in hopes this nation implodes so our oil won't compete with theirs."

"I gather that's exactly what happened."

"And they probably permitted him to carry a load of weapons in the hold." Ferdinand Poe picked up his gun. He stared at it, hefted it familiarly in his scarred hand, and mused, "I never thought I would be a soldier. Or die a soldier's death."

"The latter's a bit premature," said Janson. "You've got good men at the prison, and a few good men here." He nodded at the old men and the boy. "And I have a small but powerful unit to help them. Iboga can do nothing until he releases his officers."

"How long will I last defending my palace? An hour? Two? Maybe three. Time and again I have proved tougher than I thought I was."

"Don't even *try* to defend this palace. Consolidate your forces and lead your men defending Black Sand Prison."

Poe shook his grizzled head. "I will consolidate my forces here."

"That will play into Iboga's hands. If you defend the palace instead of the prison his officers will escape and rouse the army."

"You see the dilemma. Even with your help, I don't have enough men to defend both the palace and the prison."

"But it is not a dilemma. All you have to do is defend the prison long enough for me to neutralize Iboga."

"No. I cannot go to the prison."

"Why not?"

"I cannot. I will not."

"I don't understand," said Janson.

An elderly man interrupted. "Acting President Poe suffered in Black Sand. Felt fear and pain you could not imagine."

"I *can* imagine," said Janson.

Poe said, "Then you understand that every man has his limit. This is mine. I cannot go to that place. I will fight here in the Presidential Palace."

"You'll die in the Presidential Palace," said Janson.

"If need be. I am not afraid to die."

"Dying won't help your country, Mr. President."

Jessica Kincaid, who had been listening in the doorway, stepped into the office. "Why don't we take you away to Lisbon or London? While we defend the prison and hunt Iboga."

"Good idea," said Janson.

"No," said Poe. "Once off Isle de Foree I am nothing but a pretender to the throne. I must remain in command of sovereign territory."

"Back to the mountains," said one of the older men.

"No, my friend, we aren't strong enough to hide in the mountains. At best, I would be isolated. At worst, hunted down like an animal."

"We did before."

"Before we went en masse," Poe said patiently. "I'm sorry. We had time to build defenses, time to get support from outside, money, gunrunners. Iboga underestimated us last time. He won't give us such time again."

Kincaid gestured for a word with Janson. He stood close and she whispered, "He's talking about defending the undefendable, Paul. I do not want to die defending the undefendable."

"Agreed."

The boy piped up with another idea. "Could we ask Nigeria to send soldiers to help us?"

"*Not Nigeria!*" every Isle de Foreen in the room chorused, which evoked sudden laughter. For a moment the tension was broken.

"There is another way," said Janson.

Poe interrupted bitterly, "To be valuable to giants is a curse."

Paul Janson repeated, "There is another way."

"What way?"

He felt Kincaid staring at him.

"Did they gas the helicopter?" he asked her.

"Topped up."

"Freddy, are you there?"

Freddy Ramirez stepped in from the hall, filling the doorway like a bull.

Janson addressed the room. "Listen up! Every fighter to the prison. Hold it at all costs. On the double." He turned back to Kincaid. "Take your rifle."

"Yes, sir."

"President Poe, let's get aboard that helicopter."

"No," Poe protested. "Where are you taking me?"

"You and I will slay giants."

"But where?"

"The one place," said Paul Janson, "where the president of Isle de Foree will be safe, visible, and totally in command."

FORTY-ONE

The anorexic French pilot of LibreLift's ancient Sikorsky S-76 had developed a severe cough in the weeks since he had ferried Janson and Kincaid out to the gunrunners' freighter. Janson thought the pilot sounded like a man dying of throat cancer. The sharp stink of leaking fuel irritated inflamed membranes. The burly Angolan co-pilot cast his partner worried looks as he hacked and hacked.

The cough interfered with his light touch and the helicopter flew clumsily as it skimmed the waves. Janson pressed a reassuring hand to Ferdinand Poe's shoulder. The lights of Porto Clarence faded in the equatorial haze. Ahead the ocean was dark and featureless.

Janson listened to the marine VHF radio, waiting for a hail on Channel 16 when an alert watch officer noticed an unidentified radar blip. After fifteen minutes flying in the dark at 130 knots—the most the old machine could make without the turbines rattling the rotors off—he saw a faint glow on the horizon.

It grew slowly brighter.

They were only five miles from the source of the light when the radio suddenly spoke. "Aircraft making one-three-five knots on course one-niner-four, this is *Vulcan Queen*. Do you read me?"

The query was routine. The drill ship's radar had spotted them and calculated their speed and course but was not likely to get an accurate fix on their altitude without receiving a transponder signal. The watch officer could see no transponder response and would logically attribute it to instrument failure or operator error.

Janson checked the time. Twenty-three-forty. As he had hoped, they were arriving before midnight. The *Vulcan Queen*'s third mate—the youngest, least experienced ship's officer—would still be standing the eight-to-twelve watch. The busy night of ASC helicopters coming and going should lull him into concluding that the unidentified craft was routine traffic. The trick was to stall to get as close as possible, but not so long that the watch officer would get nervous and call the captain, who would be sleeping in his quarters below the bridge.

Janson rigged the fast rope in the side door.

"Aircraft making one-three-five knots on course one-niner-four, this is *Vulcan Queen*. Please identify yourself and your intention."

"This is madness," said Poe. "They'll think we're pirates. They'll shoot us out of the sky."

"Pirates don't fly helicopters."

At a range of less than a mile, the ship looked brilliant as a city. Electric lights covered every inch of her, illuminating the tall square stacks in the stern, the full height of her forty-story drill towers, and the enormous bridge house on the bow. The thousand-foot-long, eighty-foot-high hull was so big it cast a wind shadow. Upwind of it, seas were breaking in whitecaps and slamming against the hull. In its lee the water was flat calm. A supply boat sheltered on that side, moored under a loading boom, bathed in work lamps.

Other offshore service vessels circled, waiting their turn. All three vessels bristled with firefighting monitors, a vivid reminder that the purpose of the vast and complex floating factory was to exploit explosively volatile hydrocarbons. The *Vulcan Queen* herself was festooned with bright orange fireproof lifeboats. They were free-fall escape craft, perched to slide down sharply sloped slipways and plunge into the sea.

White domes studded the roof of the six-story bridge house. They protected the satellite antennas that received GPS data for the dynamic positioning system that controlled the thrusters and propulsion pods that held the ship in place. Battered by wind and water, the *Vulcan Queen* neither rolled nor drifted. The DP held her in as firmly as a continent.

"Aircraft making one-three-five knots on course one-niner-four, this is *Vulcan Queen*."

Janson answered with a nonchalant oil patch drawl, "ASC 44 Crew Bird dropping in with a load of worms." "Worms" were novices, new men on the job.

The helicopter was so close now that Janson could distinguish individual derricks and deck cranes. The ship was drilling 24-7. Riggers climbed high in the draw works. Movement on the main deck caught his eye. A squad of security men was unlimbering the ship's sonic cannon and water guns, though it was hard to believe that any Gulf of Guinea pirates would risk suicide attacking such a big ship.

"ASC 44, I'm still negative on your transponder."

"I've been catching grief on that all day," Janson apologized.

Janson tapped the pilot's shoulder.

The Frenchman aimed straight at the helipad that was cantilevered out from the bridge and over the bow of the ship. The landing zone was mere yards from *Vulcan Queen's* DP control center, her most vulnerable asset.

The young voice on the radio was suddenly panicky: "Negative! Negative! You can't land without clearance."

"I got a whole crew of worms," Janson protested. "What do I do with these guys?"

He ripped off the headset and pulled on his rope gloves.

Coughing violently, the Frenchman put the machine in a hover fifty feet above the helipad. Janson dropped the fast rope and plunged down the braided line. Four seconds after his boots hit the helipad, he was racing down a flight of steel steps. He hit the landing and swung the corner to the second flight. Two uniformed security officers racing up the flight saw him coming.

They raised short-barrel shotguns to sweep the steps with buckshot.

Janson fired first. The muffled reports of the sound-suppressed MP5 were drowned out by the rotor thud and turbine whine of the helicopter racketing back up into the dark night sky.

He vaulted over the fallen guards and burst through the side door of the bridge.

The quiet, dark room was lit by computer screens and nav instruments.

Janson found only two men, neither a security officer, and knew that he had bet right. Private jets, fleets of helicopters, and giant ships made corporation men feel safe, even when they weren't.

The DP unit operator and the officer of the watch Janson had snowed on the radio gaped at his weapons and the balaclava that masked his face. The DP operator stayed at his keyboard and monitors. The frightened third mate, who looked twenty years old, fled to the opposite bridge wing door.

Janson got there first with his MP5 leveled at his chest.

"Easy, son. No one'll get hurt." He herded the third mate next to the DP operator, who was hunched over his instruments. "Do your job," Janson told the DP man. "Move only to maintain your ship's position. Do not let her drift. Understood?"

"Yes, sir."

To the third mate Janson said, "Call Captain Titus. When he answers, give me the handset."

The mate did as he was told and passed Janson the phone with a trembling hand. Janson spoke. "Captain Titus, come up to the bridge to greet the president of Isle de Foree."

"Who the hell is this?"

"We have secured the bridge of your ship, Captain Titus," said Janson, the "we" intended to keep them guessing about the size of his force. "Tell no one. Do not permit your security people to come with you. The first armed man we see, we start shooting DP computers."

"Are you out of your mind? The ship—"

"Your ship will immediately fall off-station. She will drift out of control. She will tear up the six miles of riser pipe and drill string that American Synergy Corporation has driven to the seabed at a cost of a hundred million dollars. Come now. Alone. Use the stairs, not the elevator. *Now!*"

Janson backed against a bulkhead where he could cover the elevator and the stairs and the doors to the bridge wings. "Open the door for the captain," he ordered.

The third mate did. Janson heard pounding footsteps. Only one man storming up the companionway. The captain burst into the bridge. He was a bull-necked, close-cropped bad-tempered-looking man in khaki, and if he feared a heavily armed, masked commando it did not show.

"Who in hell are you? What are you doing on my ship?"

"We've taken your ship," Janson repeated. "There will be no killing and no damage if you do exactly what you're told. If you don't, I'll take out the DP." Janson gestured at the third mate. "Radio the helicopter; clear him to land."

The mate looked at the captain.

"Do it!" shouted the captain.

The S-76 thundered down from the sky, the noise only slightly muffled by the pad over the bridge. After an agonizingly long wait, Ferdinand Poe appeared at the bridge wing door, leaning heavily on the Angolan co-pilot. The co-pilot helped him in, handed Poe the machine gun he had carried for him, and fled.

"Are you all right, sir?" Janson asked him.

Poe caught his breath and said, "Perfectly."

Janson said, "Captain Titus, this is your host, Acting President of Isle de Foree Ferdinand Poe."

Titus roared, "Who the hell do you think you are, boarding my ship on the high seas? Goddamned pirates."

Ferdinand Poe bristled. "We are not on the high seas, Captain."

"What?"

"We are on the sovereign territory of Isle de Foree. And you are my country's guest."

"Maritime law—"

"Maritime law permits you to sail through our territorial waters. But as long as your drill strings and risers attach you to our seabed, you are on Isle de Foree's property."

"Detaching them," Paul Janson noted, "is a simple matter of me shooting up those computers." He pointed his MP5 at the DP controller.

"I get the picture, goddammit. What do you want?"

"What ASC brass are aboard?"

"All of 'em. Half of goddamned Texas."

"What sort of security do they have?"

Captain Titus hesitated.

Janson said coldly, "This no place for a shoot-out. You have two hundred hands working aboard your ship, Captain—sailors, technicians, tool pushers, drillers, roughnecks, stewards, and cooks. Answer me very carefully."

"I have a four-man ASC security detail."

"How many more did Mr. Case bring with him?"

The captain's shoulders sagged. "Ten."

"What sort?"

"Militia."

Janson and Poe exchanged a quick glance.

Captain Titus straightened up again. He looked Janson in the eye and spoke like an officer accustomed to leavening authority with common sense. "Mister, they've got you outmanned and outgunned. Why don't you save a lot of innocent people a lot of sorrow and put down your weapons?"

FORTY-TWO

Three decks below the *Vulcan Queen*'s bridge, fifteen men and three women who had flown most of the night and day from Houston ate at a long table in the drill ship's conference room. The table was laid in white linen and heavy silver. Quietly efficient black stewards served.

Doug Case hid an amused smile at the diners' pasty faces and stringy hair. ASC company lore held that no one in the oil business worked harder than ASC's so-called officer corps. No matter how long they'd traveled, no matter how far they'd come, ASC executives hit the ground running, rolled up their sleeves, and went straight to work. All the while pretending they didn't wish they were showering off the sixteen-hour plane ride and falling face-down on their mattresses.

Tonight, work was a full-press media massage to sell the special partnership between benevolent American Synergy Corporation and the grateful, stable island nation of Isle de Foree. Straight to work meant hosting egghead reporters from NPR, PBS, the BBC, and the *New York Times*, at a sustainable dinner of Isle de Foreen reef fish caught by artisanal fishermen. Rolling up sleeves involved sharing exclusive news of a major commercial ultradeepwater oil discovery. How major? The mother of all reserves. "Oh, and by the way, our old friend President for Life Iboga has come home to stabilize his nation."

The fabled, ancient, and rarely seen "Buddha," CEO Bruce Danforth himself, led the charm attack, demonstrating that he respected the media by being bluntly unapologetic. Despite Doug Case's vaunted title President of Global Security, this was the first time he had been in the same room with the reclusive CEO, and he was deeply impressed. The Buddha was pushing ninety, but he was a damned sharp ninety.

"Coal," Buddha addressed the dinner table in a roundabout answer to an NPR query, "will be the primary source of energy in the world for another hundred years. Oil will be the secondary source. Natural gas the third. Whether we like it or not, the methods of energy conversion established by James Watt's steam engine and Charles Parsons's steam turbine are still with us. Heat is power. Improved, refined, enhanced—heat is *still* power. And we will create eighty-five percent of that heat—that power—by burning fossil fuel."

Case glanced at ASC's vice president of media relations. The poor fool, who spent a large portion of his workdays attempting to convince dubious reporters that ASC was a green corporation passionately committed to renewable energy, winced.

Danforth noticed and did not look pleased. "Young man," he said in a dangerous tone that brooked no argument, "you look tired from your journey. You should go to your cabin and rest. Now."

The PR man left the table, ashen faced.

Danforth raised a wrinkled finger and when he had everyone's attention, again, repeated the NPR question that had prompted his blunt statement. "Will American Synergy impede the development of renewable sources of energy that currently supply the other fifteen percent? Of course not. We don't have to. ASC has no need to limit the potential of renewable energy. Physics will do it for us."

"Physics or the free market?" came a question down the table.

Case's phone vibrated. News from Black Sand Prison. Hopefully getting better.

He backed his chair from the table to take the call while the Buddha gave the woman who had asked a smile that had melted female hearts for decades before she was born and proceeded not to answer her question. "ASC invests millions to develop renewable sources. We reap a tax deduction. And if ASC's scientists do stumble past the current laws of physics, we will hold the patents."

Clearly, Bruce Danforth loved running the biggest oil corporation in America and would stay in charge until they carried him out in a coffin. Long enough time for Doug Case to develop a lasting relationship with the man. Particularly if Buddha, not Helms, was his private mentor, The Voice.

Case put his phone down and drove his wheelchair between Bruce Danforth and Kingsman Helms.

"Poe's people are putting up a hell of a fight at the prison. Iboga's advance party is falling back."

The Buddha's old, yellowish eyes fixed unpleasantly on Case. Nearby executives and reporters pretended not to be trying to hear, which they could not, as the CEO of American Synergy Corporation was an expertly quiet mutterer and his words did not carry. "You did not predict this, Douglas."

"No, Mr. Danforth," Case admitted with a sinking heart. Acting President Poe's hotly fought defense of the prison was not in the plan. At this moment Iboga's freed officers were supposed to be welcoming him at the airport for a triumphal march to the Presidential Palace.

"Nor did you, Kingsman."

"No, sir."

Buddha's dry, cracked lips barely moved. "What the fuck are you going to do about it?"

Kingsman Helms looked stricken. As well he should, thought Doug Case. The oil executive had never been in a gunfight. Case had. He took charge.

"I had hoped that Iboga's advance party would wrap things up before he landed, Mr. Danforth. But I guarantee that the moment Iboga himself steps off that plane with fresh men and weapons, he will turn the tide."

FORTY-THREE

Iboga, who had purchased every seat in the Business Class section of the TAAG 224 from Luanda, spread out a topo map of Porto Clarence and rehearsed the run from the airport to Black Sand Prison. Nine mercenary commandos sat nearby, paying close attention to the returning dictator. Victory, the release of Iboga's officers, would depend on disciplined adherence to his bold plan. None of this small force doubted it would work. Regardless of rumors of drug-addled cannibalism and his almost comical rolls of neck fat bulging from his yellow kaffiyeh, it was immediately apparent that Iboga was first and foremost a soldier who knew his business.

The snipers were first off the plane when they landed.

Their mission was to break up checkpoints and ambushes with long-range fire. While the rest of the assault force bullied the ground crew into quickly unloading their rocket launchers from the cargo hold, a waiting taxi raced the marksmen through the empty streets, dropping one at a key intersection with the beach road and delivering the other to Parliament House, a neoclassical building with a tall, spindly clock tower. The clock read ten minutes until midnight. An Iboga loyalist pointed the way to circular stairs. From the open belfry the sniper could cover the last mile of the beach road that Iboga would travel to Black Sand Prison.

The tower was a hundred feet tall, the stairs steep. The sniper was sweating in the humid night air and his weapon case was growing heavy when he reached the four-sided clock. One more story to the bell. He dragged himself up that last flight and stepped into the open. It was pitch-black. In the distance he could see the front of Black Sand Prison harshly bathed in floodlights. He scoped it through binoculars. Dead soldiers were scattered on the ground in front of the walls. The walls themselves were pocked by hundreds of rounds of assault rifle fire and scorched by grenade explosions. But the gates were still closed.

The defenders, who were sure to be spooked and bloodied from repelling the first attack, were in for a shock when Iboga's force attacked with rockets. The sniper pulled down his night goggles and knelt to open his gun case.

"This seat is taken."

He whirled toward the sound of a woman's voice and pawed his pistol from its thigh holster.

"Don't," she said.

He had missed her in the dark before he donned his night gear. She was crouched like an elf, close enough to touch, an eerie vision tinted phosphorus green. She had light-enhancing glasses, too. Panoramics that covered most of her face. She had a pistol with a noise and flash suppressor in her hand and a Knight's M110 SASS on a bipod. The semiautomatic sniper rifle was pointed at the prison.

Stupid woman. What the hell did she think she could hit at a thousand meters? Excellent gun, though, better than his; excellent night glasses, too, far better than his. An unexpected opportunity to upgrade. He faked a clumsy lunge at her to force her off-balance and sprang sideways, drawing his pistol. His last sight on earth was a flash from hers.

* * *

JESSICA KINCAID LISTENED until she was sure no one else was coming up the stairs. Then she lay prone on the stone floor of the bell tower and zeroed her rifle in on the prison's iron doors. In five minutes she heard a car on the beach road moving at high speed. Headlights flicked through the palm trees that lined the road. A second vehicle was right behind it. And then a third. They passed her position and kept going.

"Let them get close," she muttered, but Freddy and his boys were pumped by the first fight to defend the prison. They opened fire too soon on the lead car.

Sure enough, the car stopped in time. Three guys with guns piled out, unscathed, and dove for cover in the trees. The second car stopped behind the first, the third behind that. Three more men tumbled out of each, professionals moving fast and low.

Iboga appeared brighter in the thermal-enhanced panoramics than the commandos around him. The fat man emitted more heat. His kaffiyeh headdress showed up darker than his skull, as did the rocket launcher that he was waving like a drum major's mace to rally his men and coordinate their attack.

Using the first car for cover, two aimed rocket launchers at the gates. Others flitted through the trees to fire from flanking positions. Kincaid could see Iboga's plan clearly in her mind. It was neat, clean, and ballsy. Freddy and four operators and Poe's old men were now trapped between a potent assault force outside the prison and a mob of army officers inside who were primed to attack their jailors at the sound of rocket fire.

FORTY-FOUR

Doug Case's phone vibrated. He checked the screen: Paul Janson, enabling his phone to prompt caller ID—the sort of thing you would do if you were calling for help from an Italian jail.

"I better answer this," Case said.

"Don't roll off," said the Buddha. "Stay right here."

"Hello, Paul. How is sunny Italy?"

"Bring the reporters up to the bridge to meet President Poe."

"What bridge— *What?* Are you on this ship?"

"Bring the press up here to meet President Poe or I will disable the dynamic positioning units. Both of them. Do you understand what that means?"

Case had trouble catching his breath. "Yes."

"Do you also understand what a blood-soaked catastrophe it would be if you brought your shooters?"

"Yes."

"Do you understand that I feel betrayed?"

Case steadied himself. This situation could be dealt with. "Yeah," he said. "I understand you feel betrayed, but you don't know by whom."

"No witness, no crime?"

"I'm not the villain."

"Is Helms there?"

"Right here."

"Put him on."

Doug Case did not bother covering the phone as he whispered, "It's Paul Janson. He's here! On the *Vulcan Queen*, demanding we bring the press up to the bridge—*of this ship*—to meet Ferdinand Poe."

"The bridge? The DP is up there."

"He figured that out. Here!" He offered the phone. "Try not to piss him off."

"Janson," Helms said smoothly. "I hope you are in your right mind and not about to do anything rash."

"I'm staying alive by threatening rash. I am not sure who is behind all this. I will find out. In the meantime, I have stopped you cold."

"Surely we can work something out."

"Is the Buddha there?"

Kingsman Helms pressed the phone into the CEO's wrinkled hand.

* * *

BRUCE DANFORTH HAD heard a helicopter land a minute ago and had wondered who was on it. Now he knew. He put a smile on his face for the benefit of the reporters and executives and muttered so they could not hear, "Bruce Danforth here, Janson. You know I always wanted to shake your hand back in the day. But your old boss, Derek Collins, informed me that the lawyers said that we were better off never shaking hands in the event I had to deny your existence."

"I learned to trust Derek," Janson said coldly.

"I was Derek's boss."

"That's news to me."

"Way back in the day. By the time you came along I had retired into the private sector. But I keep up with the top people, the best. Perhaps I'll get my wish tonight."

"I can't shake your hand. I'm holding a weapon."

"You could put it down."

"I don't think so."

"You could name a price to leave quietly."

"You could name who murdered my pilots and Dr. Terry Flannigan."

"I do not know what you are talking about." ·

"You could also tell me who called in the Reaper attack on Pico Clarence."

"Now I'm truly baffled," the Buddha said smoothly.

* * *

PAUL JANSON KNEW that he was beaten, for the moment, in his desire to connect crimes perpetrated by faceless minions to the masterminds on high. He had just *proven* that private jets, fleets of helicopters, and giant ships made corporation men feel safe, even when they weren't. But the sense of entitlement bestowed by those layers upon layers upon layers of separation from ordinary people empowered the corporation with the mighty strength of bland denial. Janson could rail at ASC's CEO until he was blue in the face, but Bruce Danforth and Kingsman Helms and Doug Case could shelter for years in a castle built of layers and layers and layers of hidden truths, half-truths, and unknowable lies. For years. But not forever, Janson promised himself. To attack the masterminds on high, he would have to dismantle their castle stone by stone.

"Bring the media," he told Danforth. "You, Helms, Case, and the reporters only. No one else."

* * *

KINCAID RESTED HER cheek against the M110's stock and searched for Iboga in the night scope's circle of fire.

The commandos had crept within a hundred yards of the prison gates. Iboga was in the lead. She wondered why they were waiting so long to fire their rockets. Iboga signaled with his, waving them ahead, urging them even closer, and Kincaid realized that he wanted them so close that they could storm the gates the instant they blew them open.

Iboga commanded like a born leader. For what had to be a quickly thrown-together unit, their discipline was impressive. Only if they saw him dead would they give up the attack.

Iboga crouched behind a palm tree eighty yards from the gates.

He had finally stopped moving.

Nine hundred meters was a very long shot.

Kincaid aligned her rifle on him. She moved her heels to lie straight with the gun. She held her head upright. She peered with her right eye directly behind the night scope. She closed both eyes, took several measured breaths. She opened her eyes. The crosshairs were on the tree an inch from Iboga's head. She moved her heels a quarter inch, lined up, and lay still. She found her point of aim three inches below the *agal* cord that tied his kaffiyeh to his skull.

She inhaled. She exhaled. She touched the trigger. The crosshairs drifted right. She released pressure on the trigger, inhaled, exhaled, and regained her point of aim. She touched the trigger and pulled it steadily back, back, back, back—

The clock tower bell pealed the first stroke of midnight. It clanged thunderously and shook the stone floor.

Miss!

She could hear her daddy laughing like he was sitting on her shoulder. Eight years old, practicing and practicing to show him she could shoot as good as any damned son he never had. *Lookit, Didder.* She hadn't yet overcome the speech impediment that made her mispronounce certain words, so she made up words, "Didder" for "Daddy." "Squirrel" was "skizzy." *Skizzy up a seventy-foot oak tree. Lookit, Didder!*

The damn squirrel zigged when it should have zagged.

Miss. Didder laughed.

She'd practiced loading, too—loading quick and firing fast till her shoulder ached from the recoils. Bolt-action .22. She popped a fresh round in the chamber faster than that little sucker could climb and at least on that one day won her father's heart. "The second shot," he told her proudly that night, scrambling eggs and squirrel brains for their supper, "the shot after you missed, *that shot* separated the men from the boys."

Iboga must have felt the bullet pass. But he didn't know from where, assumed it came from the prison instead of half a mile in back of him, and stayed behind his tree while the parliament clock boomed twelve strokes and Kincaid lined up her second shot.

* * *

PAUL JANSON CROUCHED in shadow at the front of the bridge with his back to a steel bulkhead and his eyes raking the doors and windows in case someone in ASC security planned to be stupid. The *Vulcan Queen*'s DP controllers that flanked the helm were so critical to the deepwater drilling operation that there were redundant units in the event of system failure. Janson aimed his MP5 at the one on the left, which was currently offline. Swiveling the barrel would take out the one on the right.

Kingsman Helms came first, bounding up the stairs. The captain intercepted him, as Janson had instructed, and kept him by the elevators. Both elevator doors opened simultaneously and an old man who had to be Bruce Danforth stepped out of the first one, followed by Doug Case in his wheelchair, which he immediately raised to full height. The other elevator delivered the reporters. Janson counted three men and two women, one of whom he recognized as a brave and beautiful NPR correspondent he had slept with years ago in Afghanistan.

Those wielding mini video cameras for their Web sites suddenly focused on Ferdinand Poe, who walked slowly in from the bridge wing. He looked tired and weary and too old to be cradling an FN P90 personal defense weapon.

"There you are, Mr. Acting President. Everyone wants to meet you, sir."

Helms reached out to sling a comradely arm around Ferdinand Poe. The old man eluded him and stood aloof for his introduction. Helms uttered the bare minimum.

"Ladies and Gentlemen, I present to you a brave patriot: Acting President of Isle de Foree Ferdinand Poe."

"Good evening," said Poe. "Or night. It's late. I know you all traveled a long, long way to our island nation and I will make two brief remarks. One, a splendid commercial oil discovery is being confirmed in Isle de Foreen waters by this drill ship on which we stand—good news for the people of Isle de Foree and good news for consuming nations dependent on Nigeria's dwindling reserves."

He stared past them as though collecting his thoughts, but he was looking into the shadow where Janson hid, waiting for news about Iboga. One of the reporters, a tall man in a white shirt, followed Poe's gaze.

Tsk.

Janson had his earpiece plugged into his sat phone. He brought the phone to his lips. "Go ahead."

"It's over." She sounded utterly wiped out.

"Good job."

"Can we go home now?"

Paul Janson stood and flashed Poe the thumbs-up.

As he did, the reporter in the white shirt dropped his camera. Stooping as if to pick it up, the reporter slid a pistol from an ankle holster and charged straight at Janson, cocking the gun with the practiced grace of a trained professional. Janson barely had time to raise the MP5 and thumb the fire selector off AUTO. But the real reporters were directly behind the imposter, and he couldn't fire—even on semiautomatic—without risking killing an innocent.

Janson dropped his weapon and stepped forward, raising his hands.

"No prisoners," the gunman said, and Janson could see in his eyes that he meant to kill him. A woman screamed. Men shouted and dove to the deck. But by then Janson's step forward had brought the gunman within range of his combat boots. The sound of a knee breaking was almost as loud as the shot the gunman managed to squeeze off as he fell.

The bullet burned across Janson's leg and pierced the online DP unit. An alarm shrilled and the backup cut in automatically.

Janson kicked his fallen attacker twice more and the man lay still. "Case!" Janson shouted. "Call your boys off. You've only got one DP left."

Bruce Danforth raised his voice before Case could speak. "Security, stand down. No one move. No one." With a tight smile, he added, "Excepting the masked operator with the gun. Your call, sir. What do you want?"

Paul Janson stepped back into the shadows. "I want President Poe to complete his remarks. I want the reporters to listen carefully. Continue, please, President Poe."

"Two," said Ferdinand Poe. "I am gratified to announce that a clumsy attempt to overthrow my government by former dictator Iboga has been put down. Bloodshed was minimal. I stand before you alive and well, and the former dictator has been captured."

"Killed," Janson interrupted.

"Killed," Poe echoed. He stooped to lay his machine gun on the deck and stood displaying empty hands.

Janson smiled. He had backed a winner.

"I say to my soldiers and their officers—all their officers—the brutal days of Iboga are done forever. Iboga is gone forever. I am also pleased to announce that a sizable portion of the treasury Iboga stole has been recovered. It is a good day in Isle de Foree.... Do you have any questions?"

The reporters looked over their shoulders to where Janson had stood, looked at the fallen security man with one leg twisted at a terrible angle, and turned around again to look agape at Poe. The woman Janson remembered from Afghanistan recovered first.

"Would you call it a fortunate coincidence, or did you just happen to be aboard the *Vulcan Queen* when the coup was launched?"

"Fortunate, in that I was not present to be killed."

The bridge rang with laugher.

"And a happy coincidence," said Poe. "Because when the good news came of Iboga's surrender we were already celebrating negotiating new terms of our royalty contract with the fine people of the American Synergy Corporation who have agreed to allow other oil companies to participate in developing Isle de Foree's spectacular new reserves. A consortium will be formed. Its board of directors will include Isle de Foreen government ministers."

Ferdinand Poe thrust his scarred hand at Kingsman Helms.

Helms shook it with a ghastly smile.

Janson watched Doug Case's face as the journalists pushed past his wheelchair to get close to Poe and Helms. For the life of him, he could not read what Doug was thinking.

* * *

THE EMBRAER HELD too many ghosts. They flew commercial to Lisbon, slept round the clock in a fine hotel, then boarded a plane to New York. Janson read about Czar Alexander's defeat of Napoléon. Kincaid watched movies, stared out the window, and paced the aisles. They caught a cab into Midtown and walked the sidewalks, working out the travel kinks.

"You still don't believe in revenge?" Kincaid asked.

Janson hesitated. "Generally that is still true. I wish I could say never, but not this time."

"But you didn't kill them."

"I don't know which one to kill. I do not know which of them is the bad guy. One of them? Two of them? All of them? But at least I took away what they wanted."

"You took away Isle de Foree."

"And left them alive to live with their defeat."

"What makes you think they won't try again?"

Paul Janson grinned, suddenly optimistic, hoping that he could fix what was broken. "What makes *them* think I won't stop them again?"

"Why do you have such an Achilles' heel for Doug Case?"

Taken aback, Janson asked, "In what way? What do you mean?"

"You're so quick to believe him. The story you told me about how he shot the operator who was torturing an asset? How do you know it's true? Who knows what really happened and why he shot the guy?"

"Doug's story is true."

"How do you know for sure?"

"I was there."

"You were there? *You were there?* I didn't realize that.... I'm surprised you didn't shoot the guy yourself."

"It wasn't an option."

"Why not?"

"My hands were tied."

Kincaid looked at him, her big eyes growing bigger. "*You* were the asset being tortured by the agent Doug Case shot?"

"The agent was a sadistic lunatic—one of those people who look for an excuse to feel righteous causing pain. He convinced himself I was a traitor. I wasn't. Doug intervened on my behalf. But it was traumatic. He knew the guy well, had been through the wars with him. It pretty much destroyed him."

Kincaid nodded her head for a long time. At last, she said, "Wow."

Janson said, "The experience left me with warm feelings toward Doug."

They crossed Broadway and walked a half block through tourists and crowds of people getting out of the theaters. Somewhere a loudspeaker was blaring "Shake That Thing."

Kincaid asked, "Can we agree on something?"

"Anything."

"Can we agree that you are not entirely clearheaded on the subject of American Synergy Corporation's president of security?"

"Agreed," said Paul Janson.

They walked into the Hotel Edison and down a steep flight of stairs.

The Nighthawks were playing "Blue Skies."

The curly-haired brunette knockout who took the cover charge never forgot a face. "Welcome back," she said to Kincaid. "Good to see you, again."

Paul Janson got the dazzling smile reserved for new customers.

Acknowledgments

I want to thank my old shipmate Hunt Hatch; my old schoolmate Mike Coligny; my generous cockpit host Ed Daugherty; and Old Rhinebeck Aerodrome "mechanician" Christopher Ford for helping me understand airplanes. And thank you Alasdair Lyon and Ken Pike for showing me what astonishing machines helicopters are.

Afterword

For a young writer starting out in New York, few pleasures equaled being hailed across a crowded publishing party by Robert Ludlum He would burst from a circle of admirers, his big, cheery face alight with a welcoming smile, throw an arm around my shoulders, hug hard with astonishing strength, and announce to the scores of literary kings and queens within range of his mighty voice, "Meet the best writer I know." This style of introduction was pure Bob Ludlum. That it was typical of his generous support and boundless enthusiasm toward new writers in no way diminished the thrill.

When, years later, I was invited to create a new series based on Consular Operations "Machine" Paul Janson, the haunted hero of one of Bob's later novels, the first thing I remembered was basking in the affectionate glow of his enthusiasm. I remembered, too, the upbeat ending of *The Janson Directive*—a finely plotted thriller of betrayal that was a stylistic throwback to the taut novels he was writing way back when he and I first met.

I recalled that the end of the novel reflected the Robert Ludlum I knew—the big fellow with his arms wide, a scotch in one hand, a smoke in the other, flashing the hope-filled smile of a man who celebrated everyone's dreams.

I reread *The Janson Directive* to see what, if anything, I could bring to it. It was good. It was exciting. It had some dauntingly gorgeous writing, and some equally daunting research, and the end was even better than I remembered.

In the end, Paul Janson wins a partner—a deadly young woman whom he admires for her strength, bravery, skills, and determination to be the best she can be. Paul Janson, "The Machine," the best of the best and the deadliest, is in awe of young Jessica Kincaid's fighting skills and has never seen a better sniper. And Jessica is equally in awe of the older Janson's experience and undiminished strength and his chameleon-like ability to be almost invisible.

But the best part is that Paul Janson is keenly aware that in Jessica Kincaid he has been given a great gift. This reflected deeper layers of the writer I had known, the married Robert Ludlum whom I had observed at smaller, more intimate gatherings minus the mob of publishers. For no man ever loved a wife more madly than he loved Mary. He was thrilled by her existence.

The gift of Paul Janson that Robert Ludlum left his readers is a hero who has faced his grim past and now hungers to atone. Paul Janson is a man who reviews his life in small ways on a constant basis. He is a man who is against his own record, who has come to wonder whether sanctioned killings in the service of his country were also serial killings.

From my point of view—that of a writer invited to create Janson's future—a hero who looks into the mirror with a cold eye and swears to redeem himself is a dramatic hero who hungers to stand up to huge challenges and immense danger. That Janson has a partner covering his back makes him all the more formidable. That he might fear for her makes even "The Machine" vulnerable.

The Janson Directive's ending was the essence of the man Robert Ludlum was. But it was also an invitation to continue the story. Ludlum's hero had journeyed to a new place. A new place is a jumping-off point for new journeys, and if that isn't the definition of a splendid series, it ought to be the rule for how to write one. Clearly, Robert Ludlum was not thinking of *The Janson Directive* as a one-off book but the beginning of something new. That was all the freedom I needed to accept the invitation to journey on with *The Janson Command*.

Paul Garrison
Connecticut
2012

About the Authors

ROBERT LUDLUM was the author of twenty-six international best-selling novels, published in thirty-two languages and forty countries. He is perhaps best known as the creator and author of three novels featuring Jason Bourne: *The Bourne Identity*, *The Bourne Supremacy*, and *The Bourne Ultimatum*. Ludlum passed away in March 2001.

PAUL GARRISON is the author of the critically acclaimed thrillers *Fire and Ice*, *Red Sky at Morning*, *Buried at Sea*, *Sea Hunter*, and *The Ripple Effect*. Raised on the stories of his grandfather who wandered the South Seas in the last of the square-rigged copra-trading vessels, he has worked with boats, tugs, and ships. He is currently writing the next novel in the new Paul Janson series.

SNEAK PREVIEW!

With U.S. intelligence agencies wracked by internal power struggles and paralyzed by bureaucracy, the president had been forced to establish his own clandestine group—Covert-One. With operators selected from the very best America has to offer, this team is only activated as a last resort, when the threat is on a global scale and time is running out.

Welcome to Robert Ludlum's blockbuster international thriller series Covert-One.

Please turn the page for an early look at

THE ARES DECISION

A new Covert-One novel written by *New York Times* best-selling writer Kyle Mills.

Available wherever books are sold.

ONE

Above Northern Uganda
November 12, 0203 Hours GMT +3

The roar in Craig Rivera's ears combined with the darkness to make everything he knew—everything real—disappear. He wondered if astronauts felt the same sense of emptiness, if they wondered like he did whether God was just at the edge of their vision.

He looked at a dial glowing faint green on his wrist. The letters were Cyrillic, but the numbers tracking his altitude and coordinates were the same as the government-issue unit he trained with.

Rivera tilted his body slightly, angling north as he fell through fifteen thousand feet. A hint of warmth and humidity began to thaw the skin around his oxygen mask, and below the blackness was now punctured by widely scattered, barely perceptible points of light.

Campfires.

When his GPS confirmed that he was directly over the drop zone, he rolled on his back for a moment, staring up at a sky full of stars and searching futilely for the outline of the plane he'd jumped from.

They were alone. That, if anything, had been made perfectly clear.

He knew little about the country he was falling into at 125 miles an hour and even less about the man they'd been sent to find. Caleb Bahame was a terrorist and a murderer so cruel that it was difficult to know if the intelligence on him was accurate or just a bizarre tapestry of legends created by a terrified populace. Some of the stories, though, were undeniable. The fact that he demanded his men heat the machetes they used to hack the limbs from infants, for instance, had considerable photo evidence. As did the suffering of the children as they slowly died from their cauterized wounds.

The existence of men like this made Rivera wonder if God wasn't perfect—if even He made mistakes. And if so, perhaps His hand was directly involved in this mission.

Not that those kinds of philosophical questions really mattered. While Bahame wasn't good for much, he would probably be just fine at stopping bullets—a hypothesis that Rivera was looking forward to testing. Preferably with multiple clips.

He glanced at his altimeter again and rolled back over, squinting through his goggles at the jungle canopy rushing toward him in the starlight. After a few more seconds, the glowing numbers turned red and he pulled his chute, sending himself into a fast spiral toward a clearing that he couldn't yet see but that the intel geeks swore was there.

He was just over a hundred feet from the ground when he spotted his LZ and aimed for it, beginning a sharp descent that sent him crashing to earth with a well-practiced roll. After gathering up his canopy, he ran for the cover of the jungle, dropping his pack and retrieving his night-vision goggles and rifle.

The well-worn AK-47 felt a little strange in his hands as he swept it along the tree line and listened to his team touch down at thirty-second intervals. When he counted four, he activated his throat mike.

"Sound off. Everyone okay?"

These kinds of jumps were impossible to fully control, and he felt a little of the tension in his stomach ease when all his men checked in uninjured.

Rivera moved silently through the jungle, the roar of the wind now replaced by the buzz of insects and the screech of tropical birds. They'd picked this area because the brutal terrain discouraged people from settling it. About twenty miles into the hike out he imagined he'd be cursing the choice, but right now the fact that no one was chasing them with red-hot machetes was a big check in the plus column.

His team coalesced into an optimally spaced line as they moved north. Rivera fell in behind a short, wiry man wearing a black sweatshirt with cut-off sleeves revealing arms streaked with green paint. The Israeli machine gun in his hands swept smoothly from left to right as he glided over terrain that would have left a normal man stumbling hopelessly from one tree to another. But he wasn't a normal man. None of them were.

Their equipment and clothing were a patchwork collected from around the world. None of them had any tattoos or other identifying marks—even their dental work had been altered to make its country of origin indeterminate. If they were captured or killed, there would be no fanfare or place in history. No heroic stories for relatives and friends to take comfort in. Just a tiny headstone over an empty grave.

"Approaching rendezvous point," the man on point said, his voice slightly distorted by Rivera's over-the-counter earpiece. "Approximately ten meters."

The neat line of men dissolved into the jungle again, surrounding a small patch of land that had been recently burned by a lightning strike. Rivera peered through the foliage at the blackened trees, finally spotting a tall Ugandan standing alone in the ash. He was completely motionless except for his head, which jerked back and forth at every sound, as though the earth was jolting him with leftover electricity.

"Move in," Rivera said into his throat mike.

He'd seen it a hundred times in training, but watching his men melt from the jungle always made him feel a twinge of pride. On neutral ground, he'd put them up against anyone in the world, be they the SAS, Shayetet 13, or hell's own army.

The man in the clearing let out a quiet yelp at the ghosts materializing around him and then threw an arm over his face. "Take off your night-vision equipment," he said in heavily accented English. "It was our agreement."

"Why?" Rivera said, peeling his goggles off and signaling for his men to do the same. It had been a bizarre precondition, but it was indeed part of the deal.

"You must not look at my face," the man replied. "Bahame can see through your eyes. He can read minds."

"Then you know him?" Rivera said.

The Ugandan was only a shadowy outline, but he sagged visibly as he answered. "He took me as a child. I fought for many years in his army. I did things that cannot be spoken of."

"But you escaped."

"Yes. I chased a family that ran into the jungle when we attacked their village. I didn't harm them, though. I just ran. I ran for days."

"You told our people that you know how to find him."

When he didn't respond, Rivera dug a sack full of euros from his pack and held it out. The Ugandan accepted it but still didn't speak. He just stared down at the nylon bag in his hands.

"I have six children. One—my son—is very sick."

"Well, you should be able to get him help with that money."

"Yes."

He held out a piece of paper and Rivera took it, sliding his night-vision goggles in front of his eyes for a moment to examine the hand-drawn map. The level of detail was impressive and it seemed to more or less match the satellite photos of the area.

"I have done my part," the Ugandan said.

Rivera nodded and turned back toward the trees, but the man grabbed his shoulder.

"Run," he said. "Tell the men who hired you that you could not find him."

"Why would I do that?"

"He leads an army of demons. They cannot be frightened. They cannot be killed. Some even say they can fly."

Rivera shrugged off the man's hand and slipped back into the jungle.

Hell's own army.

TWO

The light of dawn was beginning to penetrate the jungle canopy, dispelling the darkness that had become so comfortable. Lt. Craig Rivera slipped past the man in front of him, wanting to take point personally until the confusing twilight finally gave way to day.

The condensation on the leaves was already starting to heat up, turning into mist that weighed down his clothes and felt thick in his lungs. He eased up a steep, rocky slope, dropping into a prone position at its crest. More than a minute passed as he scanned the tangle of leaves and branches for a human outline. Nothing. Just the endless shimmer of wet leaves.

He started to move again but froze when a voice crackled over his earpiece. "Keep your eyes on the sky."

Rivera pressed himself against the broad trunk of a tree and looked up, putting a hand to his throat mike. "What have you got?"

"Bahame could swoop down on us at any minute shooting fireballs from his ass."

The quiet snickers of the men closest to Rivera were audible in the silence and he started forward again, trying to decide how to respond. "Radio discipline. Let's not forget what happened to the other guys."

An African Union team had gotten a tip on Bahame's location and come after him about six months ago. All that was left of them was an audio recording.

Rivera would never admit it to his men, but he could still hear it in his head—the calm chatter and controlled fire devolving into panicked shouts and wild bursts on full automatic, the screams of attackers who sounded more animal than human. And finally the crash of body against body, the grunts of hand-to-hand combat, the bloody gurgles of death.

After he and his team had listened to it, they'd blown it off with the expected bravado. African Union forces? Hadn't they gotten taken down by a Girl Scout troop in Cameroon? Weren't they the guys whose mascot was a toy poodle?

As team leader, though, Rivera has seen the dead soldiers' files. They weren't reassigned meter maids from Congo, as one of his men had suggested after polishing off the better part of a twelve-pack. They were solid operators working in their own backyard.

Rivera threw up a fist and crouched, aiming his AK through the trees at a flash of tan in the sea of emerald. Behind him, he could hear nothing but knew his men were fanning out into defensive positions.

He eased onto his stomach and slithered forward, controlling his breathing and being careful not to cause the bushes above him to sway with his movement. It took more than five minutes to cover twenty yards, but finally the jungle thinned and he found himself at the edge of a small village.

The woven straw wall of the hut in front of him was about the only thing that hadn't been burned—and that included the residents. It was hard to determine precisely how many blackened bodies were piled next to what may have once been a soccer goal, but forty was a reasonable guess. It seemed that their intel was good. This was Bahame country.

Behind him, he heard a quiet grunt and something that sounded like a body hitting the soft ground. Swearing under his breath, he headed back toward the noise, finger hooked lightly around the trigger of his gun.

"Sorry, boss. Nothin' I could do. She came right up on me."

The woman was cowering against a tree, holding her hands in front of her in frozen panic. Her eyes darted back and forth as his men materialized from the foliage and surrounded her.

"Who you figure she is?" one of them said quietly.

"There's a village up there," Rivera responded. "Or at least there was. Bahame got to it. She must have given him the slip. Probably been living on her own out here for the past few days."

There was an infected gash in her arm and her ankle was grotesquely twisted to the right, bones pushing at the skin but not quite breaking through. Rivera tried to determine her age, but there were too many contradictions—skin the color and texture of an old tire, strong, wiry arms, straight white teeth. The truth was he didn't know anything about her and he never would.

"What are we going to do with her?" one of his men asked.

"Do you speak English?" Rivera said, enunciating carefully.

She started to talk in her native language, the volume of her voice startling in the silence. He clamped a hand over her mouth and held a finger to his lips. *"Do you speak any English?"*

When he pulled his hand away, she spoke more quietly, but still in the local dialect.

"What do you think, boss?"

Rivera took a step back, a trickle of salty sweat running over his lips and into his mouth. He didn't know what he thought. He wanted to call back to Command, but he knew what Admiral Kaye would say—that he wasn't there on the ground. That it wasn't his call.

"She's no friend of Bahame's based on what he did to her village."

"Yeah," one of Rivera's men agreed. "But people are afraid of him and don't want to piss him off. They think he's magic."

"So what are you saying?" Rivera said.

"If we let her go, how do we know she won't talk? Hell, we can't even tell her not to."

He was right. What was it their contact had said? That Bahame could see through people's eyes? Legends had roots in reality. Maybe people were so terrified of the man that even the ones who hated him told him everything they knew in hopes of working their way into his good graces.

"We could tie her to the tree and gag her," another of Rivera's men said.

This was stupid. They were exposed and wasting time.

"Boss?"

"We can't tie her to a tree. She'd die of thirst or an animal would get her."

The man standing behind her silently unsheathed his knife. "She's not going to last out here on her own anyway. We'd be doing her a favor."

Rivera stood frozen for what he knew must have seemed like far too long to his men. Indecisiveness was not a particularly attractive quality in his profession.

The knee-jerk reaction was always to fall back on his training, but this kind of a situation had never been dealt with in a way that meant anything when you were actually faced with contemplating ending the life of an innocent woman.

"We're moving out," he said, turning and starting in a direction that skirted the burned-out village. There would already be a lot of explaining to do in the unlikely event he ever laid eyes on the Pearly Gates. Murdering helpless women wasn't something he wanted to add to his list.